"RANDY WAYNE WHITE TAKES US PLACES THAT
NO OTHER FLORIDA MYSTERY WRITER CAN
HOPE TO FIND."
—Carl Hiaasen

DEAD SILENCE

"Straight-ahead, nonstop action and full of the varying
shades of light and dark that White has honed to a super-
lative craft. In *Dead Silence*, one gets not only a dead-on
thriller, with all the twists, surprises, and action one expects,
but a sense that each of the Ford books is a sort of über
chapter in the development of one of the most compelling
characters in the genre."   —*The Miami Herald*

"Florida author Randy Wayne White wastes no time plunging his hero Marion 'Doc' Ford into a thriller that doesn't
stop for a breath until the last sentence. [It] soars with an
energetic plot, characters who show their mettle against the
odds, and a sense of terror. His best novel to date."
                                        —*South Florida Sun-Sentinel*

"The action, typical for White, is relentless, and the tension
builds agonizingly (nothing like burying somebody alive to
ratchet up the suspense)."   —*Booklist*

"[A] high-octane . . . thriller. The action roars along as Doc
does what Doc does best: kick butt."   —*Publishers Weekly*

"A fabulous action-packed thriller . . . fascinating."
                                        —*Midwest Book Review*

continued . . .

TITLES BY RANDY WAYNE WHITE

NONFICTION

FICTION AS RANDY STRIKER

DEAD SILENCE

RANDY WAYNE WHITE

BERKLEY BOOKS

NEW YORK

THE BERKLEY PUBLISHING GROUP
Published by the Penguin Group
Penguin Group (USA) Inc.
375 Hudson Street, New York, New York 10014, USA
Penguin Group (Canada), 90 Eglinton Avenue East, Suite 700, Toronto, Ontario M4P 2Y3, Canada
(a division of Pearson Penguin Canada Inc.)
Penguin Books Ltd., 80 Strand, London WC2R 0RL, England
Penguin Group Ireland, 25 St. Stephen's Green, Dublin 2, Ireland (a division of Penguin Books Ltd.)
Penguin Group (Australia), 250 Camberwell Road, Camberwell, Victoria 3124, Australia
(a division of Pearson Australia Group Pty. Ltd.)
Penguin Books India Pvt. Ltd., 11 Community Centre, Panchsheel Park, New Delhi—110 017, India
Penguin Group (NZ), 67 Apollo Drive, Rosedale, North Shore 0632, New Zealand
(a division of Pearson New Zealand Ltd.)
Penguin Books (South Africa) (Pty.) Ltd., 24 Sturdee Avenue, Rosebank, Johannesburg 2196,
South Africa

Penguin Books Ltd., Registered Offices: 80 Strand, London WC2R 0RL, England

Sanibel and Captiva Islands, and Long Island, New York, are real places, faithfully described but used
fictitiously in this novel. The same is true of certain businesses, marinas, bars and other places frequented
by Doc Ford, Tomlinson and pals.

In all other respects, however, this is a work of fiction. Names, characters, places, and incidents either
are the product of the author's imagination or are used fictitiously, and any resemblance to actual
persons, living or dead, business establishments, events, or locales is entirely coincidental. The publisher
does not have any control over and does not assume any responsibility for author or third-party websites
or their content.

DEAD SILENCE

A Berkley Book / published by arrangement with the author

PRINTING HISTORY
G. P. Putnam's Sons hardcover edition / March 2009
Berkley premium edition / March 2010

Copyright © 2009 by Randy Wayne White.
Interior map copyright © 2007 by Randy Wayne White. Rendering by Meighan Cavanaugh.
Cover art and design by Marc J. Cohen.

ISBN: 978-0-425-23330-6

BERKLEY®
Berkley Books are published by The Berkley Publishing Group,
a division of Penguin Group (USA) Inc.,
375 Hudson Street, New York, New York 10014.
BERKLEY® is a registered trademark of Penguin Group (USA) Inc.
The "B" design is a trademark of Penguin Group (USA) Inc.

PRINTED IN THE UNITED STATES OF AMERICA

10 9 8 7 6 5 4 3 2 1

To friends and teachers at two superb schools,
North Central High, Pioneer, Ohio,
and Davenport Central, Davenport, Iowa.
An object in motion tends to stay in motion—
thanks for the boost.

AUTHOR'S NOTE

This manuscript traveled with me inside and outside the country during the last twelve months and benefited from kindnesses extended to the author.

Special thanks go to Marvin and Helene Gralnick for sharing Casa de Chico's with Ford and Tomlinson. The bead board and pine floors still radiate the couple's gifted energy, and, when the moon's just right, the rattle of a VW van sometimes echoes from the garage.

In Cuba, Roberto, Ela and Temis Lopez were hugely helpful, as were Raul and Maura Corrales, and special thanks to my friend Gilberto Torrente Santiesteba, Secretario de la Logia Masonica, Havana.

Jim and Donna Lane, owners of the Ellerbe Springs Inn (about eighty miles east of Charlotte, North Carolina), were extraordinary hosts as usual. The inn is an aging but elegant outpost, removed from noise and the tourist herd. I spend a week or two there every year because it's a great place to write. It also serves, without question, the best southern breakfast of any restaurant in my experience.

Thanks to Rue Matthiessen, I had a great place to work while in Sag Harbor, Long Island, which is not far from the home of Tomlinson's pal the Mad Monk of Sagaponack.

Special thanks to John and Mitzu MacNeil for providing a productive work space (an office at Moody Street Pictures) when our "deluxe rental" in Concord, Massachusetts, turned out to be a dud. Swimming daily in Walden Pond was also a big plus.

A lot of this novel was written at a corner table, before and after hours, at Doc Ford's Sanibel Rum Bar and Grille on Sanibel Island, Florida, where staff were tolerant beyond the call of duty.

Thanks to my friends and partners Marty and Brenda Harrity, Mark and Heidi Marinello, Greg Nelson, Dan Howes, Brian Cunningham, Liz Harris, Capt. Bryce Randall Harris, Milita Kennedy, Kevin Filliowich, Kevin Boyce, Eric Breland, Sam Hussan Ismatullaev, Rachel Songalewiski of Michigan, Jean and Abigail Crenshaw, Lindsay Kuleza, Greg Barker, Roberto Cruz, Amanda Rodriquez, Juan Gomex, Olga Guryanova, Mary McBeath, Kim McGonnell, Allyson Parzero, Cindy Porter, Big Matt Powell, Laurie and Jake Yukobov, Bette Roberts, Jose Rosas, Jorge Sanchez, Travis Zeigler, Arturo, Sammy, Feliciano, Enrique and Ms. Dawn Oliveri.

At Timber's Sanibel Grille, my pals Matt Asen, Mary Jo, Audrey, Becky, Debbie, Brian, Bart and Bobby were, once again, stalwarts.

Finally, I would like to thank my two sons, Rogan and Lee White, for helping me finish, yet again, another book.

—RANDY WAYNE WHITE

CASA DE CHICO'S

SANIBEL ISLAND, FLORIDA

The universities of Cuba are available only to those
who share my revolutionary beliefs.—FIDEL CASTRO

As a child I was taught the Supernatural Powers
(Taku Wakan) were powerful and could do
strange things.—RED CLOUD (1903),
Peter Matthiessen, *In the Spirit of Crazy Horse*

It is not the mission of Freemasonry to engage in plots
and conspiracies against the civil government.
It is not the fanatical propagandist of any creed or theory.
It is the apostle of liberty and equality.
—ALBERT PIKE, *Morals and Dogma* (1871)

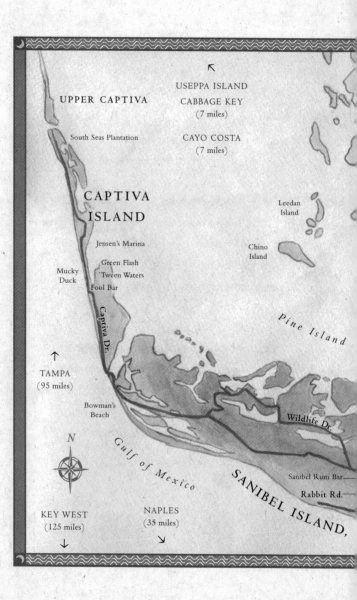

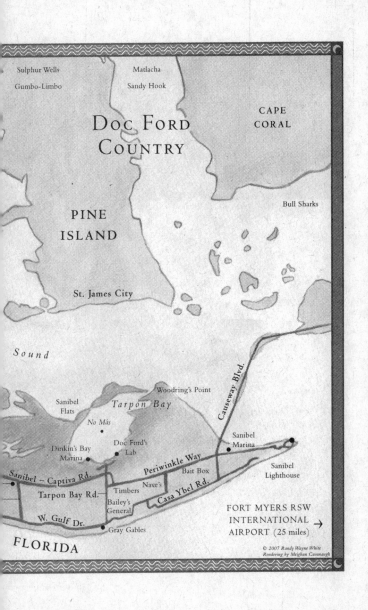

DEAD SILENCE

PROLOGUE

On a moonless winter night, after working late in the lab, Marion Ford anchored his boat and swam to a yacht owned by a killer.

Ford wore swim fins, a black wool cap and cargo pants. His glasses were around his neck on fishing line, as usual. He had a tactical light in one pocket, a broken wristwatch in another.

Aboard the forty-three-foot Viking was a man named Bern Heller. Heller had played two years in the NFL, then sold Cadillacs while living a secret life as a serial rapist. He'd murdered a Cuban fishing guide, one of Ford's friends.

Heller was free after eleven months in Raiford spent lifting weights, talking sports with the brothers, waiting for his idiot attorneys to get him a retrial.

Sometimes, alone in his cell, Bern would fantasize about women, the noise they made when they'd given up. A mewing sound. The way their thighs went limp—total submission. After years on steroids, remembering that sound was the only way it worked, unless Bern had his fingers on a real live girl. Something he planned to do soon.

Ford had spotted Bern that afternoon. Huge man, beer in hand, Bermuda shorts and an orange ankle monitor that looked heavy. Ford had approached, smiling, thinking Bern might take a swing, but hoping he wouldn't because Ford knew then, looking into the crazy man's eyes, what he would do.

"The beating I gave you wasn't enough, I guess. You want more?"

Ford had straightened his glasses, eyes shifting from a marina-foreclosure notice to Heller's gold Rolex. "I could use the work. It's been a while."

"Is that supposed to mean something?"

"Not to you. I was thinking of Javier Castillo."

"Your dink fisherman pal. If I was guilty, you think they would've let me out of Raiford?"

Ford was thinking, *He's stoned,* as he said, "Okay. I'll give you a second chance."

"I don't want shit from you. Damn weirdo with your microscopes and dead fish. You gonna stand there talking or take your shot?"

"Maybe later. I've got an early flight." Now Ford was looking at the yacht where Heller lived. "I'll knock first."

"*Sure* you will. I won't hold my breath."

When Ford said, "You'll try," Bern blinked.

Ford knocked now, standing outside the yacht's salon, ready when Heller pushed the door open, wearing shorts, no shirt, a stubnose revolver in his hand.

Ten minutes later, Heller was in the water, trying to say, "Let's talk about this. *Seriously,*" but there was a rag stuffed in his mouth.

He tried to say "My goddamn elbow's busted!"— knowing what it felt like because of that game in Green Bay when he got blindsided by one of the Frozen Chosen. But not as cold then as now, with water sloshing in his ears, his wrists tie-wrapped, floating on his back as the weirdo biologist towed him, kicking with fins.

Bern tried to wrestle free but inhaled water up his nose. Tried again, panicking, and felt the ammonia sting of salt water.

He screamed, *"Please,"* but made only a mewing noise because of the gag.

The sound—a helpless-kitten sound—scared him. It was familiar. Thinking about it, Bern stopped struggling. When he remembered, his muscles went slack.

Ford continued swimming from the lights of the marina, kicking harder, using his right arm to pull.

He had a plane to catch.

At 6:45 a.m., Ford was aboard Delta's direct to Newark, sitting starboard side, first class, reading the *Miami Herald*. A story about Cuba. Secret documents were surfacing, now that Castro was gone.

Disturbing.

Ford had worked in Cuba. He had also worked in Central America, South America, Asia and Africa.

Ford had told Bern the truth. His skills were rusty.

As the plane banked over the Gulf of Mexico, he folded the *Herald* and cleaned his glasses. Below, wind glittered on water a mile from shore, where Ford had untied Bern Heller, then pushed him overboard, yelling, *"Swim!"*

At 3:30 a.m., the lights of Sanibel Island were bright.

By five, Ford had returned to his home and lab on Dinkin's Bay, secured his boat, was showered and packed. He'd also stowed cash from Heller's safe and the Rolex in a hidden floor compartment.

Thinking about it now, Heller's voice—*"Don't leave. I'm begging you!"*—Ford felt an unfocused anxiety that startled him. A sinking sadness—a dense, unlighted space beneath his heart.

It passed.

An emotional response? No . . . a paralimbic reaction. The distinction was interesting—but unimportant.

Ford was working again.

Below, green water became granite as the jetliner ascended.

They'll think Heller fell overboard, escaping to Mexico . . . if the cops find him.

They might not.

That orange ankle monitor looked heavy.

HOTEL NACIONAL, HAVANA, CUBA

Farfel told the Venezuelan, "More than a month ago, I warned you. Now it's too late. The U.S. government has Castro's files." He exhaled through his nose, touching a finger to his glasses: *Amateurs.*

The young Venezuelan, his face lathered, sat reading the *Miami Herald*, Spanish edition. Farfel, the hotel barber, could see over his shoulder.

SENATE SUBPOENAS CUBAN DOCUMENTS

There was a photo. A good-looking woman, weight of breasts beneath her charcoal blouse. A powerful man with teeth. Cochairs of an intelligence subcommittee, they'd been bickering about the files for months, mostly with the world political community, but also with the CIA.

"Five weeks ago. What did I tell you?"

The Venezuelan had a partner, an aloof New Yorker. What Farfel had told them was, "You want the files? Bury one of the politicians alive. Bury them with oxygen, a little water. Enough for a couple of days. It'll work, I read about it in a book. The Americans will give you anything you want."

They'd thought he was joking.

Now, because Farfel had a razor in his hand, the Venezuelan closed the newspaper. He sat straighter, thinking, *He has cut men's throats. I wouldn't be the first.*

True.

Farfel began stropping the razor fast—a rare display of emotion for the precise little man with silver hair, mustache and glittering silver eyes. They were alone in the shop with Koken chairs, mirrors, combs in blue disinfectant, the smell of powder and cigars, a calendar on the wall showing Havana's skyline.

"The article means nothing," the young Venezuelan said. He was worried the barber would be insulted if he stood and wiped lather from his face but was thinking it over as he added, "I have good news."

"Save your breath. No more excuses."

"At least listen."

"Why bother? I should be looking for a way to disappear. They will hunt me the way Jews hunt Nazis. A boat, maybe."

The Venezuelan stood and found a towel. *To hell with etiquette.* He gave it a moment for effect, but also to move closer to the door. "Yesterday it was decided," he said. "The grave will be dug."

Farfel folded the razor slowly.

"We were going to tell you."

"The coffin, too?" The barber's dentures made a clacking *snap* sound.

"Yes, as you ordered. A wooden box with an oxygen bottle. A container for water—a *canteen,* I think it is called."

"Where?"

The Venezuelan said, "Only two people know." Said it in a way that implied the New Yorker knew but the Venezuelan didn't. He lobbed the newspaper in the trash, his confidence returning. "There's something else. We also have the senator's schedule."

He was talking about the good-looking woman in the charcoal blouse.

Farfel had told them, "Abduct the female. Snap photos with the coffin open, the woman staring up. The FBI will soil their pants, do whatever we want. Old files in exchange for the life of a senator? Force the Americans to *react*, not *act*."

Farfel's former assistant, Hump, the son of a dead friend, had made a cinematic gesture, framing the scene. "I like photos," he said in his simple way. "I own a camera."

The Venezuelan ignored the man. His deformity was unsettling.

This was back in December, Hump and Farfel, former members of the Cuban Socialist Party, talking with the young Venezuelan and the New Yorker on a seawall where the Gulf Stream swept close to Havana, a river of green on a purple sea.

"Maximum leverage without killing. You told me no one can be killed."

"But burying a woman—"

"*Exactly.*"

"You're asking me to imagine—"

"To imagine the worst way to die. People will say fire. They will say falling from the sky in a plane. Cancer . . . a few will speak of disease."

Hump and Farfel had exchanged looks, as if old pros on the subject of torture and death. They were.

"To understand fear, listen to your spine, not your brain.".

The idea had floated in silence. *Buried alive.*

Even the New Yorker, a cold one, had grimaced.

"When FBI agents get the assignment, they'll feel like *they're* suffocating. If we tell them to shit, they'll ask what color."

"I don't know . . ."

Hump had said to the Venezuelan, "We do," as he removed his cap, looking at the man's face for a reaction.

He got it.

The Venezuelan swallowed and turned away. "I'm not criticizing. But as a practical approach—"

Farfel said, "You're an expert? In Florida, a convict buried a rich man's daughter. This was years ago. A fan for air, some water. She was buried four days. The rich man delivered the cash. The FBI *helped* him deliver the cash. They concentrated on saving the girl. Not searching for the kidnappers. Understand the concept? We put the victim's life in their hands. They'll be so busy, they won't waste time looking for us."

"Did the daughter live?"

Farfel took a deep breath, his expression asking *Why do I bother?*

Hump answered, "Yes, the girl lived," speaking in his simpleminded way, sounding disappointed.

For five weeks, the foreigners had delayed, insisting on more time. Even the New Yorker, who'd started it all, appearing in Farfel's shop one morning, then pressing a note in his hand instead of a tip.

Reading the note, Farfel had felt like a man again. He'd told Hump, "I don't care if it is a trap," as they walked to their first meeting.

It wasn't a trap.

Castro's personal possessions, files included, had been stolen by the Americans and shipped to Maryland in industrial cartons. Four cartons to a container, thousands of items and documents that had been grouped, not cataloged. Collectively, the Americans were calling them the *Castro Files*.

A carton labeled C/C-103 (1976–'96) contained details of experiments the Soviets had conducted on American POWs in Vietnam, then Angola, Panama and Grenada. Administrators of the study, working as private contractors, had continued the experiments in Iraq and Afghanistan. Pain and fear: What were the human limits? The study ended in 1998 when the last POW from Vietnam finally gave up and died.

The Cuban Program. The Soviets called it that because Castro had provided three unusual interrogators with special skills. The men were scientists, in their way, and were so determined, so exacting, that they soon usurped control from their Russian bosses.

One of the interrogators was a small, fastidious man named René Soyinka Navárro. He was the son of a Russian mother and a Cuban KGB officer.

In Afghanistan and Iraq, Navárro had been hired by Al-Qaeda as an expert contractor, an interrogator who could obtain information from even the most determined prisoners. To those countries, he had brought along an apprentice, the son of a fellow interrogator named Angel Yanguez, Jr.

From his late father, Yanguez had inherited a genetic deformity—*Seborrheic keratosis*—in the form of a cutaneous horn just beginning to grow. He'd also inherited the nickname Hump, which he didn't mind, unlike Navárro who despised his nickname, Farfel. It had shadowed him since Hoa Lo Prison in Vietnam, where POWs had named him for the Nestlé's Quik TV puppet that clicked his wooden teeth shut at the end of every sentence. Navárro, who wore dentures, made a similar sound when he wanted to emphasize a point.

In Vietnam, prisoners had referred to the Cubans, collectively, as the *Malvados*—fiends.

The New Yorker's note had read: *Americans once begged for your mercy. Are you willing to beg for theirs?*

How could the New Yorker know the truth about Navárro if the documents didn't exist?

The New Yorker and Venezuelan weren't partners. They were working for someone. Farfel had overheard them whisper a name in English. The name sounded like *Tenth Man*. Possibly *Tenman*.

The Venezuelan was a twenty-three-year-old *maricon*, his face smooth, like an angel's. He was a Communist, a young fool with ideals. The New Yorker was a Muslim who used whores and marijuana but not alcohol. They had no interest in the Cuban Program. Carton C/C-103 contained something else their employer wanted. Something worth only money, Farfel believed, if they weren't willing to kill for it.

Didn't matter.

The grave will be dug.

Since the Soviet collapse, Farfel and Hump had been in government protection, living like peons in Havana. False identities, menial jobs. Humiliating after living like gods in Vietnam, Panama and Iraq.

Now, though, they were working again. Professionals with unusual skills.

1

On a snowy January evening in Manhattan, I was in the Trophy Room of the Explorers Club when I saw, through frosted windows, men abducting a woman as she exited her limousine.

It wouldn't have made a difference, but I knew the woman. She was Barbara Hayes-Sorrento—*Senator* Barbara Hayes-Sorrento—a first-term powerhouse from the west who had won the office once held by her late husband.

Well, not much difference. The senator was my dinner date for the evening. No romantic sparks, but I liked the lady.

It was six p.m., already dark outside. The Trophy Room was a cozy place. Fireplace framed by elephant tusks, maps of the Amazon scattered around, a mug of rum-laced tea within easy reach. I was the guest of an explorer who was also a British spy: Sir James Montbard. Friends called him Hooker because of the steel prosthetic that had replaced his left hand.

Hooker was a secondary reason for visiting New York. The primary reason was the hope of a new assignment from my old boss, a U.S. intelligence chief. Clandestine work sometimes requires a cover story. Friends sometimes provide it.

It was no coincidence that Barbara Hayes-Sorrento was free for dinner, or that my neighbor, Tomlinson, had been in the city until the day before, lecturing on "psychic surveillance" at an international symposium.

I had kept my social calendar high-profile, and I'd stayed busy.

Hooker and I had been planning a trip to Central America. He believed that warrior monks had sailed west in the 1300s, escaping with plunder from the Crusades. He said it explained why, two centuries later, the Maya believed in a blond, blue-eyed god, Quetzalcoatl, and so made a fatal mistake by welcoming the murderous Conquistadors.

I wasn't convinced. But renewing contacts in Latin America was important now, so I'd agreed to join his expedition. This was our third night at the Explorers Club using its superb library.

When Hooker excused himself to freshen his whiskey, I stood, stretched and strolled to the window because it was snowing—a rare opportunity for a man from the tropics. I had an unobstructed view of the street below.

It was 70th Street, a quiet one-way, two blocks from Central Park. It connects Park Avenue and Madison.

I could see Barbara Hayes-Sorrento as she got out of her car. She wore a charcoal coat, stockings and high heels. Her briefcase looked darker for the confetti swirl of snowflakes

The woman was leaning into a limo, saying good-bye to a fellow passenger, when a taxi rear-ended the limo. Not hard.

I knew that the passenger was a teenager she had mentioned earlier on the phone, a kid who'd won an essay contest and an escorted trip around the city. Something to do with the United Nations. Barbara had volunteered to meet him at the airport.

When Barbara jumped back, surprised, a man wearing coveralls and an odd pointed cap stepped to the driver's door, blocking it. A smaller man grabbed Barbara's shoulder. Her reaction was a warning glare.

The woman's expression changed when the man didn't let go. Barbara swung her briefcase but missed. It tumbled into the slush. Barbara tried kicking. One sensible black shoe went flying.

I was turning toward the stairs as the man began pushing her toward a taxi that had stopped in front of the limo. The woman's lips formed a cartoon *O* of shock. Her mouth widened into a scream.

It was a silent scream. The building that houses the Explorers Club is one of the brick-and-marble tall ships from a previous century. Neither car horns nor a lady's scream could pierce that elegant armor.

The club's stairs are wooden. They creaked beneath my weight as I charged down the steps.

On the street, the few pedestrians watching probably thought Hollywood was filming a movie. But I'd noted the careful choreography that is the signature of a professional hit.

Taxi A blocks the narrow street. Taxi B rear-ends the limo but gently, sandwiching it. Things appear normal when men in coveralls rush to inspect the damage. But the men are not city employees. They are bagmen. *Bag,* as in *bagging game.*

The unfolding scene had registered on a subconscious level that is ever alert—me, the eager student of other professionals. I knew before I knew that a well-planned kidnapping was taking place.

As I charged down the steps, I calculated how many operators it would take to snatch a U.S. senator. Both taxi drivers, of course, plus a support crew. There also might be a shooter stationed atop a nearby building. Possibly atop the Explorers Club—it had six floors. And possibly more than one shooter, if it was a bag-and-tag operation.

Tag, as in *coroner's tag.*

So there were at least four men, but maybe eight, presumably all armed.

On the bottom floor of the Explorers Club, near the stairs, is a world globe, museum-sized. On a nearby wall, I'd noticed a climbing ax from some Himalayan expedition. An ice ax, spiked at one end, a blade on the other.

I yelled to the desk attendant, "Where's Sir James?,"

as I pulled the ax from its mount, stumbled and nearly fell over the globe.

The attendant stared at me like I was insane. She pointed toward the restroom, her lips moving to tell me, "Sir James is . . . unavailable."

I told the woman to call 911. A United States senator was being abducted.

2

As I exited the Explorers Club, the kid Barbara had met at the airport was stepping out of the limo, a cowboy hat pulled low, boots ankle-deep in slush.

The essay winner? It was a boy who couldn't have been more than fifteen. He looked like a bull rider, all shoulders and legs.

I yelled, "Kid! Get back in the car!"

The kid looked at me, his expression surly. "Huh?" Maybe he was masking confusion.

I hollered, "Back in the car—*now*," aware that the man with the pointed cap was watching the boy, maybe thinking about grabbing him.

The teen yelled to me, "*Kid?* . . . A goat ever kicked your ass, mister?" as I turned toward taxi A, parked in front of the limo.

An unusual vocabulary for a high school scholar.

The taxi's rear door was open, exhaust condensing in the cold. Hands from inside pulled at Barbara's coat while the guy in coveralls wrestled her legs into the car.

Barbara was getting in some shots, panty hose showing, as she hammered with her feet. But she was losing.

I could have thrown the ax but risked hitting her. Instead, I yelled, "Stop—I'll shoot!," imitating a television cop. Disciplined, but eager to squeeze the trigger.

It earned me a couple of seconds. The guy in coveralls straightened. His head pivoted. I saw a choirboy face, Mediterranean, maybe Spanish, which could mean anywhere. His dark eyes met mine as I raised the ax, running hard.

I don't care who you are, an ax is unnerving.

I saw his eyes widen, and gained another second, ten yards separating us now. Close enough to lower a shoulder and use my momentum to hit him so hard we'd spring the door off its hinges.

Instead, I changed my mind at the last second—always a mistake. Ask any football coach. Decided I could use the ice ax to scare all three men, so why disable just one?

Sensible. But when I tried to stop, I hit a patch of ice and my feet went flying. I landed hard on my back, momentum unchecked, and ass-sledded into a tangle of legs, then under the taxi, Choirboy atop me, Senator Hayes-Sorrento in the slush nearby.

Barbara called, *"Ford?"* as if reluctant to believe I was her bungling rescuer.

"Run! Get out of the street!" I was worried about a shooter, high above, watching through a rifle scope.

Several things then happened at once: The taxi driver

panicked, and hit the gas. The spinning tires somehow kicked Choirboy free. The vehicle began a slow-motion doughnut that would have crushed my head if the ax hadn't snagged the doorframe.

I grabbed the handle with both hands and levered my body away from the tires. I was half under the car, rotating with it. Let go, I'd be run over.

The car straightened, then slowly gained speed in the fresh snow, dragging me down the street.

I got my right hand higher on the ax handle. I lifted my butt off the pavement to reduce drag. Using the ax as a fulcrum, I was powering my legs from beneath the chassis when the guy in the backseat started kicking at the ax.

Because I had no other option, I made a wild lunge for the door. I got lucky. I caught the man's ankle—but only for a moment before he yanked his foot free.

The additional lift was enough. I swung clear, expecting the bumper to clip me when I let go of the ax. It didn't. I skidded through slush until I banged against the tire of a parked motorcycle. The ax clanked to a stop nearby.

I stood. Anticipated my legs buckling if something was broken. They didn't. I used the motorcycle to steady myself and watched the taxi continue down the street.

A hand appeared from the backseat and pulled the door closed. The driver accelerated.

Dazed and cold, I turned, hoping to see Barbara. Instead, I saw her limo speeding toward me, its headlights blinding. It was a Lincoln Town Car. Black. The driver was silhouetted by the lights of the vehicle behind it, taxi B.

I knelt and grabbed the ax, assuming the taxi was chasing the limo. Maybe I could smash the windshield if I timed it right. So I stood my ground—until the limo veered to hit me.

I dove for the curb and felt the fender brush close. Taxi B tried next. Its right bumper smacked the motorcycle, knocking it onto the sidewalk.

What the hell?

I jumped up, hoping the driver would lose control. He'd almost crushed my legs. I wanted to grab the guy by the neck and squeeze until his eyes bulged like muscat grapes.

But he didn't lose control. I chased him for a few steps, then stopped, watching the town car. The silhouettes of three people were visible in the rear window. It looked like two men were struggling to control a person sandwiched between them.

Barbara?

Brake lights flashed in tandem, then both vehicles turned right into the fast traffic of Madison Avenue. There were sirens now, squad cars converging from several directions

I pivoted toward the Explorers Club. I'd been dragged about fifty yards. A couple of men were jogging toward me, calling, "You okay?" My Brit friend, Hooker, wasn't one of them.

Near the entrance was a cluster of people, none obviously female, none the obvious center of attention. U.S.

senators are usually the center of attention, whether they welcome it or not. She was gone.

Goddamn it!

On the opposite side of the street, I saw a man walking fast toward Madison Avenue, head down. People who don't want to be noticed also attract attention. He wasn't wearing coveralls, but he could've trashed them.

I stepped into the street, interested in his reaction. The man glanced, then walked faster.

When he snuck another look, I followed. It was the Spanish-looking guy, Choirboy.

He ran.

I dropped the ax and ran, sirens close now.

I was losing ground until Choirboy fell when he tried to vault a stone wall that bordered Central Park. I was on the other side of Fifth Avenue, lanes of fast traffic separating us.

I got another break when a car actually pulled over for law enforcement vehicles threading their way from up-town, blue strobes pinging off a dome of falling snow. It stopped one lane of traffic and slowed others. I used the hole to juke my way across, ignoring the horns. I almost made it clean.

Almost.

A car locked its brakes and got rear-ended. As drivers swerved, I jumped behind a power pole and watched the chain reaction, cars skidding, spinning and colliding. The soft-metal percussion of fenders traced a firecracker progression.

When it was safe, I stepped back into the street as drivers got out to inspect the damage. Choirboy had disappeared into the park. The smart thing to do, I decided, was flag down a cop. I was cold and needed help. They needed information.

It wasn't easy. Squad cars were snaking through the mess, sirens howling, fixated on getting to the Explorers Club. No time for fender benders. No time for the big tan tourist, alternately waving his arms, then blowing on his hands for warmth.

Then I heard someone yell, "That's the guy! The stupid sonuvabitch that caused it!" A guy was pointing in my direction. People stared.

It took a moment. Me, the stupid sonuvabitch.

"Dumbass—*you*. You're not going anywhere!"

Yes, I was.

I went over the wall, into the park, where the tree canopy was dark above, silver beneath.

The snow was candescent.

In the distance, horses pulled carriages over asphalt trails, and I could see a small building. Some kind of concession. People had gathered there, music playing.

I could also see Choirboy's snow trail. I jogged and skidded, following his tracks downhill. Soon I got a glimpse of him through the trees. He had resumed the role of innocent stroller. He was walking. It looked like he'd been headed for the music but changed his mind.

Not enough people there for him to disappear. So now he was angling north, where it was darker, but also where a white, unlighted space showed, a pond.

He hadn't spotted me, so I circled uphill, keeping trees between us. I jogged, watching his shadow appear, then disappear. The footing was iffy and my feet were freezing. Also, my right knee was throbbing where my khakis were torn, blood-splattered from road rash.

Adrenaline was losing its kick. I couldn't outrun him now. I needed to surprise him.

I found a fountain near the pond. The pumps were off. Stone encircled a potage of ice and maple leaves. A foot-path curved along the pond where lamps created pools of light that followed the path uphill to the carriage road.

I knelt behind the fountain.

After a couple of minutes, I began to worry the guy had changed directions again. But then he appeared, hands in his pockets, still checking over his shoulder every few seconds. As he neared the fountain, I could see that he wore slacks and a windbreaker.

I crouched—an atavistic reflex incongruous with the Manhattan skyline. I wished now I hadn't left the ax behind.

The best place to jump him was at the edge of the pond. The surface was frozen but not solid. In the middle, a pump maintained a melted-water space, where ducks and geese squabbled. With the pond at his back, Choirboy had fewer options.

As he neared, I crept toward him along the wall of the

fountain. Because of the damn geese, I didn't hear a policeman on horseback approaching until he was close enough to zap me with his spotlight.

"You lost, mister? Or running from something?"

Two men were with him, civilians, both on foot—probably because their cars were being towed.

The cop told me, "Turn and face this way. Show me your hands."

Caught in the same beam of light, Choirboy reacted before I did. I saw him straighten, hesitate, then raise his hands.

I got my hands up, too, fingers wide, but didn't take my eyes off Choirboy, as one of the civilians said, "That's the asshole. Me with a brand-new Chrysler, this jerk runs into the street like he's drunk."

Choirboy looked at me, then at the cop, his brain putting it together, as I said, "My name's Ford. I'm a friend of Senator Barbara Hayes-Sorrento—the FBI will confirm that."

The cop leaned toward me, interested, as the man pissed off about his Chrysler said, "FBI—hear that? He's not drunk, he's crazy."

I continued speaking directly to the cop. "The senator was abducted about ten minutes ago. They used two taxis. Four to eight men, maybe one of them posing as her limo driver. The guy in the Windbreaker—this guy—was involved. I was chasing him."

When I used an index finger to point, the cop snapped, "Keep them where I can see them," shifting the spotlight to his left hand so he could unsnap his holster. His tone was different now. He was dealing with a crime that carried the death penalty. Less volume, more edge.

"You heard the call go out about a kidnapping?"

I said, "No. As I just explained, I was—"

"You work in law enforcement? That was a clean report you gave."

I shook my head to mask exasperation. "I'm a marine biologist. I'm here on vacation from Florida."

"Just a tourist doing his civic duty, huh? How do you know four people were involved?"

"Four, but as many as eight, I'm guessing. The point is—"

"Two taxis and a limo—another lucky guess? You know a lot of details."

The cop had drawn his weapon, holding it against his riding boot, barrel down, so it wasn't obvious. A revolver, not a Glock 9, which told me the guy had been with NYPD a lot of years. The civilians could see the gun. They were backing away

"You're a close personal friend of this U.S. senator, is that what you're telling me?"

"I'm a friend."

"Friends with the FBI, too?"

"I said they can confirm my story. If agents aren't already interviewing people, they will be."

Staring at me, the cop said, "Cops and criminals—no one understands the system better. And you're not a cop."

I waited.

"Why'd you cause that pileup, running across Fifth Avenue?"

Before I could answer, Choirboy attempted a finesse. "This man was not chasing me. I was walking. I hear order to stop, I stop. I have read about the police of New York. They say you are the finest."

Spanish-speaking, but from South America, not Spain.

Looking at me, the cop said to Choirboy, "I suppose you're on vacation, too?"

He answered, "No. I am here for the United Nations. The Embassy of Venezuela."

It was tough not to react. Even if the man was lying, it was a clever lie. Diplomats can be detained but not arrested.

"As a diplomat, I must protect myself for my safety, so I notice things. I think he is a robber, this man. Or a crazy person. I ask myself, why is he not wearing a coat?"

The cop and the civilians stared at me, seeing torn pants and my short-sleeved polo, as the horse snorted frosted plumes, saddle creaking in the cold.

When I started to explain, the cop told me, "On your knees. *Now*," not raising his voice much. He holstered his weapon temporarily to dismount the horse.

The Venezuelan lowered his hands, a hint of a smile for me—just me—as he said, "I must go meet American friends because I am late. Thank you for arresting this dangerous man." He was looking at the cop who had both feet on the ground now, gun still holstered, as he keyed a radio to call for backup.

When the cop told him, "Sorry, sir. Not until I see some identification," the Venezuelan's expression read *I don't understand*. He turned and began walking.

"I'm talking to you, sir. Do you hear me?"

The Venezuelan smiled and gave a friendly wave, still walking. Then walked faster as the cop drew his weapon, telling him, "Stop now! I'm not going to tell you again."

Because I saw it coming, I was already moving when the Venezuelan ran. Got a good jump as, behind me, the cop shouted, "Freeze! I'll blow your fucking heads off!" not sounding like an actor.

He yelled something else as I closed in on the Venezuelan, already at full speed because I was running downhill. Legs driving, head up as I lowered my shoulder, I hit the man so hard I heard the cartilage pop of his ribs as we went spinning out across the frozen pond.

On the ice, sliding, there was the illusion that we gained speed, and I could hear the honk of surprised waterfowl as they scattered. I wrestled my way atop the Venezuelan as we stopped and had my fist hammered back in case he tried to run again.

The man wasn't going anywhere. He was bug-eyed, fighting to breathe with his broken ribs.

I got to my feet, shielding my face from the spotlight. When I took a step, my feet skated out from under me and I almost fell.

I hollered, "Get that damn light out of my eyes! I didn't run. He did."

The cop thought about it a beat before telling me,

"I've got people on the way. Keep your hands where I can see them."

I wasn't in the mood. "Deal with it. You try walking on this shit with your hands up."

The cop raised his voice to insist but stopped talking when I stopped—froze, more accurately—both of us listening to a cracking sound. The noise spiderwebbed across the pond.

I looked at my feet, then into the spotlight. I was asking the cop, "Do you have a rope?" as I went through the ice.

The Venezuelan dropped next.

3

The kidnappers didn't get the senator. They grabbed the teenager instead. Will Chaser, a high school freshman from Minneapolis.

Apparently, Minnesota had cowboys.

The mounted cop, Marvin Esterline, gave me the news. Fitting. The man had twenty-seven years with NYPD, the last eight as a member of the elite mounted division. He stuck around after they'd driven us from the pond, then moved me from the Central Park office to the 19th Precinct, a five-story building on East 67th, red brick with blue trim.

For two hours, I answered questions. Every time I took a break, Esterline was in the lounge waiting. "Unlike a certain South American perp," he explained, "you didn't demand an attorney."

"You can't question him until a lawyer shows up?" I asked.

"No, Einstein," the cop replied. "No questions because his attorney *did* show up. It burns my ass how tight the regs are now."

The perp was Louis Duarte, a twenty-three-year-old university student from Caracas who had a couple of minor dings on his record, both associated with protest rallies, one in Rome. *Interesting.*

"A political activist," the cop told me, showing his own politics the way he said it. Maybe because of his contempt, Esterline continued to refer to Duarte as the perp or the Venezuelan. And once or twice, as the greaser, even though Esterline looked Italian, the mother's side probably.

Esterline was a veteran who wasn't afraid to bend the rules. He made sure I got a shower in the precinct locker room, telling the duty officer, "There's so much duck shit in that pond, this guy will be quacking. How you gonna question a man who quacks?"

He had a couple of uniforms talk their way into my hotel and bring me dry clothes. He also delivered a thermos of coffee spiked with whiskey.

"You still cold?" Esterline kept asking.

Yes, I was still cold. I was also in a hurry—in a hurry because of something Choirboy had said while we were struggling to pull ourselves out of the water. But there was no way to speed up the questioning without inviting suspicion. Esterline had good instincts. I got the impression he'd guessed why I was in a hurry because he kept bringing the subject back to Choirboy, the two of us alone out there in water.

More than once, he said, "That Venezuelan owes you his life."

It was true.

Maybe Esterline felt like he owed me, too. Two corpses would have cost him a lot of paperwork. Instead, I had handed him Choirboy alive, a big-time collar that might help his career.

Esterline wasn't doing the questioning. In charge were detectives from NYPD's Major Crimes Unit and agents from the FBI. A couple of other men entered the room and left without a word. Maybe cops, or maybe reps from one of the U.S. intelligence agencies—my old boss keeping an eye on me? No way to know.

I cooperated, but in the careful way men in my profession have been trained to cooperate. I went off on tangents. I misunderstood questions. Esterline's comment about my "clean report" was a reminder that civilians behave like civilians.

Presumably, Choirboy would soon be questioned, but in a more secure setting. I wondered if he would tell his interrogators what he had already confessed to me. I had given Louis Duarte a choice when the two of us were in the water, trying to pull ourselves from the ice: Tell me the truth or I'll leave you to die. So he had told me the truth. Maybe.

It was another reminder: Civilians give information. Professionals barter it. Choirboy had placed a major chip on my side of the table.

I didn't waste that chip on the detectives. Our sessions weren't contentious. They could confirm most of my story. I had hand-delivered one of the kidnappers, so they rewarded me with bits of information in trade. But it was Esterline who provided details as reports came in.

Sir James Montbard had rescued Barbara while I was being dragged down the street, he told me. The Brit had led her through some secret entrance into the Explorers Club basement.

I smiled, picturing it. The Brit had a debonair ease that made everything he did seem effortless. The fact that he was seventy years old mitigated my envy, but only a little.

Because of Hooker, the kidnappers had to settle for the teenager. Apparently, the kid had taken my bad advice and stayed in the limo. Esterline didn't know if the driver was one of the bad guys or another victim because it was a limo service, not the senator's personal car. They were still searching for the vehicle.

Barbara had been assigned a security team, then driven to her suite at the Waldorf. Esterline told me she had requested that one of my friends keep her company until her staff arrived.

"The report says either the British guy or someone referred to as 'the Buddhist psychic'—whatever that means."

My neighbor, Tomlinson, is what it meant.

When Esterline became diplomatic, adding, "Either guy, I'm sure she's in good hands," I didn't tell him that Tomlinson's hands were far less trustworthy when a woman was involved. Nor did I inform him that the Buddhist psychic had already returned to Florida and was probably aboard his sailboat smoking something harvested personally.

For Tomlinson, lecturing provides ancillary income. The good earth provides the money crop. I was eager to see the man.

Physically, Esterline said, the senator was okay. From the way he said it, I guessed she was fast becoming a pain in the ass for NYPD—a woman with power and contacts who knew how to use both.

Her sense of responsibility was magnified because she didn't represent the teenager's home state. Barbara had been doing a favor for a senate colleague. Meet and greet the essay winner, ride in a limo with a U.S. senator: big thrill.

The teen had been entrusted to her and she'd failed. So she had converted her suite at the Waldorf into a communications center and was now hammering at law enforcement, pushing them to find the kid.

So far, no luck.

"She wants to see you when we're done here," Esterline told me.

When the detectives were finished, he offered me a ride.

"I can tell you're in a hurry," he said.

I thought, *Here we go.*

I didn't doubt that the Central Park cop felt indebted, but I also knew he wanted something. Esterline was an

NYPD vet who lived by the code of the barter system. He had produced information for me. Now it was my turn.

It was obvious what he was after when, for the fifth or sixth time, he said, "That Latin guy, you could have let him die right there. He would've never made it out of that shithole on his own."

We were in a squad car, moving with late traffic on Park Avenue. I replied, "Yeah, I guess that's true."

It was.

When Choirboy and I went through the ice, I knew I only had a couple of minutes before my system shut down. Plunge the human body into near-freezing water and an emergency switch clicks in the brain, a phenomenon named the *mammalian diving reflex*. All motor skills are short-circuited as blood is shunted to the heart. In three minutes, I wouldn't be able to move my arms. Ten minutes, we'd be dead.

Maybe Choirboy knew. He panicked when he couldn't get out. Every time he tried, he slid back into the water. It wasn't like climbing onto a table. Our fingers couldn't find traction on the ice.

Esterline and the two civilians had tried forming a three-man chain, but the ice wouldn't hold. So there was nothing they could do but watch, hoping firefighters arrived with a ladder before hypothermia killed us.

The cop saw every move Choirboy and I made. But he couldn't hear everything we said. That's what Esterline wanted to find out. What had Louis Duarte told me while we were alone out there? Why was I in a hurry?

Slowing for a stoplight, I listened to the cop say, "I

thought you were both goners. I figured, shit, the water-rescue boys will have to go after you with tongs and an ice pick. Take three days before you thawed enough for an autopsy."

I sat back and listened, letting the cop set it up.

"You know what convinced me that you'd lost it out there?"

I could guess, but said, "It's hard to remember details, it happened so fast."

Esterline said, "Uh-huh," not buying it.

I said, "The EMTs told me freezing water can affect the brain that way. What's the phrase, *temporary amnesia*?"

The cop said to me, "*Right*. From what I saw, your brain worked just fine. Until you took your shirts off—that's what I'm talking about, when I thought you'd lost it. Two guys go through the ice, the last thing you expect is for them to start taking off their clothes. But then I saw you talking to the Venezuelan, getting in his face about something. And I heard the guy answering. So I figured you were okay."

As if interested, I said, "Weird, that's hazy, too. Do you remember what we said?"

The cop gave me a sharp look. "I couldn't hear because of those damn geese. But there you were, the two of you, having a conversation. Like you were in no hurry, not worried about dying."

"I was trying to make him understand," I said. "We were running out of time. He had to listen."

"You told him that you knew how to get out—right?"

"I wasn't positive, but that's what I told him."

"That's when you took off your shirts, after you convinced him. Then you told him what to do, how to pull himself onto the ice."

I said, "Yes."

I got another sharp look. "Information that saved his life. You *gave* it to him." Esterline's tone said I was a fool or a liar.

"It was our only chance."

"You had that asshole by the short hairs. You'd just watched him rough up the senator. She was your date for the evening and the bastard tried to kidnap her. You could've made that guy tell you anything you wanted to know. Or just left the asshole out there."

I stared out the window, waiting for him to ask a key question the detectives had not asked.

Instead, Esterline said, "Almost thirty years, I've done this job. Ford, I'm not stupid, but tonight you made me feel stupid. When I popped you with the flashlight, I would've bet you were some nerd math teacher, in town for a convention but ended up at too many strip bars."

"Thanks," I said, smiling.

"Then you pitch yourself as a biologist on vacation. Just doing your civic duty. Bullshit. I saw how you handled yourself in the park. I watched how you handled those FBI preppies."

I said nothing.

"When you were in the water, the Venezuelan told you something. I couldn't hear. But I saw how you reacted. Every word, you filed away. See why I'm interested?" He took his eyes off traffic long enough to see me nod.

"If I thought it'd help that boy, I'd have a couple cops waiting for us at a quiet place. Old-school types. You'd get real talkative real quick. *Kapeesh?*"

He looked again. I didn't nod.

"What'd you tell the big shots when they asked about you and the greaser, all alone in the water with time to talk?"

"They didn't ask."

"You're kidding. I asked you twice before we got to the station. But you went off on some tangent."

I said it again. "They never asked."

"Figures. The whole damn world is gone to shit."

Looking at him, I said, "Marv, if I knew where the boy was, I would have volunteered it."

It was true. In the water, Choirboy had answered three questions in exchange for my help. My first question was: *Where are they taking the senator?*

Because he said he didn't know, I let him live. If he was lying, I wanted the feds to have a chance to pry it out of him.

"All that talking, the Venezuelan didn't give you anything?"

I said carefully, "If it was something your people could use, I'd tell you. Or the bureau."

"Then why such a rush? You keep looking at your watch. Couldn't wait to get to a pay phone, even after I offered you my cell. I didn't imagine it."

"I booked a morning flight to Florida, six forty-five, out of Newark. I wanted to get back tonight, but it's too late." True.

When he said, "Okay, you got nothing that would interest us or the feds. But what about Interpol?"

I answered, "Believe me, if I knew where the kid was you wouldn't have to ask."

After several seconds, Esterline said, "That's the way it's gonna be, huh?"

When he glanced at me, I was looking out the passenger window.

"Then let's leave it like this: If your memory improves, you call me. Not those assholes from the bureau. And not those brownnose detectives. Mostly, they're a good bunch. But not those two. Okay?"

I was watching storefronts blur past—delicatessens, clothing stores, the marquee of the Waldorf-Astoria Hotel two blocks ahead—as I replied, "I owe you, Marv. I appreciate what you did for me tonight."

He laughed—a cynical, wise-guy laugh—done with it. "Okay, we'll see. At least explain how you came up with the shirt gambit. Or are you gonna play dumb about that, too?"

I said, "I wasn't positive it would work."

"But it *did* work. How'd you think of it, that's what I'm asking. You wrapped a shirt around each hand like a glove, then smacked both hands down hard on the ice. I saw you."

I said, "After clearing away the snow."

"Yeah, brushed it away and splashed some water. Only maybe that was accidental."

"It wasn't," I said.

"Then smacked your hands down flat on the ice. After five, ten seconds, you hollered at the Latin guy, 'Now!' I heard that clear enough. He used your shoulder to boost himself up. You pulled yourself out, no problem. Then the two of you belly-crawled to shore."

"That was the scariest part," I said, "those last few yards."

"So what was the deal, using the shirts? They gave you a better grip because your hands were warmer?"

I said, "Just the opposite. The temperature's in the twenties, our shirts were soaked. That's what gave me the idea. When you were a kid, did you ever stick your tongue on a Popsicle?"

Esterline said, "A couple times every winter, we get a call, some kid's tongue is stuck to a pole or something."

"That's the concept," I said.

After a few seconds, he smiled. "I'll be goddamned. I get it. The shirts froze to the ice, huh? Your arms were like the two sticks."

"Sort of," I told him.

For the next block, I followed that tangent, explaining the tensile strength of water molecules as they bonded, crystallizing as ice. But what I was thinking about was the kid, in his rodeo clothes, and his smart-assed reply when I ordered him back into the limo.

I wished him well, and hoped he really was as tough as he talked. Young William Chaser would have to be a survivor to endure the nightmare he was living—if he was still alive.

4

Curled in a dark space he knew was the trunk of a car, Will Chaser had vomited and nearly messed his jeans, he was so scared at first. Now, though, he was numb enough to do some thinking.

Long as I live, I'll never enter another essay contest, doesn't matter the prize. I shoulda written the goddamn thing myself.

Which he hadn't. Not a word. Was amazed, in fact, the contest people never doubted.

"We are pleased to recognize a young Indigenous American who comprehends the complexities of international relationships . . ."

A line from the official letter of congratulations. Using "Indigenous" instead of "Native," which was irritating, because Will had to go looking for a dictionary. Then using "comprehends," like the judges were surprised to discover a Skin who wasn't too damn stupid.

"You don't have to be a genius not to be stupid." A

line from his so-called foster granddad, Old Man Bull Guttersen.

As a kid on the Rez, Will had done some dumb things. He'd been kicked out of three schools and arrested twice. Math was weak, his spelling worse. But he wasn't stupid. *Ever.*

Will was aware early on it would take a special effort for someone like him to win a statewide writing contest. Five pages, neatly typed? Margins just so, with a title page and numbers at the top? Not with so much competition in a state filled with brainy, corn-fed Minnesotans, half of them know-it-all splittails with parents who acted like their crap didn't stink. Faces might crack if they smiled and not because of the damn windchill factor—windchill being Minnesotans' way of bragging about their shitty weather while sounding smart enough to move south if they wanted.

Great Falls registered the lowest temperature in the nation this morning, 30° below, not counting windchill.

They were proud of that?

"Somewhere in Minnesota, there's a freakin' tombstone reads, 'One below, not counting windchill,' I shit thee not." Bull Guttersen again.

On the plus side there were blond girls who showed a warm interest in Will's dark skin, his rodeo muscles and warrior hair, girls being what had gotten him into this mess to begin with. After the Rez in Seminole County, Oklahoma, blondes appealed to him because they were exotic.

When Will showed Old Man Guttersen the contest

booklet, Bull had read aloud, "Win five days in New York City . . . United Nations tour . . . Run for Secretary-General, International Youth Council . . . Teens from all over the world."

The old man had tossed the booklet on the table. "Left-wing candy-asses, that's who's behind this baloney. Never made a payroll in their lives. What hooked you is them pictures. Splittails from Sweden, Denmark, Berlin."

Which was true, of course. That was the good thing about the old man, Will didn't have to lie.

Bull, who was experienced at promotion, had done some thinking. "Know what? You being a half-breed minority Injun might just scratch their itch. A delinquent, too—that can't hurt. But you ain't suggesting you write this article yourself?"

Will had replied, "What? You think I'm a dope? There's a teacher at school who likes me: Mrs. Thinglestadt. I'll get her to write it."

Which won the boy a nodding smile of approval from the old man. "Never thought I'd be saying this, considering you once offered to shoot me, but there are times I'd be proud to call you my son. I shit thee not, Pony Chaser."

Bull used *thee* and *thou*, having grown up Amish, driving a buggy and putting up hay, until he went into pro wrestling and became worldly. *Pony* was a name from a bit on *Garage Logic*, three hours of radio better than HBO. The old man was a reliable judge of entertainment after years in a wheelchair.

Bull had a bias for TV westerns, which he admitted. *Gunsmoke*, Roy Rogers, anything John Wayne ever did. All related to his profession, six years wrestling as Outlaw Bull Gutter, four years as Sheriff Bull Gutter. Still had the cowboy hats, one black, one white.

Pony Chaser, Bull told Will, was a decent ring name if Will ever showed an interest. Not as good as Bull Gutter or Crazy Horse Chaser, but better than Shadow Chaser, which sounded like a candy-ass name, or Whiskey Chaser, which risked having a negative influence on teenage boys who didn't have the benefit of Will's experience in life.

"Get some size on you—earn it, so to speak—Crazy Horse might be the name that gets you into the World Wrestling Federation. I'll let you know."

As the car hummed along, Will was surprised how strong the old man was in his mind. Sour old white guy—*Caspers*, they called white guys on the Rez, which had something to do with a cartoon ghost. But Guttersen still had backbone even though his spine had been broken doing a cage show in Muscatine.

"Act fearless—the world's full of cowards eager to believe." Otto Guttersen, the philosopher.

"Life's not like poker. Win or lose, attack, keep gambling, because once you cash those chips you're screwed." The man could go on for hours and often claimed the boys down at Berserker's Grill said he should write a book.

Attack. Exactly the way Will had decided to handle this situation.

First thing he did was stop blaming himself. While it

was true he'd cheated his way to New York, the moron really to blame was the big, goofy-looking guy wearing glasses.

"Get back in the car!" the man had yelled, an order which Will had obeyed out of respect for being in such a big city. That's who was to blame for getting him into this mess.

If Will had kept going—helped the woman senator, as he intended—no telling how things might have worked out.

The senator was rich—she had to be—and had a nice smile. She smelled good, too, with interesting curves for a woman so old, which she pretended to want to hide. But she didn't—not really—wearing her jacket open to give Will a look at her blouse, the way buttons strained, then showing him a flash of black bra as if it were accidental.

It wasn't accidental, as his English teacher, Mrs. Thinglestadt, had proven to him back in Minnesota.

Pretty girls: something else that had gotten him into this fix. Well . . . a pretty woman, because Will couldn't justly think of a teacher as a girl. Not after charming Mrs. Thinglestadt for three careful months and finally getting her to invite him home to seduce him.

Bull had agreed it was smart, the way Will had made her beholden by proving his trust. Meeting the woman late in the park off Minnehaha and 46th, no one around but a few drunken Skins. Handing her the baggie of weed, then pocketing her money, before telling her how heavy it made his heart seeing his ancestors living like shit-faced bums.

Will had almost used the word *firewater* but decided no, not everybody watched westerns.

Mrs. Thinglestadt was a type. A milky-skinned female eager to prove she was open indeed by helping her inferiors one at a time. But smart in her way, obviously smart enough to write a prizewinning essay.

So he couldn't rightly blame her . . . unlike the jerk who'd ordered him back in the limo.

Big, goofy-looking dork. If I ever lay eyes on him again, just wait!

For now, though, Will was focusing on attacking the problem at hand. He'd been awake for more than an hour and was working in spurts to free himself even though his stomach was queasy from the ether.

He knew he was in a rental car—the assholes driving didn't realize he understood Tex-Mex Spanish. And because of the steady speed, he also knew they were on a highway and he'd be safe until the car began to slow.

The men had duct-taped his hands behind his back. It wasn't hard to wiggle his knees to his chest, then thread his feet through. Will had used his fingers to peel the tape from his mouth, then chewed his hands free. Next, his ankles, before tearing through the garbage bag they'd stuffed him into, not caring if he suffocated. He almost had suffocated when he vomited, the burn of upchuck being what saved him.

A garbage bag, like he was damn garbage or trash or an oil-patch 'groid. How many times had he been called names like that on the Rez or by drunk foster parents who hated kids but needed that good money the government paid?

Candy-asses.

First thing he did after peeling away that plastic bag was use the trunk liner to wipe has hands and face clean as he spit, spit, spit, trying to get the sick ether taste out of his mouth. No water. Nothing to piss in either. His new beaver cowboy hat was gone, too—the sonuvabitches wouldn't say where; they had no appreciation for fine western headgear. They'd also taken his wallet, which had almost two hundred dollars in it, plus a debit card good for seven hundred and forty dollars more, which Will had earned himself, saving for something special he'd wanted to buy . . . if he ever got the chance. Which he probably wouldn't, not after this.

They're gonna kill me, didn't even give me a can to piss in. Shows how much they don't care.

Will came close to retching again, thinking about dying, because he knew it was true.

Now he was at the rear of the trunk, his nose burrowed close to the taillight, where air filtered free of exhaust, cold off the highway. It was eerie red inside the trunk because of the taillights, the carpet hotter over the wheel wells.

Beside him was a tire jack, a lug wrench and a screwdriver that he'd found under the floorboard. Still working in spurts, Will squared the jack on the frame and ratcheted the jack until it was wedged tight against the trunk lid. He continued ratcheting, hearing metal creak as if the lid was about to burst open. It didn't.

Just wait 'til you open this sonuvabitch, you morons!

Will left the jack and rested for a few minutes before prying open the backside of a taillight. Every Skin on the Rez was a shade-tree mechanic. What he wanted was to short out the electrical system, but the damn fuses would blow first. Also, he didn't have a stripper or side cuts.

Instead, Will grounded a secondary wire just to see what would happen. The brake light began blinking. On the other side of the car, he yanked the ground wire free. The light went out.

Good. Give the cops a reason to stop us.

It was peculiar, lying there in the car's trunk, as the red taillight flashed. Piercing red, even with his eyes closed, while thinking about what they'd done to him.

Garbage . . . trash . . . oil-patch bucks. No water, his wallet stolen, no ID.

Yep, they were gonna murder him.

After several minutes of fuming about his situation, being killed by two spic-speaking strangers, Will felt a chemical sensation bloom in the back of his brain that caused his heart to pound. He sat up as the sensation radiated. He felt fear, then a suffocating panic.

"Stop! Stop this goddamn car!"

Will began kicking the floor, hammering at the trunk, wanting the assholes up front to hear. Kept yelling when the car veered right and began to slow. He didn't care about signaling the cops now. The panic was fading, yet the chemical burn remained. The pulsing red light remained, too—even as he got on his knees and ripped both taillights from their harnesses.

The red light he saw was behind his eyes, Will realized. Red, a color so bright he could smell it. He opened his eyes, then closed them. Red—still there, now strong enough to muffle his hearing.

"A grand mal seizure or anger-management problems," a government shrink had told Will's parole officer the first time Will had screwed up and actually told the shrink how it sometimes felt when he got mad.

What he didn't tell the shrink was that it had happened before. Happened again tonight, in fact, when the big Cuban-speaking asshole grabbed him by the back of the neck and shook him as if Will was a rag, no more valuable than a dog's toy.

Flash.

The man had snapped a photograph, causing more searing red dots to bloom.

Whenever the fear inside Will changed to rage, he saw that pungent color. His vision sharpened, the world quieted. Will saw only his adversary, alone in a tunnel of red, red silence.

The darkness of the trunk was red-hued now, as the vehicle bounced off the road and braked to a stop. Will checked the jack and cranked it one more notch, putting so much pressure on the lid that the trunk's hinges creaked like springs on a steel trap.

Will heard the car's front door open, passenger side, a voice saying, in Spanish, "Hurry, check on the brat—it's nine-thirty already!"

Door closed . . . Then Will listened to the heavy steps of a man walking on gravel, coming toward the back of the car to check the noise Will'd been making in the trunk.

Come on, you bastard, open it . . . Open it! Just you wait!

Will felt his brain burning, the anger was so strong. In his right hand, he gripped the lug wrench, while air molecules circulated around the trunk space in darkness, tracing pale gray contrails when the boy's eyes were closed . . . but sparking silver-red when they collided with Will's hard, dark eyes.

5

At 9:30 p.m., a security guard signed me into Barbara Hayes-Sorrento's suite, which was actually two suites, courtesy of hotel management. They'd donated the adjoining rooms because there were almost as many staffers inside working for the senator as there were reporters outside waiting for a statement.

Hooker was expecting me because the front desk had called. He wore a corduroy shooting jacket with patches at the elbows, a blue cravat tucked into his shirt. Same clothes he'd worn when he'd excused himself to freshen his whiskey four hours earlier at the Explorers Club. Not a stain or a scratch on him.

"Any word from the kidnappers?" I asked, taking off gloves that Esterline had loaned me. From the next room, I could hear one-sided phone conversations, the voices of men and women blending with the clatter of a printer.

"No news, I'm afraid. We've put a few pieces of the puzzle together, but nothing at all on the boy. The senator's been trying to contact his parents. Apparently, the father abandoned the family long ago. And staff can't seem to locate the mother."

Because the Brit read my expression correctly, he added, "It wasn't his parents. The boy lives with a foster family in Minneapolis. The men were after Barbara, no one doubts that. Thanks to you, I was able to steer her out of harm's way. Taking the child wasn't planned. It may be true of the limo driver as well, but that's not been confirmed."

I said, "William Chaser, a teenager from Minnesota. The police kept me updated."

"Yes—Will I think he's called. Good organization, the NYPD. They've assigned liaison officers to keep the senator informed. She's very pleased you got one of the kidnappers but worried about you catching pneumonia."

I was picturing the kid in his cowboy hat and boots, seeing his tough-guy expression when I ordered him back in the limo. By now, he had probably bawled himself dry, too scared to risk his cowboy act.

I said, "No father, living with a foster family? Jesus, a high school freshman. That makes him about thirteen years old."

Hooker said, "Fourteen. He was held back last term."

"Huh?" I didn't know details, but the essay contest had to be a big deal if the prize was a trip to New York. Statewide, maybe nationwide. And from Minnesota? He was no dummy.

"Perhaps troubled," Hooker offered. Barbara's staff

had assembled all the info they could gather on the teen—
not easily done because they couldn't contact his teachers
or friends until a parent had been notified. The foster parents didn't count because they weren't adopting, they
were volunteers with Lutheran Social Services. The program provided temporary homes for teens at risk.

Will Chaser had actually grown up on an Indian reservation south of Oklahoma City, Hooker told me. It
explained the cowboy connection. The reservation was in
Seminole County, oil and gas country, but also a stronghold of federally funded ghettos and the apparatus associated with despair: day care, public housing, programs for
substance abusers, which included about sixty percent of
the adult male population.

Two years ago, the Indian Opportunities Center had
"relocated" the boy to a Sioux reservation near Fond du
Lac. Maybe he had gotten in trouble, or maybe he'd dis-
played uncommon talent. A few months later, Lutheran
Social Services accepted him into their Foster Grandparents Program. He had been living in Minneapolis ever
since with a couple in their fifties, Ruth and Otto Guttersen. If the senator's staff couldn't contact the birth
parents by midnight, the FBI would notify the Guttersens
that Will had been abducted.

Hooker said, "The child has already had his share of
trouble. A bloody pity he has to go through something
like this."

"Fourteen years old," I repeated, feeling a renewed
urgency. I checked my watch: 9:40 p.m.

An abduction fires the irrational in rational people. The brain's flight-or-fight response triggers a craving to do *something* even when waiting is the only option and there is no visible foe to fight. I'd been through it.

Maybe the Brit understood because he made an effort to lighten the mood, waving me into the kitchen as he said, "While awaiting battle, the wise knight oils his armor." He took a six-pack from the refrigerator. "Care for a drop or two?"

Rolling Rock, green bottles. When I reached for one, he warned, "Not yet," then used his steel pincers to pop the tops.

"Handy."

"That's why it's attached to my wrist. But this doesn't compare to an ice ax. You made an unusual choice of weapons, Ford. If memory serves, the intelligence services haven't used an ice ax since your people summited Leon Trotsky in Mexico."

I took a step and winced because of my knee. "I'd forgotten. But they left the business end in Trotsky's head, didn't they? I left mine in the street. If it's valuable, I hope someone returned it."

"The last man to use that ax was Sir Edmund on Everest. Thanks to you, I may lose my fellowship next committee vote." The Brit smiled. "Don't worry, the ax is back on the wall. And Hilly would have approved, I think."

I followed him around the corner into the sitting room, where management had set up a buffet table. In the adjoining suite, they had also installed desks and additional computer lines.

The room was crowded. A half dozen people, a plain-clothes bodyguard, plus Senator Hayes-Sorrento, who was pacing the terrace, a phone wedged against her ear. Staffers were also on phones or frowning at their computer screens. When the woman noticed me, she waved and managed a wan smile but continued talking, emphasizing a point to some subordinate.

The senator looked good for a woman who had just been assaulted. Blue blouse, gray slacks—the first female on the hill to wear men's suits. She had been a TV anchor before inheriting a congressional seat from her late husband. The woman still had the requisite good chin and eyes, the photogenic jaw that could flex on cue. She was also smart as hell. The Senate was the next logical step.

Writers described her as *handsome,* a word safely attached because the mix of feminine and masculine reflected her political style but also transmitted a sexuality that was pure female. It was no charade. On a recent Caribbean vacation, it had almost ruined the senator's career. A blackmailer, a hidden camera and a beachboy were involved.

Thanks to random good luck, I was able to snatch the video and return it. Barbara and I had had a few dates since, but I didn't feel the abdominal awareness that signals sexual chemistry—possibly because those signals weren't being sent by Barbara.

I liked the woman. She was driven and complex, and aggressively private in the way some public figures are. Because of the way I'd dealt with the video, she trusted me. Because I knew the video's content, pretense was pointless. The woman felt free to say damn-near anything when we were alone together. We hadn't known each other long, we weren't lovers, yet were becoming confidants. It was an unusual relationship for two healthy heterosexual adults.

As I stood in the doorway, talking with Hooker, I glanced toward the terrace to confirm Barbara was still on the phone. She'd been looking at me, hoping to get my attention. I saw her confidential nod, as she held up a finger, eyes posing the question *Can you give me a few minutes?*

No problem.

Hooker noticed the exchange. He took out a cell phone, touched a button or two, then slipped it into his pocket. "This might be a good time."

I said, "For what?"

He put his hand on my shoulder and leaned so he could say privately, "There's a gentleman who would like to have a word with you."

"Who?" I was unfolding the paper he had slipped into my hand. There was a key, too.

"It's a room number. Just down the hall."

"Do I know this person?"

Hooker replied, "I couldn't say," meaning exactly that.

The room was empty but the phone was ringing. It was my old boss, Harrington, the man who'd summoned me to New York.

When I recognized the voice, I said, "The gentleman who gave me the message. A new member of your staff?"

"No, just returning a favor. You sound irritated."

I was, but it wasn't because he'd used Hooker as a messenger. "I had a date tonight, but something pulled me away. Your people? I need the truth."

Harrington said, "*Our* people, you mean?"

"Depends on the answer."

"Why do you think I called? You're suspicious because of the timing. I would've been suspicious myself."

I said, "As a general rule, I'm suspicious of anyone who invites me to lunch. Almost getting killed proves it's a good rule."

In the last week, Harrington and I had met several times, usually at the Lotos Club, but once at the Café Vivaldi, in Greenwich Village, where we'd interviewed a member of Alpha 66, a Cuban militant group. Fidel Castro's personal possessions—the contents of a secret home, including his private papers—had been discovered, seized and shipped to Langley. That was the story leaked to the international press anyway. *Castro Files* was the phrase being used to underplay that more than three tons of personal effects, books, photos and papers had been confiscated.

Harrington had a personal interest in what the files contained. So did I. It was my main reason for coming to New York.

I changed my question to eliminate wiggle room. "Did you have any prior knowledge about what happened tonight? Even a hint?"

With the phone to my ear, I was searching the room, opening closets, switching on lights. Empty rooms make me nervous. So do telephones.

Harrington said, "Zero. No involvement. It's not the way we operate. Even off the reservation, it would mean breaking all the rules. Can you think of an exception?"

He was talking about the kidnapping. Anywhere outside the United States was off the reservation.

I said, "The only rule is, there are no rules," quoting one of the organization's own maxims. But he was right. I couldn't think of an exception.

"Besides, do you really think I would've okayed anything involving an exemption? How long have we known each other?"

An exemption was a noncombatant minor. *Exceptions are exempt*—another rule of a black ops team that had no rules.

I wanted to believe him. Harrington had a daughter. Like me, he had lived through a kidnapping. Plus, the man had changed in a way I'd yet to quantify. In our meetings, he'd been personable, not cold. He'd admitted past mistakes and made comments that were introspective, even philosophical—totally out of character. Maybe years of accumulated guilt had snapped some internal guy wire.

It happens. It has happened to stronger, smarter men than me, which is why I focus on the present, not the past. I am aware of the dangers of exploring murky demarcations between principles and morals, obligations and duty. I prefer sunnier places, like the Amazon.

A more compelling reason to believe Harrington was what Choirboy had told me while we were in the water. My second question was: *Why kidnap the senator?*

Choirboy's answer had implicated a group of religious crazies. But even if he spoke the truth, it didn't guarantee he knew the truth.

I said to Harrington, "If the tables were turned, wouldn't I be your first suspect?"

He replied, "You're right about the timing. Yes, I understand. But this is a business call, not social. Do you mind?"

Someone could be listening. A warning in his tone. I sighed, preparing myself for a code protocol that was outdated but still part of the game.

Harrington said, "I think what happened tonight has to do with the library collection we discussed. Are you with me?"

He gave me a moment to translate: *Castro Files.*

"I want that collection. Sure. At least, take a look. But I'm not the only one. There are people all over the world who want it. And powerful organizations. A library that extensive? No telling what it's worth on the open market."

I said, "I know, I know. People are dying to get their hands on it."

"I'm not that desperate. Not yet. Move too fast, I overpay. But moving too slow could be even worse—for both of us. That's another reason I called. I'm counting on you to keep me updated. That shouldn't be hard. Same hotel, right?"

He was referring to Barbara.

"It's like you're a mind reader."

"Odd, that you should make that reference. I enjoyed your friend's lecture. It was interesting. Maybe you should consult him on the matter."

He had heard Tomlinson speak on psychic surveillance? The new, open-minded Harrington.

I listened to him say, "The people who screwed up your dinner plans tonight are making a bid on the collection. That's what happened."

"A theory?"

"If your girlfriend's people haven't heard, they soon will. The info's coming in right now. Hold on." The phone went silent. I guessed he was reading a bulletin on the SIGINT web, a high-clearance intelligence source. "The party crashers don't want the entire library. They want four volumes."

Harrington was telling me the kidnappers had made contact with a ransom demand. I looked at the door, wondering if Barbara knew.

"The same volumes we want?" *We* wasn't used editorially. It was possible that a carton labeled C/CN-103 contained information on an illegal organization. Harrington was still involved. I was once a member. It was the Negotiating and Systems Analysis Group—the Negotiators. Information about the organization could be filed under c for *Castro* and cn for *Clandestine*.

If there was such a file, it contained the last documents anywhere that proved the Negotiators existed—or so Harrington had promised me.

Harrington said, "Different volumes. There's proof, if you need it. What they're after wouldn't interest you or me. Feel better?"

I asked about the boy, saying, "Do they still have something to trade?"

Harrington said, "Looks like they might—there's a photo. I'm reading their offer right now." There was another long pause before he said, "Do me a favor, stick by the phone, okay?"

He hung up.

More than just files and property had been seized. Harrington had finally told me the whole story after our meeting with the Alpha 66 militant.

Cuba was not a peaceful place, despite the death of the man Cubans once called the Maximum Leader, or the Bearded One.

Fidel Castro's secret retreat had been uncovered on a tiny island off the southern coast of Cuba, Playa Giron. The island had been declared a military zone in 1962 but, in fact, Castro owned the island. Used it for vacations, then as his home in later years, finally as a sanctuary when he became ill.

After officially transferring control of Cuba to his

brother, Raul, Fidel had spent his last year on Playa Giron, writing his memoirs, almost a hermit except for medical attendants, visiting physicians and a few friends. His most valued possessions were brought to him—a common request for a dying man but Fidel Castro was anything but common. He ordered his valuables hidden, anticipating that his regime might have to live in exile for years before returning to power.

He was at least partly right. The Castro regime collapsed soon after his death in December, although not as soon as some expected, and the main players had fled to a sympathetic Venezuela, either unaware of what the Maximum Leader had left behind or where the valuables were hidden.

When the U.S. military discovered the cache, Castro's assets—Playa Giron included—were declared to be without legal provenance and so were confiscated. The collection now filled an entire warehouse at a secret facility in Maryland, not Langley, Virginia.

Fifty years of secrets, tens of thousands of documents censored to protect only Castro, plus a hidden cache of Fidel's personal possessions. Because the Senate and the CIA had been in a tug-of-war, courts had sealed the containers soon after they were grouped and before most were cataloged or analyzed.

There was worldwide political interest because of the files, but there was also a treasure trove of valuables—literally.

Two decades before his death, Castro started a government-funded salvage company, Carisub. Several dozen

Spanish treasure galleons had sunk in Cuban waters, and Carisub's mission was simple: Find the treasure and notify Fidel, who was an avid diver.

Carisub used four boats and employed sixty divers, who were trained in archaeology, epigraphy and numismatics. They were an elite team, all loyal members of the Cuban Communist Party.

Cuba is a treasure diver's dream, and Carisub's pros found a lot of wrecks and salvaged a fortune in Spanish gold, silver, coins, emeralds, rubies and jewelry.

It was known that the Cuban dictator had invested in small rarities to shield his own wealth and also to give him a quick out. Fifty million in gold was fifty kilos of trouble. But fifty million in rare stamps and gems could be hidden in a hatband and converted into cash anywhere in the world.

To the world's clandestine organizations, though, the cache of private papers was more valuable. Unknown facts about the Cuban Missile Crisis, President Kennedy's assassination, the Soviet collapse, funding of anti-Western terrorist organizations, the truth about Angola and Granada—surprising data might surface.

The same groups were worried that other secrets might surface, too.

Appointed as cochair of a Senate intelligence subcommittee, Barbara had been at the center of the political firestorm that followed. Fidel's private papers and files were a small part of what had been seized, but their contents might have a big impact in terms of national security or intelligence. Barbara Hayes-Sorrento, backed by the powerful Cuban-American lobby, wanted the papers to be made public.

Harrington and I did not want them made public, not until we knew what the files contained anyway, something I hadn't told the senator.

My friendship with Barbara Hayes-Sorrento was coincidental but was now potentially useful. It put me in a helluva tough position. My standards of morality change with border crossings. But never in my life have I set up a friend or allowed anyone to use me as bait to harm a friend.

That's exactly what Harrington had been asking me to do. But it was different now—in my mind anyway—because the kidnapping gave me a legitimate reason to stay in close contact with Barbara. I had been there when it happened. I was the one who had told the teenager to stay in the car—the worst possible advice, it turned out.

I wanted an active role in tracking the bastards and catching them. When Harrington finally called back, I tried to make that clear.

I said, "I'm more of a hands-on sort of person. We should get together and discuss the next step." He had confirmed the kidnappers had made contact before returning to the subject of Castro's files and Senator Hayes-Sorrento.

"More questions?"

"A request, really."

Harrington said, "I'm all ears."

"I want an application."

"A job, you mean. A real job . . . with us."

"That's right."

"No need to apply. The answer is yes."

I stopped by a window. The room was on the eighth floor. Snowflakes convexed skyward on a monoxide thermal, car lights eight stories below. "You're sure you understand what I'm asking—"

"I offered you two research positions. You nixed both. Finally, we've found something that meets your high standards. I'm relieved."

The sarcasm wasn't imaginary. I was working on my own terms now. I'd told him I would accept only assignments that meshed with my interests as a biologist or that presented an unusual technical challenge. I was a private contractor, in theory, who had yet to accept my first job.

Harrington had offered me missions in Venezuela and Pakistan. I already had enough enemies in South America. For the Pakistan job, I needed at least six weeks to get in the kind of shape the job required.

I had said no to both.

Going after the teenager, though, was a good fit. Because I had a personal interest, I would have requested the job even if hack amateurs had abducted him. But these people weren't hacks, they were pros—I'd seen their work. If they kept the boy alive, I had a decent chance of doing a reverse snatch-and-bag. The kidnappers would expect law-abiding cops, not someone like me.

I said, "Then I can pursue the matter." The kidnappers and boy, I meant.

"I'm all for it. But gloves on while you're on the reservation."

I said, "Of course," because it's what I was required to say. "What else do you know?"

"They want four cartons, two labeled J, two labeled S. Why? I don't know yet."

The image of a semi came into my mind, the cartons like oversized blocks, filling the trailer. J for *jewelry*, S for *salvage*.

"They sound like businessmen, not collectors."

"Or salesmen. Too early to say."

"A straight trade?"

"With a deadline. Sunday morning at eight." I was looking at my watch as he added, "A little more than sixty hours. But that's their guess, so it could be way off. It depends on the battery."

I didn't know what that meant. "Maybe we can humor them, get an extension."

"Not a chance. They don't have control over the deadline."

"You just lost me."

"I'm thinking of your home state. Do you remember the name Mackle? As in *Mackle Brothers*? Think back. You'll understand the deadline."

Mackle—the name had a distant familiarity.

I said, "They were developers. Maybe still are. Are those the—"

"Yes, the same."

The Mackle Brothers did Florida megaprojects. Marco Island was one. Port Charlotte was another. Turnkey cities. Big money. I said, "One of the brothers had a daughter who was in the news because—" I caught myself because I remembered now. The Mackle girl had been kidnapped. Her abductors had devised an ingenious way to put responsibility for the girl's life into the hands of law enforcement.

I said carefully, "She was detained."

"That's right."

"In a . . . small room."

"She might as well have been underground."

I didn't remember how long the girl had been buried. "Thirty-six hours?"

"Almost four days. With only the basics: a little water, a battery-powered fan. Very motivational."

I understood now about the deadline. I whispered, "The sonsuvbitches."

"I hope you can pass the message along personally, Doctor."

Suddenly, my transportation problems were more urgent. I needed to get home. I had weapons there, and other equipment. A commercial flight home wasn't good enough.

When I told Harrington, he said, "There are some fairly decent outfitters closer to your hotel. Langley, Beltsville. How about Little Creek?"

If I needed weapons, he was telling me, I could choose from the best armories.

I said, "No need. A quick trip to Florida, down and back. Then anyplace else I need to go."

Harrington knew what I was requesting. He said check

back in a hour, he would see what he could do, then added, "But stay focused on your research. You're working two jobs now—don't forget."

He was referring to Barbara and Castro's files again. What did the woman know?

6

They've threatened to bury Will alive," Barbara told me when I returned to her suite. "We have until eight a.m. on Sunday. They mean it. Our driver was found dead, stuffed into the trunk of the car."

She'd just gotten the news.

The woman gave me an emotional hug, her eyes clear, not red as I'd expected, but she sounded dazed. "I'm sorry I dragged you into this, Doc. I'm like poison lately. I hurt everyone I touch."

The woman thought I was being kind when I replied, "I can empathize. But it's not true of you."

An FBI agent and a uniformed NYPD captain were in the operations suite when Barbara led me in. I had interrupted a briefing. Barbara's staff was seated around the room, heads down. Phones had been muted but message lights pulsed at random on each desk.

There is an airless quality to a room filled with people in shock, a pheromone tension that depletes oxygen and leaches sweat. Small sounds echo. A cough is an occasional mask of the unchecked sob. Airports have a designated room. This room at the Waldorf was too richly lighted for the dark space it had become.

Hooker stood in the back, his expression attentive, not somber—a man accustomed to conflict. He nodded at me, then used his eyes to steer my attention to a computer.

On the screen was a photo of the teenage boy, Will Chaser. His abductors had used a flash. The black background was a garbage bag, possibly in the trunk of a car. His mouth was taped, cheeks inflated, and his brown eyes bulged as if surprised by the sudden light. They'd just removed his blindfold.

It was a close-up, head and shoulders. The pearl buttons of his western shirt matched the boots and cowboy hat I'd seen earlier. So did the untanned line on his forehead where black hair spilled over, thick as a brush. Because the boy's chin was thrust forward, I guessed his hands were taped behind his back.

Looking at the photo, the image of Bern Heller sparked behind my eyes, then dissipated due to clinical indifference. In the Darwinian paradigm, a self-culling mechanism is requisite.

The image was replaced by the face of Will Chaser, the country boy newly arrived in the big city, all polished and brushed. I'd been amused by his tough guy posturing. "A goat ever kicked your ass, mister?" He'd said that when I'd hollered, "Kid!" Just off the plane, a teen who'd been miniaturized by skyscrapers, atomized by crowds, reduced to a speck, but he still had enough Oklahoma grit on his boots to fire back at a stranger.

No more tough-guy attitude. Not now. Adults go into shock when taped, gagged and blindfolded. This was a small-town boy. In the photo, he looked helpless as an infant.

As I followed Barbara across the room, the police captain, a woman named Tiffany Denzler, frowned her disapproval, saying, "Another outsider, Senator? This briefing was intended to be confidential."

Hooker and I, the outsiders. Or maybe she meant staff, too. The captain had a point. Any of us could have ties with the bad guys.

Turning to the FBI agent, Denzler added, "I wouldn't allow it, normally. I'm not sure I'm going to allow it tonight," her tone less differential, her body language letting the room know that she was in charge—a bird-sized woman claiming more space, the way she stood, elbows out, hands on her familiar gun belt where there was a 9mm Glock, right side, in a speed holster.

The cop's attitude changed when Barbara released my arm, saying, "Captain, were you sent to make decisions? You're here to follow orders, that's my understanding."

"If that's your understanding, Senator, I'm not going to burst your bubble—"

"A wise choice, Captain Denzler. You would disappoint the police commissioner and the head of your NYPD Captains Union—they've been very supportive in our phone conferences. The commissioner spoke well of you."

Denzler cleared her throat. "Senator Hayes-Sorrento, if you expect us to find these people we can't share information with every out-of-town visitor who happens to be in the neighborhood—"

"Visitors, Captain? How many of the kidnappers do you have in custody?"

Denzler said, "Pardon me, Senator?" to give herself a second before she answered, "I have one suspect in custody. He hasn't been charged yet because—"

"He's not your suspect, you didn't catch him." Barbara motioned to me. "This gentleman did . . . and almost died. And the man in the back of the room got me out of one hell of a dangerous spot. You haven't met Sir James Montbard and Dr. Ford. When you do, take a moment and thank them. If you're smart, you'll ask for their input."

Barbara's voice softened but not her tone as she added, "I don't expect miracles. I know the numbers and they're not encouraging. There are twelve thousand taxis and limos in this city. And, what, forty-some thousand taxi and limo drivers? It's impossible to search every vehicle. Or to seal off the island. The NYPD is as good as it gets. But you personally, Captain, haven't done a goddamn thing to impress me. Until you do, don't presume to give orders. You will treat my staff and associates with respect. Is that understood?"

It was like a balloon deflating, the way Denzler looked in her starched uniform, arms at her sides now, while the FBI agent took an imperceptible step, distancing himself. The cop's eyes moved from me to Hooker as if seeing us for the first time. "I didn't realize, gentlemen. I apologize. I read the report on the abduction and what happened at the park. Outstanding, the way you responded, especially for civilians."

Hooker said, "High praise indeed," sounding sincere but smiling.

Barbara had moved close enough to put her hand on the policewoman's shoulder but didn't. The positioning suggested endorsement yet withheld approval. The woman knew how to manipulate people and control a room.

"The important thing, Captain, is that we work together. You're the expert. We're the amateurs. We need your help."

"Senator, I think we got off on the wrong foot—"

"Don't we all occasionally? I should have discussed protocol with you privately. But let's get down to business"—Barbara was pouring herself a glass of wine—"so please continue with your briefing. Hold all questions until you're done?"

Denzler replied, "That works for me," sounding grateful and eager to please.

Senator Hayes-Sorrento poured a second glass of wine. As she offered it to me, I gave her a look: *Impressive*.

The woman shrugged, her eyes looking into mine: *Part of the job*.

Nice eyes. Gray-green with flecks of gold. *Power flecks*, my friend Tomlinson calls them. *Sensuality transceivers*.

I hadn't noticed before.

W_{hile} Denzler briefed us, the FBI agent's cell phone buzzed. He went outside to take the call. When he returned, his projected detachment told me it was important. But not too important it couldn't wait, because he took a seat and listened with the rest of us while the policewoman told us the latest.

At 8:45 p.m., the kidnappers had e-mailed a ransom note to three general Internet addresses used by the NYPD. Nearly an hour later, the photo arrived sent as an attachment.

The note was written in precise English, but the syntax suggested it was composed by someone whose native language was Spanish. Probably male. He had written "interned" instead of "buried." He had written "the air cylinder in testament produces" rather than "the oxygen tank will produce." The name William Chaser was used in the subject line of the photo, but the note referred to their captive as "she" or "the politician." The note had been written in advance of the abduction, anticipating the senator, not a teenage boy.

Denzler said she couldn't show us the note or the exact wording. Instead, she had created a computer document outlining key points. I understood the purpose but found it irritating.

The kidnapper's note said the Minnesota teenager would be put into a box, then buried. The box contained an air cylinder with enough oxygen for approximately thirty-six hours. A tube running from a canteen would be taped to the boy's mouth, so he would have a limited amount of water.

If certain demands were met, the kidnappers would post the GPS coordinates of the box on a popular third-party website. It didn't name the site. If the American government responded before eight a.m. on Sunday, the boy might live. If there was an attempt to negotiate, or to pursue, the boy would die.

The kidnappers had effectively placed the boy's life in the hands of the people they were extorting. They claimed to be Castro Revivalists and wanted Cuba to return to National Socialism. They called themselves the *Bearded Ones*.

In the frozen pond, Choirboy hadn't mentioned Castro Socialists. Judging from the FBI agent's physical response—he looked at the floor, nose wrinkled as if sniffing—he didn't believe it either. Captain Denzler did.

"It explains why they were after you, Senator Hayes-Sorrento. Your committee has authority over the materials they're demanding—it's been on the news."

Denzler touched a remote; the computer screen changed. "Here's what they want. They refer to them as files. Files C/J-116 through C/sa-120. We've been unable to confirm that these files exist." The woman gave it a second. "Do they exist, Senator?"

Barbara was sitting between her chief of staff and her attorney. Both were taking notes. I watched the woman nod. "They're not just files. Our people discovered a . . . a place, where the former dictator's personal papers were being warehoused. Some personal possessions, too."

Some personal possessions? The woman was good.

She said, "But because the information has been"—Barbara glanced at her attorney, who was shaking her head—"because the information is classified, my staff will investigate the steps necessary to arrange a private deposition. I want to do everything I can to help this child."

The FBI agent said, "You can confirm, though, these designations match materials that have been cataloged?"

"Not cataloged—not yet. Grouped under very general terms. Subgrouped, really. C for *Castro*, then subgrouped, A for *apple*, B for *baseball*. Like that. The number refers to the carton. C/J-116, for instance, means *Castro Files*, letter J, carton 116. You might find something related to Japan inside. Or jewelry. I'm not saying there is jewelry, understand. It's just an example."

Denzler asked, "What about this one: C/sa? Carton 120."

Becoming impatient, Barbara replied, "As I said, everything's alphabetized. I assume fewer items begin with the letter J, so there's only one carton. More items are in subgroup S, so there are two or three cartons. Sometimes dates were also added. A sort of sub-subgrouping. The work had to be done"—Barbara hesitated—"in a limited amount of time."

"How many people know about the labeling system?"

"Too many, obviously."

The policewoman started to ask another question but decided to let it go. "Then it fits. A pro-Castro organization demanding Fidel Castro's files. Certain items, I'm saying, that's what they're demanding."

Barbara was looking at the screen, way ahead of Denzler, maybe thinking what I had already concluded: The kidnappers had insider information. They knew how the items had been organized and at least an idea of what the cartons contained.

After a long silence, the FBI agent said, "That's very helpful, Senator Hayes-Sorrento, thank you," then looked at Denzler, who got the hint, and stepped back so he could talk.

The FBI agent said, "There was a kidnapping that has interesting similarities. A college student named Barbara Mackle was abducted and buried in a specially constructed box. She was targeted because her father was a wealthy Florida developer. Her abductor was an escaped convict, Gary Krist. Krist spent a month at the Miami Public Library searching for the perfect victim for what he considered the perfect crime . . ."

I tuned out the agent, less interested. Harrington had made the connection with the Mackle case. As an intelligence consultant, he would've had no trouble piping information to the FBI.

I was thinking about the third question I had asked Choirboy when we were in the water: *Who is your contact in America?* His organization had known the senator's schedule. There had to be an informer.

Choirboy gave me a name. A code name, really. If I hadn't been freezing, I might have experienced my first emotional chill. The name was linked to my own personal history. If I believed in evil, the name might have once defined it.

"Tenth Man," Choirboy told me, although it was difficult to hear because of his chattering teeth and the congealing fluid in my inner ears. Salt water and blood both crystallize at thirty degrees Fahrenheit.

Tenth Man made no sense. An alternative translation had come to me later while under a hot shower at the station house.

Tenth Man . . . ? Ten Man . . . ?

No, Choirboy had said *Tinman*.

Maybe the same person, maybe not. I had my suspicions, nothing confirmed.

Tomlinson, my friend and neighbor on Sanibel Island, sometimes worked as a roadie for the classic rock band America. His favorite song: "Tinman." It didn't prove a connection, but the song wasn't his only linkage. Like me, he'd traveled the world. Like me, his past life was a gray region, an old map with unexplored territories. Because returning to Florida was now a priority—there was equipment I needed—I would also have my chance to discuss the significance.

I was eager to talk with Tomlinson.

My eyes moved around the room, seeing James Montbard at the back of it. He'd lost interest, too. Was it because he'd already heard the story from Harrington?

Barbara listened while going through a stack of faxes. Her face, seen in profile, showed the patrician nose, the strong chin. The starched collar of her blouse framed a glossy sweep of hair, and my eye moved naturally downward, the curvature of buttons incongruous with the detached expression on her face.

I pictured Barbara, not the Mackle girl, when the agent said, ". . . if it's not a hoax, we expect a second photo before they bury him. A photo of the box with the boy inside. Showing off. Like a trophy. Probably taken just before they close the lid."

By the time I had forced the image out of my head, the agent was saying, "Krist told Ms. Mackle the batteries would last a week if she was careful, but the fan would quit in two days if she wasted power. Understandably, she became hysterical when Krist sealed the box and she heard dirt being shoveled onto the lid.

"He told her, 'Shut up and stop acting like a baby.' That's an exact quote from the report." The agent's expression read *See the kind of people we're dealing with?*

He continued, "Two important points: If they bury Mr. Chaser, there's a chance we will get him back alive. Ms. Mackle was found—almost accidentally, by the way—eighty-six hours later, weak and dehydrated but still alive. Almost four full days. It proves a person can endure what these people are threatening to do. The key is giving the kidnappers what they want. That's hard for the FBI to say, but there it is.

"The second point isn't pleasant. The note mentions an air cylinder and a water tube. Nothing else. Ms. Mackle's abductor was a megalomaniac, a loser by every definition of the word, but he at least exhibited some empathy. He provided a little food, a few personal items and enough room for Ms. Mackle to bend her legs and arms."

The agent was referring to the tube that would be taped to Will Chaser's mouth. Either the coffin was too cramped to lift a canteen or the kidnappers planned to bury Will with his hands bound. Why else make him drink through a tube?

When the agent described the tube and how Will's hands were taped, Barbara's attorney stood, made a coughing sound, then rushed from the room. Two staffers followed, maybe to help but more likely not.

"He's better off dead," I heard one of them say.

7

When Hump leaned over the rental car and pressed the button, the trunk shot open as if on springs. The Chrysler emblem whacked the man hard on the chin, and his knees buckled as he backpedaled.

Hump let himself fall, expecting to land in weeds and trash, like in the ditches in Havana. But Farfel had stopped at the edge of a ravine on an off-ramp where there was no traffic, only the window lights of a distant home—a ranch or farmhouse—the world starry-skied and silent at ten p.m.

Dazed, the huge man braced for impact. But instead of a ditch, he dropped fifteen feet off the hill's sheer lip and landed hard, shoulders first. Hump made a high-pitched whine of surprise, then a wheezing *whufff* when he hit.

Out of control, he tumbled down the hill through bushes and nettles, his arms covering his head because of the rocks—and also because of his bloody ear, which the sonuvabitching kid had bitten almost off, after promising to cooperate when they'd stopped to kill the limo driver.

Hump kept his head covered several seconds after banging against what might have been a fence, unconvinced he had reached the bottom, or that this wasn't another of the kid's vicious tricks.

Then Hump raised his head to look because he heard something. No, someone . . . Yes, cowboy boots on rock.

Mamoncete!

Instead of trying to escape, the insane boy was chasing him down the hill.

Scrambling to his feet, Hump called in Spanish to his partner, "Farfel, I have captured him. He is here—," then made the wheezing *whufff* noise again when the boy tackled him, shoulder down, swinging wildly at Hump's head with a lug wrench.

"Farfel! Come quickly. I have the little goat turd!"

Will Chaser spoke Tex-Mex Spanish and understood enough Cuban to yell in reply, "You're the turd! I'll use your horn as a damn gun rack!," referring to what he'd said before biting Hump's ear in the limo: "A head like yours needs glass eyes and a plaque on the wall."

Will was on the huge Cuban's back, trying to fight the man's hands away so he could get a clean shot with the lug wrench. When Hump tried to elbow him, Will countered with his own elbow, hammering at Hump's neck. When Hump tried to buck free, Will locked his legs around Hump's waist, the toes of his boots cinched tight.

"Get off me, you little *maricon*! Get off me and I won't hurt you, I swear."

Will yelled, "Stop moving—I'll surrender," hoping to knock the Cuban unconscious with the wrench, but Hump continued to buck and roll.

No way could the huge man buck him free. It was because the boy was experienced in riding animals that bucked. Before Will was expelled from school and sent north, to Minnesota, he was on the Seminole Oklahoma Rodeo Team, top steer wrestler and bull rider, Junior Division. He would have won a third All-Around Cowboy title if the cops hadn't discovered that his horse, Blue Jacket, was actually Paddy's Painted Darling, a famous roping pony and quarter horse stud that had disappeared six months earlier from Lexington Farms, Texas.

Only twice in his life had Will Chaser ever cried, not counting when he was an infant, which he couldn't remember. First time was when the cops trailered Blue Jacket and drove away. He had cried in private, of course, where no one could hear.

The second time was just a few hours before Hump opened the trunk. Stuffed in a garbage bag, his hands, feet and mouth duct-taped, Will had listened to the limo driver begging for his life and then to his screams as the Cuban assholes stabbed him.

In the abrupt, rattling silence that followed, Will had wept, convinced he would be the next to die, regretting only then that he had insulted the Cuban, telling him his head would make a nice trophy.

Now, though, Will was filled with rage, not regret.

The thing growing from the side of Hump's head was spiked, like a tooth. It made a good target for Will. He had the man on the ground now and he swung the lug wrench with intent.

The big Cuban was quick, though, deflecting the boy's arms when he swung the wrench, metal sparking off rocks with each miss. That ancient sound, steel striking stone—*cha-leenk*—was scary so close to Hump's bloody ear. The Cuban had been surprised, but now he was getting mad.

"Get off me!"

"Hold still."

Cha-leenk.

"I'm warning you."

"Quit bouncing, you candy-ass!"

Cha-leenk. Sparks showed Hump's black eyes.

"You little queer, I'll kill you!"

The huge man stood, Will's legs still cinched around his waist. Using the butt of the lug wrench, Will pounded Hump's neck as Hump staggered to a fence, turned and slammed hard against it, crushing Will against the boards.

Will lost the wrench in the first collision. Hump rammed the fence again and Will fell to the ground. Hump leaned over the boy—*"Maricon!"*—and began kicking.

"Don't kill him. Not yet!" Farfel was yelling as he zigzagged down the hill, careful not to fall. He had a pistol in his left hand. The pistol had a laser sight that painted a narrow band of light over the tree canopy as it sought the boy.

Hump kicked again and Will felt a rib snap. He screamed and rolled away in a fetal position.

Now Farfel was yelling, "You idiot! Not until we get another photograph!"

Will remained balled up, expecting to be kicked again. A moment passed. He looked up. A couple of yards separated him from the huge man, who was looking at the older Cuban.

It was time to let the men know he spoke Spanish. Will said, "I'm sorry. Please don't hurt me no more," as he got to his feet. Because Hump was coming at him again, Will added quickly, "Promise, I'll do what you tell me. Goddamn, you busted up my ribs! I'll do anything you say."

Hump stopped and touched the back of his head, then squinted at his fingers: blood. His head was ringing from the blows and his ear was throbbing. "You crazy brat, you hurt me with that tire tool. I will have a knife next time. I will cut you like a frog!"

Will had his hands on his knees, groaning like he was going to be sick—and he *did* feel sick—but he was also examining the nearby fence: four boards high, on the back side of a pasture, with strands of electric wire strung tight on insulators. There were probably horses or bulls grazing inside or maybe buffalo. Will had noticed the lights of the ranch, which had sparked a homesick-like feeling inside him.

The older Cuban called, "Come back to the car. We won't tie you this time." He was motioning for Will to follow. The man had nasty metallic eyes. He was lying, of course.

Will yelled, "I will. I promise. But first I have to do something."

As the two Cubans looked at each other wondering if maybe Will had to piss, Will threw the rock he'd been palming. The rock was baseball smooth, oval shaped and heavy. It bounced off Hump's forehead, making a melon sound.

Tú cabrón!

Will scrambled over the fence, jumped clear of the insulators and ran. Seconds later, he heard the huge man bellow again. Will made a chortling-crying sound, a mix of laughter and pain from the broken rib, but he continued running.

The dumbass grabbed the electric fence.

Across a hundred yards of pasture, Will could see the elegant silhouettes of dozing horses and the yellow windows of a ranch house. A larger house, mansion-sized, lay beyond. The boy ran, one hand holding his ribs, legs taking long strides, his boots familiar with the cobble work of hoofprints in a frozen meadow.

Every few seconds, Will glanced over his shoulder. No sign of the Cubans.

As he ran, the nickname old Otto Guttersen had invented came into his brain: *Pony Chaser.* For the first time, the name fit, like in the TV westerns. The tough kid running from the bad guys . . . only, on TV, the bad guys were usually Skins, not Cubans, men who really would kill him if they caught him.

Will no longer felt tough. *A knife?* The thought of a blade puncturing his body until he quit breathing? The limo driver's screams displaced everything in his head. He could hear the man begging, then screaming in rhythm with Will's boots as he ran across the field of rank grass and horse pies.

That's when he noticed the headlights: a car beyond the ridge, invisible until it crested the hill, its lights now teetering downhill, illuminating poles and gravel road, dust boiling behind as it accelerated toward the ranch house—a black Chrysler.

The Cubans.

Will ran harder, still favoring his rib, not sure if he could get to the house and bang on the door before the Cubans turned into the driveway

Should he keep running or hide?

Will was thinking, *It's going to be close.*

8

At midnight, I heard Barbara Hayes-Sorrento's finger-nails on my door. I checked the peephole, then flipped the bolt.

The woman said, "What a night," as she slipped into the room, nodding over her shoulder to someone in the hall. I got a glimpse of her chief of staff, his face illustrating patient disapproval. Maybe because he recognized me, he rolled his eyes: *I can't control her.*

I knew better than to try, not just because Barbara was a political star. Women perfect the subtleties of control—how to deflect, when to pressure—long before the small percentage of males who finally understand that control is acquired through skillful restraint, not won through confrontation.

"Were you asleep?" Barbara's shoulder brushed my ribs as she passed me, and I felt her tremble as I turned the dead bolt.

I said, "I was on the computer." I didn't add that a car

was picking me up in five hours. Harrington had arranged a direct flight to the municipal airport in Fort Myers.

"If I'm interrupting, I can—"

"No," I told her, "I was researching the kid's background. I found the place where he grew up. It was in Oklahoma. The reservation's not as bad as some. And the little town, Wewoka?—I'm not sure how to pronounce it—it looks like a nice place. A good high school rodeo team."

We were in the room where I'd used the phone earlier. I had spoken with Harrington again, twice. It was a room, not a suite. I slipped my arm into Barbara's and led her to the desk where my laptop was open, the lights of neighboring offices showing through the window, snow crested on the windowsill.

I wore Navy-issue swim shorts, khaki with brass rings for a buckle, no shirt and wire-rimmed glasses tied around my neck on fishing line as always. She was in the same business suit she'd worn at the briefing, the charcoal jacket on but not buttoned. It gave the impression she wasn't going to stay. Or that she had stopped, hoping I would invite her to come back after she had showered and changed.

Gesturing to my computer, I said, "The boy's foster parents, Otto and Ruth Guttersen, right?"

"They're not adopting, it's temporary. He's been in Minnesota for eighteen months."

"Otto Guttersen—there can't be many guys with that name—he was a pro wrestler. Not real wrestling, the soap opera stuff. Ten years on the Great Lakes circuit, shows in Minneapolis, Keokuk, Cleveland, Davenport. Small-time. Take a look."

Barbara was sitting at the desk. I leaned over her to retrieve a fifteen-year-old photo from the *St. Paul Pioneer*. A wide-bodied man, overstuffed in his hairless body, biceps and big belly flexed, showing the camera a crazed grin. He wore chaps, boots with spurs and a black cowboy hat. The caption read, "Outlaw Bull Gutter vs. Bobo Godzilla Tonight, Civic Auditorium." I said, "Minnesota has cowboys, too."

Sounding weary, Barbara laughed. "An Indian kid living with a make-believe cowboy . . . I don't know if it's sad or funny."

"Ironic anyway."

"Or maybe it's worked out. Half an hour it took us, from the airport to Midtown, and Will hardly said a word. But he took off his hat when we met. Shy but polite, you know? 'Very nice to meet you, ma'am.' That type. And he loved riding in a limo. But I could tell he was . . . different, somehow."

"Oh?"

"I expected a scholar, I guess. A nerd with glasses . . . No offense."

I said, "None taken," thinking about the kid's vocabulary.

"Maybe I understand now, one foster home after another. Tonight, he was reserved because he was overwhelmed—flying in at night, his first look at New

York City, skyscrapers and all those lights. But he loosened up by the time we got to the Explorers Club. In fact, he asked if I wanted to get together later for a drink."

"An adolescent boy?"

"That's what I'm saying. It was unexpected. A boy without a male role model. No one permanent anyway. Maybe thinking that's what men in the big city say to women. A line he heard in a movie."

"Have a drink, as in have a *drink*—coming on to you?"

She shook her head. "Of course not. At fourteen? He was trying to fit in. His whole life, Will has probably been trying to fit in. Dressing like a cowboy after a year with Outlaw Bull Gutter. He wears whatever costume it takes."

I was thinking twelve years on an Oklahoma reservation was a more likely explanation as I opened the courtesy bar. "I have bottled water, beer . . . wine, too. But I might have to call room service for a corkscrew . . . "

Barbara said, "No need to do that for me," meaning the shirt I'd grabbed, not the corkscrew. Her staff had delivered my things from the Explorers Club and my hotel.

I put the shirt on anyway but left it unbuttoned, as the woman said, "Let's talk about this," then explained that one glass of wine wouldn't help. It was impossible to sleep after what had happened.

"When I'm this wired, there are only a couple of

things that relax me. But I have to be with someone I can trust."

I didn't know what that meant. Because she saw me look at the clock radio, she added, "Plus, there's something personal I'd like to discuss."

I'd hoped to get five hours of sleep, but maybe the car Harrington was sending would be late.

I said, "Anything you want."

She said, "Don't volunteer before you know the mission," a line she'd probably heard at some military briefing, giving it an inflection that made me think, *Uh-oh!* "I'll be back in a minute."

I was buttoning my shirt as she went out the door.

Now she was sitting at the desk, sipping wine from a water tumbler, a half-empty bottle of red next to my laptop. She had closed the computer and rearranged the desk before using the corkscrew—a woman accustomed to taking charge.

She was wearing jeans and a green denim blouse, no makeup, her hair still wet from the shower. Barefoot, I noticed, as if she'd dressed in a rush, the emotional overload showing. I sat and listened, hoping she would burn adrenaline by talking.

The boy wasn't the only thing on her mind.

Her in-laws were flying in from Chicago, she told me. She was talking about her late husband's parents. Favar Sorrento had been an entertainment mogul before he went into politics and married Barbara, a TV anchor who was twenty-five years younger than the wife he'd just divorced.

Barbara said, "His mother's bearable in a passive-aggressive sort of way, but the father's a bastard. He's old-school Castilian Spanish. Left Havana just before Castro took power and still thinks a woman's place is on her back when she's wearing shoes and in the kitchen when she's not." The woman folded her hands behind her head and leaned back in the chair. "When Favar was alive, Favar Senior tried to undermine my influence in every imaginable way. Now he tries to take advantage of my influence in ways you can't imagine. He still treats me like a brainless trophy wife. Like the only reason I won the election is because I'm his dead son's proxy. Next election, I finally drop the hyphen and the *Sorrento* and run under my own name."

Mostly, though, Barbara was awake because she was worried about the boy.

I stood, took the wine bottle and filled her glass, watching her nervous hands as she drank, her gray-green eyes showing more color when she turned from the window, saturated with light from the desk lamp. It was touching listening to her fret about a boy she barely knew. She had collected a lot of background and shared it with a harried energy that was symptomatic of guilt.

"Every time I close my eyes, I feel like I can't get enough air. Like it's me inside that coffin. When the agent described the convict shoveling dirt, the girl hysterical inside the box . . . my God, that's what happens when I start to drift off. I hear dirt hitting the lid"—she touched the palm of her hand to her nose—"this close to my face. God!"

She stood, too agitated to sit, and began to pace and talk.

Her staff still had a hell of a lot to do and was working around the clock. Everything in the cartons the kidnappers wanted was being cataloged and copied. A team had been assigned to arrange for a plane and crew to deliver the cartons—through the military or State Department possibly—hoping Barbara could convince her committee, along with other layers of government, to cooperate with the kidnappers.

"They have to," she said, but in a wistful way that told me she knew it wasn't true. "Goddamn them! They wanted me! Why did they have to take a fourteen-year-old boy?"

I stood and took her hands in mine. Held her, trying to stem an escalating panic that signaled hysteria. "Maybe someone on your staff has a sleeping pill or something. You need rest."

I was startled by an unexpected mood change. Barbara yanked her hands free and turned her back.

"Are you okay?"

"Ford, I need to ask you something. I want an honest answer."

"I'll try."

"I was hoping for a yes."

"A *maybe* is better than starting with a lie."

"If that's the way it has to be . . . The vacation video they were using to blackmail me . . . you said you discovered it accidentally?"

"Not accidentally. But it wasn't a priority. I knew there were videos of other people, some powerful."

"You said you took it because it was the right thing to do. A good deed for a stranger. You wouldn't accept money and didn't want anything in return from me."

I hesitated before putting a hand on her shoulder, thinking she might shrug it away. She didn't.

I said, "All true. But I was aware there are benefits to having a U.S. senator for a friend. Power radiates. I won't pretend I didn't know. You've done favors for me that you probably aren't aware of."

That's when she shrugged my hand away. I let it fall from her shoulder as she turned, looking up into my eyes. "I'm aware of more than you realize. Did you know that James Montbard is a British intelligence agent? *Covert.* He's been with MI6 for years."

"I didn't think the UK was our enemy."

"If you're going to play word games, I'm leaving."

I took a step back. "I'm sorry." I meant it. Then stupidly tried to add, "But I wasn't sure that Hooker was—"

The woman cut me off. "If you can't tell the truth, I'd prefer you said nothing."

I cleared my throat, said nothing.

Barbara faced the window, the reflection showing her eyes as she stared out, the night air cleaner now that it had stopped snowing. "What about Harrington?"

"You see him more than I do. What are you asking?"

I took a seat on the bed, with a bottle of water, as she said, "I'm curious about your relationship," then explained that her subcommittee relied on Harrington for information. He was a respected analyst in the world of intelligence gathering—also true. She didn't know, of course, it provided the perfect cover for Harrington's covert work.

Barbara said, "When I wanted you checked out, Hal was the person I asked. He gave you full marks. Do you know what strikes me as odd?"

She wasn't going to wait for an answer so I didn't offer one.

"I find it odd that you and Montbard, and Harrington, are all here, in New York, the same week I agreed to meet the boy. And only a few days after the court assigned control of the Castro Files to me. My subcommittee, I mean."

She cut me off when I tried to remind her that we'd made our date weeks before.

"I also find it strange that you know each other. Some might even say that you and Montbard made an effort to ingratiate yourselves. Returning the video, for instance. A coincidence?"

I was tempted to comment on the egocentric slip—*my subcommittee*—but said instead, "Or saving your life? If that's currying favor, your friendship bar is pretty high."

"You know I didn't mean that."

"I know you're making too much of it. Tomlinson's lecture was booked months ago. When Hooker found out, he decided to visit the Explorers Club while I was in town instead of coming in March. Seeing you was a nice perk, but—"

"Tomlinson," she said, "is someone else I find oddly suspicious."

I said, "Who doesn't?," unsettled that she'd made the connection, hoping she would smile. She didn't.

Instead, she got out of the chair, sighing as she stood over me, communicating something—disappointment? suspicion?—then went to the phone on the nightstand. She opened the drawer and took out a palm-sized tape recorder. *Surprise!* I overcame the urge to sit up straighter.

"This is voice-activated, a common security measure for rooms I book and pay for. When Sir James said he needed a phone, I gave him the key. Have you ever felt like someone is spying on you?"

"As of now."

"Good. I want you to know what it's like." Barbara hit FAST REVERSE and waited for the garbled voices to stop. "I haven't listened yet. Your call, Doc. Should I? You know things about me no one else knows. I find that scary."

She tossed the recorder onto the bed, stared at me. "Is there something in the Castro Files that scares you? I've had a look through those cartons, remember."

I cleared my throat again.

She sighed, this time communicating *I thought so,* then sat on the bed close enough to put her hand on my arm but didn't. I hadn't earned her approval. "I've heard rumors about a covert cell that's more like a secret society. *Clandestino*, in Spanish. Wouldn't that be filed under cn? If it's true, how many countries do you think would demand extradition? There's no statute of limitations on murder."

I was sitting straighter now, my brain alternately scanning a list of lawyers while reviewing an escape procedure put in place long ago.

Her voice softened but not her tone. "But that's ancient history. The important thing, Doc, is that we work together. I don't care what you've done or who you've worked for, I need your help now."

I said, "What?," not trusting the surge of relief I felt. She'd used the same finesse to manipulate the policewoman.

"You think I'm being tricky."

"Aren't you?"

"My motive is right up front. It's an offer. Find Will Chaser. Find him alive and bring him back. I don't give a goddamn what it takes. I'm halfway through my first term. Three years in a row, my staff expenses were way under budget. I can afford you." She let that settle a few beats, then added, "Or would you rather barter?"

"I don't understand what that has to do with—"

"I'm hiring you as a special consultant. At least twice a day, every day, you will report by phone. I'll give you every piece of information my contacts provide."

"But the FBI, the New York police—"

"They'll do a brilliant job . . . but within the constraints of the law. The boy, if he's still alive, doesn't have time for legalities. You're working for me now, understood?"

I was thinking, *Jesus Christ, what about Harrington?*

The woman swung her legs onto the bed and leaned in close enough that I could smell her shampoo. "When the FBI agent left the room to take that phone call, it was Ruth Guttersen, Will's foster mother. Fifty-eight years old, a Minnesota native. Her husband may be a fake cowboy, but she's pure Middle America. When the agent gave her the bad news, know what she said? She said, 'God help them.' Can you imagine? Worried about Will, but also the kidnappers, asking God to forgive them." Barbara's expression was a mix of admiration and remorse.

"In D.C., it's easy to forget there are decent people out there. People who follow the rules, who keep their word, people who care even about the jerks of the earth. It's the America I'd like to believe in, but I don't. Did you read Will's essay?"

Yes, the first two pages, but I shook my head no. The writing was feminine, flowery, tough to stomach because of its smug naïveté.

"Mrs. Guttersen is only a foster parent, but the boy has the same values. He's decent. A good kid."

I was thinking of another way to interpret *God help them*. That Will Chaser was dangerous—which was ridiculous, unless Ruth Guttersen had somehow anticipated the wrath of Barbara Hayes-Sorrento.

Barbara was back on the subject of the men who'd attacked her, saying, "I don't give a damn what you do to them. It's your business as long as my name's not involved. Bring the boy home, that's all I care about." She turned to the window, as if to say, *Kill them—whatever—I don't want to know.*

I nodded slowly. Drained the last of my water, thinking about it. "No one can find out."

The woman looked at me a moment, then smiled—a savvy, knowing smile. "We've got a deal."

"Did you hear what I said? It never leaves this room."

"There's not much I don't understand." Her smile became recreational, signaling that she was done with business. "This could be the beginning of an interesting friendship. Maybe even beautiful. But I doubt if I'll ever be able to call you Frenchy."

"I appreciate that."

"Don't worry, Doc." She stood and fished something from her pocket. A lighter and a cigarette. No . . . a joint, long and thin. "People like me—people who know what they want—we spend our lives hiding who we really are. You're among the few who've seen the real me."

"I never watched the video." How many times had I told her?

"You had it in your hands, though. Holding is more intimate than seeing. You held me, the way I am when no one is watching. That's close enough."

"Give me some credit."

Barbara said, "I'm trying to," then flicked the lighter and leaned back, inhaling deeply, her face softening as she inhaled again.

Through a veil of smoke, she told me, "I rarely get the opportunity, but this is how I relax. I become recreationally indecent. When I come out of the bathroom, I don't expect you to be decent either."

With her free hand, she was unbuttoning her blouse.

9

On my flight back to Florida, Barbara Hayes-Sorrento confirmed, via computer, what I had suspected but didn't want to believe:

> Re: Documents >Castro Files> (search incomplete.)
> *No entries as T-I-N-M-A-N. However, several references to T-E-N (space) M-A-N. Identified as U.S. citizen, male, no criminal record, address: (indecipherable). Birthplace: East Hampton, Long Island.*
>
> First name unknown. Surname: T-O-M-L-I-N-S-O-N.

In my hotel room, Barbara had said, "He's another one I find oddly suspicious."

Now I understood.

If I had been on a commercial flight, I would've ordered a couple of vodkas for the Virgin Marys I usually drink. But this plane wasn't carrying liquor. There might have been weapons in the hold—machine pistols, Stinger rocket launchers, no telling what—but no booze, no beer.

The airline wasn't in the business of recreation and it wasn't carrying paying passengers . . . not in a conventional sense.

Harrington had gotten me on a SAT-FG (Security Air Transport, Federal Government) flight. The charter group was used by the State Department and all thirteen federal intelligence agencies. In certain code-oriented circles, SAT was known as *Spook Airway Tours.*

Depending on the classification, if your name was on the SAT roster, as mine now was, the charter company would get you to your destination, day or night, holidays included. It was an elite shuttle service for most. But if you were ASP—Authorized Security Principal—as I now was, you could check bags that would not be inspected and bring aboard unnamed associates, although prior notice was required.

Snow had changed to sleet when I climbed the boarding ladder at Fort Dix at six a.m. on a black New Jersey morning. Military personnel wore aircraft-carrier earmuffs and mittens, staring into cups of steaming coffee, as the copilot levered the hatch closed.

This civilian Learjet was reason enough to avert the eyes. The ground crew was Air Force personnel. They knew it was a Special Operations Flight, Destinations Classified. Presumably, so did my fellow passengers: a naval officer in dress whites sitting aft and a woman sit-

ting amidships. There were no greetings as I seated myself at the forward bulkhead, no attempts to make
conversation, no polite inquiries about personal interests
or destinations while the plane deiced.

I spent the flight using my laptop, taking advantage of
the plane's communications perks. I traded instant messages with Barbara, who was exhausted, then contacted a
relentless Harrington, using cloaking software that en-
coded and decoded our correspondence.

No news about the missing teen. Harrington believed
that if a second photo wasn't provided within twenty-
four hours of the abduction, the boy was dead. "Unless
subject has escaped," Harrington added, "but improba-
ble for a child that age."

I wondered.

God help them, Ruth Guttersen had said to the FBI
agent. *A goat ever kicked your ass?* the kid had snapped at
me. The teen had fire. Some people are born old, others
skip childhood to survive. Foster homes might have made
Will Chaser tougher, shrewder. Could have added some
protective armor.

Because I hoped it was true, I wanted to speak with
the Guttersens myself. Maybe a former teacher or two.
Barbara had provided me with phone numbers. She'd
also provided a satellite cellular phone, a contact list and
temporary credentials, all with an efficiency unexpected
of a woman who was wine-tempered and very stoned.
This performance, I decided, was not her début.

Somewhere over the Carolinas, I received the senator's

e-mail about Tomlinson. A surprise not just because of the content but because I thought she was finally asleep.

I didn't trouble her with a reply. Instead, I checked the time—7:10 a.m.—and decided to e-mail the psychic philosopher myself. Normally, e-mail is not the quickest way to contact Tomlinson. He has purged his sailboat of all electronics he considers worldly and intrusive, keeping only necessities: a VHF radio, a turntable and a complicated stereo system.

Every morning, though, he dinghied to the marina around seven, if he wasn't too hungover. He checked messages, bought a paper, then pedaled to Baileys General Store for a scone.

The timing was about right.

Tomlinson and I have a convoluted history that goes way, way back. Years ago, before either of us had chosen Sanibel Island as home, a group of so-called political revolutionaries sent a letter bomb to a U.S. naval base. One of the men killed was a friend.

Tomlinson was a member of the group but had nothing to do with the bombing, although it was years before I was convinced. A government agency believed otherwise and declared that all members of his group were a clear and present danger to national security. Agents were sent to track them.

As Harrington told me at the time, "We're not the CIA. We can operate inside the reservation."

I have never admitted that I was sent after Tomlinson,

although he suspects. The man has an uncanny knack for perceptual reasoning that he insists is clairvoyance. I credit his gift for observing nuances and minutiae that most people miss, myself included.

In that way, he is different. It's impossible to say whether the ability is due to enlightenment, as he claims, or because his neural pathways have been oversensitized by years of chemical abuse.

Ninety minutes later, the jet banked southeast along the sun-bright beaches of Clearwater and Saint Pete, then landed at what I recognized as MacDill Air Force Base, Tampa. The Navy lieutenant got off, carrying a briefcase. I noticed there was no rating emblem on his uniform— meaningful to someone who has worked with naval intelligence. We were soon airborne again.

The Learjet made a short arc over Siesta Key and Englewood before it reduced speed, maneuvering to land. Below, I saw toy cars, coconut palms, seaside estates and the domino concretion that is Cape Coral.

Sanibel Island drifted into view, a green raft on a blue horizon. The island's shape was impressionistic, like a totem on the Nazca desert of Peru, a giant shrimp petroglyph, tail curved. The totem's belly was hollow, formed by Dinkin's Bay, a brackish lake ringed by mangroves. Home.

After landing, I asked the pilot about the plane's return schedule. "We have another stop or two after we refuel," he told me vaguely, and handed me his card, his cell number on the back.

When I trotted down the steps onto the tarmac of the civic airport in Fort Myers, it was a little after nine, temperature already seventy-four degrees.

Page Field had been a gunnery school during the Second War. Now it was the namesake of an adjacent mall where six lanes of traffic filed as methodically as leaf-cutter ants, the driver of each anonymous car resigned.

I got a cab and joined the procession. Told the driver, "Dinkin's Bay, Sanibel," which was an hour away because of tourist season. After nearly freezing in a Central Park pond, I understood Florida's allure better than ever.

My note to Tomlinson had read, "What is significance of term *Tenth Man*? Need all interpretations, derivatives, variations. MDF."

He would assume I was still in New York. Surprise the man. That's what I wanted to do. How, I hadn't decided. I didn't believe Tomlinson was involved with the abduction. The guy was not capable of hurting anyone. But he was also wildly complicated and prone to talking jags when intoxicated, which was often.

Because Tomlinson knew my schedule, he also knew Senator Hayes-Sorrento's schedule. He would've had ample opportunity to talk. He had lectured in Manhattan after spending three days on nearby Long Island, where there was a Zen master he visited regularly. A little village near the Hamptons that statistically was the wealthiest enclave in America. Billionaire estates. Old money, Internet tycoons. International rock stars and actors.

Sag Harbor, I remembered, was the little village near the Hamptons.

It was possible Tomlinson had been used once again by one or more of his dilettante associates, the trust-fund revolutionaries who flirted with violence like children pulling wings off flies.

Ruthless, arrogant: the very definition of crimes I associated with the name Tinman.

Tomlinson was no dilettante. He didn't use his spiritual convictions to manipulate or fly his counterculture lifestyle as a flag of contempt. That's not true of the typical cast of New Age mystics, born-againers, crystal worshipers, alien advocates, astrology goofs, conspiracy saps or thought-Nazi elitists, along with their politically correct mimics.

Tomlinson has a stray-dog purity, without ego or malice. I have never met anyone, anywhere, who didn't like and trust the guy.

Yet the man was also easily manipulated.

A Tomlinson quote: "I'm prone to exaggerate when I'm sober."

Accurate. It was also unsettling if he had information that should not be shared.

My home on Dinkin's Bay is a pair of weathered gray cottages on stilts fifty yards from shore. Tomlinson secures his sailboat, *No Mas,* on nearby moorings. When his mood is monastic or he's dodging a jealous husband, Tomlinson anchors far from the marina. Usually, though, *No Mas* sits just beyond the channel within hailing distance of my porch.

I was looking for the boat's sun-bleached hull as I made my way through the mangroves, walking quietly on the boardwalk that leads to my home and lab. I've installed a gate at the water's edge to discourage unwelcome visitors. One of the fishing guides made the sign that hangs there:

SANIBEL BIOLOGICAL SUPPLY
MARINE RESEARCH STATION

The sign is hand-routed teak. Much nicer than the plywood tag some comedian or activist had nailed beneath:

KILL IT & STUDY IT—THE WHITE MAN'S WAY

I disengaged the alarm system, closed the gate and could soon see Tomlinson's boat, moored where it was supposed to be.

As I walked toward the house, I thought about the surest way of surprising the man. I could borrow a canoe. Or swim?

No, stealth wasn't necessary. I wasn't going to accuse him. My e-mail about Tenth Man might, hopefully, key the retrieval of similar code names from his unconscious, which then would be left to ferment in his short-term memory. I wanted Tomlinson's unedited reaction, then maybe a brief talk before I collected my gear, got another taxi and headed back to the airport.

As I approached the house, though, a voice called,

"Hey, compadre! Didn't think you'd get here for another hour. Delta added a new direct from Newark?"

I stopped at the stairs. Tomlinson was on the upper deck on a beach chair in the sun using two pie pans as reflectors, holding them near his face.

So much for surprising him.

As I climbed the stairs, I said, "I chartered a private jet," expecting him to laugh and he did. I stowed my computer and satchel in the lab, then stepped outside. "You were expecting me?"

Tomlinson didn't open his eyes, but he moved the pie pans enough so I could see his face: stringy bleached hair hanging over one shoulder, bikini underwear, bony toes visible over the rims of his Birkenstocks.

He said, "I was expecting you or the cops. Maybe both. I spent most of the night in the lab waiting. Think I ought to get dressed?"

I was thinking, *Cops because of the abduction?*, but knew better than to rush to assumptions with Tomlinson. I said, "This is possibly a new record. Four seconds and you've already confused me."

"Kidnapping and murder, man. Don't kid a kidder. Cops still make house calls for that sort of thing . . . don't they?"

"I've heard the rumor."

"Good. I neatened up the place just in case."

I stepped closer. "You're admitting it?"

"Why shouldn't I admit it? The house was a mess—well, a little messy after some tourist ladies stopped by last night for refreshments . . . "

"Not that," I said, "the kidnapping. You're telling me you were involved? The driver was stabbed to death, for godsakes."

Tomlinson opened his eyes. *"Huh?"*

"Isn't that what you're talking about? Now you're lying around, soaking up rays, while you wait to be arrested for an abduction that—"

"Arrest *me*?" He sat up. "Marion Ford, are you high? They're not gonna arrest me. I keep an emergency stash in the lab over one of the rafters. Just because you never found it doesn't mean the pigs won't. Now it's gone—that's all I meant."

Stash. Even after all the years I've known the man, my brain took a moment to translate. *Drugs.* Marijuana for sure, and God knows what else.

He said, "Not that there was much left after the tourist ladies visited. But what there was, I took and put in a nice safe place. So the cops won't pin it on you when they show up with a search warrant." He looked at the sky, recalculating the sun's angle, then moved the beach lounger a few inches, his dreamy expression telling me the women tourists were a lot of fun, I should've been there.

"Search warrant," I said, trying to be patient. "We're not all telepathic, Tomlinson. A lot of people might expect, you know, some sort of explanation. The *reason* you think the police are coming to search my place."

He lay back in the chair, looking at me. "You know what I'm talking about. You're the one they're gonna arrest, not me. Marion, the kimchee is about to hit the fan. You don't think I know who killed that mutant?"

Mutant—Tomlinson's nickname for Bern Heller.

I thought, *Uh-oh.*

He said, "That's why I came to get rid of evidence. A murder charge will cause some gossip, no doubt. But Doc Ford taking a fall for drug possession? Your whole image would be screwed. Next stop, Freaksville. Once again, marijuana will get a bum wrap for being a gateway drug."

The man made a weary sound, getting serious. "You used to claim Tucker Gatrell was the twisted seed in your family. But this thing you've got for killing bad guys— whew, Doc, it's risky karma all around. I'm starting to feel like the loyal sidekick, a Caucasoid Joe Egret. Not as noble, but much hipper of course."

"Oh, for sure," I agreed.

He was referring to an Everglades legend, also a friend. Joseph Egret had been devoted to my crazed uncle and had a strong influence on me when I was a kid. Both men were dead now. The state had given special permission to bury Joe in a Calusa Indian mound in the 'Glades. The mounds had been built by contemporaries of the Maya, a tribe that predated the Seminoles by several thousand years.

"Joseph Egret," Tomlinson added, "that's exactly who came into my mind as I neatened up after the recent homicide. I'll stick by you, Doctor, but, *man,* you've got a demon in that noggin of yours that psychotropics just might help. Seriously."

Never rush to assumptions with Tomlinson. Abso-damn-lutely right. Staying quiet was the way to deal with this.

If I didn't play it right, instead of looking for the kid I'd end up like him: a prisoner, or worse.

10

When the black Chrysler skidded into the driveway, Will Chaser gave up pounding on the farmer's door and sprinted toward the barn. Tried to anyway. The broken rib was like a razor in his chest.

Headlights swept across him. He heard a door open and the Cuban with the freaky horn hollered, "Stop, you little goat turd!" But the smaller man, the one with metallic eyes, was smart. He yelled in pretty good English, "Your parents are worried! We want to help you."

Already explaining why they were chasing him in case someone in the house was listening.

Adults could say anything. Tell another adult that a kid was a runaway or the cops wanted him for stealing a horse or selling pot, they would believe it. Didn't matter a goddamn what a kid said, adults listened to adults. Will had lived it.

Fact was, he was screwed either way. If the Cubans didn't catch him, cops could jail him after contacting

Minneapolis. Police there had a couple of reasons to lock him up, particularly if they'd discovered why his ninth-grade English teacher, Mrs. Thinglestadt, had written the award-winning essay that got him into this mess to begin with.

"You're blackmailing me!" she had complained to Will.

"Laws about buying weed and screwing students got nothing to do with asking a little favor," he'd replied.

What if the good-looking older woman had squealed?

Will popped the barn-door latch, stepped into the warm odor of hay, leather, horses, and then banged the dead bolt solid. Security lights outside were bright enough for him to know he was in the fanciest stable he'd ever seen. A dozen stalls, polished hardwood everywhere, doors with brass bars and carved name placards for each horse. Bricks on the floor were soft, like rubber. Glass chandeliers were suspended from a beam that ran the length of the barn. Like a whorehouse for purebreds.

Nothing like this in Oklahoma. Where the hell am I?

In a shitpot full of trouble is exactly where he was. In the distance, he heard someone knocking politely on the farmhouse door, while someone else—the buffalo-headed Cuban probably—rattled the dead bolt, trying to get into the barn.

Convinced the doors were locked, the man put his lips to the crack and said, "My little friend, I have frightened you. I have come to apologize, my *new* little friend."

Buffalo-head.

Will had never met anyone so goddamn dumb. He raised his voice to be heard. "We're friends? Are you serious?"

"Yes!"

"I don't believe you."

"My head has stopped bleeding. It is nothing. Look for yourself."

"Then say it. Say you promise."

"Open this door, you little—" The Cuban caught himself. "Yes, I promise!"

"Okay. If you *mean* it, I'll come out. But I have to use the bathroom. Just a couple of minutes, to take a crap. Please."

"Of course! We were stupid, not providing a place for you to crap. Relax and enjoy, my spirited new friend."

Truth was, Will did have to crap. And he was also so thirsty, he was shaking. But first . . .

He looked around. Will knew barns. Didn't matter how fancy, they all had at least two entrances aside from the sliding doors, and usually a loft door to pulley in hay. He ran to the opposite doors and confirmed they were locked, then sprinted to the manager's office when he heard a noise coming from there. Got to that door just as Buffalo-head was turning the knob.

"Hey, I'm taking a dump in here! How about some privacy!"

The idiot hesitated just long enough for Will to flip the spring lock, then step back.

Close!

Buffalo-head tried the knob, getting frustrated. "You don't trust me! You are not the only one who needs to use the toilet. Do you mind?"

"Two minutes, it's all yours." Will's eyes were adjusting to the dark. There was a phone on the manager's desk. An old phone, with a dial. As he dialed 911, he said to the door, "How is your ear?," wanting Buffalo-head to keep talking.

"My *ear*? Perhaps you will find my ear in the toilet with your shit! But . . . of course, I am *joking*! I am not angry. I feel almost no pain, I swear. Barely noticeable, thanks to God, because of the pounding in my head. The rock you threw . . . it did me a great favor!"

Will had dialed but too fast, because he got a recording.

Damn old phone.

He dialed again, listening to Buffalo-head say, "What is an ear? Or a bump on the head? We will laugh about this someday!"

Then he heard the Cuban with metal eyes coming, calling, "You idiot! Don't you see what the brat is doing?"

The phone was ringing.

"The junction box," the man yelled, "it's right there. There . . . in front of your eyes."

The phone rang a second time.

There was a thud on the other side of the wall, then the sound of wire and staples ripping, as a woman's voice said, "Nine-one-one, what's your emergency?"

Will cupped his hands around the phone. "I need help. Two men are trying to kill me. Two Cubans. But I don't know where I am! My name is William Chaser. I'm from . . . Oklahoma." He'd almost said Minnesota but remembered the police.

The big Cuban began ramming his shoulder against the door as Will waited for the woman to respond.

Silence.

"Hello? You hear me? I need help!"

The phone was dead.

Now the older Cuban was telling Buffalo-head, "Find a brick. Knock the lock off. Hurry, before the man gets here. We'll look like fools!"

Gets here? What man? Someone was coming to help the Cubans.

Will began ransacking drawers, looking for a weapon. Every office, in every barn, on every ranch he'd ever worked, the manager kept a handgun in the top-right drawer for quick access—a revolver if it was an older guy and a semiauto if he was younger. Plus a Winchester rifle in the corner or over the door. A shotgun at least.

Not this ranch.

Eastern shitheels . . . Who runs this place? The candy-asses should be raising sheep.

Will was getting mad. Could feel the heat of it, like a chemical moving from his temples to his heart. One of the drawers spilled out. He slammed it against the door where the Cubans were now hammering at the lock. Pulled out another drawer and threw it.

He yelled, "Come on in, you assholes! I'll blow your damn heads off!" He was looking for something else to throw and found a lead paperweight.

Will screamed, "What's the matter, afraid?" He threw the paperweight at the door. It made a *whap* sound, like a hammer smacking wood. "I'll open the damn door myself!" Said it knowing, even as he spoke, it was a mistake. He was mad, not crazy. No way in hell was he going out that door.

Never make a threat that'll get your ass kicked or prove you're a pussy—Old Man Guttersen on the subject of how a man should conduct himself in life.

On the far wall, Will saw the breaker box for the barn's electric. Beneath it was the medicine cooler, padlock open. Even eastern ranchers had to know horse doctoring. Will had been working with vets since he was seven years old.

The boy rushed to the cooler, hoping to find a weapon—a scalpel or razor, anything sharp—then paused, listening. The banging had stopped. No whisper of voices outside.

He decided the Cubans were probably waiting quietly for him to exit. A stupid thing, telling them he had a gun and was coming out.

A few seconds passed, still no sound. He continued listening, as he opened the medicine cooler and scanned the rows of familiar veterinarian supplies: liniments, vitamins, bottles of vaccine and tranquilizers, wrapping tape, syringes . . .

As he scanned the rows of supplies, the period of extended quiet caused him to wonder, *Maybe the Cubans ran for cover, afraid of being shot.*

Possible.

Three or four minutes later, when the men still hadn't resumed breaking into the barn, Will was sure of it. *Maybe it wasn't so dumb telling them I have a gun.*

Old Man Guttersen was wrong for once.

So now he had to find a way to make the lie work for him. He needed a weapon. Give those candy-ass kidnappers a reason to be afraid of him.

His attention returned to the medicine cooler. And there it was. Not a weapon, exactly, but something that might do the job.

Will knew that the kidnappers would soon come back to the barn with a crowbar maybe . . . or use keys when the man they were waiting for arrived.

Their partner—whoever that was—worried Will, as if things weren't already worrisome enough. Which is why the boy had kept busy until now.

After he'd flipped the main breaker, killing the lights, Will had watched the metal-eyed Cuban talking on a cell phone, standing by the farmhouse, its windows still bright. He couldn't hear what the man was saying. But he could feel it, sort of. More like a taste or smell. Metal-eyes was talking to someone who was coming to help them. Self-assured, his posture upright.

How was it the two Cubans had a friend out here in horse country, the middle of nowhere? Unless . . .

unless—Will's brain was now inspecting different scenarios—unless the Cubans had pulled off the road because this ranch was their destination. Had nothing to do with Will screwing with the taillights, then kicking like a crazy fool. The Cubans had turned because they were meeting someone here. Possible?

Whatever . . .

The Cubans were coming for him, that's all that mattered. Will knew it as sure as he knew Buffalo-head was watching the back of the barn while Metal-eyes was in front, talking on the phone.

No escape, not yet. Nothing he could do until it happened. So Will had focused on getting ready, which meant choosing the best damn horse he could find. To which he gave some thought, carrying a bag he'd taken from the medicine cooler, moving from stall to stall.

There were a dozen stalls but only eight horses. One was a mare that would foal in a month or so, four geldings and a big gray stallion that had to be sixteen hands tall.

There also were two good-looking geldings. One of them, a Morgan, was colored like Blue Jacket and had bright, intelligent eyes.

But Will kept coming back to the stallion. CAZZIO, was the name over the door. There was a ton of trophies on the mantle and a ton more blue ribbons and medals pinned on a board outside the stall.

Will cracked the stall door, then leaned his face in and waited, letting Cazzio decide. The horse had puffed up and snorted, no petting-zoo whore—*Good!*—then took his time before touching his muzzle to Will's hair, then his face.

The stallion sniffed, then snorted. Sniffed again, then banged Will's face with his muzzle in a testing sort of way. Snorted again and shied, letting the clatter of his hooves communicate a warning.

Will considered backing out and trying the Morgan gelding with the intelligent eyes. Stallions were risky. Two years back, he had watched a rank Arabian stud clamp his teeth on a man's neck and fling him like a rag doll before trying to stomp him to death. A decent hand with horses, too, an experienced wrangler.

It's the way stallions were. Slip a grain sack over their head, tip them and clove-hitch their legs—all that might dull the fire for an hour or two but it was only a temporary fix. On the other hand . . . certain stallions, you didn't want the fire dulled. Some were worth the risk.

Will put the medicine bag on the floor, aware of what the horse was smelling—horse tranquilizers and some other stuff—then stepped into the stall and closed the door.

"Easy . . . Whoa, easy . . . "

The gray horse shook his head and pawed at the floor. Didn't even have to move to dominate the darkness, his energy so radiant it shrunk the airspace.

"You look like the Real McCoy to me," Will whispered.

I ain't no vet, I'm a hand, he thought.

Then he waited, arms at his sides, for Cazzio to make up his mind.

Now Will was on the stallion, lying forward, his arms loose around the horse's neck, the stall door closed, not locked, which the horse knew but was tolerating.

Go when it's time to go.

A stallion like this one—by God, he would *go.*

Will had his boots up on Cazzio's hindquarters, chest flat on his withers, so it was like lying on a wide, warm couch. He was under a blanket that he had pulled over them, but not until the air was right and the horse was ready—a feeling alive in the darkness, transmitted flesh through flesh. Not consent but tolerance, a gradual calming of muscle, subtle as first light.

Who the hell braided your mane? A real ranch, we'd open the gate before allowing this bullshit . . .

Right flank, left wither, the animal's skin fluttered beneath Will's belly. Muscles flexed independently, mechanics of a complicated instrument that, if played expertly, produced pure kick-ass flow. Part dance, all power.

Will's nose rested near Cazzio's mane, close as he could get to home: horse sweat and leather, the ammoniac mix of manure and grain. Crying wasn't an option, but it was right there if Will allowed himself.

Waiting. They both were. Ten minutes, at most, he had been in the barn, but it felt like hours.

You like that?

He scratched Cazzio's neck and Cazzio stretched his head forward, lips wide, teeth bared, as if laughing. He wasn't laughing, of course, although people who treated horses as pets, as almost human, might believe it. Not Will. Horses were horses, a few better than most. The same with hands. It was just something some stallions did.

Blue Jacket, another example.

As Will lay on Cazzio, he told himself to relax, he needed to conserve his energy. Cazzio already had drunk his belly full from the water trough and found residue in the feed bin. Oats and sorghum plus a supplement powder, which smelled sweet but Will knew tasted awful. What farm kid hadn't tried it? He'd squeezed the mash into a ball and swallowed it anyway. Will needed food. He didn't want the crazy feeling to come back, which happened more often when he ran out of gas.

Will knew he did stupid things when he got mad. Not something to admit to that government shrink, the one who'd told the parole officer, "A grand mal seizure or anger-management problems." A lesson for him, telling the truth instead of lying about how it felt, the chemical sensation when he got seriously pissed off.

This was after a couple of tests which he also should have lied about, although he had lied quite a bit, faking some of the answers, but not enough.

"The boy's not abnormal, but he lacks certain normal qualities," the shrink had told the parole officer and a social worker, talking as if Will wasn't in the room. "He demonstrates behavior associated with emotional scarring, typical of abandoned children. Rage mixed with antisocial behavior. But he has highly developed survival skills. He's an expert manipulator. Again, all typical, considering his background."

William wasn't abnormal, but that didn't mean he was normal either, the woman shrink had added—which was lying flattery, something adults often tried. But then it got interesting:

"It's the way the boy's brain translates outside stimuli," the woman had said, before asking, "William? Isn't it true that certain things come into your mind as colors or smells? Numbers have colors, you said. Days of the week, too. Friday is yellow, you told me. Thursday is purple, the number ten is silver. Fear is bluish gray. Fear has an odor, a mix of copper and pears, you said." The shrink was reading from notes, finally including him in the conversation.

Everyone wasn't that way? That was a surprise to Will.

"Will has a condition—a gift perhaps—that's been well documented. It's called *synesthesia*. Synesthesia is not a paranormal power. It's a heightened awareness. Just like some people have exceptional eyesight or hearing. Very rare.

"It's been linked with unusual artistic abilities. Sexuality, too: It's possible that synesthetes radiate pheromones that are abnormally potent—that's anecdotal data but fascinating, isn't it?" The shrink had smiled but avoided Will's eyes, oddly uncomfortable. "Intense rage is also associated," she'd said. "There's a lot we don't understand about synesthesia.

"I've contacted the psychology department at the university. We want to pay Will to participate in a research program designed just for him. Wouldn't that be wonderful, Will? We could work together, the two of us! And no more living in stinky barns, doing manual labor."

Will had smiled but was thinking, *No way, José*.

It wasn't that easy getting out of it, though, because the shrink was determined. Didn't matter that the cops had just nailed him for stealing Blue Jacket.

A week later, though, when the principal surprised the school librarian seducing Will in the stacks, it was farewell Oklahoma and hello Land of a Thousand Lakes. The timing hadn't been easy because the principal seldom left his office and the librarian was fickle.

Minnesota was okay, mostly because of Old Man Guttersen. Guttersen got a kick out of Will's stories, when he shut up long enough to listen. Will could tell the old man anything, including the truth. Selling weed, gambling, diddling teachers didn't bother him a bit. Same with stealing: as long as it was in a different neighborhood and former U.S. military personnel weren't targeted. Even if Will hadn't been stealing for a good reason—saving to buy Blue Jacket—it would've been just fine with the old man.

"We're both sneaky, lying, shitheel frauds," Guttersen had confided, "and we're screwed if the world finds out."

Luckiest thing that had ever happened to Will, being assigned a foster granddad who understood.

"The word *unique*," his English teacher, Mrs.

Thinglestadt, had told him, "is commonly misused. It is incorrect to say 'very unique' or 'extremely unique' because unique is *unique*. One of a kind."

She had corrected him as they were showering—Will had made the error while complimenting Mrs. Thinglestadt's breasts—and after they'd celebrated the good news about winning the essay contest and his trip to New York.

Only Old Man Guttersen knew how he'd won. First time in Will's life he didn't have to pretend. Will Chaser could be himself when the two of them were together, listening to *Garage Logic* or sharing a beer while watching cowboy westerns.

Usually, Bull called him "Pony," but sometimes "Rookie," like the young guy on *Garage Logic*, depending on whatever fit the old man's mood. Maybe Guttersen would call him "Crazy Horse Chaser" after this . . . if Will ever made it home to tell.

Unique. The word for his relationship with the old man.

Bull . . . Goddamn it, Bull, I wish you were here right now.

Especially now. Because a familiar sound stirred the darkness: the Chrysler pulling up so close to the barn that for a moment Will worried the Cubans would use the car to crash on through. But the car stopped, its headlights filtering through windows, under the double doors, filling the barn with dusty, diffused light.

Next to Will, on a hook meant for tack, he had hung the handle from a broken rake. Taped to the handle was a syringe with a four-inch needle—taped to the plunger actually—so it looked sort of like a spear point.

Pony Chaser, on his horse with a spear, ready to charge.

Will liked the Indian feel of that—unusual 'cause anyone who grows up on the Rez knows the whole Indian act is bullshit. Rubber arrows, drunken Skins wearing feathers and blankets dancing for tourists, the only thing real being a mesquite fire and the sad, hungover weariness of shuffling feet.

The feeling Will experienced, though, was real. A solitary sensation that was brave-hearted, aloof and alone. It was a soaring feeling, unafraid despite the inevitable.

Warrior. For the first time in Will's life, the word had substance, dense as granite yet weightless enough to whistle like a faraway wind in his ears.

Warrior. Yeah . . .

A ceremony, that's what the moment deserved. So Will took a scalpel, grabbed a handful of his own hair and lopped it off. He tied a length of hair to the spear, sort of like a scalp, then knotted the rest to Cazzio's candy-ass braids.

Looks nice . . .

Yeah, it did, the way their shadows combined on the stall's gray wall. Shadow of the stallion's body capped with Will's. The spear angled vertically from his hip, its shadow silhouetted as black as a charcoal drawing. An image came into the boy's brain: a painting sold at the souvenir shop on the Rez, *End of the Trail*.

Watching his own shadow, Will touched his chin to his chest, imitating what he remembered, and there it was, the painting's ghost—*Ouch!*—Will's broken rib stabbed his lungs and he lay forward again.

Then he heard another familiar sound: a crowbar prying wood . . . then barn doors sliding open on their tracks.

The doors were open wide now, and the Chrysler's headlights projected giant shadows. Buffalo-head came first, hunched over as if ready to flee, moving carefully into the uncertain space of the barn.

A second shadow appeared: Metal-eyes, who stopped and leaned against the fender of the car.

Will put his mouth close to the horse's ear. "It's time."

He nudged the blanket back enough to free his right arm.

Cazzio snorted, skin fluttering. He whinnied and tested his legs, steel shoes on the floor, an animal that was born for business. He sensed the Cubans approaching, a subtle change of air.

Will felt it, too: a color sensation, tan turning red.

Easy. You'll know.

In the medicine cooler, there had been a lot to choose from once Will saw there wasn't a weapon worth a damn in it aside from veterinarian syringes and some scalpels. Also a pack of big-gauge needles and several vials of tranquilizers, a few with familiar names.

There was Dormo, which was fast but didn't last, and Rompon—a horse on Rompon could remain tart enough to kick. He also found a vial of Ace, a mixture of stuff that would have been Will's choice if it was for Cazzio but it wasn't.

He had chosen Ketamine. Ket caused quick paralysis but didn't deaden what a horse could feel. One-third syringe would drop a horse, but Will had emptied a whole vial and part of another filling a syringe. He didn't bother plunging out any air bubbles either before lashing the syringe to the pole.

The pole was now a spear. No, a lance, the way Will held it: the end locked beneath his arm, the point extending beyond the horse's muzzle.

"Check the stalls! The man just called from his car, he's only a few kilometers away," Metal-eyes was yelling at Buffalo-head, who was now peering into Cazzio's stall.

The man—someone the Cubans were counting on to do . . . what?

It worried Will, this unknown person. He wanted to be gone by the time the stranger arrived, so he was thinking, *Don't stop, keep coming* . . .

Buffalo-head did just that but slowly, slowly. The large Cuban appeared unsteady as he drew close enough to see into Cazzio's stall. Sounded nervous, too, as he reported to Metal-eyes, "Nothing in here but a very big horse."

"Keep looking!"

Hump didn't want to keep looking. "You have never seen such a large animal. I should have the gun. Horses bite, I have been told."

"You can't have the gun."

"Then come with me. On my grave, this horse is a giant, I swear."

"Idiot! Would you rather be in an American jail?"

Will could feel Cazzio's body heat as he wrapped his left hand in the horse's mane, watching from beneath the blanket, as the big Cuban cracked the door and looked into the stall. Because of the headlights, Will could see the man's shape: the sloped shoulders, the nub of horn that curved like a stem out of his pumpkin-sized head.

Cazzio nickered, sniffing the Cuban's odor, and tested his steel shoes on the floor, as Will patted the horse's neck and thought, *Ready?*

A second later, Buffalo-head called to Metal-eyes, "If the man's only a few miles away, why not wait? It would be better if there are three of us."

Will heard the older Cuban snap, "You're afraid of a child? We're not waiting!"

Buffalo-head pulled the door wider, as he turned toward the headlights, saying, "Want to know what I think?"

"No! Stop wasting time. The man is already convinced we are incompetent fools."

"Then I won't tell you that I believe the boy is cursed. Or possessed by demons—I have heard that it happens to teenagers."

Will was thinking, *Wait and see!*, his shoulders tense, still hiding beneath the blanket. He knew he had to time it right. Move too soon, the Cubans would trap him inside the barn. So he kept his eyes focused on the angle of light, watching the door open wider . . . wider . . . until only the huge man was standing in the doorway, blocking their escape.

When Buffalo-head looked away to complain to Metal-eyes, "But the Devil Child is insane. A monster!," Will used his boots to signal the stallion and yelled, "Now!"

The stallion was already lunging out the door.

11

Bern Heller's body had washed ashore. There was a story about it in the regional newspaper, the *News-Press*. That's why Tomlinson expected the police to show up with a search warrant.

Sections of paper were scattered beneath the man's beach chair, where he was still stretched out sunning himself. The front page of the local section was folded open.

When I saw the headlines, I felt a constricting anxiety and thought, *I've got to get out of here*.

EX-NFL PLAYER FOUND
POLICE TO PROBE DROWNING OF
CONVICTED MURDERER, RAPIST

It explained Tomlinson's fears about a search warrant. A lot of people had reason to hate the man, yet my pal sounded convinced that I was the killer.

Why?

He had placed a book on the newspaper because of a breeze freshening off the bay. Wind roiled the water, whitecaps flashing near the oyster bar where pelicans and cormorants perched, leeward side, heavy in the rubbery mangroves.

I removed the book—*Shadow Country* by Peter Matthiessen—and placed it on the deck before grabbing the newspaper. The front section was still in the plastic baggie untouched.

To demonstrate I wasn't worried and wasn't in a hurry, I ignored the local section, with its headlines about Bern Heller, and read the front-page national section.

The lead story was about the attempted abduction of Senator Barbara Hayes-Sorrento and the missing boy. Only a dozen paragraphs had made this early island edition, but there was a photo of Barbara and a photo of one of the entrances to the Explorers Club. There was also a sidebar about the murdered limo driver.

The boy, Will Chaser, wasn't named. An "unidentified pedestrian" was credited with detaining one of the kidnappers.

I asked Tomlinson, "You didn't read the national section?"

"Never made it that far." He motioned vaguely to the deck beneath his chair. "No need to play it cool with me. I can tell you're worried shitless. Take a look at the story about Heller, you'll understand."

As I knelt to retrieve the local pages, he added, "You don't have to worry about me narcing you to the cops. I'm no Judas."

"It's unusual for you to make biblical references on a Friday. Getting a jump on the weekend guilts?"

"In your e-mail, isn't that why you mentioned Tenth Man? Thirty pieces of silver—hell, they could offer me thirty blotters of Frisco '68, I still wouldn't blabber."

I said, "Here's a concept: Some people ask questions because they want an answer. Me, for instance."

"That's my answer: Judas was the Tenth Man, the tenth disciple. You sent the e-mail, worried I was going to rat you out to the cops. That's the way I interpreted it."

Had Choirboy said *Tenth Man* or *Tinman*? Interesting distinction. It offered an entirely different meaning, but I was concentrating on the newspaper now.

The body of a man found floating off Naples Pier has been identified as former NFL lineman Bern Heller, 38, of Indian Harbour. Heller was sentenced to life in prison but released from Florida State Penitentiary, Raiford, last month pending a hearing.

Heller, who was principal owner of Indian Harbour Marina, was found guilty of second-degree murder seven months ago and was awaiting trial for additional charges that included murder, kidnapping and multiple rapes. Heller was reported missing from his live-aboard yacht at Indian Harbour six days ago by a friend and occasional roommate, Tripper Oswald of Fort Myers.

The marina is in the final stages of foreclosure. Only Heller was living on the property, according to Citi Management Corporation, the mortgage holder.

A Wisconsin native, Heller was convicted of the shooting death of Capt. Javier Castillo, a popular local fishing guide. Capt. Castillo's widow and two children have been the benefactors of recent charity functions sponsored by Dinkin's Bay Marina on Sanibel.

Heller's arrest made national headlines, and his testimony may have contributed to investigations into the effects of steroid rage associated with crimes committed by professional athletes.

According to the Lee County Medical Examiner's Office, the cause of death will not be released until police finish their investigation. According to a statement issued yesterday by Heller's attorney, there are "sufficient anomalies" to suggest the former football star was a victim of foul play.

Oswald and members of Heller's family have retained a private investigator. According to the sheriff's department, the investigation into the former star's death is continuing . . .

I had tuned out Tomlinson but now looked up from the paper after he banged me on the shoulder, asking, "Are you listening to me? This is serious shit, man."

I said, "Heller's dead. Good. I don't see what that has to do with me." I folded the paper and carried it to the railing. My shark pen was below: a rectangle of net and wire kept afloat by basketball-sized buoys at each corner.

Sharks are delicate, complex animals. The bull shark, *Carcharhinus Leucas,* is one of my primary interests as a researcher. *Leucas* is known by several names worldwide, including Zambezi River shark and Lake Nicaragua shark. It swims hundreds of miles up rivers to feed and possibly reproduce in freshwater lakes. The shark is also responsible for more attacks on humans than great whites or tiger sharks.

Because I had been traveling, the pen was empty. A five-hundred-pound shark is not the invincible killer portrayed in films. The animal requires constant care and is fussy about what it eats in captivity. I no longer take risks with the sharks I use for research. I would rather release a dozen of them than return home after a trip to find one dead.

Through the clear water, I saw a school of mullet daisy-chaining, stirring detritus clouds with their tails. Angel-striped spadefish flashed in slow arcs near pilings. Where water deepened, snook were stacked in shadows, muscled densities orderly as rungs.

Tomlinson was still talking. "That investigator the paper mentions, I met him. He was nosing around the marina last night, asking questions at Sanibel Marina, and Tween Waters, too. Seedy little gumshoe of a guy, you ask me."

I nodded: *Good.*

"The county fuzz, that's who you need to worry about. They showed up last night, the lead detective in an unmarked Chevy. Her name's Palmer, Detective Palmer, an interesting-looking woman. She's got the typical hard-ass attitude, but there's some wisdom in her face. Palmer's smart. She's also ambitious."

I shrugged: *Bad?*

I was scanning the rest of the story, hoping to see a mention of the watch Heller was wearing, as Tomlinson said, "Detective Palmer was interested in the Cheesehead's wristwatch," breaking into my thoughts. It wasn't the first time he had done something like that.

I played it straight. "What's his watch have to do with anything?"

"When they found him, Heller was wearing a cheap rubber watch. Not waterproof. They figure it stopped the day he drowned. Like in the movies, you know, the broken watch determines the time of death. The paper says he's been missing since"—because Tomlinson was reaching, I handed him the newspaper—"Heller was reported missing six days ago. It was also the day the watch stopped. So the date would have been . . . Saturday, January seventeenth?"

I said, "The detective told you all this?"

"Yeah . . . I mean, no. Yes, it was the seventeenth. No, Palmer didn't tell me. I pieced it together from the questions she asked the fishing guides."

He rattled the paper for emphasis, then stuffed it under the chair. "You flew to New York last Friday, the sixteenth, right, Doc?"

Tomlinson was staring at me now. I stared back. "You know I did. Apparently, I left the day before Heller died. Which means you're wrong. Police have no reason to come after me."

"I'm not an expert on watches, but couldn't a killer click the date ahead, then break the thing on purpose? A really shrewd person, I'm talking about."

I said, "With saltwater drowning, it's not easy to pin-point the time of death. Because fish and crabs and things aren't fussy about what they eat. A smart killer wouldn't bother planting a broken watch. And a dumb killer wouldn't think of it. That makes the watch gambit unlikely."

Tomlinson got up, nodding. I watched him go into the lab, giving me a look, before he let the screen door swing closed, his expression saying *Okay, okay, if that's the way you want to play it . . .*

I went downstairs to double-check my boat. Heller's family was pushing police to look for his killer? I had a lot to do.

A few minutes later, I heard a screen door swing closed. Tomlinson came down the steps, wearing faded jeans and a tie-dyed T-shirt that read RELIGION IS A COMPASS, NOT A HARNESS.

He was carrying an antique bag, once called a Gladstone, leather and brass.

I was coiling a water hose. Before leaving for New York, I had double-scrubbed the boat's deck. An extra shot of water and half a bottle of degreaser couldn't hurt. DNA can be as stubborn as any stain.

"Going somewhere?" I asked him.

As Tomlinson said, "That's up to you, man," the cell phone Barbara Hayes-Sorrento gave me began to buzz. I wiped my hands on a towel and fished the thing from my pocket. The senator had sent a text message.

Tomlinson said, "Doc, there're a couple things you should know. First is, Detective Palmer told one of the guides Heller hated rubber watches. She was asking around about a gold Rolex. I remember good ol' Bern wearing a gold Rolex when he showed up at the marina party last week and also the day he slugged you. Loud and gaudy, a watch just like him. Remember that day?"

"If I didn't, the headaches would remind me," I said, studying the phone. I was squinting at the menu, trying to figure out how to retrieve Barbara's message.

"There's something else. It hasn't made the news." Because Tomlinson paused, wanting me to look at him, I intentionally did not look away from the phone.

"Heller had a girl aboard his boat that night—the night before you left for New York."

Now I looked. A shocker. I tried not to show it but the man knew me too well.

"It's such a bummer, I didn't even want to tell you," he said, sounding worried. "There's a witness, Doc. Nothing we can do about it. You don't need a compass to know when karma turns south. And sometimes I wish we were all born with an anchor hooked to our ass. A way to stop the negative flow, I'm talking about?"

"A witness to what?" I said, thinking back, trying to picture the interior of Heller's boat. The place had been a pigsty, but I'd seen no signs of a female guest.

Tomlinson said, "She claims Heller abducted her and was trying to rape her. He'd torn off most of her clothes but stopped when a man knocked at the cabin door. It was late: two a.m. or later. She told police it was a big guy, clean-shaven. He wore his glasses strung around his neck with fishing line."

"How do you know this?" I had opened Barbara's message but was now giving Tomlinson my full attention.

"Someone involved in law enforcement told me. That's all I can say."

"A reliable source?"

"Better than just reliable. And no more questions, okay?"

"There are a lot of boaters who use fishing line to secure their glasses," I offered, then realized I was doing what guilty people always do, trying to impeach the facts.

Tomlinson said, "No need to convince me. But I'm worried you might have to try and convince a jury. If you'd spent your life abusing drugs, like a normal person, your skills as a liar would be more highly evolved. As it is, I think your ass is on the line, pal. The witness got a good, long look at the killer, my friend in law enforcement says."

I didn't want to risk mentioning that there was no moon that night so I kept it safe, asking, "What did she see exactly?"

"Heller and the guy started fighting, the woman told the police. She was in the forward stateroom, they were in the salon. She grabbed what was left of her clothes and climbed out the front hatch to get away. She lay there and listened to the whole thing. Saw some of it.

"She said the fighting stopped after a minute or two. Then, she says, the guy wearing glasses tied up Heller and swam off, towing him like a wagon. Heller kicked and splashed, but the guy kept swimming. He had to have been one hell of a strong swimmer to haul a tub like that mutant."

Tomlinson let the sun bake his face for a moment, letting me think about that, before saying, "Your daily workouts are about as public as it gets, compadre. You either jog to the pool and swim laps there or you run a couple miles on the beach, then swim to the NO WAKE markers off the Island Inn. How many miles a week are you doing now, five or six? I've never seen you in better shape in your life. And the way you do it, so public and all, it won't be hard to find witnesses."

I said, "There's nothing illegal about working out. You were telling me about the girl Heller tried to rape."

"Oh . . . well . . . she grabbed her stuff and got the hell off that boat, while you . . . while *the guy* wearing glasses . . . swam Heller out beyond the lights. She says she ran to the main road, and called her sister.

"Because she was afraid, or maybe embarrassed, she didn't tell anyone what happened until three days ago, when she finally went to a doctor. But she chose a private clinic in Miami for some reason. And she tried to use a fake name."

I said, "Hmm," not sure what that was supposed to mean. Miami was across the Everglades on the Atlantic Coast.

Tomlinson said, "The doctor didn't buy her story so he contacted social services. They're the ones who called the police. Amazing story, huh?"

I said, "Lucky timing. I'm glad for her," and meant it.

"There's nothing lucky about Universal Mind and divine intervention."

"If you say so."

"The girl thinks Heller would have killed her. He'd already beaten her pretty bad, which is why the sister made her get X-rays. The guy wearing glasses saved her life."

I caught myself as I reached to straighten my glasses and instead looked at my watch. "I hope she's okay. But if Heller was still alive the last time she saw him, it doesn't prove anything."

Tomlinson agreed. "He was struggling, splashing, definitely alive, from what my law enforcement friend told me. But isn't a dead Cheesehead in the water a little like a trout in the milk? Considering who you are, I mean, and what that asshole mutant did to Javier?"

"*Cheesehead,*" I said. "I get it, Heller's from Wisconsin. Who's the cop?"

"You know him. He's one of the few I trust."

I was impressed that Tomlinson wouldn't compromise the guy by using his name. My friend's contempt for the police borders on pathology. But there are a few he likes: the head sheriff's deputy on Captiva and a surfing pal from Naples. And there were rumors that the island's marshal might have been his distant relative.

I said, "He didn't tell you the girl's name?"

"No. She's in some sort of profession but young. Smart, too, from the way she handled herself. Smart enough to know her guardian angel dropped everything else that night to save her. She saw what she saw, though."

I started up the steps that led to my house and lab, saying, "The girl was in shock, that's the way it sounds to me. People in shock imagine all sorts of things."

At the door, I added, "I've got to pack a few things, then button up the place and get going . . . with your permission, of course."

Now was not the time to press for the meaning of Ten Man, or Tenth Man. I couldn't stay on Sanibel. The investigation into Heller's death was just getting started. Most serious crimes are solved within the first seventy-two hours or not at all. I didn't want to be around when the investigation peaked.

Inside the house, I checked the message on my new phone. It was from Harrington, not Barbara.

Return New York fastest possible means. Subject may have escaped, possibly hiding. More info when airborne.

Subject: He was referring to Will Chaser.

The boy had escaped? Well . . . possibly, he'd escaped. Even so, it was good news, and a relief to have something to smile about. Maybe the kid wasn't a typical teen after all. I'd put off contacting his foster guardians but was now eager to talk to them and learn what sort of boy the kidnappers were dealing with.

I found the SAT pilot's card in my wallet and dialed his number. He'd told me a smaller aircraft was available out of nearby Naples if I wasn't carrying "unconventional" personal items. He also said that his plane would be at Fort Myers Municipal, refueled and ready, by two.

I chose Fort Myers, adding that I would call to confirm.

I had a little more than an hour to collect my things and get to the airport.

In the lab, I checked the aquaria, reconfirmed I was still in possession of a few small, important ancillary items, a passive-electronic fish tag among them, and left a note for Janet Nichols, who takes care of the place when I'm away.

I also put out a new gadget: a bulk feeder loaded with food for Crunch & Des, a black cat who has granted me intermittent ownership obligations. I try to keep the cat happy because otherwise he'll omit the lab from his rounds for weeks if I miss a single day's feeding.

Finally, I pushed my bed aside and opened the hidden compartment under it built flush into the floor. It contained items I couldn't risk leaving for the cops to find.

When I looked in the fireproof compartment, though, I was suddenly no longer smiling.

Tomlinson was waiting at the bottom of the steps when I exited a few minutes later, my briefcase several pounds heavier than when I had arrived.

Glaring down at the man, I said, "Where is it?" I reached for the key ring inside the breezeway, preparing to lock the doors.

He didn't reply.

I said, "You know what I'm talking about. No one but you could've figured it out."

As I flipped through keys, Tomlinson said, "I swept the lab for evidence, I already told you, but not just my

stash. I called your hotel last night and there was no answer. It was an emergency. Doc, I had to do something.
My cop friend had just told me about the witness."

I said, "Rooting through my private property is going
way too far, pal." I hung the key ring in its regular place
and turned, adding, "But thanks, I guess. I can see your
point."

I could also see something else, too. Dangling from
Tomlinson's index finger was Bern Heller's gold Rolex.

He smiled. "Your prints aren't on it, just mine. I made
sure of that."

"Masterful," I told him. "When you talk about astrology, I do my best not to listen, but aren't you a Gemini?
I'm trying to decide which twin to slap."

Tomlinson liked that. "Twins would've gone schizoid,
man, dealing with the crap I've got going on. I've got a
full-time staff. Are you mad?"

"For trying to save my butt? No. But it won't work
even if I went along with it, which I won't. You were out
of the state, staying with your rich Long Island friends,
the week of the sixteenth."

"Sort of, sort of not," he countered. "I was in Sag
Harbor, which is more like a foreign country, not just a
different state. Out there, people like me are considered
entertainment, not houseguests. My name won't be on
any lists. Plus, the superrich don't talk to cops. The cops
go straight to their attorneys, don't even bother
trying."

I said, "That doesn't give you much of an alibi."

"So what, man? If it wasn't for thin ice, I never

would've learned to skate. If the cops question me, I'll have a clear conscience for the first time. A new experience: It's what I live for."

He was twirling the watch on his finger now. I sighed as I took a look around. In the distance, tourists milled on docks at the marina. JoAnn Smallwood and Kathleen Rhodes, both looking good in beach wraps, were swaying toward the Red Pelican carrying what looked like covered dishes for the weekend party.

Reading my mind again, Tomlinson said, "I hate it, too, missing another Friday night at the marina." He curled his bony fingers around the watch. "Doc? I called your hotel at least ten times last night. I don't want you to think I make a habit of snooping through your private stuff. This is his, isn't it?" He meant the watch.

I said, "I wouldn't want you to think I make a habit of doing what you've just implied. I don't believe in revenge."

Tomlinson was listening, his eyes serious, but he was still keeping it light. "Cool, I can relate. Why even the score when the objective is to win?"

I said, "You took it the wrong way. For me to do something so . . . so extreme, I would give it a whole lot of thought. Benefits would have to outweigh risks. I would need a credible motive—intellectually credible, not some emotional rationalization. Pyromania is to arson what homicide is to getting rid of a predator like Bern Heller."

Tomlinson said, "You're not a part-timer looking for a hobby, in other words."

I held out my hand for the Rolex. "I'm not a murderer."

"Is a murderer different than a killer?"

I wasn't going to answer that. I shook my head.

Tomlinson said, "Well, amigo, it doesn't matter, because I'm no saint." I watched him bounce the watch in the air and catch it. "If it had been me knocking at Heller's door that night, a woman would have been raped and killed. Because it wasn't me—because it was someone else, a man with a whole different set of moral convictions—she's alive. Maybe that's the thin line between murder and killing. Cowardice, in some form. Proactive or passive, it's still the same as murder. It's a crime."

I said, "I don't understand what you're getting at and I'm not sure I want to."

"For the first time in my life," Tomlinson replied, "I'm struggling with the concept of nonviolence as a form of violence."

I said, "A facilitator anyway."

"No, violence, the real deal. The woman would have died if I'd been there that night. Just because I wasn't at the cabin door doesn't make it any less valid. I would've chosen passive resistance—maybe out of conviction, but also maybe from being a coward. Either way, Heller would have brutalized her and she would now be dead."

The man was serious.

He was still bouncing the Rolex in his hand as I said, "Your fingerprints on Heller's watch won't ease your guilt or help my case. What worries me is, you'll have a few shots of rum at some bar after smoking a joint and want to talk philosophy with someone who—"

"A doobie mixed with demon rum is God's own truth serum," he interrupted. "I get talkative. Hey, I admit it. Which is why"—he bounced the watch twice before lobbing it to me—"I've decided we should disappear for a few days. I'm thinking Pensacola. It's Key West without the cruise ships or bondage crowd. An easy four-day sail." He lifted his antique bag. "Boat's ready, I'm packed. Want to come along as crew?"

I said, "I love Pensacola, but it's got to be New York. I'm looking for the boy they kidnapped." Because of my special clearance, a friend could travel with me on the SAT flight, so I added, "Interested?"

Tomlinson stood, folded his chair and stacked the pie pans. "New York—perfect," he said, unaware I had a plane waiting. "Screw the Intracoastal, we'll sail offshore. It'll be spring before we raise the Statue of Liberty, but that's okay. I don't own any winter clothes."

12

Lying on the horse waiting for Buffalo-head to pull the stall door wider, Will heard the man clearly as he turned to Metal-eyes and said, "But the Devil Child is insane. A monster!"

Will was thinking, *Not a monster, candy-ass, a warrior,* his voice loud inside his own head, as he threw back the blanket and used his boots to signal the stallion, but Cazzio was already moving toward the stall door, the horse's collective musculature vibrating through the boy's body like shock waves from an explosion.

Even Blue Jacket couldn't jump a six-foot fence, but this horse could, judging by his trophies, so Will was prepared for the rocket acceleration, leaning forward, staying low, as he heard Buffalo-head scream "Mother of God!" as he dove for safety when Cazzio lunged.

The next moment, though, Will was on the floor. His shoulder had clipped something—the doorframe?—but he wasn't hurt. Or was he?

Yeah . . . his shoulder was throbbing, that's all. But his legs were still solid. Will was getting up . . . getting up faster than Buffalo-head, who was also on the floor, as the stallion whined and reared, his eyes wild in the blinding headlights of the automobile parked outside, almost blocking the open barn doors.

"Here he is! I have captured the Devil Child!" Buffalo-head was yelling to Metal-eyes, still nervous but excited, keeping his eyes fixed on Will. "Bring the gun, quick!"

Then the big Cuban's expression changed. There was something he noticed about Will, that he was gimped over, that it hurt when he moved. As the older Cuban came into the barn, Buffalo-head said to him, "Wait, I don't need a gun," sounding relieved. "The Devil Child has been injured. He will be easy to catch now."

Will was backing away, watching the big man but also stealing looks at his shoulder. *Blood?* No, there was no blood, but it hurt. What the hell had happened to his shoulder? Or maybe Buffalo-head had noticed Will favoring one side because of the broken rib. His ribs *hurt*.

Then Will became more confused because the older Cuban stepped into the light close enough that Will could see the man's metallic eyes and also the revolver he was holding, dust particles illuminated by its red laser beam. The man said calmly to Buffalo-head, "Step away. I won't miss again."

Again? Will took another look at his shoulder. If he'd been shot, why wasn't there blood? More likely, he'd banged the doorframe, but he didn't dwell on the pain because Metal-eyes was now walking toward the stallion, who had calmed a little. The man was pointing the gun at the horse's head.

"Watch the boy. I want a clear shot."

Will was thinking, *He doesn't mean it, he's bluffing. No man in his right mind would shoot a good horse.*

But the Cuban wasn't like most men. He had his finger on the trigger, ready to fire.

Will yelled, "No! Don't do it!" as he stepped toward Metal-eyes, then screamed, "You sonuvabitch, you're after me, not the horse. The horse didn't do nothing!" but could barely hear his own words because of a fresh roaring in his ears.

Metal-eyes ignored him, waiting for the horse to stop moving, the gun only a few yards from Cazzio's head.

"You old bastard—I'm talking to *you*!" As Will said it, he knelt to grab the pole with the hypodermic needle taped to the tip.

That got the old Cuban's attention. He called to Buffalo-head, "Take that damn thing away from him," then extended the gun, squinting at the horse.

Will sensed Buffalo-head's bulk coming at him from the side. He turned in time to jab at him with the spear but the needle missed. The Cuban was still quick.

The boy took a step back—an intentional decoy—then lunged forward as Buffalo-head moved toward him. This time, the needle glanced off a rib or something, then sunk deep into the man's belly flesh, before he jumped back, yelling, "*Pendejo!* Damn you, that hurt!"

Metal-eyes called, "What did the brat do now?," as he

watched his partner touch his stomach, then study his fingers. "You oaf, you're bleeding again. Had I known you were helpless against a child, I would have left you to shovel shit in Havana!"

Eager to prove him wrong, Buffalo-head held his hand out, relieved. "It's nothing. He pricked me with a pin. Only a speck of blood." He grinned. "The little Indian thinks his toy spear can hurt a *Habañaro*! A spanking, that is what this little Indian *puta* deserves."

Metal-eyes's eyes warned *Be careful* but Buffalo-head waved him away, his swagger saying *Stop worrying!* as he marched toward Will, who was now taunting him. "My pecker's bigger than your horn! I won't look so small when you're on the floor!"

It *happened*.

Buffalo-head completed three steps before he slowed to a halt, breathing heavily as he turned toward Metal-eyes, who was saying, "What is wrong? You look sick!"

Now Buffalo-head had an odd, confused expression on his face, and he was sweating. He attempted another step but almost fell. He looked from Metal-eyes to Will, as he took a big, dizzy breath and gasped, "This child is not normal. He is bad luck. We must . . . must—"

The man couldn't finish. His eyes rolled back and his knees buckled. With a flesh-and-bones *whump*, his body hit the floor.

Suddenly, Metal-eyes didn't care about the horse. He swung the gun's red laser beam to Will's chest, saying, "You're insane."

Will turned toward the old man, still holding the spear,

and began walking toward him. "Why? 'Cause I'm gonna scalp you?"

Metal-eyes backed up a few steps. He said, "You *are* crazy," sounding surprised but also suddenly interested.

"Not enough to kill a good horse, you sonuvabitch." Will shifted the spear so that he was holding it over his shoulder, ready to throw.

Talking to himself, Metal-eyes said, "Insensitive to fear . . . rage compensation. I wonder if the child has abnormal pain tolerance." The Cuban squinted through his glasses as if studying a bug. He said, "I'll find out," aiming the pistol at Will's stomach, then at his pelvis, where nerve endings terminated in mass.

Will yelled, "You're not the first man to point a gun at me!" because that's what came into his mind, the image of Old Man Guttersen holding a pearl-handled revolver the first time they'd laid eyes on each other.

Fast talking had saved Will back in Minnesota.

Not this time. The Cuban wasn't chatty like Bull Guttersen. Will could see a deadness behind those silver eyes—an aloof, clinical interest—which Will didn't understand, but he knew what was about to happen unless he could get the needle in the guy.

When the gun muzzle flashed, Will was focused on the man's chest and already jumping to the side as he threw the spear, thinking, *Just like in the westerns except real bullets.*

The gun was so loud, the boy thought he'd been hit, but he'd jumped at just the right time and that saved him. But his spear missed, too . . . or had it?

Metal-eyes appeared to have swatted the shaft away
before the needle got to him, yet now the old bastard was
hunched over, crabbing fast toward one of the stalls, as
Cazzio reared. The horse reared again and tried to stomp
the man.

Will was hustling to retrieve his spear, yelling, "Get
'em, get 'em!" as the stallion's steel shoes made a coco-
nut-popping sound on the floor, just missing the man as
he pulled his legs into a stall, then reached to slam the
door closed.

Spear in his right hand, Will touched his left fingers
to Cazzio's rump, not wanting to surprise the stallion,
then traced his hand along Cazzio's body until he was
close enough to grab the halter. The boy was hurrying,
but also cooing, "Calm down . . . it's okay . . . we'll
stomp the candy-ass later . . . easy . . ." as he watched
Metal-eyes peek through the stall bars. When Will drew
his arm back to throw the spear, Metal-eyes ducked
from sight.

"My spear's tipped with deadly poison!" Will yelled in
Tex-Mex Spanish, then had to switch to English to add,
"One touch, that's all she wrote!"

Buffalo-head wasn't dead, but he was facedown in
straw, making weird, drunken noises. Near him was a
fifty-gallon drum of feed. Will used the drum to boost
himself aboard the huge horse.

He got his fingers knotted in the braided mane, ready
for the lunging acceleration, then signaled Cazzio with
his boots, yelling, "Go!" as he heard a gunshot so close
that his ears rang. Metal-eyes fired three more times—

whap-whap-whap—as Cazzio charged toward the blinding headlights.

Beneath the boy, the horse stumbled for an instant, then surprised Will by hurtling airborne, in a brief, arching silence, over the car's fender, then jumped again two strides later, clearing a four-board fence, into the pasture.

Will was shaking, not only because he was scared as hell but also because he had never been aboard an animal so sure, so powerful.

"Go . . . Go! Yah!"

Cazzio galloped into the frozen darkness, the drumming of his hooves in synch with plumes of steam spouting from his nostrils. Will's ears were attuned as his body matched the rhythm, hearing the countersynch snorting of the horse's breathing, an occasional grunt and the slosh of belly water.

He risked a glance over his shoulder. The Chrysler was fishtailing down the driveway toward the road. Metaleyes was trying to beat the horse to the overpass, where the pasture ended.

Fat chance!

The boy grinned as he leaned forward, finding Cazzio's rhythm, once again. For a glorious minute, he felt that soaring warrior feeling, aloof, alone and free . . .

It didn't last.

Cazzio stumbled . . . then stumbled again. The sound of his breathing was changing. Instead of snorting, the horse was wheezing, the air in his lungs making a bubbling sound as if leaking through a secondary exit.

"What's wrong? You hurt?"

Will spoke into the stallion's ear. As he leaned over Cazzio's neck, he saw that bubbles had joined the plumes of steam coming from the animal's nostrils. The boy's nose isolated a metallic taste in the air.

Blood!

Cazzio had been shot, Will realized. The bullet had gone into the horse's lungs, judging from the bloody bubbles, but Cazzio's heart was so big that he'd continued running.

"Stop, it's okay. I'll call a vet!"

Will pulled back on the braided mane but Cazzio wouldn't stop even though he was slowing. Because Will had once possessed an uncommon horse—Blue Jacket—he understood what was happening, and the knowledge created a vacuum of pain beneath his heart.

Cazzio would continue running, no matter what. He would run and run, and keep running, until the last of his life had seeped away.

The fence marking the edge of the pasture was ahead. Cazzio had ten lengths on the car but was now struggling between a gallop and a canter. Will leaned low, like a jockey, and didn't realize he was crying until his voice broke when he called, "Go! . . . Go! . . . Go!"

At the fence, Cazzio rallied, marshaling speed. His body swooped low before attempting takeoff, ascending, but with difficulty, fighting gravity's terrible weight, and his front hooves clipped the top railing of the fence.

The horse was still ahead of the Chrysler when he landed and gained another length before his rear legs buckled.

Will anticipated the fall. He threw himself clear as the horse crashed headfirst into the weeds, then made a high-pitched whinny of frustration.

As Will got to his feet, he stared at Cazzio for a moment but had to turn away. The horse was on his side, blood pouring from a wound in his chest. His legs were moving, clawing at weeds and empty air, still trying to run.

Above, on the overpass, the Chrysler had stopped, headlights bright. Seconds later, another car pulled in. Will guessed it was the man the Cubans had mentioned, the one they'd been waiting for.

Will was ducking beneath the lights and starting for the trees when he heard Cazzio whinny again. The cry was different this time. It communicated fear.

Will looked and saw that the horse's eyes were wide and wild, terrified. He could also see two men working their way down the rock ledge, Metal-eyes, with his gun, in the lead.

It didn't matter. Will ran to Cazzio and knelt beside him, his hands kneading the loose skin on the stallion's neck.

The boy was whispering, "I'll take you away from this. It'll all be okay," when Metal-eyes got close enough to say to Will, "Move—or I'll shoot you, too."

13

Even from a distance, I could see a horse's bloated body lying in a clearing on the far side of a fence.

White fence, gray horse. Conspicuous on a landscape of hills and winter oaks. At dusk, in January, rural Long Island was as colorless as a woodcut on parchment.

The horse had been shot, maybe while jumping the fence, maybe as he touched down. It was possible that Will Chaser had been aboard.

The animal lay in waist-high sedge, his body mass creating an indentation in the grass. Tail and mane were darker than the Appaloosa spots on his rump. He had been dead for at least eight hours, but vapor continued condensing on his coat as heat dissipated from his body.

We had crossed a hundred yards of pasture. Behind us was one of Long Island's elite equestrian estates, Shelter Point: dressage ring, boarding barn, breeding lab, staff quarters, forty acres of white fencing, a castle-sized mansion in the distance, an orange wind sock that told me the horsey set used private jets.

The practice arena was patched with snow. Jump stations were fabricated with a theatrical precision that reminded me of a miniature golf course.

A quarter mile down the road was a farmhouse where Shelter Point's manager lived. Beside it was a semitrailer converted to haul horses in style. The trailer was hooked to a new Range Rover, which was typical of the area, opulence that was elaborately, unmistakably, aggressively understated. Welcome to the Hamptons, a cluster of villages, beach estates and ranches that, for most property owners, constituted the most expensive hobbies in the Western Hemisphere.

Ahead of us, the fence's top rail had snapped midcenter. It looked as if someone might have hit it with a sledgehammer, but the horse had busted it as he jumped the fence—or attempted to jump the fence.

The fence was five feet high. Heavy two-by-sixes bolted to posts. Solid and unforgiving—obviously.

The horse had ended up twenty yards beyond the fence, to the right of the break. Looked as if he caught the top rail with a hoof, then struggled a few strides trying to recover before he fell.

But it wasn't the fall that had killed the horse. The FBI agent who'd met us at an East Hampton jetport had already provided some details. That night, around ten p.m., a 911 call was placed from a stable near the manager's house, but the phone went dead before the operator heard the caller's voice. The operator made the required call back and the manager answered—the number had been forwarded to his cell, he told her. He was in town, no one was at the ranch, so maybe he'd sat on his phone wrong.

When the manager got home, though, he called 911 and said he needed police, it was an emergency.

Police discovered that the phone line had been ripped from an outside wall of a barn. Inside was evidence of a fight, and the ranch's prize hunter-jumper stallion was missing. They'd found the horse's body only four hours ago.

The evidence was still fresh, but it was a difficult scene to read. That's why the agent, Jibreel Sudderram, wanted to have another look. The FBI had instructed Sudderram to let us tag along because a powerful senator had insisted.

"I heard the boy was a competent horseman," Sudderram had said as we drove from the airstrip, his inflection asking if we knew anything else about Will Chase.

I did. During the flight, I'd slept for a while, then made phone calls. I'd spoken with one of the boy's former teachers and also to Ruth and Otto Guttersen. Most of the information came from Otto, a crippled ex-wrestler who seemed to genuinely care about the kid. As we talked, the smart-assed teen became a person—complex, troubled, gifted, tough, tricky and, most all, different.

All three said that about the boy: "Will is *different*."

I told the FBI agent that Chaser was more than just a decent horseman, he'd been a rising star on the Oklahoma junior-rodeo circuit.

"I suppose they take rodeo seriously in that region."

I said, "Chaser was qualifying for senior competitions before he was thirteen. At a regular school, the equivalent would be a seventh grader playing varsity football starting at quarterback."

William Chaser had lived on three reservations and in six different homes before he was twelve, I told the agent. "The only consistent thing in his life was working on ranches. A former teacher said the boy's a better barrel rider and roper than most men."

"Barrel riding . . . He was that good, huh?"

I said, "Hopefully, he still is," and paid close attention to the agent's shielded reaction. The man had seen or heard something that convinced him the boy was dead or soon would be.

Because the agent noticed, he amended, "That was a slip. We're not even sure the boy was in the area. But some strange things took place last night . . . or early this morning, more likely. We're still putting it together."

I wasn't convinced he wasn't convinced. Using the past tense might have been careless but it wasn't accidental. And there was a reason we'd seen a pair of helicopters working both shorelines as we landed and why there were police cruisers and unmarked cars on most of the roads.

Long Island's eastern tip forks like a lobster's claw. The South Fork is a summer retreat, not a winter destination. From the air, the estates had looked as deserted as the shoreline, miles and miles of beach where for two hundred years whalers hunted.

What surprised me was the wild landscape, acres of

wooded hills, swamps, kettle ponds and corn stubble. Before today, when I heard the name Long Island, I pictured Brooklyn slums, not a hundred miles of glaciated seacoast, dunes and archaic farms.

I hoped Will Chaser was still alive and on the loose. There was space here to hide from men who had every reason to kill him. Seeing a roadful of cops might not lure a boy with his background from hiding. He had been arrested twice for dealing grass and was also suspected of growing it. And he'd almost gone to jail for stealing a quarter-million-dollar horse. I had discovered all that and more about William J. Chaser, *J* for *Joseph*.

The kid was a survivor. The more I learned, the more I wanted to meet him. Not just to save him—I am a rescuer by nature, or so I'm told—but to find out how the boy had managed to escape, if he had indeed escaped. He *was* unusual and I wanted to know how . . . and why.

"It's because you see yourself in the kid," Tomlinson had told me on the plane. "Or want to. Not all homeless kids are functioning, independent adults by the time they're sixteen. You were. Maybe Will is, too. But it's unfair to hang those kind of expectations on him, man."

I had chided Tomlinson, accusing him of being in a foul mood because the plane didn't serve booze. That's what got him started. Maybe he read my refusal to debate as an admission of guilt. Or disinterest. Whatever the reason, it irritated him and he pressed the issue.

"If Will outsmarts the people who snatched him, it validates you, Doc. If he's too tough for them to break, it validates your totally unsympathetic view of what makes a man strong. Of what constitutes ballsiness in a *real* man."

When I replied, "Are you thirsty or just going through withdrawal?," his irritation escalated a notch.

"I'm talking about *your* definition of manhood, not mine. You say you're interested in the boy because he's different? Baloney. You have no interest whatsoever in people who are *really* different: old souls with artistic sensibilities, a telekinetic awareness of other dimensions and previous lives."

I shouldn't have smiled, because he interpreted my skepticism as derision.

"Laugh all you want, but you're too honest to say it's not true. If the kid really is different, it's not because he has unusual qualities. It's because he lacks the common qualities that make people human. That's what you're hoping anyway. It fits with your Darwinian, no-emotion, no-excuses, start-thinking, quit-whining view of what constitutes a competent male. *Competent:* the ultimate compliment when you speak of a man. Did you realize that?"

I had almost finished the thought, "Next trip, I pack a pint of rum instead of extra socks . . . ," but Tomlinson's voice drowned me out.

"I knew you were hooked the moment you said the kid fired back at you, the way your eyes lit up. Then, on the phone, Otto Guttersen saying the boy was as fearless as an alley cat. Self-reliant, independent. Doesn't take shit off anybody. What it sounds like to me is, the boy's a certifiable thug if someone gets in his way or crosses him, because you two share the same simple rules of life: The weak survive only if the strong prevail. And all damn quitters should be eaten like breadsticks along life's highway.

"You don't think I know why you're pulling for young Will Chaser, Doc? What you see as 'different,' others might define as 'deviant.' If the kid's anything like he's been described, you two are like peas in a fucking pod!"

Tomlinson calmed a little when I said, "He'll need to be shrewder than I was at fourteen to survive. And a lot tougher to stay sane if they do what they're threatening to do."

It was unfair to play a rational, serious card while Tomlinson was on one of his irrational tirades venting because of the stress.

But he laughed when I added, "What might help you is attending a meeting. You stand up and say, 'Hi, my name's Sighurdhr.'"

I pronounced it correctly—Sea-*guard*-er—which was risky because few people know his first name. He thought the name was pretentious, he had once confided. Associated it with his aristocratic roots and the privileged, yacht-club society he had spent his adult life denouncing.

I knew Tomlinson was okay when he responded with a cheerful "Screw you!" then resumed his nervous finger drumming, twisting and gnawing at a strand of his hair.

He was right about a couple of things, though. The kid had his hooks in me. Whether he was different or deviant, I was interested. Science is fueled by anomalies. I am driven accordingly.

I had learned something else while on the phone: William J. Chaser scared people. Ruth Guttersen had told me the boy sometimes made her nervous but sounded more than nervous when she explained, "He's a completely different child when he gets mad. He's so . . . silent!"

His teacher tried to hide it, too, but twice during our conversation paused to remind me, "This conversation is confidential, right? You're not going to tell Will . . . *Right?*"

The information provided me with a secret, speculative hope . . . until just before we landed when my phone rang.

It was Harrington. A security camera outside the Explorers Club had produced grainy images of the kidnappers. One was Choirboy. But the FBI couldn't identify the other two.

Harrington's sources could. No surprise. They had access to cross-reference files that included people the FBI had no reason to log.

"The Cuban Program," Harrington said. "How much do you know?"

I knew enough to feel an adrenal charge.

"Castro trained three interrogators. All graduated from medical school, University of Havana. The staff that worked for them varied, but one of the three took on an apprentice late in the game. Vietnam, Panama, Iraq and Afghanistan—the team got around. Twenty years spent learning their craft."

"Medical research," I said. I meant "experiments"—an attempt at maintaining code protocol.

"The campers gave them nicknames. That's never been made public."

Campers were POWs.

Harrington asked, "Remember the Nestlé's commercial, the ventriloquist—nice guy, seemed like—and Farfel?"

A floppy-eared puppet came into my mind, Farfel the dog. Snap a wooden ruler on a table, that was the sound Farfel made when his mouth slapped shut. "Choc-laaaate"—*snap*.

"One of the interrogators had the same mannerism," Harrington told me. "He clicked his teeth to make a point. Farfel: His real name is René Navárro."

Another interrogator was nicknamed Hump because of a subcutaneous horn growing from his forehead—a pathology less rare in the Caribbean than in other parts of the world.

"In the security photo, Hump should be a lot older," Harrington said. "Either Hump hasn't aged or Farfel is using Hump's son. A relative maybe. Or a Soviet special edition: part human, part something else. They tried that, you know."

Yes, I knew.

Harrington had given physical descriptions to the FBI, minus details about the Cuban Program. There'd been rumors, but the information was still classified. "Not many POWs survived, but the few left don't want it made public what Farfel and the other two did to them. The Americans called them *Malvados*, a Spanish word."

Fiends. I didn't have to ask why.

I said, "You're sure about this." I was thinking, *They'll torture the boy before he dies. Just for fun.*

"I'm convinced. It's their way of showing they're serious about getting the library. It's political." Harrington's warning tone again.

I said, "Screw protocol. A fourteen-year-old boy from Oklahoma is alone with Soviet-trained sociopaths." *Damn.* "The gloves come off, right?"

Harrington said, "Rules are rules," then switched subjects, his way of closing the door. He was asking, "Did you see the news story about the football player they thought drowned?," as I hung up.

As we crossed the pasture, Frederick Gardiner, who managed the ranch and had trained horses for forty years, told us, "Reason Long Island's warmer here on the South Fork is 'cause the ocean pushes the snow up island. Gulf Stream sweeps close to the Springs, from away down by Florida—like you three." He chuckled, surprised by the accidental irony, a man unaccustomed to making jokes.

The FBI agent told him, "I thought I mentioned that I'm from Boston, Mr. Gardiner. These men work for Senator Hayes-Sorrento, not the agency."

The horseman stopped. He tossed a blanket over the

shoulder of his Barbour jacket, gray hair showing beneath his wool hat. "Boston, eh?"

"Near Concord, like I told you. It couldn't have been more than an hour ago."

"Well, maybe so, but Boston's *Boston*. And maybe you heard me mention I'd appreciate not hearing no smart comments about the Yankees, if you happen to be a Red Sox man. Don't think I didn't notice that sticker on your vehicle. Now here you are back again."

When I started to laugh, Tomlinson elbowed me. Gardiner had already exceeded his joke quota. The man was serious.

"Red Sox people, they always got some damn smart remark. A way of being clever, I suppose, to those b'low the bridge, but they'll get no smile from me. Which I think you should be aware of, Mr. . . . Mr. . . . " He'd lost the name. "Oh, here we are. Why you gotta take another look at the saddest thing that ever happened here, it don't make no sense to me."

It was a little after six but felt later because of a waxen light that blew off the North Atlantic. We had stopped at the broken fence. Death creates its own silence, a silence with boundaries that extend beyond the body mass of the corpse. We stood without speaking for a minute. I got the feeling Gardiner would have been offended if we'd scrambled over the fence to get closer.

Maybe Sudderram had tried earlier, because he was taking his time. "Would you mind telling these men what you told me? About horses jumping fences, Mr. Gardiner—this horse, I mean."

Gardiner replied, "If I could pronounce your name, I'd use it."

"Uhh . . . it's Egyptian. Jah-*bah*-reel," the agent began, then gave up as he watched the trainer shaking his head impatiently.

"I'm not talking about you, I'm talking about him." Gardiner gestured toward the horse. "The registered name's Alacazar-Alacazam, but he answered to Cazzio. A horse as fine as Cazzy, you ought to at least call him by name."

Sudderram sighed. "My apologies," he said, but with a false deference that told me he and the trainer hadn't gotten along earlier in the day and their relationship wasn't going to improve.

"We wouldn't of sold Cazzy for a million dollars, and that there's an accurate dollars-and-cents figure. How many folks can claim they're worth half as much? FBI agents, doctors, politicians"—the trainer glanced at me and Tomlinson—"I'd take ol' Cazzy back alive before any of 'em."

Tomlinson spoke for the first time. "It's got to be a pain in the butt for an old hand like you, Fred, dealing with summer people in January." He glanced at the agent, then me, to confirm he'd surprised us calling Frederick *Fred*. "Winter's the only time this man gets a break from dealing with outsiders. I don't blame him for being upset."

It was obviously meant to be ingratiating, but it meant something to the horse trainer. "You hit the nail on the head with that one, bub. First night since Christmas I went up-street for beers and the place goes all catty-fucked. When the nine-one-one woman called, I should'a known and come home right away. Vandals, is what did this. City-idiot kids looking for drugs. Rich little fucks with nothin' better to do than cause a workingman more work."

Tomlinson, who looked respectable but cold in jeans and a black sports coat I'd loaned him, said, "Summer people! Like the old saying, huh? Some are people, summer not," his shrug adding *What're you gonna do?*

Gardiner liked that but didn't want to show it. "You're from Florida, someone said?" Talking as if Sudderram wasn't there.

"West Coast, not Palm Beach."

"Not all summer people go to Palm Beach nowadays," Gardiner told him. "Sarasota, that's become big with the money families."

"I'm about an hour south," Tomlinson said as if I'd vanished, too. Local knowledge. He had it and was making the most of it.

On the plane, I had asked Tomlinson about growing up in the nearby Hamptons, which may have fueled his irrational rant. It wasn't the first time I had asked and it wasn't the first time he'd dodged the question, switching subjects after a long silence spent twisting and tugging at his hair. Just before landing, though, he'd tried to explain, telling me, "I have friends in the Hamptons who'd be very bummed if they heard I was hanging with cops. You mind introducing me as Thomas?"

If he wanted to keep his past a secret, I didn't mind. He knew the area and understood how to interact with locals. That was obvious when Gardiner began speaking only to Tomlinson.

"I'd think even people who didn't know nothin' about horses would see it's more likely Cazzy would jump a fence with a rider than without."

"Seems obvious, when you think about it," Tomlinson said.

"Yes . . . yes, sure does. But that doesn't mean there weren't something else that caused him to do it. He wouldn't have jumped just to leave what he knew was his home."

"That's the way you trained him," Tomlinson offered.

"Damn right, I trained him! Like you said, I shouldn't have to explain what's pretty goddamn obvious."

Tomlinson told him, "Well, Fred, I don't know much about horses, but I know the best way to learn from an expert is keep my ears open and my mouth closed."

"By God, ain't that the truth? Pay attention, don't make me do twice the work. You said your name was Thomas?"

"Call me Tom. I don't like all the formal crap."

When Sudderram saw that Tomlinson had bridged some invisible social barrier, his relief was apparent. He took a step back, content to let Tom serve as interpreter. Maybe we would learn more.

Gardiner looked at the dead horse and spit. "Cazzy was one of the country's finest hunters and jumpers. It's the rare horse that can do both. He was a prime actor in the dressage ring, too. A warm-blood, just full of music."

When I said, "He looks like an Appaloosa," the old trainer made a sound of irritation, then continued talking as if he hadn't heard me.

"Eight years back, maybe you saw Cazzy in the Olympics—a bitch from the Jerseys, a woman whose name I won't say, she leased him for the trials, then again for the Games. He was on the television ten, fifteen times. We figured he could win the next Olympics. Age didn't bother him. Sorta like that mare Fein Cera. Hell, she won the World Championship when she was sixteen!"

As Gardiner explained why Cazzy hadn't retired even though he'd been put out to stud, I was trying to auger my heel into the frozen pasture. I had a question but wanted to time it right. In January, how do you bury a valued horse . . . or an abducted teenager of great value?

I ducked through an unbroken section of fence, but only after Tomlinson, then Sudderram, gave me private nods telling me it was okay.

14

I waded through the grass, then cleaned my glasses before taking a close look. Big horse, with a back as long and broad as a couch. His coat was the same dappled gray as the horse in the painting of Robert E. Lee, the Confederate general, on his gelding, Traveller.

A backhoe would have to be brought in—no problem punching through the frozen ground or digging a hole big enough for more than just the horse.

Alacazar-Alacazam had been shot at least twice. There was a pock hole the size of a quarter on the rib cage, another on the neck just below the ear. Blood had coagulated into patches of ragged amber, a carpet of red on the bloated belly, probably because the bullet had punctured a lung.

Otherwise, the body was unmarked. The mane was articulately braided, as was a portion of the tail. The horse had been recently shod, the farrier's nails still shiny.

I had more questions now but waited for Gardiner to

finish talking about the horse's stud fee. "A hundred thousand dollars a shot," he said, sounding proud and giving it a bawdy edge as if he'd been in on the fun. But there wasn't much fun involved because the horse was so valuable. His owners seldom allowed natural cover. When they did allow it, Cazzy and the mare were released into a padded stall floored with rubber brick. Video cameras recorded it all.

I said, "It looks like he was ready for a show: the braids, fresh shoes. Or was he always groomed this way?"

"One of the summer girls who takes lessons does the braiding. Cazzy enjoyed the attention, and it was good practice for her. He wasn't scheduled for another show until spring."

All outsiders were summer people, I realized, even if they lived in the Hamptons year-round. The potential for resentment on both sides was implicit.

Gardiner resumed talking with Tomlinson as I circled the body. My wild-tempered uncle, Tucker Gatrell, had kept horses. Preferred his gelding, Roscoe, over a pickup truck for short trips. I had mucked enough stalls and done enough riding to distrust the animals—they were moody and manipulative—especially stallions. But I could also appreciate the marvel that is a horse with superb conformation. I had never seen one as heavily muscled or as well proportioned.

There was no bridle or saddle to hang on to. I couldn't have handled a stallion like this, never mind trying to make him jump a fence. I paused, waiting to ask another question, then realized that Gardiner was in the process of answering it.

"The thing about jumping horses is, they don't jump fences just to jump. It doesn't come natural, not like deer or dogs. If there's no rider, something's gotta be chasing 'em. Or scaring the hell out of 'em. Fire a gun a couple of times and even a great one like Cazzy would jump. That's what I think happened. Some of those rich city assholes got drunk and came out here because I was uptown." The man's voice faltered, getting emotional.

Sudderram risked another question. "But you don't know for sure someone wasn't riding him. You said that earlier."

"Yeah, but I also told you it weren't that missing kid. A fourteen-year-old boy that had never ridden Cazzy? I doubt if you remember what else I said."

"Mr. Gardiner pointed out that the horse isn't saddled," Sudderram told Tomlinson. "There's no bridle, no way to control him."

Gardiner was nodding. "It would take one hell of a horseman to take Cazzy over a four-rail fence bareback. At night? A stranger? If it was your boy who did that, find him and bring him to me. I'll buy him a milkshake, give him a full-time job and ask him to teach me a few things."

The trainer picked up the blanket he'd been carrying and walked to the fence. "You gentlemen are done here. At least I am. We're flyin' in the company vet to do an autopsy, but until Cazzy's buried he's gonna at least be covered with some respect."

Once again, I kicked at the frozen ground, before saying, "Buried where?"

"Right here where he lived. Where you think?"

Before I could press, Tomlinson said, "They don't get a solid freeze on the East End. It's because of the ocean, like Fred mentioned."

Sudderram caught my eye, both of us now possibly thinking the same thing: In the Hamptons, the kidnappers could either dig their own hole or have a hole dug.

The trainer had ducked through the fence but stopped to look at Tomlinson, his eyes making notations, taking his time as if evaluating something at an auction. "You from around here?"

"Not really. I was one of the summer people."

"But you was here year-round."

"When I was young."

"You got a familiar look to you. They was all hippies, the summer kids back awhile. But there's somethin' about your face. You do any riding?"

"I was more the surfer type."

"I could swear I've seen you . . . Tom? The name, too. Tom . . . Thomas . . ." The man was thinking about it. "You have an older brother?"

Tomlinson shifted his feet and pulled the sports coat around him. "Nope. An only child. Lived here a couple of years."

Despite the fake name, it was odd to hear the most honest man I'd ever met lie. I knew that Tomlinson had a brother, an opium addict who lived in the Far East, if he was still alive.

"Rich, I suppose. Maybe you know the man owns this place. Nelson Myles? He was one of the rich kids back then. Now he's richer. Like most of 'em, he heads for Florida before the first snow. Palm Beach, used to be, but now Sarasota."

"I remember the Myles place. It was more like a castle, but closer to Montauk."

"Only closer," Gardiner said, "if you lived that direction," which had some kind of meaning. I could read Tomlinson's gentle nod.

The trainer stared for another long second, more interested in what he was seeing than what he was hearing. Finally, he said, "The boy I'm thinkin' of had a similar name to Thomas but short hair. The same bony kind of Jesus face and eyes."

Tomlinson laughed as he blew into his hands. "I was just telling Dr. Ford, I'm no saint."

Gardiner didn't smile. "This boy weren't either. Fifteen, twenty years ago, a local girl disappeared. Found her blood and panties. The one who did it was a rich kid, too, big mansion on the dunes. His parents shipped him back to college before the cops could prove anything."

Tomlinson crossed his arms for warmth and appeared to settle into himself as Sudderram said, "We're going to check along the perimeter of the fence, then the road . . . if that's okay with you, Mr. Gardiner."

Gardiner didn't look at me as he brushed past. He opened the blanket to cover his horse. "You're the FBI, do whatever you damn well please. But get that vehicle with the Red Sox sticker off my drive, you don't mind."

On an overpass, a quarter mile from the trainer's house, Sudderram showed us where police had found fresh tire tracks, a ball of duct tape, then a lug wrench at the bottom of a hill.

A stain on the wrench had tested positive for human blood. They were still waiting to hear from Oklahoma and Minnesota about the Indian kid's blood type. The agency had also collected hair samples from Guttersen's home to compare DNA with hair on the wrench, possibly on the tape.

A search team with dogs had been here earlier. Sudderram said he didn't expect to find anything new but wanted us to have a look.

Tomlinson's focus was still inward but in a different way, as I watched him go down the hill, moving sideways because it was steep. Psychic mode, I had seen it before.

Paranormal powers or not, he is a fastidious observer, with a knack for making intuitive leaps that are nonlinear, empathic, from illogical effect to logical cause. He can arrive at conclusions that for most require a methodical process of assembly, myself included.

There are times I don't take him seriously, but neither do I discount what he says. More than once, I've experimented with his methods without telling him. Admit it and I would've been bombarded with theories on Universal Streaming, "remote viewing." It is impossible to function when someone is yammering away with step-by-step instructions on how to let go, to empty your mind.

He had repeated the basics more than enough. Objects are electrically charged. Events create electromagnetic patterns similar to shadows. Observe with eyes closed. To perceive, cease projecting. Feel, don't think.

Absurd in many ways, but I'm aware that absurd beliefs are sometimes anchored in undiscovered fact. A hundred years ago, doctors were convinced swamp air was poisonous, long before mosquitoes were proven to carry the malaria virus.

As Sudderram worked the edge of the road, walking toward Gardiner's place, I stood on the hill near the tire tracks. I accepted the premise that the boy and his Cuban abductors had been here and tried it Tomlinson's way.

Will Chaser would have been in the back of a truck, or a car trunk, or beneath a blanket in the backseat. It would have been dark. The car stopped for a reason, then hurried off for a reason: Tire tracks and duct tape had been left on the road. A bloodied wrench nearby. The Cuban Program produced three bona fide monsters, *Malvados*, but they were also pros. They wouldn't have made stupid mistakes.

I interrupted myself. Realized my brain was plodding along, projecting a scaffolding of probabilities instead of perceiving—typical.

Screw it.

Tomlinson was Tomlinson. I was me, a cognitive plodder like most people.

I angled down the hill just to see what there was to see, testing bits of scaffolding as I went, discarding most pieces, accepting a few.

A bloodstained wrench. Left by the Cubans, it meant Will Chaser was dead. If the kid had escaped, he wouldn't have stuck around to do battle using a tire iron. Anyone in their right mind would have run and kept running.

Dead, yes. Logical.

What wasn't logical was the Cubans leaving behind the murder weapon. I had witnessed their articulate abduction. More likely, some local guy had knocked part of a knuckle off while changing a tire and thrown the damn wrench in a rage.

I was near the fence. I knelt and picked up a baseball-sized rock, intending to see if I could lob it to the road. For some reason, I stopped. Stood there feeling the weight of the rock, its mineral density. Smooth, river-sculpted.

I studied the rock for no particular reason. Brown rock, a glacial oval. One point was stained black: earth tannin, I guessed. Or . . .

I was cleaning my glasses when Sudderram called, "Have you gentlemen seen enough? They spent three hours here."

The search team, he meant.

I looked from the rock to the road as a bit of scaffolding returned to my mind for review. If left by the kidnappers, did a bloody wrench guarantee the Indian kid was dead? Will Chaser was different, I had been told. Handled anger differently: *He's so silent!*

Maybe the teen had attacked one of the Cubans. The interrogator nicknamed Farfel had to be in his late fifties. Hump looked a lot younger, Harrington had said, a giant. Even so . . . The kid had a temper. Maybe he'd gotten so mad that he couldn't stop himself. Possibly got some solid licks in before he ran.

I bounced the rock in my hand, thinking about it. Imagined the kid with the wrench in his hand, hammering at some hulking guy POWs had called Hump; the guy spinning, trying to get away, before the kid lunged toward the fence, possibly injured—the size difference made it likely—then ran for the barn because horses were familiar. The only home a kid like Will Chaser had ever known . . .

Wasting time, Ford. It's a Tomlinson fantasy.

I realized I was playing a game. I was seeing what I wanted to believe. Astrologers and Tarot-card frauds made their living playing the same game.

I dropped the rock in the weeds. I returned to the car.

15

Will Chaser was reviewing, punishing himself with what he could've done and what he should've done, a key moment being when he'd bounced the rock off the Cuban's head and run.

Instead of throwing the damn thing, he should've pulled the rock from his pocket when he was on Buffalohead's back and beat him unconscious. A lug wrench is unwieldy, badly balanced. But a smooth chunk of granite had heft to it. It was as dependable as a hammer and wasn't as easily deflected as a light piece of steel manufactured by Chrysler.

A tomahawk. Same concept.

The boy winced when he made the association.

A tomahawk. I had a damn tomahawk! But I threw it instead of using it the way it was meant to be used.

Some warrior. A dope, that's what he was.

Will replayed the encounter but changed his selection of weaponry. He pictured himself swinging the rock, like a hatchet, dispatching Buffalo-head, before turning his attention to Metal-eyes, who he would charge and . . . do what?

Metal-eyes had a pistol with laser sights. A tomahawk didn't stand much chance against a gun, unless . . .

That's when I should have thrown the rock! Drill the old bastard right between the eyes. Grab his gun and kick him a few times for luck, see how he likes having his ribs busted.

Metal-eyes, that's who the boy wanted to beat into unconsciousness. After what he'd done to Cazzio?

That sonuvabitch!

It was painful even thinking about it, so Will allowed the fantasy to drift, then vanish. He was making excuses for what had happened to the horse and he knew it.

Hindsight isn't twenty-twenty, it's an excuse for following some asshole know-it-all instead of your own instincts.

Otto Guttersen—a man who didn't feel kindly toward assholes or excuses.

It was true. What had happened *happened.*

Will was on his back, hands, legs and mouth taped once again, in the darkness of what his nose told him was a horse trailer or possibly a stall, although a trailer created a distinctive echoing effect when there was a noise outside.

Yeah, a horse trailer most likely. A big one, fairly new.

Fresh paint, a recent grease job. He could smell that, too.

Over the last few hours, there had been some noise. Sound of vehicles coming and going, the mumble of distant conversations. But nothing close, until Will heard what might have been the panting of a dog as it sniffed around, taking his time, acting important, the way dogs do before choosing a tire to piss on. The boy had tried to make some noise of his own, inchworming over the floor, until a distant whistle called the dog away.

The only other noise he heard was every hour or so when Buffalo-head returned to make sure Will wasn't chewing himself free again. The man walked like Frankenstein in the movies, his feet slow and heavy. He would crack the door, shine a flashlight, then hurry away. The Cuban was afraid of him, that was obvious, never spoke a word.

Will liked that. But during the hours of darkness, even the satisfaction of scaring the hell out of Buffalo-head grew boring, so he spent most of his time replaying his escape attempt.

It came back so clearly, it was like there was a movie screen behind Will's eyes, but the movie didn't play beyond that instant when he heard the *whap* of the first gunshot and then later felt Cazzio's muscles spasm rock-hard as the horse struggled to run, shuddering as if jolted by electricity.

Up to that frame of the movie, though, Will's memory could review it all scene by scene, seeing himself, seeing the horse, and the Cubans, too, as if a camera was mounted above them on tracks. Will knew how TV westerns were filmed—he and Old Man Guttersen had watched a documentary on the great director John

Ford—so he could imagine the camera placement if he wanted to.

He wanted to. What had happened *happened*, but that didn't mean Will couldn't change a few scenes here and there. It made events more tolerable because if they had been filmed for a movie, it was all pretend. Something he could do over until he got it right, replaying scenes, editing, cutting, muting sounds he didn't want to hear. A horse's scream, a whinny that bubbled from Cazzio's chest—just one of the sounds he never wanted to hear again.

Pretending there was a camera made it bearable, so that's what he did.

Will's favorite scene: He was back in Cazzio's stall, mounted on the horse, holding the syringe-tipped spear. He could watch his own silhouette, as he cut a handful of hair, tied some to the spear and knotted the rest into the horse's mane.

It brought the feeling back: a warrior sensation. Powerful . . . *real,* not like the drunks playing Indian back on the Rez. Will clung to that feeling. Wanted to hold on to it.

Why not? Gives me something good to think about until they bury me . . . or I get another chance to escape.

Maybe he would. Will had been chewing at the tape and now almost had his hands free. Buffalo-head didn't have the nerve to take a close look.

Idiot!

Will hadn't given up yet and he wouldn't. Not now,

not ever—just like Cazzio—because Will had heard the Cubans talking with their American partner. Two graves had been dug somewhere out there in the pasture, one of them just for Will.

"The box is prepared, specially constructed," the American had told them. "That's where you'll place the hostage."

The American was a skinny, straggly-haired man who had money and knew the area, judging from the way the Cubans deferred to him, and he also had a snooty, educated way of speaking.

The hostage. Saying it in such an impersonal way to distance himself from this bullshit, like he was too good to get his hands dirty.

Will found it unsettling that the American, for some reason, hadn't said anything about killing him first. But they would, of course. They had to—not that Will wanted to die, but you couldn't bury someone alive. So the American, Will guessed, was leaving it up to Metal-eyes and Buffalo-head to decide, which was good.

The Cubans scared him. But the American scared him more, with his silence, the way he stayed in shadows, never allowing Will a solid look at him.

Something else that was good: The American was seriously pissed off that the Cubans had bungled things so badly and he was leaving.

"Try to finish what you've started, but please do it on your own. We have a schedule to keep and I'm keeping it. If you're not there to meet the boat, that's your problem!"

By now, hopefully, the man was gone. Escaping would be easier with only the Cubans to watch him. And he would escape. He had to! The thought of being murdered and buried, even next to a great horse like Cazzio, pushed Will close to panic if he let himself linger on the idea, so he didn't.

To get his mind off the subject, Will decided to risk chewing some more at the tape before Buffalo-head returned. Will's hands were behind him, so he drew his knees to his chest, then threaded his boots through his arms. To manage it, he had to expel all the air from his lungs, but it wasn't that hard.

With his hands now in front of him, Will could have ripped away the tape covering his eyes. But even a moron like Buffalo-head might notice, so Will used his lips to feel around until he found the break in the tape he'd already created. A couple more layers and he would be free.

In fact, if he had only five more minutes—

"Devil Child? I'm coming in—I'm warning you."

Shit. Buffalo-head was right outside.

Will was still struggling to step through his hands again when he heard the creaking of the trailer door.

The boy lay still, focusing on the silence of the Cuban's labored breathing, feeling the man's eyes on him, sensing the beam of a flashlight panning over his body.

Will heard Buffalo-head's nervous laughter. "You are freezing. Good. Balled up like a dog. That is what you deserve for poisoning me! To live like a dog before I come back with a gun. Do you hear me?"

Will didn't move.

"You say you're not afraid of guns? Hah! Then how do you feel about being buried in the cold ground? We will see!"

The trailer door slammed shut, not as loud as a gunshot but almost, and Will jumped. In his mind was this image of the hole the American had mentioned, the empty horse's grave.

Moments later, the door opened again, and Will knew it was Metal-eyes. He could smell the man's hair lotion. He could feel the man stalking closer and soon could smell another distinctive odor, familiar and medicinal.

Ketamine.

Damn it.

Will forced his muscles not to flex when the Cuban jammed a syringe needle into his thigh. Will could feel the horse tranquilizer flooding his system but didn't react.

Seconds later, Will couldn't move even if he had wanted to.

16

At ten, Tomlinson banged at my hotel door and said, "Demons have returned to the bell tower. Want to go for a drive? I was twitchy to begin with. Now I'm having visions. I think he's there."

"The boy, you mean. Where?"

"I mean my brother. Or father. Maybe both—God help us." He had the keys to the rental car and rattled them in his hand. "I should have told you about the missing girl Fred mentioned, but I never let myself be convinced."

Earlier, he'd made only a vague reference to her after admitting that he knew his father had not sold the family estate. Their only contact over the years had been a few phone calls and cards. "The day I began to suspect was the last time I set foot on the property."

Not long afterward, his father, a gifted paleontologist, and his brother, a Yale graduate with two years at Johns

Hopkins, both left the country while Tomlinson was still at Harvard. Now he wasn't even sure they were alive.

Standing at my door, he said, "I swore I'd never go back. But everything in its time, man. The dream was bizarre, now it's like a tractor pulling me home." He looked over my shoulder into the room. "You mind grabbing an extra jacket? It's freezing out here."

I was awake. I had spent two hours cross-referencing new information related to William Chaser's abduction. E-mails from Barbara's staff and one from Harrington. Now I was trying to get my mind off the puzzle of the boy's disappearance by reading an article in *National Geographic Adventurer* about the puzzle that is the precise magnetic navigation system in sea turtles.

I closed the magazine and tossed it on the desk. "Someone could be living in your old place. Maybe it's been leased, you don't know. And it's late."

"Tell that to my demons. Last I heard, Dr. Tomlinson was working in Brazil and my brother was growing poppies on the far side of the world. But it doesn't mean they gave away the family jewels." He rattled the keys.

Tomlinson's manic reaction to alcohol mixed with guilt takes many forms, most of them familiar to me by now. This was different. His eyes were wild but not glazed. He was dressed in layers: jeans, shirts and at least two pairs of socks—a scarecrow's costume for most but for him bedrock proof that he'd given the matter sober consideration.

Fifteen minutes later, I was standing outside a hedged compound, a deserted hulk of a house that Tomlinson said was once his family's estate. MELVILLE PLACE read a weathered sign at the stone entranceway—the author had spent part of a whaling season here. When Tomlinson said the family had money, I'd assumed millions, not hundreds of millions. There was a light on in a staff cottage. He asked me to wait while he went to the door.

I watched the door open. A buxom woman in a housecoat appeared. I heard a hoot of surprise, then watched the woman hug Tomlinson. He lifted her off the floor as if they were dancing.

"It's okay," he yelled. "Give me a minute!"

As the door closed, I could hear the woman weeping.

I walked to the back of the property to a dune overlooking the sea. I was there for only a few minutes when I noticed the silhouette of a man approaching. I looked at the house, then at the silhouette.

Physical characteristics in a family vary, but the person coming toward me was Tomlinson's ectomorphic opposite: broad and squat, not tall and lean—unlikely it was his father or brother. And his movements were mechanical, like a robot tracking unfamiliar ground.

I looked far down the beach. No lights. The nearest estate was two miles away. Even so, I wondered if it might be a neighbor sleepwalking.

No . . . the man was awake. His course didn't vary. I realized it was because he saw me. As he approached, I expected a signal of acknowledgment, at least a tentative greeting, typical of strangers meeting at night in an isolated place.

Nothing. The closer he got, the faster the man walked. Maybe he expected me to turn and leave—or run.

I didn't.

"Are you him? The liar that says his name is Thomas?"

When the man spoke, I backed up a step, couldn't help it. By now he had breached what academics call the *alarm perimeter* and hadn't slowed. Friends stop at three feet, acquaintances at four, strangers at nine. He kept coming. It wasn't until I stepped toward the man that he halted.

"You scared, bub? I'm waiting for an answer." The man was a local, his accent similar to the horse trainer's.

I said, "Here's the way it works: You introduce yourself, then I explain my name's not Thomas. Afterward, we both go on our merry ways."

"Didn't say that. I said you was the liar pretending his name was Thomas."

The man stepped closer.

Wind blew off the ocean, topping the dunes. I could smell creosote and diesel, odors I associate with commercial fishing. Not a tall man but big. His face was shadowed because the sea was behind him, a pale band of beach where waves boomed, water blacker than the squall-black sky. Age was in his voice and the way he moved, not old but getting there.

I wondered if he could see my face. Realized he couldn't when he said, "If you don't remember me, bub, maybe you need glasses."

My foul-weather jacket wasn't zipped. I said, "Maybe

we both do," as I took off my glasses and cleaned them on my sweater. "If you've got a problem, mister, I can't help unless I know what it is."

The mansion behind me was five stories, all the windows dark except for the lights on the porch and in the windows of the cottage. I turned toward the cottage, the mansion to my left, the sea to my right.

After a moment, the man said, surprised, "You're not him," but it was also an accusation. He looked at the mansion, took a few steps toward it, then stopped. "You must be the other guy. The one who's a cop looking for some missing boy. Only strangers come out on this point in winter. Alone anyway."

I said, "Because it's private property? Maybe I should be asking the questions."

The man took another slow step toward the house, his anger draining along with his certainty. "I was sure you were him. Fifteen years, I've waited." He stopped and turned. "Always knew what I was gonna do when we finally come face-to-face."

I said, "So I see," because I could make out details now. He had the gaunt eyes, thick forehead, the nose, skin and ears, a distant mix of slave islanders and North Sea fishermen. He wore suspenders beneath a heavy coat. In his hand was a gaff, a steel hook lashed to a handle.

"If you're going to use that, I should at least know your name."

After a long silence, he said, "Sylvester. Virgil Sylvester," before repeating, "Fifteen years, I've watched this place. In summer, it's a rental. Billionaires and film stars. But winters, it's just him who sneaks in."

I couldn't bring myself to ask who because I expected him to add a name: *Tomlinson.*

"Word used to travel fast on the South Fork. Now there ain't many locals left. Those still here are afraid to tell me who comes 'n' goes at this place. He killed my Annie—you know that, bub? We never found her body, but it was plain what happened. He raped her, then beat her to death with a golf club. *A golf club.*"

I had never heard such bitterness attached to these words.

"A rich kid. One of the summer brats. He used my girl like some damn country-club sport before taking the luxury bus back to college. A plaything to screw, then put on a tee." His chest was heaving. "He's up there, ain't he?"

I said, "I have children. What you just described, it's the worst imaginable. How old was your daughter?"

"Thirteen. Pretty girl. She'd read me little poems and stories sometimes."

"Something like that sticks. I'm sorry, Virgil."

"Yeah, yeah." The man still faced the mansion but his breathing was slowing. "Since that morning, I've been a dead man just waiting for the lights to go out."

I glanced toward the cottage, hoping Tomlinson wouldn't choose that moment to exit and call my name. I was calculating the possibilities. Virgil Sylvester would either come at me with the gaff, or charge the house, or realize that attacking was pointless and contrive an excuse for doing nothing.

I relaxed a little when he turned and said, "You really a cop?"

"No. Someone asked me to help find the boy. He's fourteen. Lives in Minnesota, but has an Oklahoma accent."

"Why tell me?"

"He might still be around."

The man nodded as if it made sense. "I can't picture anybody being friend to a child killer."

"I'm not. I don't know the person who killed Annie."

"Looking for a missing child, it's the only hell I believe in. You think one of the summer people took the boy?"

"If I was sure, I think I'd ask to borrow that gaff."

Sylvester faced me, and I could smell his clothing again. "Sounds like you mean it. But you don't. You're just trying to talk me out of it."

"I'd want someone to talk me out of it. Kill a man for revenge and he lives with you the rest of your life."

"Let the cops handle it, I suppose?"

There wasn't much I could say to that.

"You don't know what it's like out here. The power these summer people have."

On the drive to this remote peninsula, we had passed estates that were small sovereignties, mansions as ornate as cathedrals, visible only because their twelve-foot hedges were frost-barren.

"A man can't fight that kind of power. Since Annie died, I've visited family in California . . . Texas, too. Rich people everywhere, but it's spread out. Not like here, the

Hamptons. I saw an iceberg once, fishing in Nova Scotia. It comes into my head when I try to tell people. Peaks lit up like fire at sunrise, but the ocean was dark under the surface, a whole mountain of ice down there, and cold. It's that kind of power they got. Even when they use it, you don't see it."

Sylvester looked at the mansion. "Is someone up there? Besides the caretakers, I mean."

"A friend of mine."

He said, "One of the Tomlinsons." It wasn't a question.

"My friend didn't kill your daughter. Even if he'd lied to me, I would know."

Because I had provided a reason to retreat, I wasn't surprised when Sylvester used me as a target for self-contempt. "If you're such a fuckin' genius about who did what, why is that boy still missing?"

I said, "You've got a point. I shouldn't be standing here wasting time."

The man said, "Hah! Cops"—I was watching the way he held the gaff—"they sell coffee and doughnuts uptown at the 7-Eleven."

"Probably my next stop—once you're gone."

"Uh-huh, now you're tellin' me to leave. I'm fifth-generation Bonnacker. My people killed whales on this beach."

I said, "Virgil, if I ever hear anything about your daughter, I'll find a way to get in touch. I'll let you know, okay?"

The man appeared to sag. I had robbed him of his

anger. "You cops, you think you know so much. Let me tell you something about them Tomlinsons. They're evil. Big brains and dried-up hearts. You know how the old man made his fortune?"

I did, but he didn't expect an answer.

"It's blood money. Three generations fed on it. Everything crazy all rolled into one family, that's the Tomlinsons. I should know. I worked for those sonuvabitches. When one of them murdered my Annie, they gave me a month's bonus and fired me after they was all safe, gone back to Florida for winter."

17

Tomlinson's brother, Norvin, had been a member of an elite secret fraternity, Skull and Bones, at Yale. Tomlinson hadn't volunteered the information, which irritated me. I knew because of things I saw in Norvin's room.

Tomlinson pretended not to hear me say, "I've read that Skull and Bones stole Geronimo's skull. Pancho Villa's, too. They have a place off campus, not a typical frat house, called the Tomb. Some say they still have the skulls."

I was looking at a photograph of fifteen young men standing in front of a grandfather clock. Norvin Tomlinson was near the center. The family resemblance was eerie. Norvin was a little taller, with short pale hair, but the haunted eyes were familiar. The brothers had the same look of sinew, bone and muscle.

Norvin was near the fraternity banner, which I recognized. It was similar to a Masonic symbol I had seen on rings: a primitive skull and crossbones, the lower jaw of the skull missing. The number 322 was prominent.

My uncle had been a Freemason, as was Hooker Montbard. He wore an antique Skull and Bones ring. It was Hooker's interest in Masonry and the Knights Templar that had fired his conviction that artifacts from the Crusades were somewhere in the jungles of South America.

I stood, looking at the photo, until Tomlinson finally had no choice but to comment.

"That was Norvin's senior year at Yale. It's a weird fraternity, but our father was so stoked he bought Norry an MG convertible when he was tapped."

"Tapped?"

"Chosen. Members of Skull and Bones are considered chosen people. I didn't realize it's such a huge deal until later, because Norry's best friend was tapped the same year."

Tomlinson pointed to one of the men in the photo. It was Nelson Myles, he said, the man who owned Shelter Point. I now understood the horse trainer's reaction.

"They were our neighbors practically, that's why I took it for granted being tapped. It seemed common. But it's not."

I turned to him. "You don't think I've heard of Skull and Bones? Why didn't you tell me your brother was a member?"

"I didn't think it was important."

I said, "Hey, old buddy, it's *me*."

His smile was a mix of chagrin and admission. "Sorry. I've got a problem with power, you know that. The Bonesmen scare the hell out of me. That fraternity produced how many presidents and vice presidents? A couple of Supreme Court justices and at least two directors of the Central Intelligence Agency. In almost two hundred years, no Bonesman has ever gone public with the fraternity's secrets. Do you have any idea how much power they have?"

Fifteen minutes earlier, I had heard Virgil Sylvester say something similar about the Hamptons.

"But, hey, I *did* tell you I'm pretty sure Norvin was recruited by the CIA. It was almost the same as telling you."

Sort of. Skull and Bones is a favorite of conspiracy kooks. The fraternity's tradition of secrecy invites wild theories, but so do the few known facts. The OSS, the forerunner of the CIA, was founded by Ivy League graduates. Most, if not all, Bonesmen are offered interviews by the various intelligence agencies. The amount of wealth and power the fraternity wields is remarkably disproportionate to its tiny membership.

Even so, the theories are ridiculous. I don't believe that secret societies hatch international plots, for the same reason I don't use comic books as research material. When I meet more than three people who can keep a secret when their lives aren't on the line, I'll start giving conspiracy theories another look.

Tomlinson said, "They recruited us heavy back at Harvard, too, of course, spook agencies. Thank God I couldn't remember my Social Security number or they might have hired me full-time instead of just cashing in on my special skills. But you know about that."

"Yes," I said, "I know." Tomlinson's credentials to lecture on clairvoyance were better than most. He had participated in a program called Stargate by its many critics. The Pentagon preferred Asymmetrical Intelligence Gathering Research, and funded the study after discovering the Soviets were recruiting telepathic savants to work as "psychic spies."

This wasn't conspiracy theory fantasy, it was documented fact.

My friends in the intelligence community had confirmed that Tomlinson turned in one of the highest scores ever recorded on what must have been a bizarre test used to cull prospects.

We were in Norvin's room—an apartment, really. One of several in the family's thirty-room "summer residence." The place had been built during the days of mustang capitalism, back when the Du Ponts, Rockefellers and Kennedys were making their fortunes.

Tomlinson had introduced me to the family maid, Greta Finnmark, now one of the caretakers. Good-looking older woman, blondish and busty, with Nordic eyes and a Nordic accent, who had to have been a knockout in her day. She slipped her arm through Tomlinson's, cooing and smiling, saying, "Guards, my dear sweet boy, it is so good to have you home!"

Guards, short for *Guardian*—her strange pet name for Sighurdhr.

"Because, even as a child, he was always looking after people, trying to raise their spirits if they were sad," she explained to me. Sincere, too, because she didn't get it when I replied, "Oh, yeah, he's a regular Boy Scout. Still raising everything he can."

Greta led us through the restaurant-sized kitchen, then turned us loose in the first of two great halls. The furniture was covered with tarps, and it was cold as a cave. Greta had confirmed that the main house was rented each summer, then closed in the off-season.

"The rent charged by your family's trust company is incredible!" she had said. "For the same money, you could buy a house most places. But they pay. Oh yes, the rich people from New York, they wait in line to pay!"

There was a grand piano near the fireplace. Tomlinson tossed back the cover and played the first plaintive notes of "Clair de Lune" before he noticed that I was staring at a painting over the mantle. It had to be his great-grandfather, the man who'd built the estate. Remove the tux, add a decade of tropic seas, taverns, midnight water, rock 'n' roll plus salt-bleached hair, and it was Tomlinson.

I wasn't surprised when my pal stood and motioned me along, saying, "Speak of the devil, huh? Say good-bye to Hank—friendly name for a coldhearted genius."

"That was your father's name, wasn't it?"

"No, Dad's name was Hank, as in *Hank*. The old man's name was Hank, as in *Henry*. I told you how he made his dough. Blood money, which is why I'll never take a cent of it."

There it was again.

During World War I, the elder Tomlinson had made a fortune off of royalties from a couple of patents. Something to do with a synchronizing device that allowed airplanes to fire machine guns through spinning propellers.

I had read that the invention had changed the course of the war—maybe history—and accounted for huge kill ratios. In that war alone, the invention had facilitated many thousands of deaths.

From the great hall, Tomlinson led me to the west wing, which was sealed by massive doors. He was perturbed they were locked. "It's the only modern section of the house, if you catch my meaning. There's a five-car garage, so if anyone's around . . ." I didn't hear the rest because he jogged back to the kitchen for the key. But Greta said she didn't have it.

"She's got keys," Tomlinson told me as I followed him outside, "but she can't let me use them. It's the same reason she pretends not to know anything about my brother or father. She's scared."

I said, "If her job's on the line, can you blame her?"

"For sure. I loved that lady, man. With a rack like that, who wouldn't? She was my wet nurse."

I said, "Huh?"

He wagged his eyebrows—*End of subject*—before saying, "If there's a trust company running the place, it means my father's still alive. Hell, he could be on the property right now and she'd be a fool to tell me. Or my brother could be holed up here. Fifteen acres—there used to be anyway—including two guesthouses, staff cottages and a machine shop the size of a barn.

"Old Hank would crap his burial skivvies if he knew

the place was being rented. Commoners? Yuppies? God forbid, a Protestant. Damn, I should've brought a flashlight. But you've got one, I bet. The ultimate flashlight snob."

I said, "I do, and you might be right," as I took a mini ASP Triad from my pocket. Palm-sized, but it fired a beam so bright it was considered dangerous. I shined it through a garage window. Empty. Next, we went to the machine shop. It was a museum piece of 1890s technology. Industrial lathes, metal stock, instruments for precise threading and tolerances. Both guesthouses were locked, no sign of activity through the windows.

In a wooded area was a cabin where Tomlinson said he'd often slept on summer nights. I watched him stand on tiptoes, feeling along an overhead beam, until he said, "I'll be damned," then showed me what looked like a Wonder Bread bag twisted into a knot. Inside were two brittle Trojan packets and a rusted harmonica. Unfortunately, the harmonica still worked.

Outside was a faded outline of a catcher painted on the wall. Sixty feet six inches away was an indentation where there had once been a pitching rubber. Tomlinson stopped blowing on the harmonica long enough to tell me, "Fifty to a hundred pitches a day," then showed me where his first and only dog, Elvis, a springer spaniel, was buried.

He was right, the estate was huge, at one time a self-sufficient village. It would take a full day to search the place.

We returned to the main house. As I followed Tomlinson up a winding staircase, I said, "When you told me rich, I had no idea," hoping he'd put the damn harmonica away if I kept him talking.

He clomped up the steps, eyes sweeping over familiar details. "The only difference between doves and pigeons is where they crap. I was one of the fortunate ones—materialism sucks if you've had everything. Plus, my old man made us get jobs, so I learned at an early age that employment sucks, too. I didn't choose to be a boat bum, God chose me. He replaced my thirst for status with a thirst for beer. It's a calling, sort of like religion or drug exploration."

He still had his sense of humor, and the harmonica was in his pocket. Good.

We'd reached the fourth floor. There was another door, this one sealed with a steel bar used as a dead bolt. Greta had told us only the first three floors were used by renters. The top floors were family storage.

I said, "If it's okay, I think I can get in," then took out a tiny restraint cutter. As I worked on the top bolt, I asked Tomlinson what it was like to return after almost twenty years.

"Weird, man. But it could get weirder if the old digs haven't changed. My room was on the fourth floor, Norry's on the fifth. It matched his elevated opinion of himself. What's the antonym for identical twins? Mirror opposites? That works. Never once did I see him shed a tear. Farting was as close as he came to showing emotion. He was a mathematical wizard. And talk about a damn know-it-all!"

I said, "I'm convinced. As different as night and day, you and your brother. Know-it-alls get tiresome quick."

"Okay, okay, but he was obsessive, too. You'll see, if his room's the same."

It was. Library shelves alphabetized. Model cars and airplanes, a '68 Corvette fastback, surfer blue I wanted to touch but the place was too much like a museum. Trophies for chess, basketball and . . . golf. Tomlinson gave me a knowing look before I leaned to inspect a bag of clubs.

"Is the nine iron still missing?"

I checked again. "No. Just the cover."

He nodded slowly, thinking about it but not surprised. "My mother was still alive then. That woman would have gone to the gallows for Norvin. But me? She threatened adoption after my first arrest for possession. On the phone, I said, 'Mother, I chose LSD, not IBM. Think of it as a business trip.' She didn't think it was funny either. What's funnier is how some parents say they don't have favorites."

I smiled but was picturing something else, the mother sneaking in to replace the nine iron. If true, a young girl's death had taken seed in this space, a room that was more like a shrine.

Virgil Sylvester's bitterness was not misplaced.

Put her head on a tee, he had said. A commercial fisherman, not a golfer. Or were rules about using tees different in the Hamptons?

I looked at Tomlinson, who wasn't smiling now. I didn't ask.

After finding the Yale photo, I began picking out other mementos associated with Skull and Bones. Miniature death's-heads, a map of Deer Island—Bonesmen owned the place, supposedly. There were also caricatures of a flat-faced Indian holding a Winchester: Geronimo.

Tomlinson told me he'd heard the same thing: Bonesmen had stolen Geronimo's skull from an Apache cemetery out west and kept it locked away in their Tomb stronghold.

"We got into a big fight after I jumped Norry's case about it. It was just after he'd joined. You know me, simpatico with the Skins. I kept pushing, but he wouldn't answer the question. Simple: Do you assholes have the great chief's skull?

"Some of the AIM founders, the American Indian Movement, they were like my brothers in those days. I did sweat lodges and the whole Ghost Dance thing. Four days, no food or water. Ate my first peyote button, which wasn't part of the ceremony. Not smart, it turned out. Peyote on an empty stomach. *Wow!*

"Back then," Tomlinson added, "I was an absurd adolescent only about ninety percent of the time. But there were moments of clarity."

I was looking at lists of names in a trifold frame, as Tomlinson told me that his mother's family and his father's family all went to Yale. "When I chose Harvard, it was like I'd pissed on the flag . . . which I'd actually done, by the way." He started to elaborate, then reconsidered. "No need for the nasty look. Shallow up, Doctor."

"These are all Bonesmen?" I turned the frame so he could see it.

"The oldest to the newest, left to right. Every member of Skull and Bones since whenever the hell it started. Eighteen hundreds? You'll find my father's name and Norvin's. Plus a surprise. It'll jump out at you."

The roster started with the class of 1838. The list was alphabetized. My eye slowed on familiar names. Four U.S. presidents. Lesser-known State Department and CIA icons: William Bundy; Richard Drain; Dino Pionzio, a CIA deputy chief; Winston Lord; William Draper, an early proponent of the United Nations.

Beside every name was a date, with one exception.

Henry A. Tomlinson. No date.

Tomlinson was looking over my shoulder. "Google it on the Internet. Type in 'Skull and Bones membership list.' It'll come up the same way."

"No date? I don't get it."

He shrugged, and picked up a bronze figurine of Geronimo. "No idea. We'll never find out. It's why they scare me. Part of the reason I turned traitor. But Norvin joined the corporation. Every Bonesman gets a big chunk of money from an endowment . . . and one of those." Tomlinson looked from the photo to an ornate grandfather clock in the corner. "They've got their fingers in everything, man. Oil, the military-industrial complex. The whole New World Order thing. Some people even believe they were behind the JFK assassination."

I had been nodding patiently until then. Tomlinson is among the many educated, intelligent people I know who are willing to believe that world events are steered by sinister groups and secret alliances, but I have my limits.

I said, "Skull and Bones, it's part of the great Right Wing Conspiracy. Or is it the Left Wing now? I can't keep track."

"Make fun if you want, but power attracts power, and power corrupts."

"Yeah? I think there's a genetic conspiracy that compels primates to believe in dragons and herd like dumbasses. Fraternity boys don't participate in murder just because they share a secret handshake—especially after they've become successful adults."

"I don't know, man . . ." Tomlinson lost the thread as his eyes moved to the ceiling, the walls. "Norry will inherit this place if smack doesn't kill him. He's welcome to it—and all that bad juju that's hooked to the package. I feel guilty saying that, Doc. Blood . . . family. They're still in my heart, you know? I envy the ones who stay close, but it's not my karma. Some people are born alone. I was. You were, too."

His lips were pursed as he stared at the figurine. "I knew the girl who disappeared. She was sweet. She had a pale violet aura: poetic. Her family worked for us. To hurt someone defenseless. To take a club and . . ." He grimaced. "I don't want to think my brother could do something so . . . vile. Or my dad. We never got along, but he's my *dad*, man."

I said, "It could have been someone else. Or maybe it didn't happen the way you think. Her body wasn't found, no charges filed."

"I'd like to believe that, but I don't know." He sat on the bed. "It took a while after the girl was murdered, but they both flipped out. Dad went to the Amazon to study fossils and never came back . . . that I know of. Norry went to Indonesia to study Islam but found the Poppy God instead. Running from their consciences. I think."

I said, "A Bonesman leaving the country to become Muslim?" It made no sense, unless Norvin actually had worked for an intelligence agency. He wouldn't have been the first to be consumed by his own cover story.

Tomlinson said, "Some people attack their old lives to validate their new ones. Valid point, though. Skull and Bones is a one-way religion."

I placed the frame on the desk and began going through a stack of magazines as Tomlinson opened his hand, showing me the Indian figurine.

"There's not a strip mall in the country that isn't built on Indian bones. Geronimo was a shaman. Marion, they stole his *head*. I know you don't believe, but I've seen it work too many times. It's a different kind of power." He paused. "The Apache graveyard is in Oklahoma. Did you know that?"

"No. Now that I do, I'll try to forget it." The man had littered my mind with so much oddball trivia that I was trying to do some housekeeping.

"Geronimo lived in Florida, too. With a bunch of imprisoned Florida Indians before they were all shipped west. You told me Will Chaser was from a reservation in Seminole County, Oklahoma. Synergy, man, it's becoming clear to me now . . . "

I knew what Tomlinson was implying but didn't want to hear his fairy-tale notions of spirituality and noble Indians. I was more interested in an article I had found. After years of court battles and injunctions, Skull and Bones had recently been forced to allow in female members.

"This magazine's only a few months old," I interrupted. "Someone's been here." I handed him the magazine, then looked at another that was folded open.

Tomlinson began to grin. "Women, the source of reason and light. Also, the ultimate ball-breaker cannibals. Skull and Bones has finally had its cherry busted. Older members, they've gotta be mad as hell. In a room full of Bonesmen, I bet Charles Manson would seem bedrock solid, the last nickel bargain in CEOs."

"Even for you, that's absurd." I was trying to concentrate. "Do you know if your brother ever visited Cuba?"

He appeared surprised. "Not when I knew him."

"Your father?"

"Same answer."

Tomlinson had been to Cuba at least twice. No need to ask.

I continued going through magazines. Obsessive people dog-ear pages, use a highlighter, underline passages. Someone—maybe one of the Tomlinson men—circled things. He'd been keeping track of the females petitioning to get into Skull and Bones. He'd also been following the battle for Castro's confiscated files. Key names had been circled.

I said, "On the fraternity roster, did you notice some of the other names? A couple of members helped plan the Bay of Pigs invasion. The country's first attempt to take down Castro after he came to power. A generation older than your brother, but still . . ."

"You're looking for a connection. Cuba, a kidnapping, Bonesmen."

I said, "I don't look, I collect—or try to. The Bay of Pigs was a disaster. Someone in a top spot tipped off the Soviets. No one's ever figured out who."

"A traitor."

"Depends on which side you're on."

"It's what I've been thinking all along. Castro's papers could expose the wizard behind the curtain. Like Judas— that's what I was telling you on the plane. The Tenth Man . . . Tinman. Same thing."

I said, "Since 1959 there have been a lot of men behind a lot of curtains."

Judas, the tenth disciple. *J*—the tenth letter in the alphabet—Tomlinson loved all symmetrical intersectings that suggested the world was orderly, design-driven.

I hadn't told him that the real name of the covert operative, Tinman, had been confirmed. But which Tomlinson?

"That song was in the dream—*Tinman*! The dream that pulled me back to the old homeplace. *'But Oz never did nothing to the Tin Man/That he didn't, didn't already have—'* " An old habit, perhaps, he reached for the harmonica in his pocket.

Before he got to it, I asked, "When you were in the Hamptons last week, who did you tell that you knew Senator Hayes-Sorrento? Or that I was meeting her for dinner last night?"

"A couple of people, I guess."

"Barbara and I made our dinner date almost a month ago. Any late-night gabbing? Or text-messaging with your Long Island pals?"

He said, "Hey," offended. On his computer, Tomlinson had pasted a cryptic note: "No Es or Cs while D & S"—No E-mails or Calls while Drunk and Stoned. It had saved him money and cut down on next-day apologies.

I tossed the magazine into Tomlinson's lap and watched his face change as he read.

"Sonuvabitch. It's them. Bonesmen are behind the kidnapping deal."

I said it again: "Fraternity boys don't participate in murder just because of a secret handshake."

"Well . . . it means my brother's involved, at the very least."

I said, "Is he?," studying his reaction. I was thinking about the Cuban Program, scanning for a way to link it with an Ivy Leaguer from the Hamptons. If there was a connection, what completed the triangle?

Tomlinson stood. "We've got to search this place. I mean, *really* search it."

I told him no, what we had to do was seal off the area

as best we could until an FBI crime team arrived, plus the local cops and more search choppers.

I added, "I want to go back to that horse farm. If the trainer wakes up, you'll do the explaining."

"Tonight?"

"Yes."

"Why? All day the cops were there."

"Because . . . Just because."

I didn't have an answer, but it was true when I told him that the helicopters were equipped with heat-sensing radar. The corpse of a dead horse, still cooling, could mask the heat signature of a live human.

I told him to find a phone or I'd get mine from the car.

"Call in the cavalry," the phrase I used, unaware of the irony until I referred to Will Chaser, adding, "Saving the Indian kid takes precedence."

I watched Tomlinson's hand become a fist, squeezing the little bronze statue of Geronimo.

"I'm taking this with us for luck."

I replied, "Good. Something to keep your hands busy," which he chose to ignore.

18

A harmonica . . . ?

Someone's playing a damn harmonica!

Uh-huh. Like a cartoon. Some doofus swallows a harmonica and makes *haww-heee . . . heee-haww* notes as he walks.

Will Chaser could picture it, although he couldn't see.

A man. No, two men, talking. Close.

Nothing he could do but listen, until the sound of the harmonica was transformed in his head and began to resemble Cazzio's wheezing scream.

Harmonica. Sounded like a donkey bloated on helium, something he knew about because he'd joked around with some girls using a helium balloon a few years back at the fairgrounds in Oklahoma City. Native American Rodeo Championship. Senior Division, even though he was twelve at the time. The Yavapai Apache team had brought him in as a ringer. How could he lose riding Blue Jacket?

"The kid wants to wager how much . . . ?"

Skins off the Rez loved gambling and vodka—vodka because bosses couldn't smell it on the job. The more booze in their bellies, the stupider they got, which was fine because Will had cashed in. Made . . . six bills? About that.

Shak-oh-pee!

A word from the old language. Another thing about Skins when drunk. They'd throw together the few phrases they remembered, getting belligerent, as their eyes glazed, pretending to be real Indian warriors like in the movies that Old Man Guttersen watched. Just as fake, too.

An excuse for acting like assholes, is what it was. Same as when they passed out, curling up in some alley—Will had *seen* it—then later, claimed they'd been on a Vision Quest. Visited by the Old Ones in their dreams.

Vision Quests. Dreams. All bullshit.

Haww-heee . . . heee-haww.

The harmonica again. Or maybe he was dreaming now? A nightmare, all of it. Which meant he was imagining men's voices, too.

No. The voices weren't real. More hallucinations. Same with the harmonica, although it wasn't easy to be sure, not since he'd awakened after being injected with a dose of Ketamine, the same horse tranquilizer he'd used on Buffalo-head.

The boy tried to relax. He summoned a pattern of thought that might be comforting. Into his brain floated the image of Old Man Guttersen.

Will held tight to the image as he opened his eyes. He was testing his own sanity, wondering if a mental picture would remain as lucid with his eyes open as it was when his eyes were closed.

It should have made no difference, considering what the Cubans had done to him now. One darkness was no blacker than the other.

But it did make a difference.

Will realized images in his brain were sharper with eyes closed, possibly because that's what his brain was used to: dreams and certain daylight fantasies.

So that's what Will did now, closed his eyes, breathing softly through his nose, and returned to the image of Bull Guttersen, which was more tolerable than the image Will wanted to get rid of: the old Cuban, with his dead, clinical eyes, holding a revolver, then pulling the hammer back.

Metal-eyes had blinked when his revolver jolted, the weapon making an unreal explosion as guns did in real life. But the hole the bullet had tunneled through Cazzio's head was as real as anything Will had ever seen.

Too real for Will to think about, so he levered his thoughts back to Minnesota, the way it was living there before he had boarded that damn plane and before the big nerd with glasses had ordered, "Get your ass back in the limo!" or something similar, which had contributed as much as anything else to his shitty situation.

Will took a deep breath through his nose, and let his mind settle, repeating *Minnesota . . . Minnesota* over and over in his brain, but then had to interrupt himself with an honest aside, thinking, *Never thought I'd see the day I'd dream of going back to that ass-freezing land of too many lakes and not enough ranches.*

True enough. But right now, he would have traded the box the Cubans had stuck him in for the worst hellhole foster home in Minneapolis.

"Specially constructed," the scary American with the stringy hair had described the box.

Not that Ruth Guttersen's place was a crummy box or hellhole. It was neither. Mrs. Guttersen kept her two-story house, with its white siding, with its flowers and a flag out front, as tidy as a church. Which would have been tough for Will to have endured had the old man not kept things interesting.

Bull had a knack for that, which he had proven on day one.

The first time Will met Otto Guttersen, the old man was holding a Colt .38 to his own head, only seconds from committing suicide—the suicide part, though, Bull hadn't admitted to Will until later.

Okay, so I lied. Russian roulette ain't something I normally do when bored—not with more than one round in the chamber anyway.

The gun, though, the man couldn't deny. It was a knockoff Colt, with a plastic-ivory handle but loaded with real bullets.

This was two years ago, Minneapolis. Because that first meeting had turned out okay—it had turned out *good,* in fact—the boy didn't mind remembering it, so he let his brain follow the thread.

Will had climbed through the kitchen window because no one answered the door at his new foster home, then hurried downstairs carrying a garbage bag. He had enough experience with the Lutheran Foster Grandparents Program to know Minnesotans kept many of their valuables in the basement, which they called recreation rooms after fixing them up nice with carpet and neon beer signs, a pool table or foosball and sometimes a flat-screen TV.

There sat the old man, a gun to his head, even though what Will would learn was his favorite radio program was on, *Garage Logic*. The fact it was a commercial break may have had something to do with the timing, but it didn't explain why the old man was holding a gun to his head and crying. Eyes swollen red, cheeks wet.

It was new to Will, the helpless, sad blubbering of a grown man. Stood there almost a minute before Guttersen noticed, then he watched the man slowly, slowly take the gun from his temple and point it at Will. Embarrassed, no doubt, but not too damn old to pull the trigger. No doubt about that, either, when Will saw a spark brighten the man's eyes.

"It's good you brought that garbage bag. Less mess when I blow your head off."

Will had said, "You talking to me or your hostage?," never so scared in his life but trying to keep it light, as if the situation wasn't serious, while not sounding like a smart-ass.

"I suppose you plan on robbing the place, then murdering the witnesses," Guttersen had said, his tone mean-mad but also hopeful in a spooky way. Maybe planning something in his head, a way to kill two birds with one stone. Shoot the robber, then shoot the witness. A perfect crime.

Will decided the smart thing to do was explain. "There's a pawnshop, they pay thirty cents on the dollar for old coins and gold and souvenirs from the war." Something about the old man indicated *Lie to me or try bullshitting, bang!* So Will added, "I saw the flag outside. Houses with flags, the people usually collect all three."

Click: The gun's cylinder rotated as the hammer locked back. "Stealing from American patriots makes me less inclined to offer you a beer while we're waiting for the ambulance."

Will didn't respond, didn't even put up his hands.

"Are you deaf or just slow?"

The man was motioning with the gun, so Will raised his hands, saying, "I'm scared shitless, what do you think?"

"You *can* hear."

"Yeah! I can see, too." Will nodded toward the sign over the bar: FREE BEER TOMORROW. "It's no surprise that I'm gonna go thirsty." He forced a smile.

Guttersen didn't soften. "A damn kid who's got no respect for the American flag shouldn't be robbing houses owned by patriots with guns who know their rights." He studied him for a moment. "What are you, Puerto Rican? Mexican?"

The old man was trying to fire up the situation. That's what was happening. He had a plan and didn't want to lose his momentum.

"No need to call names," Will said. "Why don't you go back to doing what you were doing? I'll promise to never steal from a house that flies the flag again. How's that sound?"

The old man was still looking at Will's face, seeing the black eyes and the shoulder-length crow hair, trying to figure it out. "Maybe Mexican mixed with something else. Ethiopian is a possibility. They've 'bout taken over the Twin Cities. Could be your daddy raped one of our local Latin girls."

Will said, "Don't say that," and lowered his hands.

"You got something against Ethiopians? Nothing to be ashamed of."

A burning sensation in his ears, Will could feel it blooming. "I ain't no damn Ethiopian, mister. Knock it off."

"You break into my house to rob me and kill witnesses. Now you're giving me orders?"

"What right you got saying my dad's Ethiopian? I'm a Native American, not some damn foreigner who wears robes and pisses in the park."

Guttersen liked that, although Will didn't see it and only got madder when the old man replied, "Don't blame me for sizing you as a welfare mutt. Hell, half the people claiming to be Indian in Minnesota, you couldn't get a bullet through their heads with a .357. It's 'cause of the gambling money."

That did it. Will felt the craziness take control—an ammonia smell mixed with sulfur—and he started yelling, "I wouldn't live in this shithole state if you gave me the keys! Wear robes just to get a welfare check? Humping Mary Tyler Moore's statue just 'cause she's white? My dad was pure-blooded Seminole from Oklahoma. And my ma was Apache!"

Which was partly a lie. Will had only heard rumors about his father being Seminole. Before his mother had died, she'd told the boy that his daddy might have been a no-good, drunken drug addict, but on *her* side of the family things were different. Her father had run a successful airboat business in the Everglades. His grandfather had been famous—in that part of the world at least.

The way his mother had talked, Will's grandfather had been seven feet tall and so damn handsome every woman in the country, white, black or Seminole, was crazy about the man, his mother included.

But screw it, Will wasn't going to waste effort convincing some old racist Casper who was on the verge of suicide anyway.

Walking toward the old man, slouched in his wheelchair, Will had yelled, "Pull the goddamn trigger or I'll show you how it's done!"

Threatening to shoot the man. Just like that.

Off to a bad start with Otto Guttersen, no question. But it had balanced out because interrupting Bull in the act of killing himself gave Will leverage. Stealing meant jail, but attempting suicide meant the loony farm.

As to shooting a foster grandchild, Lutheran Social Services was strict. Mrs. Guttersen would have been banned from the program and forced to spend her days home alone, not volunteering.

"She would've talked me to death, I shit thee not," Guttersen had said later, thanking Will. "That's a thousand times worse than a bullet."

The relationship between robber and witness had improved over the last eighteen months.

Weird, how much I think about that old bastard. Same as when I was locked in the car trunk, taped tight and scared. Like he was there with me.

To which Old Man Guttersen would have said, "You're surprised? Any situation that requires a cool head, I'm your go-to guy."

Well . . . sometimes, maybe. Guttersen was right a lot of the time, but was also dead wrong upon occasion. What he'd said about stupid threats—*Never make a threat that'll get your ass kicked or prove you're a pussy*—wasn't actually the first time he had given Will misinformation. More like the fiftieth or sixtieth.

Wish Guttersen was here right now. He'd go apeshit, stuck in a box. Back in the barn, that's where I could'a used Bull. Stalls all dark—perfect for an ambush. If the Cubans came through that door, old Bull would have . . .

The old man would have done what? Wasn't much he could do, being a cripple, except wait for events to happen.

Possibly so, yet Will would've still felt a lot better if Bull was with him. Safer, although *safer* wasn't the right word because Bull was in a wheelchair. He couldn't stick his big Norwegian finger in Metal-eyes's face, then pull his cheap pearl-handled revolver. And he couldn't beat the shit out of Buffalo-head like he would've done in the old days as Sheriff Bull Gutter.

A guy takes a swing, my best move is a quick duck-under to a fireman's carry. Then helicopter-spin him a few times— in a bar fight or a professional show, either way. Next, a body slam, followed by a knee-drop to the neck. As a professional, I've got to moderate the knee-drop or I kill the bastard. Same if it's a bar fight, although I have given more than one private citizen a little "sweet taste," we called it. Something to remember me by.

Bull Guttersen's commentary the night they'd watched John Wayne in *The Quiet Man,* a movie in which a big Irish actor knocks the Duke on his ass, the Duke having been a nice guy once too often.

No chance of me being too nice, not if I ever get my hands on Metal-eyes.

Will hated the man, and it caused his brain to return to the present. Thinking about what Metal-eyes had done to Cazzio, and now what the Cubans were doing to him, the boy felt the first cellular prickle of heat on the back of his neck.

Don't get mad. Don't.

It scared Will, the thought of what he might do if he lost control now.

After Metal-eyes had shot him full of horse tranquilizer, the Cubans had discovered that Will had been chewing at the tape on his hands. So they had wrapped him with new tape and moved him to a different place, keeping him blindfolded the entire time. Next, they shoved him into what turned out to be the box the American had mentioned.

The sound the hammer had made as Buffalo-head nailed the lid closed was the most sickening sound Will had experienced. Worse even than Cazzio's last frightened whinny.

The box was too small for the boy to move in, the lid only inches from his nose. It was like a coffin, with a padded floor and some unseen vent that let in air. Not much. Right now, though, that trickle of air was the boy's only connection to life as he'd known it.

Telling himself to breathe, to concentrate on more pleasant things, Will tried to calm down, reminding himself, *If I lose my temper in here, I could snap my own arm bones fighting against this damn tape. Animals do it all the time when they're caught in a trap.*

What would happen next, Will didn't want to explore, although he knew what would happen because a small, wise place in the boy's brain whispered the truth to him: *You can't endure much more.*

If he lost control, really lost it, Will knew what would happen and that terrified him. Insane. He would go so wild insane, so crazy insane that his brain would never come back to him.

Will took another breath through his nose, released it slowly and began once again to repeat, *Minnesota . . . Minnesota . . . Minnesota . . .*

19

I told Tomlinson it was too windy and cold and I was too damn tired to put up with his aimless sawing on a childhood harmonica, it was almost midnight.

"You're irritating the hell out of me. Aren't you usually passed out drunk by now?"

"I've convinced my liver that daylight savings has been outlawed. It's celebrating. Don't rock the boat." He did a quick scale, then slapped the instrument on his palm. "The suit's the guy I want to irritate. Maybe he'll freak out and leave us alone."

The suit wasn't wearing a suit. He was a man bundled in a hooded ski jacket, waving his arms as he approached, calling, "Hold it right there, please," as I opened the gate to Shelter Point Stables.

In a distant pasture, I could see an industrial glare of lights and heard the diesel surging of a backhoe. When the man was close enough, I identified myself, then asked,

"You're digging the horse's grave already?," letting him know I was in a hurry and had a reason to ask.

I watched the man fix a cordial expression on his face, squinting into headlights because the rental was still running, both doors open. "Who did you say you are again?"

I repeated everything, question included, as I stepped through the gate.

"Alacazam has been buried, that's right. Probably just finishing up now," the man said, handing me a card. "It's been a tough day for all of us. I'm sure you understand."

I said, "I understand. But I want to have a look at the grave." I turned toward the car for light.

ARCHIBALD HEFFNER
MANAGER/GENERAL ATTORNEY
EQUINE ACQUISITION & SALES
N.A. MYLES, INC.

"You've got to be kidding."

I shook my head. "It won't take long."

"Not tonight, gentlemen. Impossible."

Tomlinson gave it a try. "We met the trainer earlier, Gardiner—Fred Gardiner. I got the impression he runs the place. Tell him Tom's here. We're like friends, sort of. I'm sure it'll be okay."

I wasn't convinced, nor was the attorney.

"One of the finest trainers on the South Fork," Heffner said. "But Fred doesn't have"—he paused as a helicopter roared overhead, watched until the chopper's strobe was a quiet blip—"Fred handles the day-to-day operations. But Mr. Myles instructed me to oversee the ranch until things settle down. We have many millions of dollars invested in our livestock"—he was looking at Tomlinson, interpreting the ponytail, the four-day beard, the pirate earring—"animals have rights, too, you know. A lot of people don't understand that—"

"Very sensitive creatures," Tomlinson said. "Brilliant and intuitive. Discord—the emotional type—can have a cumulative effect. I understand animals."

The attorney was nodding. "First the tragedy, then a full day of noise, police coming and going. Search dogs smell like wolves to a horse, do you realize that? They know what death smells like. They sense danger, and Mr. Myles agrees. Mr. Myles is afraid things are getting out of control."

"There's a fourteen-year-old boy who would agree, if he's still alive," Tomlinson replied, his vocal pattern such an uncanny echo of Heffner's, his sincerity couldn't be doubted. "Personally, I'd rather be sitting near a hot fire with a cold rum. Give us half an hour, we'll be out of your hair."

"To do what?"

"Have another look around. Anything we find might be useful. William, that's the boy's name. You've seen his picture on the news. Put yourself in his place. Barely a teenager and he's in hell, man. An innocent child who probably hasn't stopped crying."

Heffner said, "A tragedy, I know, awful. But there's nothing here to find."

"You're probably right, but what do we have to lose? The kid's life's on the line. Forty-five minutes, we don't even need an escort—"

Heffner appeared to be softening until another chopper buzzed us and unraveled Tomlinson's spell. "I'm confused. Dr. Ford said he wanted to look at Alacazam's grave. Why?"

"My partner," Tomlinson said, "has a thing about details. You know, like going through the alphabet backward. The grave represents *z*. What we really want to do is make a quick sweep of the area, that's the main reason—"

"The FBI and police spent three hours on the property. Now you want to search the grave?"

"Not search. Just a quick look—"

"To see what? It's a mound of dirt where a great animal was buried."

"We're thinking of the boy—"

"Where Alacazam was buried has nothing to do with the boy. Five minutes ago, I talked to the police. They told me there's no evidence the boy was on Long Island, let alone this farm. What are you men implying?"

I was watching the distant lights of the backhoe, ignoring Tomlinson's sharp look. Yes, I had rushed the question, but I wasn't done. "Why such a rush to bury the horse? I thought you were waiting for an autopsy."

Heffner *was* done. "Our company vet finished hours ago—not that it's any of your business." He took a breath to calm himself. "Look, guys, some freak shot and killed a great horse. Our horse. Now he's buried. I hope you find the boy. I hope he hasn't been hurt. But the kidnapping has nothing to do with our horse. End of story. That's all I have to say." He looked at the gate. "If you don't mind . . . "

I had my cell phone out. "I mind," I said as I called Barbara.

Tomlinson put the harmonica to his lips. Because he was right about it irritating the suit, I didn't mind so much.

There were two fresh graves, not one.

"Four days ago, the trainer called. Said they had to put a gelding down," the backhoe driver told me. "Called me again this afternoon for another job. We do most of the work for the horse people around here."

Several times, I had circled the graves. I had a flashlight. The backhoe, although not running, was still lit up. I was looking at two mounds of dirt on frozen pasture ten yards apart. A single length of hollow steel pipe had been driven into each grave near the center.

"Why the pipe?"

"If snow drifts, they don't want their staff driving over a grave when it's fresh," the driver replied.

"How many horses have been buried out here?" With my flashlight, I could see a series of geometrical rises that continued beyond the lighted perimeter toward the pasture boundary.

As the driver shrugged, Heffner said, "The Myles family has owned this property for generations. They kept horses even before Mr. Myles founded Shelter Point. Horses die, Dr. Ford. It's the way life works."

The driver appeared nervous as I continued asking questions. I wondered if it was because of the two uniformed cops who were escorting us. The men weren't happy, standing outside in the cold, waiting for us to do a search they considered pointless. Heffner had added to it, giving them *These men are crazy* looks, the attorney of a wealthy resident bonding with local police.

"Dr. Ford and Mr. Thomas aren't official law enforcement," he had told the cops earlier as we hiked across the pasture. I had stopped because I noticed headlights at Fred Gardiner's house. The Range Rover was leaving, I realized, horse trailer in tow. Where were they taking a horse on a cold January night?

When I asked the cops to use their radios and request that the vehicles be searched again, that was Heffner's reaction. We had no authority, Heffner reminded the cops, and their livestock had suffered enough. "They represent the interests of a politician, a woman from D.C.," Heffner said. "We're doing this as a courtesy."

When the attorney added, "They're not even local, they're from Florida," one of the cops said, "Hey, did you guys see the story about the football player that drowned? They're saying he was murdered."

The night was cold, the mood chilly.

Aware there was no winning them over, Tomlinson was doing his obnoxious best to punish the cops, possibly for past sins of policemen he had encountered over the years. Trying to drive them away by driving us all crazy with his harmonica.

"When it's this cold, mister, metal could stick to your tongue," one of the cops warned him. "Every winter, we get calls."

When I said, "Don't you wish it would happen?," the men thought I was trying to ingratiate myself. I was tempted to give the name of a New York mounted cop as a reference.

Each grave was nine feet deep, seven feet wide, corners squared nice and neat, the backhoe driver explained.

"Laws are pretty strict. You've got to bury horses on high ground. If water starts coming in when I'm digging, I gotta stop and report it. And I would. Right away I'd call, because that's what the law says."

For the benefit of the police, Heffner put in, "It's never happened at Shelter Point. We're very careful not to contaminate the water table."

"Not only that," the driver said to me, "if water floods the grave, even after it's covered, we might have to start all over again. It's 'cause of the pressure. I've never seen it happen," he added, talking faster, "but I've heard of it. Even this time of year. On the South Fork, we don't get a solid freeze, so, you know, it's something you gotta think about."

The man was increasingly nervous, something the cops had picked up on. I could read their faces.

Horse or human, fresh graves are taboo. I had avoided it but now walked across Cazzio's grave to the pipe near the center of the mound. It was three-inch pipe, the sort used for fencing or playground equipment. I used my flashlight to look into the pipe, as Heffner said, "Now what?"

I didn't reply.

"What are you doing? Hey, Ford! I've been too damn patient. These men aren't stupid and neither am I. You're insane if you're implying—"

One of the cops interrupted, "I don't see how he's hurting anything. The sooner these men are done, Mr. Heffner, the sooner we can go home. Make sense?"

The backhoe driver was lighting a cigarette, I noted.

My little ASP Triad flashlight is military-grade aluminum. I tapped the pipe. Waited. Tapped again, then tried to move the pipe with my hand. "How deep is this thing buried? I can't budge it."

"The pipe's an eight-footer. It's what they told me to use."

"Always or just tonight?"

The driver said, "Mister, I do what they tell me. It's what we always use." He drew on his cigarette and began to pace.

"If you don't get much of a freeze, you can't get that much snow." I addressed the cops. "What's the D.O.T. use for snow markers? Fiberglass poles, something like that? This is galvanized pipe, three-inch tubing. Why use hollow pipe as a marker?"

I tapped on the pipe again. Cupped my hands and put my mouth to the opening. Hoped Heffner couldn't hear me as I hissed into the pipe, "William? Will?"

Heffner was saying, "That does it! What you're doing constitutes slander," but stopped when one of the cops got a radio call. As he stepped away, I went to the second grave and waved for Tomlinson to follow.

"What do you think?" I used the flashlight on the pipe. *Ping-ping-ping.* Cupped my hand around the opening and called the boy's name again. We both leaned to listen—nothing. I sniffed the opening. Air warmer, musky.

"The cops know what you're thinking, Doc. Heffner's about to lose it. I'm all for you, man, but . . . the vibes just aren't here for me."

"I don't care about vibes. Think about the boy."

He was silent for a moment. "Okay, I will. Step back a second. Metal's an excellent conductor."

I watched Tomlinson touch his hand to the pipe, then close his eyes. He made a humming noise: *Ommm-mmm.*

I waited.

He opened his eyes. "Blank screen. It's just not happening, man. Sorry."

I was unconvinced.

He said, "Hey, amigo, you're the logical one. Think it through. Kidnappers wouldn't bury the kid close to home, then tell the cops where to find him. If my brother's involved, he's too smart. Anyone living in the Hamptons is too smart."

I said, "Kidnappers lie. Once they get what they want, they don't have to tell us where he's buried. It's too much trouble keeping a hostage alive. Most are killed in the first twenty-four hours."

Tomlinson sighed and put his hands to the pipe again. Kept his eyes closed for several seconds. "A shape . . . bones. A scar. Neutral something. Oh . . . a gelding. I forgot." He stood, shaking his head. "Nothing human coming through. Not a spark. Even dead, I don't think the boy's down there."

I said, "Are you ever wrong?"

When Tomlinson realized I wasn't joking, he gave me an odd look. "You're admitting that I'm sometimes right? I wish I had it on tape. That kid really does have his hooks in you."

I was watching Heffner talking with the cops. "Just tell me the odds. They're about to pull the plug."

"I miss signals sometimes, sure. Especially when I try too hard. Or if someone's on a whole different frequency. Some people, it's like they've got kryptonite shields. You, for instance. Lately, though, I've been zone-solid."

I ignored Heffner, who was calling to me, saying, "Enough! We're done for the night," as Tomlinson followed me to Cazzio's grave. I nodded to the pipe. "Try again."

"You're serious."

"It can't hurt. You've got the credentials. Some people in law enforcement believe in this stuff. What you say carries weight."

Tomlinson whispered, "If you want me to lie, just say the word."

I gave him a look: *Hurry up*.

"Okay, but you first. I'm serious, man. You and that boy are on some tribal wavelength. That's what I think's going on here. A frequency not on my dial. So give it a shot—"

"Damn it, Tomlinson—"

"It can't hurt: your words."

I didn't want to tell him that I had already tried. Back on the road, holding the rock, maybe I had felt something but knew it was my imagination.

He sighed. "Okay, okay." Then went through the ceremony, hands on metal, eyes closed. After a few seconds, he said in a monotone, "Flesh . . . residual spirit. Power, very intense, relentless. An odor . . . too. Weird." He was silent. "A smell of . . . pears? Copper, like when it's been cut. Copper mixed with pears, that's the odor." He sounded puzzled but then let it go. "Bone . . . bone splinters, a fracture. Some metal. Could be the bullets." He opened his eyes. "Nothing human."

"That's all?"

"You tell me."

Tomlinson pointed at the pipe as one of the cops called to us, "Guys . . . gentlemen? I just got a call from the station. We're leaving."

I touched a hand to the galvanized metal—*Cold*—as Tomlinson whispered, "Stick with it."

The cop raised his voice. "Dr. Ford? I'm asking you nice, but only once. Tests are back from the lab. Blood on the wrench wasn't the missing boy's blood. Not a match. It's definite."

I was thinking about Harrington, wondering if there was a chance Farfel's and Hump's blood types were in the records.

Tomlinson tried to buy some time, saying, "What about the DNA? They were going to compare hair samples."

Heffner was getting madder. "Nothing matches. There is absolutely no evidence the missing kid was on this property. In fact, there's no evidence"—the attorney stopped to say something to the cop, who nodded—"they don't even think the boy was in the area. There was a possible sighting somewhere in Indiana. Another in Jersey. Can't you get it through your heads? The boy wasn't here!"

I still had my hand on the pipe, but not because I hoped for some telepathic cry for help. My willingness to believe, even temporarily, signaled a simple fact: If Will Chaser had been buried alive here, he would soon be dead. Or already was. Right or wrong, I had to press the issue. There was enough linkage to risk it. Every second mattered.

The cops were walking toward us, one of them telling me, "At the station, they're questioning some teenagers right now. There's been a series of break-ins, drug-related. Probably a couple of screwed-up kids broke into the barn, then shot the horse."

The other cop added, "Dr. Ford, one way or the other you are leaving—*now*."

Irrational, but my feet wouldn't move. "Nothing I have heard," I told them, "explains why three-inch pipes were sunk into these graves. Sorry, until I get an answer I'm going to insist that—"

The backhoe operator surprised us all, calling, "Okay, okay! I lied! But it's not my fault, I swear!"

Everyone stopped.

The man sounded exhausted as he rushed to say, "It's what they told me to do. So I did it, okay? That's the truth. But it was their idea. I've got a family to feed!"

I turned and began ramming the pipe with my shoulder, hoping to widen the size of the boy's airway, as Heffner snapped, "Shut your mouth, you idiot! Not another word!"

When he realized how damning it sounded, his tone became apologetic as he said to the police, "This has nothing to do with that missing boy. The man's a drunk, you know his record. Believe me, I can explain."

Then he did explain, saying the three-inch tubing had been inserted to relieve water pressure "in the unlikely event" that water seeped into the graves.

The backhoe driver wouldn't have fared well in an interrogation. His eagerness to confess made him far more convincing.

"There's almost always water when I dig out here," he told us, sounding panicked. "I admit it. I knew I was breaking the law but kept digging these damn holes anyway. One day, sooner or later, someone had to figure it out. I don't know what kinda doctor this guy is, but he was the first to notice what worried me from the start, 'cause it's so damn obvious. Snow's not the reason we use those pipes. We use pipe so the water has a place to go. So pressure doesn't build up."

I found out later that the backhoe operator had two DUIs on his record. He feared one more arrest, even for breaking a county ordinance, would put him in jail.

The police were convinced. One of the cops had trouble hiding a smile.

I, too, was convinced, but for a different reason. Archibald Heffner, a polished attorney, wouldn't have yelled at a backhoe driver because he feared a small fine. Not in front of police anyway.

Heffner was scared. Why did he fear a more careful search?

The cops threatened to arrest me when I refused to leave.

I said, "Then arrest me." I wasn't moving until I had spoken with Barbara and with the FBI.

"I'm getting a court order to open these graves," I told the cops. "I'm probably wrong, but what if I'm right? Why not play it safe? Scramble an emergency crew. What if it was your kid?"

I told them we needed bottled oxygen to aerate the pipes. And at least one GPR on wheels. GPR—Ground Penetrating Radar. If local Search and Rescue didn't have a unit, I suggested the nearest university with an archaeology department might.

The cops told me that even though procedure required that Tomlinson and I be handcuffed, they would wait to hear from their duty officer.

They were reasonable men. Most cops are. Tomlinson is not. As they approached, he sat down fast, arms folded, and advised me, "When the pigs try to lift you, let your body go limp. They hate that. But watch your nuts."

My first sit-in and my last.

Passive resistance is effective if you have unlimited time.

We didn't.

It was early Saturday morning, and Barbara's staff spent an hour working contacts before they'd assembled enough New York muscle to roust a judge willing to sign a search warrant. It took me slightly longer to locate a GPR machine and get a technician on-scene.

Heffner battled us every step.

Somehow, though, I'd won over the cops. They had an EMS vehicle beside the graves within fifteen minutes. They pretended not to notice when we started opening a hole around the pipe, digging with our hands.

At 12:35 p.m. we got the go-ahead to use the backhoe but were specifically limited to the two freshest graves. Same with the little GPR, which was mounted on wheels like a lawn mower.

By then, though, I suspected there was no reason to dig. Heffner didn't realize it but he had convinced me of that, too.

20

Saturday morning, 10:30 a.m., I was outside the Nelson A. Myles family mansion, deciding the best way to break into the place, when I received text messages from Barbara, then Harrington. A third text arrived seconds later. It was from James Montbard.

Across the road from the Myles estate was a wooded ridge. Bare oaks and dune grass. I sat with my back against one of the trees and opened Barbara's message.

New photo: William in coffin before burial. Air runs out 8 a.m. tomorrow. Horrible. Do something!

The news could have been worse. I remembered the meeting at the hotel, the agent saying it's what we should expect if the kidnappers weren't bluffing. A "trophy shot," he had called it. Their way of proving they meant what they said. Will Chaser might still be alive *if* the shot had been taken that morning.

I downloaded the attached photo and watched the Indian kid's face appear as an incremental scroll of pixels cascading down my screen. Messaging was the only way I could be contacted. My phone was muted, and I had been ignoring calls for an hour. The explanation was simple: I was tired of apologizing.

The search of the Tomlinson estate had produced nothing but embarrassment for a certain U.S. senator. Same with partially exhuming two dead horses while a sleepy GPR technician, two attorneys, an FBI agent and a half dozen cops and EMTs watched. What we found—or didn't find—in the graves doused whatever interest the FBI had in stretching the connection.

Magazines inside the Tomlinson mansion suggested someone was following the Castro story? Big deal.

Barbara was not happy. She had strong-armed her New York congressional colleagues to provide everything I wanted for what? Nothing. Just like Archibald Heffner had said, there was no evidence that young Will Chaser had been in the area. Call in the cavalry twice in one night, there'd better be a good reason.

Now Barbara was ready to pull the plug on Marion D. Ford—our professional relationship anyway, which included the entire relationship I was beginning to believe. I could hear it in her tone and read it between the lines of her text message.

Do something!

I was trying.

On my phone, the boy's face was being assembled line by line. I noticed there was dirt in his hair. Then I watched

Will's eyes appear, staring into the camera. Dark eyes but bright, as if sparks provided backlight. His expression was complex, a mix of fear and something else. Anger? No. More intense. Rage—that was it. Rage focused on a precise cynosure of loathing. It was laserlike, aimed straight at the photographer. It pierced the lens.

I realized I was smiling. The kid had *grit*. Still battling despite insane odds.

Insane, the right word.

The boy was in a box, looking up from a pit that might have been freshly dug. Dirt in his hair was suggestive. The angle gave the impression the hole was four or five feet deep. It was only a head-and-shoulders shot but enough to tell the story.

Will's mouth was duct-taped. A tube ran from the tape to a bottle of water, only partly visible. PCV pipe, attached to wires, had been propped next to the boy's head, along with a heavily taped battery pack. The kidnappers wanted us to see part of the fan assembly that provided air—their way of saying the boy's life was now in our hands. If we delivered before deadline, we had a chance.

I glanced at my watch. Twenty-one hours, but the kidnappers had put responsibility for the boy's life in our hands.

Shrewd, I couldn't deny.

I cleaned my glasses, then wiped the palm-sized screen. Photo analysis isn't my field. Presumably, there were experts on the case examining each pixel, assembling data. The Cubans, or whoever took the shot, had anticipated the scrutiny. That's why the photo was cropped so tight. No trees in the background, no environmental markers except for a section of the dirt pit and dirt in the boy's hair.

The dirt looked fresh, damp. Maybe sand, or a mix of sand and clay.

I looked at my hands. I'd showered, but there were still specks beneath my nails after my frenzied digging hours earlier. Was the dirt similar? Could be . . .

More obvious was that a patch of the boy's hair was missing. A ragged rectangle near the left ear, as if someone had grabbed a clump and cut it with a knife. In the first photo sent by the kidnappers, Will's hair was crow black, shoulder-length but even. Same with recent photos that newscasters had been showing on television.

Why would kidnappers want a sample of the boy's hair? DNA, my first guess, until I gave it some thought. After my talk with Harrington, I had researched the Cuban Program. Under the guise of medical experiments, interrogators had tortured American POWs using techniques so perverse it disturbed even the Vietnamese jailers. Because the government feared exposure, fifteen of the men, all irreversibly maimed, were moved secretly to a Cuban prison, where the *Malvados* continued their experiments.

The three interrogators weren't really specialists. They were freaks who enjoyed inflicting pain. *Fiends*—a word with darker connotations in Spanish. If one had cut a chunk of the boy's hair, it wasn't to collect DNA. He'd taken it as a trophy . . . or a joke: *Look, I've got the Indian kid's scalp!*

I realized I was shaking as I studied the photo, unusual for me. Disconcerting. Emotion is a symptom, the by-product of a reality that's been skewed by personal interest. I cleared the screen. Decided to check Harrington's message. Good timing.

It read: "G-R off X-F. 0-sig."

Translation: "Gloves are off. Zero signature."

I'd had only a few hours' sleep but suddenly I wasn't tired. Harrington had either seen the photo of Will or he, too, had reviewed data on the Cuban Program. Something had changed. I was now authorized to deal personally with the Cuban interrogators.

X-F. X referred to the *Executive Order of February 1976,* which Congress had revoked, thus reestablishing assassination as an option.

F was *Farfel,* the nickname assigned by men he'd tortured.

0-sig meant just that: *zero signature,* no trace. Successful assassins leave a body. Harrington's group, the Negotiators, did not. People disappear. It happens every day.

The euphemisms vary with the times and situations. *Neutralize, terminate, liquidate, eliminate* are the standards used in thriller films but never by anyone I've ever worked for or with. Pros prefer substitutes that provide built-in deniability or the hope of a legal out. *X-F.* How can you prosecute a man for writing that?

There are others: *Preemptive Solution. Assignment Tar-*

geting. ATQ—*Assignment Targeting Qualified.* PPI—*Person of Preemptive Interest.* PCC—*Post Conflict Causality.*

Eternalize was Harrington's favorite because it could be explained away as an attempt to write or say *Internalize.* It was a typo. Or a word that was misheard.

It had been a while since I'd been assigned a target and almost a decade since I'd been authorized to operate within the boundaries of the U.S. I was pleased, but also aware that it could add to the legal nightmare I might one day face. In Fidel Castro's files, it was possible my name was on a small list of American contractors with a *W* designation. *W,* as in *World License.*

There were fewer than ten of us—far fewer now, possibly. An organization like the Negotiators didn't hold reunions or pose for class photos. Each member was a self-reliant cell. In nearly two decades, I had met only three fellow members—as far as I knew anyway. No, I had met four. Only recently, I had been introduced to a great man, last name Wilson. It was just before his death.

In legalese, *W* designees were sanctioned by the Executive Branch to use lethal force against enemies or preassigned threats anywhere in the world as long as the designee operated within the parameters detailed in the National Security Act of 1947.

A World Court wouldn't consider it legal. Nor would courts in most of the countries where I have worked. There is no statute of limitations on murder, and the U.S. now had extradition treaties with almost every member of the United Nations. Harrington was risking the same nightmare.

Gloves off.

Well . . . if he was willing, I was willing. Besides, it was different this time.

I took another look at the photo. It wasn't a real casket. The box was smaller, with a towel for a pillow instead of crinoline lining. Black eyes stared at me. Rage—it was there. Unbroken. The boy was still battling the beast, even as the beast consumed him.

Spirit like that I wanted to preserve, but I'm not naïve. If they had buried the boy, I doubted he would live for more than a few hours, fan or no fan. Carbon dioxide would build up fast—a kindness, possibly, because Will's heart would survive a lot longer than his sanity if we didn't find him. Judging from what I knew, the boy was wound pretty tight to begin with.

For a moment, my mind drifted, trading places with the kid, and I felt a welling panic. How many days would I last in a box, mouth and hands taped, listening to my own heart beat in the relentless silence? Barbara Mackle had endured eighty-six hours, then continued to prove her heroism by living a full and stable life. But she at least had a small light, and her hands were free in a space large enough to roll over in . . .

Enough. Concentrate, Ford!

People died every second of every day. Will Chaser's spirit wouldn't save him, but I might if I collected the right data and reassembled it cleanly. Even if I failed, though, I would go after the Cuban. Didn't matter where he went or how long it took. One day, Farfel would turn around and I would be there.

I stood and stretched, taking a nonchalant look at the mansion, then the road. No traffic, no outside activity. I cleared the phone, then opened the message from Montbard. We had talked earlier so I knew it contained information I wanted.

It read: *Symbols—yes. Rituals—many. Connection—no, not for 150 years. Obligations—binding but benign. Covenant—sorry.*

I had asked Hooker to research Skull and Bones and comment on similarities, if any, between it and the Freemasons. Montbard's family connection to the Freemasons dated back centuries. An ancestor had been a founder of the Knights Templar: André de Montbard, a rhythmic name, so it was easy to remember.

Symbols and rituals—yes.

I had been right. Skulls, aprons, all-seeing eyes: The fraternity used Masonic symbols and similar rituals. In Hooker's opinion, there was only a historical connection, including obligations that he considered harmless. He had warned me, however, there might be information he couldn't share.

"Freemasons take an oath, you have to understand. We're bound to it or we wouldn't be Masons."

The organization's covenant? *Sorry.* He couldn't tell me.

Good enough. Unless Hooker was party to some bizarre world conspiracy, Skull and Bones was just a college fraternity—powerful, yes, but it was not a sinister cult. That didn't guarantee members weren't capable of committing crimes, murder included, but it reduced the odds that they had participated as a group.

It also narrowed the list of motives. Fear, greed or insanity: the big three when it comes to premeditated crime.

I glanced across the road at the Myles estate, alone and aloof on a hundred million dollars' worth of ocean frontage, and I narrowed the list to two.

Was Nelson Myles scared, or crazy, or none of the above?

Archibald Heffner had told police that Myles was at his winter home—Sarasota, I'd overheard him say—and was furious about us exhuming the horses. "Tell your boss he's damn lucky Nels can't fly back until next week. Maybe he'll calm down by then."

Nelson Myles didn't know it but he was damn lucky to be in Florida because I still believed the boy had been at Shelter Point Stables. Maybe still was. I would've preferred to question the man personally. Just the two of us, alone in this quiet place.

I believed the kidnappers had been here because . . . *why*?

One reason was Heffner's reaction when I mentioned ground radar. The odd sensory experience I'd had holding the rock had something to do with it, too. Irrational, no question. Part of me found that amusing, but interesting. Tomlinson's subconscious, I was convinced, assembled information so effortlessly, he wasn't even aware of the process. Had my subconscious retained a data byte that my forebrain had discarded? It was possible.

But there was also too much solid, intersecting data to dismiss as coincidence. At Dinkin's Bay, JoAnn Smallwood, one of the live-aboard ladies, collects paradoxical lines. One was an uncomfortably good fit: *Until I believe otherwise, I will act upon what I believe.* Another one applied, too: *I have no choice but to believe in free will.*

If I was right and found what I was looking for, it could lead me to Will Chaser. That was reason enough to enter the Myles estate illegally.

I switched off the phone and pocketed it. No more interruptions.

I walked down the ridge toward the mansion, pretending to study utility lines strung from pole to pole along the road. I was wearing a coat over new coveralls, a Yankees cap and a tool belt that jangled. Anyone watching would think I was a telephone repairman returning to work after a break spent dozing in the trees.

To the moneyed class, and their staffs, utility workers are an invisible essential, like plumbing.

An hour earlier, Tomlinson had dropped me in South Hampton where I'd rented a white pickup truck and bought a few things, coveralls included. Because there were tools and a ladder in the family's machine shop, I didn't need much else. On my way to the Myles estate, I had completed my costume by stealing two orange highway cones from a restaurant closed for the winter.

It was now 10:45 a.m. The truck was parked along the road, near a utility terminal. One cone was behind the truck, another next to a miniature green silo that was a connecting block for area telephones.

There couldn't be many. Along this section of coastline, mansions had been built on dunes, far off the highway, with acres of space between. The Tomlinson estate was on the point of the peninsula, two miles down the road.

"Nelson was practically our neighbor," Tomlinson had told me, explaining why it seemed commonplace when his brother and Myles were both tapped by Skull and Bones.

In an area this wealthy, maybe it was.

The Myles mansion lived up to the billing. It was a medieval-looking four-story that resembled "country houses" on England's North Sea coast, because that's where it had come from, shipped over in the nineteenth century, and reconstructed block by block. It was sandstone and slate, with turrets and roofed porticos that would have been hidden by hedges and a forest of hardwoods if it hadn't been January.

Even now, it wasn't easy to see. That's why I had been on the ridge. A stone wall, head-high, surrounded the place, interrupted by iron gates at several entrances. The main gate and the service gate opened on electronic tracks. On the seaward side, wrought-iron gates exited onto the beach.

To each gate was affixed a brass placard that read SHELTER HOUSE.

Shelter House was a castle, not a fortress. Breaking into the place wouldn't have been difficult after midnight, but it was before noon on a bright winter Saturday. At the staff entrance, two economy cars were parked near a Dumpster: resident caretakers. There was electronic security, including cameras at each gate, but the guard station at the main entrance was empty.

Getting into the house undetected should be easy. Spending ten or twenty minutes searching the place without interruption would be more difficult. Local police knew me now. If I didn't play it right, I would add to Barbara's embarrassment by calling her from jail.

I walked to the truck, pretended to put something on the front seat just so I could slam the door, then knelt by the terminal. I loosed the nut and slipped off the silo cover. Inside were dozens of brass connection strips, a maze of candy-colored wires and heavier rubber-coated wires. The candy-colored wires came from the main cable. The rubber-coated wires were for local use. Spend your life on the water, working with boats, either you learn basic wiring or you find a job inland.

Only four of the connector blocks were in use. An installer had used tape and a Sharpie to ID each of the four wires running underground to the mansion. I checked them, one by one. Two had phone numbers written on the tape. Two were DSL lines for Internet access.

I copied the numbers into a notebook, then put on gloves. Telephone systems use low voltage, but no one likes getting shocked. No normal person anyway.

Using a crescent wrench, I loosened a nut and removed a green wire. With a needle-nosed pliers, I stripped several inches of insulation, then bent the wire so it made loose contact with the positive side of the strip. All four rows were now partially grounded. Phones inside the mansion might still be usable, but there would be a lot of static.

Finally, I crossed the two DSL lines. No more Internet.

There.

I covered the terminal and crossed the road to the main gate. I pressed the intercom button and waited. Pressed it twice more before someone answered.

"Shelter House, can I help you?" A woman's voice.

I said, "I think you've got trouble on the line, ma'am."

"What line?"

Above me, a motor whirred, and I smiled up at a security camera. "Check your phone, ma'am. I'll wait."

When the woman returned, she said, "Could what's wrong cause my computer to go screwy, too? A couple minutes ago, the screen went blank and the whole system froze. I was on the Internet."

I had the notebook out, not looking at the camera, as I leafed through pages. "We're not supposed to give computer advice. It's some kind of liability deal. Let me make sure I'm at the right place before I say anything." I read off the phone numbers I had just copied.

"That's us. They're both unlisted, so we hardly ever get calls. It could've been out for days."

"Could've been," I replied.

"The kitchen phone sort of works, but the important thing is my computer. I was right in the middle of a project, using the cable instead of using the Wi-Fi. Damn it! Please tell me it's the phone. I just spent three hundred bucks for a new hard drive."

"I don't know . . ."

The woman said, "I've got a term paper due and I'm screwed if the Internet doesn't work."

Not a woman, a high school student, I decided, until she added, "I just made coffee. I can have it waiting."

No, a college student. High school girls didn't offer coffee.

I said, "There's no reason for me to come inside if it's your fuse box."

"Just for a minute, as a favor?"

I said, "Well . . . if I've got your permission, I guess it's okay," picturing myself at the police station answering questions. One of life's simple rules: Never, ever lie to a cop. Speak even a benign untruth and he will suspect you of murder.

"Thank you!"

I stepped back as the gate opened, adding, "It's not that I don't want to help," wanting her to understand that phone men could be nice but we weren't easy.

21

Through the window of Nelson Myles's third-floor office, I could sit at his desk and look inland at the ridge where I'd hidden in the trees or stand by the elliptical machine and face the ocean. Bathroom, dressing room and spa all had views.

Wind gusted off the Atlantic, west to northwest. The beach was silver, deserted for miles, an unfriendly corridor where salt foam tumbled like tumbleweed and sand blew in veils heavy as snow.

There was a loft. I went up the steps and found a bed covered with a Yale comforter, a Yale throw rug on the floor, Yale pennants and a Yale varsity jacket hanging on a hat stand. Big yellow Ys everywhere but on the bay windows. I was standing near the window when I saw a police car slow as it passed my rental truck. I watched the vehicle stop, back up, then the officer on the passenger side opened his widow. He was checking the truck's license plate. Smart cop.

I had been inspecting the jacket. Nelson Myles had lettered in golf—the man had to have been pretty good—but I let the sleeve swing free, concentrating on the squad car. Now the officer was getting out, hand on his sidearm but using it more as a support. A young guy who had hurt his back. A hockey player, I guessed . . . or maybe he'd moved furniture into a new apartment.

I was taking out my cell phone as the cop looked into the truck's bed, then put a hand on the bumper to read the license. Watching the man's reaction, I switched on my cell phone, thought for a moment, then dialed 911.

I needed more time.

Until the squad car, things had gone smoothly. I'd had only a minute or two to look around the rich man's office, with its pecky walnut library, its marble floors and fireplace, walls checkered with mementos, photos of horses competing with Geronimo statuettes and Yale for space.

Stop there and I could have allowed myself to believe that Nelson A. Myles was incapable of kidnapping a child. On the mantle were pictures of a son and a daughter, along with swimming medals and soccer trophies they had won.

I could have gone away convinced the man was a rock of stability: civic awards, photos of Myles with two presidents, plaques of recognition from charities. I'm sure other visitors had been won over.

But the office also contained hints of discontent that, when viewed in context, provided a more powerful lens.

There were no golf clubs or any golf accoutrements,

yet mementos from Skull and Bones and his years at Yale dominated the décor. Why had the collegiate golfer given up golf?

Out of the dozens of photos, there was only one of the children's mother, Connie Myles, a recent shot, but the woman was part of the background, a vague presence. Drunken eyes, a lost expression on a face that had been stretched and glossed by cosmetic surgery. And there were no photos of a new significant other, a secret lover, the clichéd confidante who was "just a friend."

The absence of golf clubs could be explained: a bad back, like the cop. But the absence of a girlfriend told me he was probably involved with the woman who had let me into the house, Roxanne Sofvia, the off-season manager. She was a thirty-four-year-old college student, working on her master's via the Internet when she wasn't overseeing this twenty-acre estate and its fifty-eight-room castle.

"You have no idea, the upkeep," Roxanne had told me as she steered me into the kitchen, and handed me a mug of coffee. "It makes me tired to talk about it."

She preferred discussing her computer problems or her field of study.

"Marine biology," she'd said. "It's something I've wanted to do since I was a kid. But it's not all playing with dolphins and saving the planet, like some people think. And there's zero money."

I'd replied, "Oh? No kidding?"

"You're surprised. Everyone is."

She resembled a woman I knew. No, a woman I had

recently met. The Tomlinson caretaker, Greta Finnmark. Milkmaid breasts beneath a wool sweater, blond hair tied back, Nordic cheeks and chin and glacial Nordic eyes. She had a vague sensuality that confused the pheromone responders, a slow-acting chemistry that invited a second look, then a third. The kitchen had smelled of tea and baking bread, the room too warm because of a clanking radiator. They became catalysts as the woman's face took form, a solemn angularity on a body that swelled, then retreated, in curvature beneath wool and denim.

"Sofvia," I'd asked her, "isn't that Slavic? Or Jewish, I suppose," which was a clumsy attempt to find out her maiden name.

"You're not allowed to talk about computers but you're allowed to discuss race?" she'd replied. I could sense her mind working. Either I was a Zionphobe or too inquisitive to be a telephone repairman. I got the impression a Ph.D. could have asked the same thing, though, and it would have been okay. As cultures mix, an affected sensitivity has replaced racial swagger. Ethnic posing—twenty-first-century mimicry and probably a healthy precursor as we evolve into an *American* race.

"I have a friend," I told her. "Her last name was Pettish until she married a pharmacist. A guy with a name that sounded a little like Sofvia. He arrived four years ago from the Czech Republic and already owns a couple of stores."

"I see," Roxanne said, giving me a chance to squirm as she stared. If she saw anything, she saw the truth because it was the truth.

There were a couple of other things that I believed were true: Roxanne Sofvia was Greta's daughter. She had inherited a full dose of maternal genes. The similarities were striking. Roxanne, I felt confident, was having an affair with Nelson Myles, lord of this castle and also her boss.

"We need to restore the coach house," she had told me. "We need to change the entire landscape theme," she'd said. "When I finally find the right person to run this place," she had confided, "I'll be able to concentrate on what I should be doing. Getting my master's degree. A full-time staff, that's what we need—"

Roxanne, the master's mistress, was already talking as if she was mistress of the house. Her confidence, though, was forced. I got the impression the relationship had banged a rock or two.

Because the woman followed me every step I took, I had to find a way to get rid of her. It wasn't just because I needed time alone to gather information, though I did. Roxanne's physical presence was distracting. It wasn't because she wasn't beautiful, although she was attractive in a bony, sleepy sort of way. She was even pretty by Hollywood standards. But Roxanne had a . . . *scent,* that was the word, an odorless scent that was atomized by her eyes, the pitch of her voice, her attitude, and by her body, too.

Mostly, by her body. It was key to her slow-acting chemistry. First look: bland face, vague shape. Second look: interesting eyes, bony hips, and—*Hmm*—the inference of a bulky sweater that wasn't bulky. Now when I looked at the woman, I saw an ovular symmetry, breasts and hips, and skin that was translucent as lingerie. The effects were cumulative.

The few women—very few—who are born with that chemistry don't lose it. Doesn't matter their age. Greta was an example. Symptoms are a twitching, internal awareness that, ultimately, disconnects the brain as the body shunts blood to a less sophisticated command center.

Distracting? You bet. I needed space.

Roxanne had discovered a useful female finesse: Accidentally touch her breasts to a man's arm and she would get what she wanted. Turn my back to her and there she was, her body pliant, communicating with mine.

"Are you too warm? It's that damn radiator system. We need to completely remodel this place."

No, I'd told her. In fact, I wanted my coat back. "Fixing your computer just moved to the top of the list. How's that sound?"

She had smiled. "Are you serious? I would be so damn thankful."

Me, too. After a few minutes alone with Greta's daughter, I felt shaky. So I had returned to my truck and switched the DSL wires. But I didn't fix the partial ground.

"Check the phone," I said when I returned to the kitchen.

"The static's worse than ever," Roxanne had replied, her tone impatient.

"What about your computer?"

"The phone's still screwed up, why bother trying?"

I lied. "I rigged an experimental thing, just to get the computer working. You mind?"

She sat at a desk and I watched her fingers parachute over the keys, attempting a dialogue with the Internet. It took a few seconds for her to smile. The glacial eyes brightened. "You did it! I think it's even faster than before."

I grumbled, "Well, we're getting there," and headed up the stairs.

Two minutes later—just enough time to orient myself in the rich man's office—I saw the police cruiser slow and the cop with the bad back step out. He was peering through my driver's window as I dialed 911.

"What's your emergency?" *Beep*.

I didn't try to disguise my voice. "It's not an emergency. Maybe I'm imagining things but is there a women's group in the area—nudists—who do the polar-bear thing? You know, jump in the water when it's cold?"

"Excuse me?"

I said, "I'm no prude, but I'm thinking women shouldn't be parading around naked on the beach behind mansion row. One girl, maybe, but four or five—it's too much. Not at eleven in the morning."

"You mean South Hampton?"

I said, "Right on the beach. The cheapest place would cost me, what? Ten million? For ten million, a family expects protection. There's gotta be some kind of law against public nudity."

"Sir, are you serious?"

Watching the cop test the door to my truck, I said, "I've never been more serious in my life. Even if it's a sorority party or some sort of initiation—whatever—the girls should be wearing bikini bottoms. Or towels. It's January!"

"You *are* serious."

I said, "More serious by the second," watching the cop try the passenger door.

"What did you say, five college girls? I need your name, please."

I lowered my voice to tell the woman, "My wife's upset, that's the only reason I'm calling. But I don't want to make the girls mad if they're my new neighbors. See what I mean?"

I turned off the phone and watched. It wasn't long before the squad car became animated with blue strobes. The officer with the bad back jumped in, moving faster than he had before.

Some people can't let go of the good old days. Maybe Nelson Myles was one. His emotional attachments to Yale and his fraternity were reaffirmed by every wall. Inside his office desk, too. I had pried the lock and was going through drawers.

The man's picture was in front of me. A recent shot, Myles and a former governor standing near a Learjet, the same as the model Learjet on the desk.

Myles was a disappointment. I expected square-jawed ascendance. Wealth, breeding, confidence. Instead, Nelson looked dour in his Wall Street suit and European glasses. His face sagged as if he'd sprung a leak. Maybe he had—many people do after college. The grinning fraternity boy I had seen in the Skull and Bones photo had lost his smile, along with his hair, a lot of muscle and some of his vision. But the man's loyalty to his alma mater was intact.

I could picture Myles on autumn weekends, wearing his varsity jacket and a yellow tie, watching his Bulldogs on cable. Or maybe he took the ferry to Connecticut and joined fellow Bonesmen at the stadium.

Yes, he had tickets in the file drawer. I found the invoice for season box seats. Expensive for the average man but not for a man who had a hefty stock portfolio, accounts with three banks, several million dollars in savings and more than half a million in a checking account. To a man like Myles, having ready cash was more important than a decent interest rate.

In recent weeks, there had been three sizable withdrawals, each for seventy-five thousand dollars, and each had been converted into euros. Cash. So . . . he had bought more horses or part interest in another jet.

Interesting, but I was looking for something that connected him to an intelligence agency or the Cuban Program. Or some indicator of mental instability. Fear or insanity: It had to be one or the other if Myles was involved with the kidnappers.

He was a qualified pilot, with a stack of FAA licenses and correspondence, all neatly filed. But there was nothing to indicate he'd had military training, as I'd hoped.

Pilots get shot down and become prisoners of war. Some are assigned freaks as interrogators. Not Myles, though.

No connection.

I found copies of prescriptions for Valtrex, Allegra, Xanax and Valium. Myles had allergies, and somewhere along the way he or his wife had picked up genital herpes. I wondered if Roxanne knew . . . or perhaps it was she who had gifted him. It could explain the tranquilizers. Presumably, the pills were for anxiety, but that didn't mean the man was crazy.

No connection . . . or was there?

I glanced around the room and realized I had made an error that good field observers aren't supposed to make. I had failed to note what I did *not* see. What this private office did not contain was alcohol. There were no rare single malts or brandies. No martini shaker, no books on vintages. A man who bought and sold million-dollar horses would be expected to keep a private stock for clients. Fraternity boys drink, even adults who are also pilots. Nelson Myles was using prescription tranquilizers but not the world's most common: alcohol. There had to be a reason.

"I am referring to the singular incident of the dog barking in the night," a London detective once said.

"But the dog wasn't barking," his assistant pointed out.

"That is the singular incident," the detective replied.

Why had the dog stopped barking? Something had caused Myles to change his lifestyle. The leading candidates: alcoholism, pathology or a powerful event.

I went to the bookshelves. The only self-help books were business oriented. Nothing on addiction or dealing with liver disease. My hasty conclusion: Something had happened. An event had caused the man to quit drinking. Maybe quit golf, too.

A judge would have laughed at the flimsy implications. The police wouldn't have wasted their time.

There was a calendar in the top drawer. As I reached for it, I heard a car door outside. I looked, saw a mail truck, and relaxed a little. Opening the calendar, I turned so I could keep an eye on the driveway while studying Myles's schedule.

Myles had been in the office eleven days ago, Tuesday, January thirteenth. On the January fourteenth block, he'd written *Return S.* I'd found documents related to a home he owned near Sarasota.

He, too, was a compulsive circler. Maybe he had marked the magazines in Norvin Tomlinson's room— Bonesmen, after all, would enjoy brotherly rights when it came to sharing property. And Greta Finnmark still wasn't talking, even when interviewed by the FBI.

Flipping through the calendar, I noticed an oddity. The numbers 7 and 8 were used often, always singularly and in contexts that made no sense. *Ferrier scheduled? 8. Yale/Harv. 7. Buy tickets. 8.*

It was a substitution cipher. Sitting at the man's desk, the first key that came into my mind might have been the first that came into Nelson's mind. H-o-r-s-e-s? No. B-u-l-l-d-o-g-s? No.

Then I got it. Fifteen new voting members were inducted into Skull and Bones each year. Never more, never less. Eight votes was a positive, seven a negative.

Ferrier schedule—yes. Yale/Harvard game—lost.

Less cryptic was a single exclamation point—!—penned beneath January twenty-second. The date was circled, an important day.

Yes, it was. That was two days ago, a Thursday. Will Chaser was kidnapped.

I paused to check my watch. Seven minutes: That's how long it had been since the squad car pulled away. The house was too solidly built for sound to carry from the first floor to the second. But the stairway was marble, and even if Roxanne used the elevator I would hear her coming. I allowed myself three more minutes and went back to work

There were several folders dedicated to Skull and Bones. Because I did not expect them to be labeled, I found them faster than Myles would have hoped.

Women being inducted into Skull and Bones had been an issue. There were copies of letters to an attorney discussing a court order to block their admission. There were copies of articles about William F. Buckley, the famous writer, who had successfully gotten the courts involved and stopped an earlier attempt.

Inevitable, Myles had scribbled on the last document in the file. The man had tried but gave up.

I found a Skull and Bones roster from the man's senior year. The fraternity assigned nicknames. On a roster, Myles had written the names in ink, along with notations. *Long Devil—long! Boaz—football capt. Gog—fag, I think.*

Pancho Villa—spook, gin martinis. Capt. Morgan— distilleries, fruit. Clark Kent—airline.

Myles's nickname was Magog. Beside it he had written, *Can't help myself!*

Was it a plea or was he boasting? Boasting, I decided. *Gog* was gibberish, but the name had been assigned to someone of ambiguous sexuality. *Magog,* with its prefix, would be the opposite: a heterosexual trooper.

Myles had been a hound and was proud of it. The script for Valtrex confirmed he was still a womanizer, and if he hadn't liked the nickname he would have scribbled it out. That's what he'd done to Norvin Tomlinson's nickname. Myles had used a different pen—no, two different pens— to blot it out. He wanted that nickname gone.

Why? They had been neighbors as boys.

I held the paper up to the light. Unreadable, but the length was right, the number of letters. Some of the nicknames were rooted in family wealth: oil, distilleries, airline stock. The Tomlinson fortune had been manufactured from small metal parts: steel, iron, brass, tin.

Tinman.

"Tenth Man," Choirboy had pronounced it through chattering teeth, revealing the name of his American contact.

There it was.

Finally, I knew the truth, but it wasn't the truth I had expected to find. I expected to discover some link between Nelson Myles and an intelligence agency or the military in particular since he was a pilot. It would have been enough to keep me on track.

Because there was no link, my other inferences collapsed. I had been wrong about the golf clubs and the abstinence. I had been wrong to demand that the graves be exhumed and wrong about Nelson Myles. Maybe Myles had been used in some way, but the man who knew where Will Chaser was buried was Norvin Tomlinson.

Damn it.

I glanced from the window to the door, then at my Rolex: nine minutes. Time to lock the desk and go. Roxanne would be checking on me soon.

Turned out I was wrong about that, too. The woman had just returned with the mail and was on the cell phone with her lover and boss. It wasn't conjecture. I could hear her yelling at Myles as I descended the stairs.

"How could you do this to me. You sonuvabitch! Even when I suspected, even when I gave you the chance to tell me the truth, you lied to me!"

Roxanne's office was off the kitchen. To spare us both embarrassment, I decided to leave through the front. It was also a prime excuse to get the hell out. I had wasted too much time following my idiotic instincts. Because of a rock—absurd! But the woman stepped into the hallway as I crossed the great room, too angry to notice me at first. She had the phone in one hand and a sheet of paper in the other. It wasn't personal stationery.

I walked faster, hearing her say to Myles, "No . . . No, it is not possible. Yes, I have the occasional glass of wine. So what? It doesn't make me a drunk. And it doesn't mean I whore around. Stop with the excuses. For once in your life, goddamn it, accept responsibility, Nelson. You did this to me!"

A lab report, that's what she was holding. Home pregnancy tests are inexpensive and the results don't arrive in the mail. There was only one explanation: Myles had given her herpes.

I was almost to the door when Roxanne saw me. When our eyes met, I waved and shook my head—*Sorry*—then offered a thumbs-up. She could take that any way she wanted. The house phones would soon work, then I would be out of there. I thought it was my last look at Roxanne Sofvia.

Wrong again.

I opened the door and there was Greta Finnmark coming up the walk toward the kitchen. She smiled, but then stopped smiling when she realized who I was. Her head swiveled toward the mansion, then back to me. Her expression was puzzled, as if she'd gotten off the wrong bus.

"You are . . . Guardian's friend," she said, using her pet name for Tomlinson.

I had to stop. No other way to handle it.

"Isn't your name . . . ?" It took Greta a moment. "You are the biologist. Yes, I know you. What are you doing here, Dr. Ford?"

I started to make up a story about helping a sick repairman but then realized that Greta wasn't listening. She was focused on Roxanne, who was standing at the window sobbing, no longer on the phone.

Greta was stricken, her reaction confirming her relationship with Roxanne. It was touching, but that's not why I didn't run for the truck.

I said, "Let's go inside. Your daughter needs your help, Greta."

I needed it, too.

22

Roxanne was ignoring me, watching a little wall-mounted TV over the breakfast bar, where a newscaster had just said, "In what is now believed to be a homicide, Florida police say they are seeking 'a person of interest' in the drowning murder of Bernard Heller, a former NFL lineman, himself a convicted murderer. Police aren't releasing the name of the individual, but on Sanibel Island local fishermen think they know who it is and they are talking. More on that story when CNN returns . . ."

I was thinking, *Bernard?*, not surprised that police wanted to question me. Bernard made me think of Barney Fife, the funny little deputy on *Andy Griffith*, not the three-hundred-pound freak who'd spent a lot of time in the weight room but not enough time in the swimming pool.

"You mind turning that thing off?" It was the second time I'd asked, but Roxanne was pretending I wasn't there, sitting at the kitchen table, while Greta flitted around making tea to cover her own aggravation. Greta was irritated because I kept pressing, rewording my question after she'd already said she hadn't seen Norvin Tomlinson in more than five years.

"Does that mean Norvin hasn't been back in five years? Or that you haven't seen him in five years? A house that size, he could stay for weeks and you might not run into each other."

Greta had started to answer when Roxanne turned the volume louder, interrupting, "I'm thinking about moving to Florida. Get the hell away from the ice and the insanity. It's warm enough, apparently, even psychos get out on the water. But wait"—she flashed me a sarcastic smile—"I forgot, you're from Florida. So maybe I'll try Grand Cayman instead."

I said, "Enough. I'm trying to save a boy's life. Give me fifteen minutes. Do you mind?"

Roxanne had not told Greta about the lab test and wasn't aware that I knew. Act sympathetic and she would suspect. A smart woman.

Big sigh, but Roxanne touched the POWER button as Greta explained, "Even if Norvin came home for one hour, I would have seen him." With her accent, it came out *I voould hap seen him.* "He would not come back and hide from me. I raised those boys! Norvey isn't affectionate—not like Guardian, who is still so sweet. But he is not rude."

I was thinking, *Tomlinson avoids contact for fifteen years, that's sweet?*

"Norvey would speak to me," Greta said. "Sometimes

he sends cards from far places. Only a word or two, but it shows he still cares. Five years ago, he looked so terrible I didn't want him to leave. But he went anyway and hasn't come back." She turned to Roxanne. "Why doesn't he believe me?"

Roxanne was holding a jar, reading the label, before spooning honey into her tea, probably already thinking of homeopathic remedies. She said, "You mean, the liar who claimed to be a phone man? The one who's pretending to be a cop now? Maybe he's hung up on the truth."

I nodded, conceding.

She said, "Everyone who comes here lies. Blame this goddamn mausoleum"—she stood and slapped a light switch—"it's so goddamn dark, only lies can survive."

Until we'd clashed over the TV, Roxanne hadn't said much. Here she was in the middle of a personal crisis being questioned by a stranger when all she wanted to do was pack her bags, maybe break a few of Nelson's personal items in the process, before slamming the door on her Nissan and on her dreams of traveling by Learjet and owning a castle in the Hamptons. She had that kind of temper. It was also possible she was that mercenary.

I was beginning to believe Greta was.

I said, "What about Norvin's father?" I had asked before but she hadn't answered me.

Greta said, "Dr. Tomlinson is the executor of the trust. The trust pays me. If I worked for you, would you want me spreading gossip?"

"I wouldn't mind if it could save a kid's life. If Hank

Tomlinson visits from time to time, what's the harm in telling me? If it's true, it's not gossip."

She said, "I don't talk about the personal business of my household. It's a code in the Hamptons."

"The service class, you mean."

"Yes, the service class."

"You protect your employer at all costs."

"Our *households,* we protect. It's different. They are sacred."

"The household is like family, so you remain loyal."

"It's expected of anyone who takes the job seriously."

"Are you devoted to the house? Or to the Tomlinson family? There's a difference."

"Both. We protect each other. And that is all I have to say."

The woman was afraid. I saw the look she gave Roxanne.

I took a chance. "Greta, which worries you most: that Dr. Tomlinson will find out you have a daughter or that you have a daughter and he will find out he's not the father?"

Greta got up, saying, "I don't have to answer that! I'm a domestic, not a slave—" as Roxanne cut her off, saying in a louder voice, "He's not my father. My father died in the war!"

That silenced the room. Suddenly, I was even more interested.

Roxanne said it again. "My father's dead, okay? He worked for the Myles family. Then he joined the Army and died. End of story."

"Which war?"

"Does it matter?"

I said, "It might."

"I don't think so, they're all the same. A bunch of macho guys like you, carrying guns on their belts instead of tools. Is it the sound of metal that gets you off? Like cowboys with spurs. Knights in armor. Grown-ups playing games until . . . until . . . " Her voice softened, her attention turning inward. "That's what men do . . . play games."

I said, "What was your father's name?"

"Billy. Is that a funny name for a man? Billy Sofvia. He was very handsome—smart, too. But not smart enough to realize what a dead end it is working for the Myles family."

Greta whispered, "Enough, Roxy!"

"Why can't I talk, Greta? You don't want *them* to hear?"

Greta said, "Please, dear."

Roxanne laughed as she looked around the room, seeing stainless-steel pots hanging above a butcher's block, the industrial appliances, a double-wide Sub-Zero that cost more than most people made in a month. "You don't know anything about the service class, Ford. Do you mind if I call you Ford? I'm really not in the mood to call you Doctor."

Greta was looking at her, asking, "What is wrong with you today?"

Roxanne continued talking, telling me, "The reason the service class keeps secrets is because we have secrets of our own. Isn't that the truth, Greta? Of course it's true. My mother and father even dated secretly. When she got pregnant, they kept that a secret, too—"

"Roxanne Sofvia! Be quiet!"

"—because the feudal system didn't end in the Middle Ages. It moved to the Hamptons, where staff is considered property. They're expected to remain faithful, particularly attractive females. You would have to grow up in the system, Ford, to understand."

I said, "As a domestic worker," to keep her going.

"Or be one of them. Wouldn't that be more fun?" Roxanne crossed her legs, becoming conversational, as if taunting the older woman. "Becoming one of them, it's what the daughters of domestics dream of: marrying into the household. Isn't that the phrase, Greta, *marrying in*? Domestics live the wealthy life, Ford. We see it every day. But we're never more than ornaments or appliances unless we get lucky and marry in. Which never happens, of course. You know the old saying . . . why buy the cow?"

She thought for a moment. "Lucky, hah! That's a laugh. Domestics grow up knowing the truth about rich families but it doesn't change the way the families think. They know they're no smarter than the domestics. They know they're not as competent, and certainly not as solid, but domestics still hang on to the dream of marrying in. Isn't that sad? I mean, if you really think about it, how damn sad! Most of them, in fact, are completely crazed fuckups. The Tomlinson family—a classic example—but it doesn't change anything."

"That does it, I am leaving!" Greta was getting her purse, looking for her keys.

"No you're not!" Roxanne said, moving toward the door. "You'll never leave and you know it. *I'm* leaving. I'm leaving this house and this sick society and never coming back. I can't believe I let you talk me into it in the first place."

Greta's anger collapsed. "Roxy . . . why? Did something happen?"

"Between me and Prince Charming, you mean? What happened is, I found out it's true what they say about frogs. I kissed one. You want proof?" Roxanne reached for the lab report but caught herself as she started to hand it across the counter. "Do you mind, Ford? I have something personal I want to share with . . . my mother."

I was nodding, unsure how to handle it, then said, "Okay," and went out the door.

I fixed the phone lines, then paced, slowing time by checking my watch too often. It was almost noon. Will Chaser had been in the ground for at least three hours, if the photo was authentic. Probably already dead, but if he wasn't—and if the air system worked, as the kidnappers claimed—I still had twenty hours, maybe a little longer, to find him.

As I paced, I battled the ridiculous notion of returning to the road and seeking mystic insights from the rock, if I could find the damn thing. Had the boy been here? Had he been riding the gray stallion when it was shot?

I fixed my thoughts on a more reasonable hope: If I waited, played nice, maybe Roxanne would come out and answer my questions, including *Which war?*

Half an hour later, Roxanne did come out.

I wasn't imagining the chill in Barbara's voice when she said, "Did you happen to read a news story about the football player who washed up on a beach near Sanibel? One of my colleagues brought it to my attention. They think he was murdered."

I said, "No, I don't follow football," then told her I wasn't being a smart-ass, there were more pressing matters to discuss.

Was there anyone in the country who didn't know of Bern Heller's recent landfall? It kept me from asking the name of the woman's colleague. Only the guilty are interested in their accusers.

Barbara replied, "That's not true. One of Tomlinson's friends is a coach with the Jets, so I know you follow football. His name is . . . well, I'm positive you told me, whatever his name is. Ask the Tin Man, *he'll* remember."

I said, "Mike Westhoff," in a way to let her know how irritating she could be. I wasn't going to argue with a woman who argues professionally, although it was grating that Barbara—like almost everyone—was charmed by Tomlinson's star power and credited the man with virtues that friends and fellow boat bums knew were undeserved. But when people got their asses in a sling, who did they come running to?"

"I stand corrected," I told her.

I was in my hotel room, phone wedged between shoulder and ear, packing to return to Florida. The dispatcher at Air Transport Services had been even frostier than the senator when I requested a flight to the Gulf Coast. Now here was Barbara going off on tangents rather than cooperating. I was beginning to suspect it wasn't a coincidence.

Barbara said, "I probably shouldn't have mentioned it. I was given the information in confidence."

I said, "No need to say another word. A secret's a secret. But back to finding a plane for me—"

"Unfortunately," she interrupted, "this could have a bearing on our relationship. Doc, just between the two of us—and please stop me if the matter's already been settled—but police are saying you're a person of interest. I don't know the legal definition, but to me when police say someone is 'a person of interest' they mean that person had something to do with it."

Two hours thrashing around in a hotel room did not constitute a relationship, but now was not the time for precise definitions. Or was it? I needed a fast flight to Sarasota, and the lady was unlikely to help unless I dealt with this first.

I said, "I have a friend, a big-time attorney, who keeps her boat at the marina. She says there is no legal definition for the phrase *person of interest*. *Material witness*, yes. *Suspect*, yes. But *person of interest*—according to my friend anyway—is what police use to manipulate journalists. It's meaningless."

"I don't know, Doc. My reputation has taken such a beating in the last twenty-four hours—"

"Barb, what probably happened is, your friend misheard. When a boat goes missing, a lot of times the Coast Guard contacts me. I chart drift patterns in the Gulf of Mexico and keep records. You know, if a boat—or a body—drifts for three days, where's the most promising area to search? That's probably why the police are interested in talking to me. They know where the football player was found, but where did he go in the water? I do that sort of consulting a lot."

There was a long pause. "Are you sure? You can trust me, if you want to talk."

Like her colleague had trusted her? I said, "Barbara, I've spent exactly four hours in Florida since I arrived in New York last week. I didn't have time to kill a pro football player. We should be talking about getting me back to Florida. The Sarasota area, but anywhere close will do."

The woman replied, "So you can spy on Nelson Myles," sounding chillier.

"No, so I can find William. It's what I need to do." I had just told her that I was now *sure* Myles knew something about the kidnapping. She had replied, "As sure as you were last night?"

Tough to argue that one. Now, being a suspect in a high-profile murder investigation wasn't helping my cause any.

Barbara asked me, "Why do you have this thing against a man who, by all accounts, is not only respected in New

York but in the national community? In fact, the international business community—and that's not an exaggeration. Nelson Myles's father was an ambassador, for godsakes!"

I said, "The man buys and sells horses. He's not a political figure, and liking animals doesn't make him a saint."

It was tempting: Give her Roxanne's number and let the two women talk. I didn't blame Barbara for her reluctance to risk more embarrassment. But I didn't expect her to jump to the man's defense.

"I have colleagues in D.C. who know Nelson Myles personally. They say it's crazy to suggest he's capable of kidnapping anyone, particularly a U.S. senator. Give me one good reason why a man with his money and background would choose to get involved with something like this?"

I said, "I don't think it was a choice. I think he's being blackmailed," and realized as I finished the sentence that I couldn't tell the woman why I believed that was true. Accuse the man of murder next? Then hint that Myles was being manipulated by an interrogator from the Cuban Program, an operation that only people with high-security clearance could confirm existed? I wouldn't have bought it. So I added a lame explanation, saying, "It's just a hunch, but I think I'm right."

"You *think* you're right. The FBI has shifted the investigation to Castro sympathizers in Miami and to an Islamic organization in Detroit. But you're still determined to hound one of the wealthiest men in the Hamptons."

I said, "*Hound* has a negative connotation. I prefer *stalk*," thinking I might hear a smile in her voice. No.

Instead, I listened to several seconds of silence before she said patiently, "I appreciate what you've done for me, Doc. And I know you're tired. How much sleep have you had since yesterday morning? You didn't get any sleep Thursday night, I can testify to that." Her laughter was ingratiating. Or was it? I found the context odd. She was probing for something . . . or politely laying the ground-work to distance herself from me.

I said, "There's something on your mind. What's wrong?"

"What could possibly be wrong? A boy whose life was entrusted to me has been buried alive. As of this minute, we have"—I could picture the woman in her D.C. office looking at her wristwatch—"eighteen hours until Will Chaser dies, and that's if the sonsuvbitches are telling the truth about the air system."

I started to ask about the deadline—"They haven't changed it . . . ?"—but she talked over me, saying, "The national press is watching every move I make, which I expected. But the international reaction is a shock, even to me. It's all about blame. The United States and poor little Cuba. The imperialist giant reaps what it has sown. Justice—finally!—after a fifty-year embargo that started as a pissing match between a president and a banana-re-public dictator. This morning, a German editorial came right out and said I invited a kidnapping because I voted to make Castro's files public. That it's my fault they got a fourteen-year-old boy instead."

Quoting someone—I wasn't sure who—I tried to slow her down, saying, "The power of a dominant nation can be gauged by the sniping of its allies, not the denouncements of its foes."

"Foes? I'm not sure who the enemy is anymore," Barbara said. "The American press is just as relentless and even dirtier. Why did I decide to *not* have children? Did my late husband consider me incompetent? Am I a closet lesbian? And Favar Senior is proving he's the father-in-law from hell by charging to my defense, saying sweet things like, '*Incompetent* might be a little strong' or 'What's wrong with a woman giving up motherhood to get what she really wants . . . or marrying a wealthy man who's twenty-five years older?' See what I mean?"

I replied, "You said your father-in-law left Cuba in 1959?"

"Fifty-*eight,* the year before Fidel marched into Havana."

"How did he feel about Castro?"

"Despised him, like every Cuban-American I've met. Having Sorrento as a surname helped me politically, I admit it. And it got me appointed cochair of my committee, which has turned out to be more like a curse. So, in that way, I understand why Favar resents me. I inherited his son's money, his office, and I've benefited from using the old man's name . . . until next election anyway."

I said, "But even if the man hates you, you still extend his perimeter of power. And you carry on his son's legacy. Why would he fire such obvious torpedoes? Unless—"

"You figure it out," Barbara said.

"He's running against you in two years. That has to be it."

"There you go."

"By dropping *Sorrento* from your name, you're opening the door for him. You realize that?"

"Of course. But the man is seventy-eight years old, so I'm not that worried. And he hasn't actually come out and said that he's running, but . . . but . . ."—there was nothing theatrical about her sigh of weariness and disgust—"but . . . shit, who *cares*? What I'm going through doesn't compare to what our boy must be dealing with. When I start feeling sorry for myself, all I have to do is look at that goddamn awful photo. You have *seen* it? My computer's set up so the updates are forwarded."

I said, "It's on the phone you gave me. I'm using the picture as the . . . whatever they call the picture you keep on the screen."

"Then you've read the updates? They're sent on the Signet-D system because of classified information."

I said, "Not the latest, but about the photo . . . "

"It's sickening, isn't it?"

I said, "Can I finish a sentence? I think whoever took it is more interested in emotional impact than leveraging assets." I was trying to bring her back to what she'd said about international interests, but she missed my meaning.

"They're sick, I agree."

"Or detached," I said carefully.

"Insane, out of their minds," she replied. "I had the

staff tack a copy on every wall to remind them why we're working so hard. The FBI says the picture is good news in a way. If the shot was taken this morning, William has been alive for"—I was carrying the phone to the bed, yawning, as she did the calculation in her head—"so William has managed to stay alive for thirty-eight hours. Some of the agency people were hinting he was already dead."

I said, "If the picture *wasn't* taken this morning, I would agree."

"Ruth Guttersen—William's foster grandmother— Ruth sent me one of his school photos. I have both pictures on the desk in front of me, but I can't bear to look at the coffin shot for more than a few seconds—" Barbara stopped. "*Detached?* Is that what you said?"

I replied, "Impersonal. Emotionally uninvolved, yes. They haven't changed the deadline?"

"Detached . . . " She was thinking about it as she continued, "No, nothing's changed. Eight o'clock tomorrow morning, if they keep their word. We're keeping ours, even though the official line is that we don't negotiate with criminals." She paused. "Detached. But you said they were after emotional impact, not financial."

"Psychological intimidation, then emotional control: It's a device, a tool interrogators use. Money or power or preserving power—it works on all three."

"How the hell do you know about things like this?"

"It's what social animals do. Wolf packs and male dolphins. We're no different."

"Then it is about money. That's why you're accusing Nelson Myles."

I said, "I haven't accused him. I want to talk to him . . . privately." She hadn't reacted to the word *interrogator,* so I added the next link. "You don't associate Myles with anything Cuban, just wealth. Is that the problem?"

"No. Money and power, it's what I think of now when someone mentions Fidel Castro. Until now, I had no idea how wealthy that man had become in fifty years. Favar Senior tried to tell me years ago and I didn't believe him. Castro may have started as a penniless dictator, but now, even dead, he is an international conglomerate with world holdings worth—are you ready for a number?—worth seven hundred billion dollars. Were you aware of that?"

I wasn't, but she had finally given me an opening to ask about something more personal. "It sounds like your people completed the manifest list."

"Not just my people. Every bureaucracy from the CIA to the Park Service's Department of Archaeology has their hands in it. It's crazy how long they're taking."

"Find anything surprising?" If my name was on a list of licensed U.S. assassins, it was no wonder she wanted to cut me loose.

Instead of answering, Barbara covered her phone. I listened to a muffled exchange between the senator and someone who had come into her office. Male . . . British accent? I couldn't be sure, but I was picturing Hooker Montbard standing in her doorway, dapperly dressed . . . or wearing khakis, which he often did on weekends.

"Doc, I'll call you back in five minutes. No more than ten, promise."

I said, "But if I don't nail down a flight—"

"Read the newest updates. We can't really talk unless we're both on the same page, now can we?" The woman hung up.

I zipped my carry-on closed, checked the room and headed down the hall toward the elevator, telling myself there was no reason to be suspicious of my pal Hooker. But it was okay to call him. We were friends, right?

I dialed. No answer, and I didn't leave a message. Next, I did what the lady suggested and opened the updates.

SIGNET-D Communiqué (Level: Classified + Secret + Brown)

Summary Report #12, Prepared by staff of Hon. Barbara B. Hayes-Sorrento, United States Senate, 1 Billings St., Washington, D.C., 24 January, Saturday, 11:00 EST

SUBJECT A: William J. Chaser, minor male, missing as of 22 January, Thursday, 16:00 EST

SUBJECT B: FBI Addendum issued 10:00 EST

SUBJECT C: NYPD Addendum issued 10:30 EST . . .

It was a typically staccato rendering, but it didn't take long to get to something interesting. As I pushed through the lobby doors headed outside, I was reading:

SUBJECT H: Jettisoning of Superfluous Chattel Properties of the late Castro, Fidel A., via Military Aircraft over an area yet to be designated . . .

Jettisoning? It was government-speak for delivering the ransom. Castro's much-coveted personal files had been officially redesignated as trash. The military didn't know where they were dropping the stuff, but the cover story had been established.

I didn't smile, but it brightened my day despite the concrete chill of another New York afternoon. With any luck, it would be my last for a while. One way or the other, I was returning to Florida. If I couldn't arrange a special flight, I would have to fly out of Kennedy International ninety minutes away.

I told the concierge desk I needed a cab, then skimmed the text, finding other interesting tidbits.

SUBJECT H/Para. 4: Transport of Superfluous Materials: Aircraft: H130 Hercules Cargo Aircraft, USAF, has been assigned as Disposition Platform.

Crew is on standby, Dulles Air Base, three watches, 8-hour rotation. The H130 was assigned despite the small amount of Superfluous Materials because the disposal area has yet to be designated.

Aircraft range: 1800 nm+/- (BRC) with refueling aircraft on station. Status: Alert Orange . . .

SUBJECT H/Para. 11: Superfluous Materials consist of three (3) Industrial Cartons containing approximately 2.3 metric tons. Loading of Superfluous Materials is being finalized pursuant to variables of an undetermined disposal area . . .

SUBJECT H/Para. 14: Industrial Cartons have been mounted on skids and fitted with LALO parachutes for wet drop or dry drop. Final Go Confirmation expected by 1900 hours EST.

FBI awaiting contact with Civilian Clients via VHF Marine Radio or electronic mail and will then advise USAF crew . . .

Civilian clients were the kidnappers. Castro's possessions had been loaded on a long-distance aircraft and rigged for a parachute drop. Everything would be packed and ready to go by five p.m., which was fifteen hours in advance of the deadline. Good!

Or was it . . . ?

I thought about it as I waited for a cab. What suddenly bothered me was that several normally inefficient bureaucracies had hammered this package together, meshing all the complicated pieces, in an extraordinarily efficient way.

Had I ever heard of a joint project being completed ahead of schedule? Hell, I had never even heard of a project that was finished on time.

Weird.

A few minutes later, sitting in the back of a cab, headed west on the road out of the Hamptons, my phone began buzzing: Barbara.

Barbara told me, "Castro was a neurotic, that was my first surprise—I'm talking about surprises in the last day or so. He was insecure when he took power in 'fifty-nine and the man never changed."

I said, "Neurotic, hmm," listening to the woman avoid discussing Nelson Myles by sharing revelations about the Castro Files. She hadn't mentioned who interrupted our conversation either. Why was she being evasive?

"Castro kept two bags packed with collectibles, ready to go, in case he had to escape in the middle of the night. *Valuables*"—her smile was audible—"is not the right word for what that man had squirreled away. It's *treasure*, the pirate variety. I'd heard that he formed a team to salvage shipwrecks around Cuba. Now we know it's true. There are some beautiful pieces from the seventeen hundreds: Spanish gold crosses, emeralds and jade. Small, not too heavy. Probably worth millions, and all of it easily converted into currency. There's an emerald necklace— my God, you've got to see it."

I said, "Spanish treasure, that's always interesting." She couldn't avoid discussing Myles, or getting me on a plane, forever.

"There are some political shockers, too. Three boxes of files on Meyer Lansky and what was called the *Jewish Mafia*. They controlled most of the gaming in Havana. If the documents are made public, some of our Middle Eastern friends are going to be upset about how Israel was financed in those early years. Everything's being photographed, of course. Still, without the original documents . . ."

She let me figure out the significance and moved on. "The Catholic Church takes a big hit. There are documents that prove—well, that suggest anyway—that some priests entered into an alliance with Castro . . . a sort-of *covenant*. But I can't go into specifics, sorry."

I didn't need specifics. Barbara was referring to a secret meeting that took place in Havana in 1966 between ten activist priests and Fidel Castro. In return for Castro's political blessing, the priests activated a plan to encourage and fund Socialism in Central and South America. Over the next two decades, newspaper readers in the United States would puzzle over the political assassinations of nuns and priests in the region. It seemed outrageous to a citizenry that knew nothing about the covert wars going on worldwide, so they suffered with mental images of murdered Flying Nuns and kindly Bing Crosbys.

I said to Barbara, "A covenant with the Catholic Church, that *is* a surprise. Was it around the time of the Bay of Pigs invasion . . . or the assassination?"

She thought she was being properly evasive, replying, "We found documents our intelligence agencies aren't going to like. One or two people could face prosecution. Men in powerful positions who betrayed us, their country . . . I mean, if the information's accurate."

I said, "Bay of Pigs. An informant gave Castro's people the landing date and time. Didn't the informant go by a code name? I'm trying to remember . . ."

Barbara said, "Why do you do this? Instead of manipulating me to get information, why not come right out and ask?"

"Okay," I said, "who was the traitor?" If it was Tinman, would she have even mentioned it?

The woman said, "I can't tell you."

"Lady, you can be so frustrating—"

"Not on the phone. There were two informants. At least two—not related to the assassination, so don't assume that please. But there is something *very* interesting I learned about the day Kennedy was shot."

The woman had lowered her voice. She was enjoying this, I realized, which I found heartening because it reminded me that I was still her confidant . . . and probably always would be her confidant. We shared an ultimate secret, the secret of her blackmail video. Barbara Hayes-Sorrento might try to distance herself from me, but if she slammed the door she would lose the one person in the world to whom she could say any damn thing she wanted to say with no fear of retribution.

"Castro kept the phone logs from the morning President Kennedy was shot," Barbara said, her voice still low. "There were more than two dozen calls to his residence within twenty minutes."

I wasn't just listening now, I was interested. I waited a few seconds before I said, "And . . . ?"

"And," she said, "that's all I can tell you right now." Her tone became more formal. "Besides, I thought you called to ask for a favor, not chat about the files. We're busy here, you know."

The woman was maddening.

I started to say, "You're the one who went off on a tangent," but dropped it, saying instead, "Okay, fine. I need transportation to Florida . . . Sarasota, ideally. What can you do for me?"

"I thought you agreed to stop pestering Mr. Myles."

"No, *you* suggested it. I didn't agree."

"But you expect me to back you? After the hoops you made me jump through to exhume those two dead horses? Waking up judges, calling in favors—for what? And you're still not convinced!"

I started to say, "You've got to trust my judgment on this—"

"I want you to stay away from Nelson Myles," she interrupted. "The man has been patient so far, but you will put both of us in a dangerous position if you keep pushing. On nothing but a hunch? I'm sorry."

I said, "Dangerous legal position?"

"Yes! But also in terms of public opinion."

"*Public opinion,*" I said. "Is that code for *getting reelected*?"

"Don't get smart, Dr. Ford."

"One of us needs to. What happened, Barb? Why are you suddenly scared of Nelson Myles?"

"Power, that's why," she said. "It doesn't scare me, but I respect it. Let's don't even get into the damage it could cause to some of my working relationships. But if I doubled my fund-raising schedule starting today, I still couldn't compete with the kind of money Myles and his friends have. Even if I had ten years left in my term, instead of only two. Plus—and this is the absolute goddamn truth—I respect the opinions of colleagues who know the man."

I was tempted to say, "*Respect*—another political euphemism for *power*?," but instead I asked, "Are some of your colleagues Yale graduates? Members of Skull and Bones maybe?"

"The fraternity? What does it matter? The point is, all I care about is getting the boy back alive, and you're wasting time."

I said, "If you've made up your mind, there's nothing I can do. I'm open to suggestions." I was going to Sarasota no matter what, but why tell Barbara and risk putting the man on alert?

"Doc," she said, "I value our friendship." There was nothing phony about the way she said it, but I didn't reply.

"The best thing for you to do—for both of us, in fact—is to stay close to me. I need your moral support more than anything, so let's let the FBI handle it, okay? I can't sleep, I'm a ball of nerves." She let that settle, then added, "You're maybe the only man in the world who really understands how hard it is for me to relax."

Nothing phony about that either, nor was there any bawdy subtext. The woman was in trouble, isolated by her own office as much as by the anxiety associated with the kidnapping. That fast, I liked her again.

I said, "How about this? I'll go home from here, spend a few days, then we can get together after this is done."

Her reply surprised me. "How far is Busch Gardens from Sanibel, a couple of hours? Could we meet there tomorrow night?"

"What?"

"I wanted to fly Mr. and Mrs. Guttersen into D.C. at my expense. You know, to be near them until this is over, but Dan O'Connell beat me to it by inviting them to tour Busch Gardens. His family has a winter home near there."

She added, "The Guttersens are meeting him in Tampa tonight—both of them, hopefully, if Ruth isn't coming down with the flu. It will be good for all of us, to see this thing through together. Plus the military base at Tampa is our primary intelligence center. It can't hurt to be within driving distance."

"Senator Dan O'Connell?" I said.

"From Minnesota. He was the friend who asked me to meet William at the airport and take him to the UN. Dan's got a place on the beach, a house and a couple of guest cottages. I won't stay with him, I'll book a suite of rooms nearby. My staff will communicate by phone and Internet. Can you meet me there?"

My brain was scanning for a way to work it to my advantage. I needed a reason why I had to return to Florida this afternoon, not tomorrow. I said, "I'd love to see you, but I've got so much catching up to do at my lab. But . . . if I could find a faster way home to Sanibel—"

"You're doing it again, trying to manipulate me," she interrupted. "I've made the offer. I need you, Doc. But you'll have to fly commercial just like everyone else. If you change planes in Atlanta, you might run into the Guttersens. Otto Guttersen is a real character, Dan told me. A military background, a real tough guy . . . You two would hit it off."

I was trying to picture the ex–pro wrestler Outlaw Bull Guttersen plowing his wheelchair through sand on some

Gulf beach, as Barbara added, "Dan was just here, that's why I had to call you back. Mr. Guttersen has been through some really bad times in his life, but nothing's hit him like this."

I said, "I was surprised by how emotional he sounded on the phone," still scanning for a way to finagle a special flight. If I flew out of JFK by three, I could be in Florida by dusk.

"It would mean a lot to me, Doc, if you were there. It would be good for the Guttersens, too. Give Mr. Guttersen someone to talk to. In Florida, at least, he and his wife can get outside instead of sitting around going stir-crazy waiting for news. Dan told me it's been freezing cold up there. Something like fifteen below in Minneapolis . . . not counting windchill."

23

Over the hours, Will dozed, he reminisced, he raged and cried, and occasionally slept, but never for long because he was awakened by nightmares.

Sometimes, Will imagined that his box was moving. Or possibly it did move, although never very much. The boy couldn't be sure because his dreams, his thoughts, his memories were all so tangled by the relentless darkness and the drug Ketamine that was still filtering through his veins.

Hours ago, Will had quit fighting his insistent bladder and decided to piss his jeans whenever he needed. For a time, pissing became his primary recreation, counting in his head to see how long he could keep the stream going. Now his jeans were sodden, but his body was empty of fluids.

Because he was thirsty, it was pleasurable—for a while anyway—to imagine himself diving into a glacial lake and drinking his fill of water that was crystalline blue like a Minnesota sky.

But Will had stopped doing that because it made him even thirstier, and also because it was so damn cold inside the box. Freezing, in fact. And Will began to suspect that Buffalo-head had carried out his threat.

How would you like to be buried in the cold, cold earth?

Now, mumbling through the tape on his mouth, Will barked a reply, "I wouldn't like it worth a damn, you creep."

My God, he was cold! No wind. No light. Maybe the bastards really had buried him!

As he pondered that, Will became aware of a red-tinted darkness blooming behind his eyes, but he stopped it, thinking, *Don't . . . Don't,* terrified of the insanity that threatened from just beyond the limits of his own anger.

It was safer to focus on how cold he was rather than the heat attempting to fire his temper, so Will moved his thoughts there.

Colder than a nun at a prison rodeo. Colder than a well-digger's ass. Colder than Custer's nuts! Colder than . . . Colder than . . . Well, it's no colder than downtown Minneapolis in January, with snow falling.

One below—not counting windchill.

Bull Guttersen's line. The man claimed to be seriously thinking of putting it on his tombstone—if no one had used it first, of course. He was a stickler about originality. *Intellectual property,* he called it, and he had confided to Will that the wrestling characters he'd invented, Outlaw

Bull Gutter or Sheriff Bull Gutter, might one day make them all wealthy.

"Just you watch," the man had said. "When Hollywood finally gets hold of its senses and stops making them candy-ass, cartoon-robot shoot-'em-ups, they'll snoop around for a new hero until they sniff gold. Never been two finer intellectual properties created than Outlaw Bull and Sheriff Bull, so I expect we'll cash in before I die."

We'll cash in, talking like Will was an actual member of the family instead of just temporary, although Bull had demanded a second-year extension to the Lutherans' usual one-year guardianship.

It was weird for Will to think of himself dead and buried before the old man beat him to it. Especially considering how they'd met that first day when Guttersen had said something flippant about the garbage bag Will had been carrying, miffed that his suicide had been interrupted.

Guttersen's revolver had been loaded with . 38 caliber Hydra-Shoks. Will could picture them in the cylinder now, as he retreated into a safer venue of thought. The bullets had looked as symmetrical as spider eggs when Guttersen lowered the gun from his own temple and pointed it at Will's chest.

The bullets had ugly, puckered golden tips. They were called *Man Stoppers* at Minneapolis gun shows and marketed exactly for such an occasion: home alone, enjoying the comforts of a remodeled basement—a little bar and a flat-screen TV—only to be interrupted by a robber whose dark skin indicated that he probably was a crack addict and also unpredictable, unlike teenagers of Norwegian descent.

Instead, Will had heard *click* as the gun's cylinder rotated and the hammer locked back, Guttersen making his smart-assed remark about him being disinclined to offer Will a beer while waiting for the ambulance.

What happened next, though, was the strangest part of what had already been a strange, strange day. Guttersen had flipped the revolver around and caught it by the barrel. The move had spooked Will so badly that he threw his hands up and closed his eyes, expecting to be shot. A second later, though, when he peeked, Will was surprised to see the man extending his arm, wanting Will to take the gun.

Guttersen had said to him, patiently, "You gotta pull the hammer back before you fire. It's single-action. And don't close your damn eyes! If you miss, I swear to God I'll testify against you in court."

Will had said, "Do what?," even though he knew what the man wanted.

"Take the damn gun!"

Will had curled his fingers around the gun's weight, his thumb automatically finding the hammer, as Guttersen told him, "My coin collection's in the pantry, what looks like a candy box. There's a Mercury dime worth five hundred bucks, I shit thee not. And a hundred seven Liberty-head silver dollars—you can figure that one out for yourself."

Will understood more about that than the old man

realized. He liked coins and had kept a few from the pawnbroker. "The dime—must be the 1940-S, huh?" he offered.

"Mint condition," Guttersen told him. "But pay attention, damn it, I'm trying to talk. My wife keeps her jewelry in the commercial freezer. One of those Tupperware-thingee containers. Most of it's fake, but, Jesus Christ, don't let word get back to her—especially the diamond necklace, which is zirconium. She'll pretend it don't bother her, but she'll do it in a way that drives everybody nuts. Not that you won't find plenty of other valuables," the man had added quickly. "Don't get me wrong."

Guttersen began moving his wheelchair as he gave instructions, positioning himself near the bar where there was Mexican tile, not carpet: less mess, and a clear shot for Will.

The old man said, "My wife left for the hairdresser's only 'bout half an hour ago, but sometimes she forgets stuff and comes back unannounced. And some of those— what do you call 'em?—*technicians* color roots faster than others, so you never know. Catch my meaning? We don't have time to waste."

The man had paused and looked at the boy for a moment before warning, "About my wife . . . don't you lay a damn hand on her. Hear me? You touch my wife, I'll come back from the grave and tear you a new asshole. Savvy?"

Jesus, talking like they were in a TV western, Will being the dumb Indian, but a fire spark glowed in the old man's eyes so Will didn't comment, even after the spark faded.

Guttersen had turned the chair so he was looking at photos that hung over the bar. He straightened his T-shirt, took a deep breath and cleared his throat. Then he said, "Okay. I'm ready. Go."

Will had looked at the gun but didn't answer.

"Hear me? I said, 'Ready.'"

Will was still staring at the revolver, seeing the fake-pearl handle, the chrome flaking on the cylinder—a piece of junk.

"Jesus-frogs, you deaf, too?"

"I heard what you said: You're ready."

"Goddamn right I'm ready. I'm *overdue* ready!" Guttersen squared his shoulders and tilted his left temple toward Will. "All righty . . ." He took another deep, slow breath. "Here we go—and keep your damn eyes open! You owe me that. You're about to come into some money."

Standing in the basement of what the Lutheran Grandparents Program had assigned as his foster home, Will had then experienced an abrupt change of aspect, a camera-on-the-ceiling view that often occurred when something unusually shitty or dangerous happened in his life—a phenomenon he had experienced too many times.

Will stood there, a head taller than the big Norwegian in his wheelchair, seeing the room from above. A darkness tinted the space, a hopelessness that smelled of brittle paper and ironing.

Through the tinted air, he could see the old man, sitting with his head bowed, waiting to die, and the pool table, a SCHMIDT BEER neon sign over the bar, a jar of pickled eggs, bottles of booze in a row, a MINNESOTA TWINS pennant, photos on the wall of what looked like wrestlers, a JOE FOR EMPEROR sticker and two cowboy hats on a deer-horn rack—big, felt bullshit hats no wrangler would ever wear. One hat black, the other white.

Will had zoomed in and was examining himself, standing like a dope, holding the stainless-steel revolver, which was brighter, bigger than everything else in the room except for an old floor-model radio that Will's ears had stopped hearing until that moment, possibly because a commercial break had just ended and the announcer now was on the subject of guns. He was saying, ". . . scientists have built a giant electromagnet in the Rocky Mountains. When they hit the switch, all the handguns in America will be sucked from holsters, bedrooms, locked closets— you name it. Guns'll bust through walls, knock holes in roofs, that's how strong the magnet is . . ."

Will's eyes descended from the ceiling as he listened. After a minute or two, he was on the floor again, right back beside the wheelchair, when the old man said, "Jesus Christ, you waiting for me to die of old age? Pull the freakin' trigger!"

Will said, "I was listening to the guy on the radio."

"Well, stop listening and start shooting, goddamn it. I'm starting to lose the mood."

"That thing about the giant magnet, is it bullshit?"

"Huh?"

"What the guy said about pulling guns through walls."

The man looked up, irritated. "It's a radio show, for chrissake! What's a matter? You afraid that magnet's gonna rip your damn arm off when that gun flies out the window?"

When Will asked, "Could it?," the man snorted, getting mad now, and saying, "How stupid are they making kids these days? Damn half-breed, you must have the IQ of a Twinkie."

Will said, "Hey!" and pulled the hammer back. "Don't talk to me that way. I've got a damn gun in my hand."

The old man snapped, "Well, you sure could've fooled the hell out of me. Maybe you'd do better with a bow and arrow."

"Knock it off. I mean it."

"Let's hope you do. My wife's probably under the dryer by now."

The old man had looked at Will, seeing the revolver, hammer back, and thought for a moment. He muttered something, then he squared his shoulders again, turned his temple toward Will and focused on the old photos of wrestlers on the wall.

"Do it!" he said. "Or I'm calling the cops." Then tried to piss off Will, adding, "You being Ethiopian, maybe we should melt the freakin' gun down and make a freakin' spear out of it. A weapon not so complicated."

Will ignored the comment because he knew what the man was doing. He looked at the radio instead. Now the radio guy was saying, ". . . So here's how we use this giant magnet. We send fancy metal belts to every sportswriter who thinks Bert should *not* be in the Hall of Fame. Engraved belts, like presents, get it? When scientists hit the magnet's switch—*Whammo!*—a hundred sportswriters are suddenly airborne, flying toward Denver without a plane."

Will had noticed the old man's chest moving like he was laughing. The joke was *kinda* funny. But then Will realized the man was crying again. Geezus, it was embarrassing. A grown man crying, Will had never seen it before. Well . . . that wasn't true. On the Rez, some of the older Skins occasionally bawled when they got drunk, but it was mad-crying because they were walled in by their lives, dead broke, with snot-nosed kids who would never amount to nothing.

That wasn't the sound Will was hearing now, this hopeless weeping without bottom, a despair that had the scent of crumbling paper.

Uncocking the gun, Will went to the radio and turned the volume louder. He wasn't going to shoot the guy, so the only thing he could think of to say was, "Who the hell is Bert? Why don't sportswriters like him?"

The old man pretended to cough into his hand. On the bar was a towel. He took his time getting the towel, then coughed a few more times and blew his nose, keeping his back to the boy.

"You ever get tired of asking questions? Jesus Christ, you oughta be stealing encyclopedias instead of hard-earned jewelry and stuff."

Will repeated the question, feeling the air in the room changing, the invisible gray tint clearing, and he thought, *Good*.

The old man said, "Bert Blyleven. Bert pitched for the Twins when they won the World Series." Then he held up an index finger, as if there was something too important to miss, but it was really to give himself more time to stop bawling as he listened to the radio guy saying:

". . . Blyleven's got almost four thousand strikeouts, plus two World Series rings. As if that's not enough to earn the Dutchman a place in Cooperstown, Bert had nearly three hundred career wins, too, despite playing for underpaid teams." Being funny, the radio announcer added, "Take it easy, Twinkie lovers, I don't want you to choke on your Grain Belts—I am not referring to our Twins, of course."

It was another minute before Will said, "I never heard of the guy."

The man who only later would introduce himself as Otto Guttersen spun his wheelchair, oblivious to the tinted air flowing through Will's brain. Like smoke, it drifted upward, the space changing from gray-blue to pearl, as Guttersen said, "You gotta be shittin' me."

Will said, "'Bout what?"

"You never heard of Bert Blyleven? He's only one of the greatest pitchers of all time, which most sportswriters know. But there're still a few dingleberries out there who won't vote him into the Hall of Fame. Didn't you just hear what Joe said?"

Joe, Will would also soon learn, was Joe Soucheray,

the host of *Garage Logic,* a local guy who even Will had to admit was pretty funny for being an old Casper from Minnesota.

Will began to relax a little when Guttersen said, "You don't follow baseball? Maybe Indian chiefs don't allow TV on the reservation. Or is it because of the Great White Father?"

Usually, Rez jokes didn't bother Will. The Skins said a lot worse than that, but they were Skins, not some racist old cripple from the Land of a Thousand Lakes.

Will told the old man, "Screw you, I ride rodeo," and knew it was okay because the man didn't say anything as he placed the gun on the counter.

"Screw me?" The man snorted and sniffed. "Screw you, kid."

"Screw you!"

"Screw *you.*"

Then Will had to listen to him say, "Every kid in the world should know something about baseball. Hell, stealing bases would come natural to someone with your experience."

Looking around for the garbage bag, Will gave the man a look: *Screw YOU!*

"Kid, you wanna talk about a real sport? Here, I'll show you." The old guy had wheeled toward the bar, where there were wrestling photos on the wall, then stopped suddenly.

"Whoa . . . Holy Christ," he whispered, "I just remembered something: My wife told me we're getting a juvenile-delinquent kid tomorrow. Said he was gonna be living with us for a month, because she signed up for this stupid program down at church. Some foster-grandparent bullshit." He had poked his big nose toward Will, the old man's face now become a face with features. "You have anything to say on that subject?"

Will had used his sullen *Why should I care?* expression and looked at the floor.

"Are you the delinquent? Seriously, I'm asking."

As the man moved the chair closer, Will knelt for the garbage bag, changing his expression to read *That's so crazy it's funny.*

Guttersen had pale, piggish blue eyes that lit up when he thought he'd done something smart. "I'll be go-to-hell," he said, "it *is* you! Christ! When she said an Indian kid, I thought she meant from freakin' *India.* Like with a turban and a dot—you know, a tea drinker who might get pretty good grades in math."

Will was looking around the room, thinking, *I've gotta get out of here,* as the man pressed on. "Her Tinkerbell friends wouldn't have said *Indian* unless it was India. They woulda said *Native American* or *Indigenous*-something. But that's what my wife meant—a juvenile-delinquent *Indian.*" The old man was grinning for some reason. "By God, you're just as advertised. I can't argue with what's staring me in the kisser!"

Will had started up the stairs.

"Hey, where you going? I wouldn't mind hearing about what it's like robbing houses."

Will kept walking.

Guttersen raised his voice when he didn't get an instant response, a habit that would irritate the hell out of Will in the future. "I'm bored, for chrissake! That's not obvious? Come back and have a seat. We still got half an hour of the radio show."

Will had turned to look at the man. "You don't want me here, mister. You're afraid I'll tell the church people I caught you trying to blow your brains out. If they hear that, they'll strap you in a straitjacket and take you to the loony farm."

"I suppose they might try," Guttersen replied. "You gonna tell?"

"Not if you don't tell the cops what I do for extra money."

"I expect you've laid up quite a pile, working with a pawnshop. What do you do with all that money, buy drugs? Saving for college?"

In that instant, Will had realized something surprising: He could answer any way he wanted, even tell the old man the truth, an opportunity that would end when he walked out the door.

"I buy marijuana seeds sometimes," Will had said, talking slow so he could feel what it was like not lying. "I grow it, then make a bunch more money selling *tacote* to rich kids. You know, weed."

"*Weed*, you call it. I thought the word you drug dealers used was *grass*. Or . . . *maryann*."

"*Grass*, sometimes. *Smoke* or *tacote*, they called it on the Rez—the reservation, I mean."

Guttersen said, "I'll be go-to-hell," interested, but not as interested as he was pretending to be. Then the man ruined it with flattery. "I was impressed, you knowing about the Mercury dime. Most people, they'd drop a 1940-S in a Coke machine, not a second thought. You're a go-getter for an orphan delinquent, I shit thee not."

Will had almost told Guttersen something else true that he'd never told anyone: He was saving to buy Blue Jacket from the snooty Texans with their fancy ranch. Instead, Will had flashed his *Whatever* expression, then started up the stairs, telling the old man, "No need to shovel it so high. I'll tell the church people I ain't living here but won't mention the gun."

"Good. None of their damn business anyway." The man had pushed his wheelchair to the stairwell, waiting until Will was almost at the top, to offer, "We still got thirty minutes of *Garage Logic*. Wouldn't hurt to stay until the wife gets back from the hair parlor."

"I got better things to do, mister."

Guttersen didn't argue—a surprise. Just sort of shrugged as he spun the chair, then settled in by the radio, his indifference saying *Leave if you want. I'm not begging*.

Will had stood on the stairs, thinking about it. He didn't like the man—who would? But there was something comfortable about being with an adult you could tell to go screw himself and he'd say it right back, no hard feelings.

But the craziness with the gun was scary. And the wife sounded like most foster grandmothers, tight-cheeked do-gooders who worked so hard pretending to be sweet, they were a pain in the ass.

No thanks.

As Will reached the top of the stairs, though, he heard the old man call, "If you steal the jewelry, at least close the damn freezer door tight. Hear? But if you're staying, there's a can of beef jerky on the cupboard, and grab me a beer. Two beers, if you're thirteen or older."

It was a couple of months before Guttersen's wife, Ruth, gave them permission to open the gun safe—Guttersen, of course, pretending he didn't have an extra key—and drive to the shooting range. That's where Will heard the pearl-handled revolver fired for the first time.

Loud, yeah, but as expected.

Back in Oklahoma, even shrinks and preachers packed guns. On the Rez, Christ, the Skins still had machine pistols hidden away from the days of the American Indian Movement. Will had grown up carrying a sidearm, provided by whatever ranch was paying him to ride fence. He could shoot.

Even so, he had to listen to Guttersen run his mouth, offering advice about the finer points of marksmanship, which Will had assumed was bullshit because competent shooters didn't buy cheap weapons like a pearl-handled knockoff.

A misjudgment, he discovered.

"This shiny piece of junk's got sentimental value," Guttersen explained, shucking brass from the cylinder, then laying the gun aside. "It's a fake peacemaker I used in my wrestling shows. Sheriff Bull Gutter and Outlaw

Bull both. Good for close range, if you catch my meaning. But I woulda never used it in the field."

When Will asked, "What field?," the man didn't answer, too busy locking the wheels on his chair, then producing a gun case from beneath his seat.

"This," he said, "is what I used in the field. Not the sort of weapon I'd want some cop to snatch because they took it as evidence. Savvy?"

It was like that all the time, now, Geezus. Cowboy Bull and his Indian sidekick, Pony Chaser.

Inside the case was a pistol Will had read about but never seen, a custom .45 caliber semiautomatic Kahr, polished stainless steel, with custom sights. A beautiful weapon, even though the gun had had some use.

"Where'd you carry it?" Will asked again, but Guttersen was loading rounds into a magazine, then turned his attention to a combat range. There were targets at twenty-five yards, fifty yards, and one target seventy-five yards away.

"If I had a rifle," Will said, making conversation, "I'd take the far target and show you something."

Guttersen shucked a round into the Kahr, and replied, "I'll show you something right now," then did.

Bull Guttersen could *shoot*.

It was another ten months before the man answered the question, "What field?," confiding in Will something that even Guttersen's wife was forbidden to mention: Bull's wrestling career didn't end in the ring, as he commonly told people.

Truth was, he had been crippled six years before in Afghanistan, at age fifty-one, after being recalled as a sergeant with his mortar unit in the Minneapolis National Guard.

Hearing that confirmed something else Will had begun to suspect. Guttersen wasn't as old as he looked. He was old but not *old*. Something had happened to the man that aged him.

"I saw some action around Kabul, slept in a tent and put on a couple of wrestling shows for the USO. Didn't even mind the scorpions too much, but then the Hummer I was in hit an IED outside Mazar-Sharif and it all went to hell."

Guttersen didn't tell Will that until days later, the two of them staying up late one night watching *The Angel and the Badman*, sitting in La-Z-Boy recliners, the fancy ones with beer holders built right into the armrests.

Guttersen had offered the information in a mild, damn-near intelligent voice Will had never heard the man use before . . . and might never hear again.

"Don't ask for details, Pony Boy," Bull had said, ending the conversation. "If you bring it up, or tell a soul, I'll say it never happened, because once folks find out the truth, they never stop asking me about it—*What was it like? Musta been hell*—as if they knew something about hell. People don't know jackshit about hell, not the Real McCoy hell. Trust me on that one."

In the same mild voice, Bull had explained, "Even if I don't answer their damn questions, I still end up thinking about the answers. And I don't want to recall how truly shitty it was. Just don't got the energy for that no more." Bull had added, being very serious, "Pony, you'd have to be a POW yourself to understand."

Buried alive, Will wondered now, his eyes open in the darkness of his coffin. *Does that count?*

24

I gave up on asking Barbara for help. Made a phone call from the cab, got lucky and hitched a ride on an Army training flight to MacDill Air Force Base, Tampa. The plane was a C-130, similar to the aircraft that was being loaded with the Castro Files. No movie but a cargo hold the size of a gymnasium where I could stretch out and sleep.

"The military's standards begin where your standards end," I enjoyed telling Tomlinson over the phone, breaking the news that he would have to find his own way home.

By eight p.m. I was standing on the patio of Nelson Myles's winter estate, near Venice Beach, watching the man through his kitchen window. He was pouring himself a scotch and soda, mostly scotch. The sober horseman was back in the saddle.

Good. He would be loose, possibly even talkative. What I had to decide was my approach. Knock on the door and introduce myself? Or lure the man outside, then drive him to a secluded spot?

If the police weren't already looking for me, I might have played it straight. But their low-key inquiries were becoming more frequent, and they'd hinted about a subpoena. Mack, owner of Dinkin's Bay Marina, had updated me on the phone, as I drove a rental car south on I-75, looking for an exit near the Sarasota County line and a development called Falcon Landing.

There are hundreds of gated communities in Florida and many hundreds more to come. Gate or no gate, few are communities. Developers bulldoze an oversized patch of scrub, truck in sod and palms to damper the stink of bruised earth, then mask their domino trap with a woodsy name—Cedar Lakes, Cypress Vista, Oak Hills—and *presto!* instant habitat for people in search of instant lives.

Falcon Landing was different. It was a thousand-acre enclave, a private retreat isolated by fencing, security and almost two miles of bay frontage and beachfront. Prices started in the eight figures, execs who owned planes were the targeted demographic and there was a strict low-density covenant that catalyzed demand and guaranteed a waiting list of buyers. Even I had heard of some of the celebrities who owned homes at the place.

There were only two entrances to Falcon Landing. The southernmost was just north of Port Charlotte, the other near the pretty seaside town of Venice.

I approached from the north. The entrance was a limestone arch with a waterfall and a Learjet logo. At the

guard station was a Wells Fargo security car and two uniformed men. The place took security more seriously than
most, so I parked at public-beach access a half mile away.
After changing into shorts and a long-sleeved T-shirt, I
belted a fanny pack around my waist and jogged back to
the entrance. The guards replied to my wave with slow,
uncertain salutes, but they didn't stop me.

I can go without sleep for a couple of days, if I work out.
But I hadn't had time to do much of either in the last forty-
eight hours. It felt good to be outside, alone and running
in the Gulf-dense night. So good, I didn't want to stop.
Running is the best way I know to scope out an area. I
picked up the pace—my way of making the run last—and
mentally logged details that might be useful later.

Falcon Landing was a well-planned package: multimil-
lion-dollar estates on ten-acre parcels, homes that looked
as if they'd been layered from a tube of chocolate icing.
There was a country club, clay courts, a banquet hall and
restaurant that was open but not busy on this balmy, blus-
tery January eve.

Every structure was efficiently screened by ficus or hi-
biscus hedges. Green zones were spacious, and there were
trails and tree canopy enough to create the illusion of a
Caribbean island retreat. The exception was the western
edge of the property where more than a dozen small jets
and prop planes were hangered on an FAA-licensed
airstrip—seventy-two hundred feet long, according to
signage. Members only, night traffic by appointment,
corporate pilots must register with the attendant at Falcon Landing.

I wondered how tight airstrip security was.

The Myles estate was beachside, the house not visible from the road. It was shielded by islands of foliage: helicoids, birds of paradise, citrus and frangipani. There was a twelve-foot gate, wrought iron on electric tracks, with a horse-sculpture cap and a small brass plaque: SHELTER COTTAGE.

We'll see . . .

I checked the street before ducking into the shadows where there was a chain-link fence. After dropping to the other side, I waited two minutes in case there was a perimeter alarm or a Doberman standing watch.

The house wasn't a cottage; it was a massive three-story mansion with two-story wings at each end.

As I approached, I could hear the drumming of waves on the beach and the compressor kick of an air conditioner. Even on a flawless winter evening, the gated community types avoid contact with the reality of Florida . . . except for someone moving on the upper floor of the south wing.

I crouched and watched a woman step out onto a balcony. The moon was three days before full, not bright because of clouds but bright enough. Nelson's wife? Yes. She was too full-bodied in her silken robe to be the daughter.

Connie Myles walked to the railing, listening to the thumping bass of New Age rock in the room behind her, then lit a cigarette. No . . . a *joint*. I had observed Tomlinson's ceremonial machinations often enough to know. She inhaled several times, then pirouetted in a solitary dance, arms thrown wide, like Wendy in *Peter Pan* yearning to fly.

I remembered the photo I'd seen in Myles's office of the wife who had appeared lost and haunted, shrinking ever smaller into the background of her family members' lives. Perhaps I was mistaken. Perhaps the woman was simply stoned. For her sake, I hoped it was true.

When she finished smoking and had locked the French doors behind her, I worked my way past a tennis court and a small empty stable to the back lawn. The main house looked deserted, but there was activity in the north wing.

I crossed to the patio, where there was a pool house, a guest cottage and a landscaped deck with a tiki hut and lounge chairs. The pool was unlit, a graphite mirror beneath moon and stars. Lights were on in the kitchen . . . and Nelson appeared. I watched him open a fresh bottle of scotch and pour a drink.

The man was wearing a dress shirt that would fit if he gained fifteen pounds, suggesting recent weight loss. That, coupled with the scotch, meshed with what Roxanne had told me.

"Two weeks ago," she'd said, "Nels went off the deep end. It started with a phone call—that much I know for sure. But he wouldn't tell me what it was about."

Nelson was going to tell me.

At the edge of the patio was a metal trash can. I imagined the gonging sound the lid would make if raccoons dumped the thing. It was a fail-safe call to duty for a man enjoying a whiskey glow. But the wife worried me, even though she was stoned and insulated by ten thousand square feet of stucco and furniture.

Instead, I scouted the side of the house, where I found a Range Rover parked outside the five-car garage. When I saw the New York plates and a trailer hitch, I felt a hunter's rush . . . until I did the math. Even nonstop, the drive from the Hamptons would've taken more than twenty hours. It was a different Range Rover.

Will Chaser wasn't here, unless they'd boxed him into one of those private jets—it was possible.

I wanted to discuss that with Myles, too.

Using my ASP Triad light, I settled on a place to hide, then checked the interior of the vehicle. It was the big luxury Rover, with navigation, and a security system that was sufficiently sensitive. Headlights and horn blared an alert when I forced a burglar's shim through the door seal.

When Nelson came hurrying out, drink in hand, I waited until he was returning to the house before I surprised him.

I used duct tape, mouth and hands. Appropriate, I hoped. I got a good look at the Skull and Bones ring Myles wore, as I took care to do a professional job with the tape, thumbs out, fingers not locked.

The ring was similar to others I had seen.

Nelson Myles didn't double the family fortune or run a successful stable or get his jet rating by being easily bullied, so I didn't expect him to go all weepy once he recovered from the shock of being hijacked in his own vehicle. But I also didn't anticipate his detached reaction after I'd parked, headlights off, parking lights on, and torn the tape from his mouth.

He said, "Let's cut to the chase and save us both some time. How much do you want?"

Extortion, the first thing to come to his mind. He was drunk, I realized, in the first articulate stages of a scotch bender. I didn't reply.

After a moment, he said, "Talk to me. I have more money than patience. Come up with a figure. If it's reasonable, I won't get the police involved. It has nothing to do with keeping my word, or any of that noble bullshit. I have too much on my plate right now to deal with police. So your timing couldn't be better." He paused, suspicious. "Or maybe someone tipped you off. Was it a woman?"

That was unexpected. He was thinking of Roxanne—also a surprise. Well . . . he knew her better than I did.

I sat looking at him, letting my eyes adjust to the dash lights, hearing the vehicle's cooling engine and the wind in melaleuca trees outside my open window. The man was working his lips, trying to get rid of tape residue, but didn't offer eye contact. I was a hired hand, beneath his station—my impression.

He said, "With a phone call, I can have forty thousand cash within half an hour, anyplace you say. If you want more, we'll have to wait until the banks open. That's risky, in my opinion. More chance of something going wrong. But it's your decision."

After two minutes of silence, he added, "Personally, I'd take the cash."

After another minute, he said, "Think it over."

After another thirty seconds, he said, "While I'm waiting, open the door, I have to pee."

I was going through the fanny pack, letting him watch from the corner of his eye as I removed a lab towel, the ASP light, then surgical gloves, finally a pistol.

The pistol was a recent acquisition. It was a .32 caliber Seecamp, a precision-made firearm not much larger than a candy bar. I'm not a gun aficionado, so I had done a month of research and fired a lot of weapons before deciding that the Seecamp was the finest phantom pistol on the tactical market.

Close my fingers around the little gun, it disappeared in my hand . . . phantomlike.

I did that now, closing my hand, then opening it, letting Myles fixate on the gun. He was a shrewd guy. The workmanship, the articulate density of stainless steel, were more persuasive than any threat I could make. A weekend thug or a drug hustler would flash a big, showy knife, not a scalpel. Nelson Myles was looking at a scalpel.

"If you think you're going to intimidate me with that, you're mistaken," he said, sounding nervous for the first time.

I popped the magazine and thumbed out six high-impact rounds before replying, "Why would I care? It all pays the same."

I let him watch me snap on the surgical gloves before

toweling the steering wheel, then each bullet, clean. I reloaded two rounds into the magazine and killed the dome light. When I opened the door, he made a reflexive, mewing sound as he inhaled, then recovered by clearing his throat.

Now the man was looking at me. "Hey, what do you think you're doing? You get some kind of power rush playing the hard-ass? If you want to negotiate, let's negotiate. We can come to an agreement. There's another friend I can call. I can guarantee you sixty thousand—no, *seventy* thousand—cash. No questions, no risk. I've got my cell on me. Cut my hands loose and I'll have the money waiting."

I replied, "I've already been paid," then pushed the door closed. I walked to the passenger side, hoping to hell police didn't choose now to cruise this dirt utility road, with its detritus of garbage and beer cans, close enough to Interstate 75 to hear the wake of traffic. No combination of lies could explain kidnapping a *Who's Who* millionaire. My own distaste for what I was doing would probably have given me away before I tried. In psychological warfare, tactical cruelty is just another arrow in the quiver.

I told myself that if I was right, what I was doing might save the boy. If wrong, Myles was tough enough to recover, then deal with it along with his long list of other personal problems.

I opened the door, grabbed the man behind the neck and tumbled him onto the ground, hearing him say, "Why is this happening to me?," his voice shaky. He repeated it several times, a sign he was going into shock, then yelled, "Say something! You're driving me crazy with the damn silence. Tell me what I did wrong. Give me a name, for godsakes."

I cracked the slide, chambered a round, then stood over him holding the gun. Parallel to the barrel, I was gripping the ASP light, but it wasn't on. "They said you won't talk. So they hired me."

"Talk? About *what*? Jesus Christ, ask me anything, I'll tell you."

I said, "I don't get paid to listen," then extended my arm, pistol a foot from his head. A moment later, I clicked on the ASP light. In the laser-white scintillation, Myles's eyes widened as if about to be hit by a car. He jerked his head away. "You're blinding me!"

I said, "I'm doing you a favor," but then dimmed the little flashlight so only the gun barrel and a wedge of the man's face were illuminated.

He cracked an eye. "Jesus Christ, I thought you pulled the trigger. It was so damn bright."

"They say it's like that."

"Being shot, you mean?"

"Close your eyes, you tell me."

He opened his eyes wider. "But you don't have to kill me now. Seriously, I'll tell you anything. But I can't answer unless I know what they want."

"I'm doing what they want."

"*Please*. At least give me a minute to think this through. Just *one minute*, I'll make it right, I swear—and I'll pay you. An entirely different business deal. Isn't that fair? I'm wealthy. I can pay you a hundred times more than they paid you."

I said nothing. After a long silence, he began to cry. The man had pissed his pants, I realized. He pulled his knees to his chest, fetal position, then squinched his eyes closed until he remembered, then opened his eyes wide, as if looking up at me was his only defense. He began to moan, "I'm begging you, please . . . *please*."

I felt a mounting contempt for myself that was proportional to a rising respect for the man at my feet. He had handled the bullying better than most and taken longer to break than it might have taken to break me under like circumstances. Dying clueless, among garbage, on a dead-end road, is sufficient reason to beg.

But my assessment was premature.

My cell phone had a digital-recorder function. I pressed the RECORD icon and dropped the phone on the ground near the man's head. "So talk. They won't believe me unless I get it on tape."

Myles opened his eyes. "*Sure.* What do you want me to say? I'll tell you anything." His eagerness to survive, his clinging devotion to hope, summarized our species yet, oddly, also debased it.

"They want the truth."

"Of course! I'm a cooperative person—you'll see. But first, I think we'd be more comfortable if—"

I interrupted before he could mention freeing his hands, saying, "They're looking for a missing kid. That's all I know. You asked for a minute to figure it out. You've got it. So tell me: What's the question you're supposed to answer?"

"I don't know. I swear it, I have no idea."

I said, "Then we're wasting time," and leaned closer with the gun.

"Wait! Maybe I do know something." I watched his face. When I saw his eyes rotate upward, I knew he was assembling a lie. I touched the gun barrel to his ear. He winced but offered the lie anyway.

"There are always questions when somebody's kid disappears. No one's to blame, it's just the way it is. And let's be honest, young girls disappear all the time. What I don't understand is—"

"How do you know it was a girl?" I said.

When he replied, "Well . . . it's only natural to assume—" I pressed the pistol into his ear.

He lied again. "You told me it was a girl! 'They're looking for a missing girl,' isn't that what you said?"

I began counting off seconds—". . . thirty-nine . . . thirty-eight . . . thirty-seven . . . "—and used my foot to pin him to the ground when he tried to wiggle away.

"Stop . . . stop, I'll talk! But I need more information. Could be, the people who hired you got the wrong idea about the missing girl—boy—whatever. Did they say anything about finding something? Or about a type of radar—this was on a farm I own in New York where someone used ground-penetrating radar—"

I kept counting—". . . thirty-one . . . thirty . . . twenty-nine . . . "

"Stop that! I'm trying to cooperate. I think what happened is, someone in that area heard about an incident, but the radar was wrong. False readings are so damn common with that sort of technology. I don't expect you to understand. But if that's what this is about, I'm sure the people who paid you—"

"You made me lose count, Nels," I said. "So we start at ten. Ten seconds. What's the question? I won't understand the answer unless I hear the question." I was studying his eyes as I counted—". . . nine . . . eight . . . seven . . ."

"Please don't. One more minute . . . "

I leaned my weight on the pistol, and said, "One? *Zero.*"

"No! You win!" He stopped squirming and lay in the sand panting. "I'll tell you. The question would be . . . I guess what anyone would want to know is . . . " I watched his eyelids blink closed, then open. As he thought about it, his eyes rotated downward. "The question," he said, "might be about a girl named Annie Sylvester. Where is the girl buried? I guess that's the first question someone would ask."

"The answer?"

It was several seconds before he could make himself say it. "She's near the Hamptons, Long Island—that's in New York. Annie is buried in a pasture. A horse farm called Shelter Point."

25

Nine p.m. I battled the urge to rush as I drove the Range Rover south on U.S. 41 toward Venice Beach Road and Falcon Landing, governing my speed with cruise control and using the blinker to shift lanes. I didn't know where Will Chaser was. Didn't know if he was dead or alive, aboveground or below, and I was convinced Nelson Myles didn't know either. But I now felt sure the boy was somewhere in Florida, probably close to Sarasota. It would be unwise to invite the attention of a traffic cop.

Myles hadn't told me the whole truth—yet. But I believed him when he said he hadn't seen the boy and didn't know where he was. I did not believe him, however, when he said he didn't know that he'd been helping the kidnappers. Too many holes in his story, too many headlines on the television news.

Myles said he didn't know the men were Cuban until I told him. They had demanded money, transportation

and shelter, no questions tolerated. That included questions about a crate the two men had off-loaded early that
morning, after Myles landed them at Falcon Landing in
his eleven-passenger Citation executive jet.

"They said they were smuggling illegal weapons. I
didn't ask what. Rocket launchers or an atomic bomb—
my God, what do I care? My life was on the line. I didn't
even see their faces. That's the truth. I didn't want to see
their faces!"

My opinion of the man continued its descent.

During the three-hour flight, Myles claimed he hadn't
opened the cockpit door. The only time he was face-to-
face with the men was just before they boarded, but it
was too dark to see details.

"The man I'd been dealing with, the one in charge, he
was older. Late fifties, early sixties, and very neat. Silver
hair, a collar that looked starched. The man with him was
twice your size and three times as wide—freakish. He was
younger, judging from his voice, in his twenties or early
thirties. And he wore a weird knit cap. Pointed, sort of.
I got the impression he wasn't smart—retarded, even—
just from the way the boss man spoke to him. But
strong—my God, he handled that crate like it was filled
with newspaper instead of—"

"Guns?" I chided.

"That's what I thought," he said. "I swear."

All other contact was by cell phone, Myles told me, or
over the Internet.

"The man told me how much money he wanted,
where to be, what to do, and I did it. Anyone in my posi-

tion would've done the same. These people have been
bleeding me dry for more than two weeks and I'm sick
of it! They have no idea how far out of their class they
are, but they'll find out one day. You, too. That's not a
threat. It's a fact."

"Poor Nelson," I replied. "You've had it rough, all
because of a girl who wasn't in your class either."

The man's story meshed with the bank records I'd
found at Shelter House and also with what I already suspected: An interrogator from the Cuban Program had
discovered that a wealthy American was a murderer—a
story he'd probably heard from an American POW. Torture a man long enough and he will spill his own personal
secrets, then volunteer secrets about everyone he knows,
hoping to earn a break from pain.

Myles hadn't yet provided the connection—who was
the POW?—but I had a pretty good idea who it was. So
I was backing off, letting him get to it in his own way.

Because it was safer to talk in a moving car, I'd been
driving for about twenty minutes, making random turns,
but gradually traveling southwest toward the Gulf of
Mexico and Falcon Landing. Myles tried subtle manipulation to hurry me back to his gated community, implying
he might talk more freely when he was close to home. I
thought I understood his motivation. But I badly misread
his intent.

I stopped only once. Got out of the car, so Myles
couldn't eavesdrop, and telephoned Barbara, then Harrington, finally Tomlinson. No one answered, so I left the
same message: "The boy's in Florida, possibly Sarasota

County. Tell the FBI and anyone else who can help. I'm right this time, *trust* me."

My determination to find Will Chaser was now fueled by an additional source: my systematic humiliation of Nelson Myles. I'm no actor. A bully within me had surfaced, and the realization added yet another blemish to my already-tattered self-image. The only justification now was finding the boy.

The better I got to know my victim, however, the easier it was to rationalize. Myles possessed a mountainous ego that didn't leave room for a conscience, or a heart, or people of value in his tiny, privileged world.

Now it was 9:15 p.m. Traffic was busy on Palmetto Road, as I turned south and crossed Bee Ridge. I was listening to Myles once again attempt to justify murdering a thirteen-year-old girl the summer of his senior year at Yale.

"She was a tease—you can ask anyone who knew Annie. Thirteen going on twenty-one, you've met the type. I was just a kid myself. Drunk, and I'd smoked grass, and it was the first time I'd ever snorted coke. I was celebrating because I'd been accepted into a very elite fraternity. Next morning, I couldn't remember anything. Don't expect me to remember every detail now."

"Don't expect me not to expect," I said.

"It's a manner of speech. I'm trying to explain how it happened. Little bits and pieces flash back, but never in order, so I've got to stitch it together even for me to understand. It was night, and I was on the beach alone. I'd been at a party and got too drunk, but I was smart enough to leave. The party was getting dangerous: a bunch of locals with an attitude had showed up. So I took a bucket of balls and a golf club down to the beach to hit a few while I sobered up.

"A driver?" I said.

He thought for a moment. "No, an iron. A seven iron."

"You're sure?"

"Yes."

I was picturing the golf bag I'd seen in Norvin Tomlinson's room, as he told me, "Next thing I remember, Annie was standing in front of me. This was in June, a warm night. She'd just gotten out of the water. She was wearing a white T-shirt, no bra, and bikini shorts. How would you react?"

I didn't answer. There was a stoplight ahead and I wanted to time it right. I'd used the master switch to lock all the doors but wasn't certain there was an override on the passenger side. If I slowed to a stop, he might try to jump.

"Women never do that sort of thing accidentally," he said. "I don't care if they're thirteen or thirty." The man buried has face in his hands and made a groaning sound. "My God . . . there ought to be a law."

I said, "There *is*," not hiding my contempt.

"But the girl started it! She wanted me to make a pass at her. When I finally did, though, she laughed and ran, so I threw the goddamn club . . . like a joke, you know, to scare her. It's what kids that age do. Jesus!"

"Twenty-one years old," I said, "and still a boy."

He missed the sarcasm. "*Exactly.* I didn't mean to hurt her. But she turned her head and the club hit her in the eye. I got scared. Even she didn't realize how bad it was. There was a lot of blood and I panicked. Anyone would've freaked out in that situation. Plus, I had my family's reputation to protect. Father was about to be named ambassador to—"

I said, "Nelson!" He was on a talking jag and didn't hear me. "Myles!"

When he was listening, I said, "What's par for killing a girl? How many strokes? After the second time you hit her, you claim she called you a name. What did she do to deserve it the third time? The fourth?"

"You don't understand how it was."

I said, "You're goddamn right I don't understand."

Myles looked out the window and rubbed his swollen ear. "I'm getting sick of your questions."

"Try a dose of truth. It might help."

"I've told you everything I remember. It was a long time ago. The boy who was on the beach that night doesn't even exist. I'm not responsible, *he* was responsible. I'm a different person now."

I said, "Prove it. The girl's dead, but maybe you can help me save the boy. Find him alive, it'll earn you points with the jury."

"How many times do I have to tell you? I don't know anything about the kid. I told you about Annie. Why wouldn't I tell you where the boy is?"

"Maybe you know more than you think. The Cuban could've said something that meant nothing to you but might make sense to me."

"Really? You're that much smarter? I find that unlikely. Know what I think?" I waited. "I think you know more than you're admitting. Why are you so sure the man is Cuban? You expect me to talk but don't share anything."

I replied patiently, "Tell me the story again. Start at the beginning—every detail."

He groaned. "Just take me home. I feel like I'm going to vomit. And I need a shower. I've never felt so filthy in my life. Take me back to Falcon Landing, maybe I'll feel better. We can talk there."

It was a typical reaction for an assault victim. It was also a symptom. The rich man's brain was reassembling his self-image, piece by piece, as he transitioned through predictable stages. He had been apologetic, then ingratiating. Pride, indignation and anger would reboot next. Myles would become increasingly contentious or closemouthed. I had to short-circuit that process. There was more I wanted to know.

I shifted lanes, looking for a place to turn around, then flicked the turn signal.

"What are you doing?"

I said, "Taking you back."

"Not to that goddamn dirt road!"

"I should've done what they hired me to do."

Myles slapped the dash, then leaned his head on his forearms. "Jesus Christ! Haven't I been through enough?

It would be easier if you asked questions. Instead, you just sit there hardly saying a word. You do it on purpose. You know it drives me crazy."

I said, "When you stack the lies high enough, they'll implode. That's when I ask questions."

"Go to hell," he said, but got serious when he realized I was still slowing to turn.

"*Jesus!* Okay, I'll tell the story again. But who the hell do you think you are, treating me this way? Do you have any idea who I am?"

I said, "Let me guess: You're rich and you know a lot of powerful people."

"An understatement. You have no idea."

"Guys like you," I said, baiting him, "you're all the same. You lie to feel important. Next, you'll start bragging about all the sports stars and famous politicians you know. Buddies from some yacht club or some rich-kid fraternity who can bury me if you just say the word." My tone told him *Bullshit,* but I didn't hit it too hard. I wanted him to talk about Skull and Bones.

Myles said, "If I told you how many senators and presidents that're in my fraternity, you wouldn't believe me."

I replied, "Then don't bother."

He was shaking his head, letting me know how dense I was. "My beach house where you jumped me? Three neighbors are from the same fraternity. One's a federal judge, one's on the board of the International Bank and the other's a leading member of Congress. That's who you're dealing with. Now do you understand?"

I asked, "A congressman? What's the name?'"

His reply was a snorting noise of refusal.

"Fraternity boys," I said, "secret handshakes and drinking songs. Big deal. Nels, *you're* the guy who's going to start at the beginning of the story and not stop until you get to the end."

He made a blowing sound of frustration, his temper rallying, but he did what I told him to do. This time, he added a few key details.

Two weeks before, Myles had received the first of several anonymous phone calls. Adult male, Spanish accent: the Cuban interrogator. The Cuban claimed he knew what had happened to Annie Sylvester. Then he proved it by providing details that couldn't have been gathered from an old police report.

The Cuban demanded that Myles send him a quarter million dollars U.S., converted into euros, to a Havana address through DSL, an international carrier. He wanted the money sent in three separate packages to increase the odds of at least one package arriving. If Myles didn't cooperate, the Cuban told him, he would send a letter telling police exactly where to find the girl's body.

"He told me I would never hear from him again if I paid," Myles said in a monotone to let me know how tiresome this was. "But I'm not stupid. I've been through it before and I knew he'd want more. But I assumed it would be money, not helping him commit a felony."

We were on East Venice Road, a quiet four-lane lined with sable palms. Manatee Civic Center and Desoto Square Mall were to the north, the entrance to Falcon Landing only a few miles away.

"You're almost home," I told him. "Keep talking."

Five days ago, Myles continued, on January twentieth—two days before the kidnapping—the Cuban telephoned again. This time, it was from a pay phone in the United States, a 305 area code—Miami. Myles said he'd checked.

The Cuban said that he and a couple of friends would be arriving on Long Island—at Shelter Point Stables—in two days. They had purchased a crate of illegal weapons and had found a buyer, but the timing had to be right. Because there was a chance the boat they were meeting might not show, the Cuban told Myles he wanted a pit dug where he could cache the weapons until later. He also told him to have his plane fueled and ready in case they needed to fly out fast.

The pit the Cuban ordered dug was to be six by eight feet and six feet deep—Will Chaser's grave. When Myles told him it would draw less attention if the pit was big enough for a horse, the man said that would be okay.

"By then," Myles said, "I think he was already worried about how they were going to get out of the country. It was just a feeling I had. His English wasn't great, but he mentioned me being a pilot often enough to make me suspicious. But I didn't want to do anything to piss him off, so I humored him. You know, so he would trust me. Digging the hole he wanted was no problem.

"We had an old gelding that had to be put down, so I told my stable manager to schedule a backhoe. I told him to have our contractor dig two holes on the far side of the pasture."

It was the first time Myles had mentioned the backhoe or his manager, or that one of the Cubans was worried about how they were getting out of the U.S. I had not asked for the same reason I hadn't asked who'd shot the expensive stallion. Questions can give more information than they provide.

"You told him the holes were for graves," I said.

"Yes," Myles said, drumming his fingers on the dash. "It's what we do when animals die: bury them. But the other hole was for the guns—or whatever it was he was bringing. The Cuban said it's what they did in the Middle East to hide weapons, bury them. Which made sense to me. It's on TV all the time."

"One old horse, two graves. Did your manager ask why?"

Myles said, "When I give an order, I don't wait for questions. Oh . . . there's something else: The Cuban said they would arrive at the stable late Thursday. He didn't want anyone else on the property. So I told my manager to go into town Thursday night and get drunk. But I didn't tell him or anyone else I was returning to the Hamptons."

I said, "You ordered him to get drunk."

"No, but I knew he would. I spent the previous two nights in Asheville—our family keeps a place there—and landed at the Hamptons jetport around ten p.m., expecting to meet the Spanish-speaking guys at my farm. But the head man called and said something had happened to screw up their plans. He told me I should wait at the landing strip. So I did."

I had to ask: "On the plane?"

He made a gesture of indifference. "Why not? I own it, along with a couple of pilot associates. No one there but a security cop at the gate."

I didn't believe him. I thought it was more likely that Myles had either returned to his farm and met with the Cubans or he'd rendezvoused with Roxanne at some secret meeting place, the Tomlinson estate possibly.

"Then what happened?"

"Around eleven Friday morning, my manager called me on the cell and told me someone had broken into one of the stables and shot our best stallion. I hadn't heard from the Cubans, so I thought, shit, they did it. But the Cuban called about an hour later and said no way, he had nothing to do with it. The police, he said, were crawling all over the place. Why would they cause trouble, give the police a reason to search, when they were sitting there with a crateful of illegal weapons? He said they'd found a good place to hide and that we would leave as soon as it was safe."

As the man talked, I was making mental notes, saving my questions until later. "Keep going," I said.

"I expected the police to take a couple of hours at most. But I found out later that a couple of low-rung bureaucrats had somehow managed to get a signed search warrant, nothing I could do. They brought the thing I mentioned earlier, the ground-penetrating radar. My idiot manager had gone back to town and was drunk again."

I didn't want him to see how pleased I was. I had screwed up their plans, maybe bought the boy more time.

Myles said he didn't hear from the Cubans until about after midnight. During that phone conversation, the head man said he wanted Myles to fly them to a safe place outside the U.S., preferably near Havana. It was the first he'd mentioned it.

"I told them I couldn't. I said my plane didn't have that kind of range, which wasn't true. But the main problem was that a private plane can't leave the country, even to Canada, without filing the proper flight plan. I tried to explain to him that we would be tracked. Leave the country and no matter where we go, someone would be waiting when we landed. I didn't think it would come as such a surprise, but the guy was furious. He acted like he'd been set up in some way and tried to blame me."

I said, "Most kidnappers aren't fussy about FAA regulations."

"No, but they worry about who meets them when they get off the plane. There aren't many truly private jetports in the country—that's why I bought at Falcon Landing. There's nothing like it in Canada, or Cuba either, judging from the man's reaction. I realized he hadn't been lying about expecting a boat. I don't know how he was supposed to make contact, but someone stood up him and his partner—as of this morning anyway."

Myles told me that when the Cuban finally decided he was telling the truth, he started asking questions. Did Myles know anyone in Florida who owned a big boat? Or an amphibious plane? And what about an airstrip in the Bahamas?

"I told him I would check my aviation charts," Myles said, "but I was lying: The Lear team took my plane to Miami this afternoon, in fact, for servicing. So then they focused on finding a boat.

"Somehow, the man already knew I keep a sixty-eight-foot Tiara at the marina, but he decided the boat was too big. They didn't have a lot of experience on the water—that's my impression. My stable manager, though—sometimes he uses one of our guest cottages—my manager owns a thirty-four-foot cabin cruiser and docks it next to my boat, which is embarrassing—a junker, you know?

"But all I wanted to do was get rid of those two, so I told them the cabin cruiser was great, it had huge range and where to find the keys. That was this morning, around six a.m., still dark. The Cubans were on the tarmac the last time I saw them. I just walked away."

I said, "Did you tell them where to find the keys to your boat?"

"I never tell anyone where to find the keys to my boat."

"Then you're sure they took the smaller boat?"

"Why should I care?" Myles snapped. "I thought I was done with the whole business . . . until you came along."

In my mind, I was comparing this version of the story with earlier versions, as Myles said, "My manager lost more than his damn ugly little boat. He doesn't realize it, but he's about to be fired."

I was picturing the Cubans aboard some junk cruiser, browsing through local charts, seeing hundreds of islands, and Havana Harbor two hundred miles to the south. "You sound heartbroken," I replied.

"No, I'll enjoy it. The man sees himself as some kind of blue-collar hero. When he really is a know-it-all jerk." Myles gave it a few beats, then decided to test my boundaries. "You and my stable manager have a lot in common. You'd probably hit it off."

I replied, "Maybe I'll come visit one day."

"Sure, I can see it—two macho guys bragging about their scars, having fun talking about guns. Stop for a few beers after work, then go bowling on Sundays. Real buddies, I can almost guarantee it." From the corner of my eye, I could see the man staring at me.

"You have something against people who work for a living?"

"See? That's exactly the sort of thing he would say. No, I don't. But men like you have something against men like me, men who are successful, who make a difference in the world. That's how you and my manager are similar. I can understand how galling that must be because there's really nothing you can do to improve your-selves. It's not your fault. Genetics—'paralyzing the hope of reform,' as Bryan put it. Do you know who I'm talking about?"

I said, "No," thinking, *William Jennings Bryan, Scopes trial.*

Myles, the Ivy Leaguer, said, "*High heritability:* Do you have any idea what that means? It has to do with ge-netics. Human IQs. It applies to animal husbandry, too."

"No kidding?"

"No kidding." He smiled. "I'm not criticizing, mind you. It's an observation. We don't choose our parents or our social class. People like you, and the people who work for me, you're all a type. There are a lot of mutts out there and not many purebreds."

I was picturing Roxanne Sofvia, her expression of hurt and surprise, as he added, "Nothing wrong with either one. Sort of like horses: Some are champions, others pull plows. I think you know where you fit in." Now the man's ego was rallying. "No offense," he said.

I replied, "Just being in the same car with you, Nels, is offensive enough."

The man had a sly, bitter way of laughing as he spoke. "Funny! What a big night it must be for you, having power over someone like me. For a short time anyway."

I said, "I think of it as being immunized against a personality disorder: *assholishness.*"

"Is that a word?"

"We use it at the bowling alley all the time. Like get-ting a shot for something contagious. Like the flu . . . " I gave it a few beats. "Or herpes."

The bully inside me enjoyed the man's sour silence.

26

At 8:30 a.m., Saturday, January twenty-fifth, Farfel used his new cell phone to snap a photo of Will Chaser staring up from his coffin, then lobbed a handful of sand at the boy's face before walking to confer with Hump, who was leaning on a shovel waiting.

The sand was a farewell gesture of contempt and punishment for the boy's recent behavior.

When Hump had pried the lid off the box, after so many hours in darkness the boy had sat up and started bawling. He had stupidly misread the photographic interlude, believing the fresh sunlight signaled freedom instead of what it actually foreshadowed: William Chaser's last living minutes on the face of the earth.

The boy had cried so hard that he started coughing, another silly mistake because his mouth was taped. Then he'd begun choking, coughing and choking with such violence that his eyes bulged.

Panicking, Hump had ripped the tape from the kid's

mouth and the kid instantly began begging for forgiveness and thanking Farfel for his life, crying through the entire scene.

Disgusting. How many times had broken men asked Farfel for forgiveness? It was a variation of the Stockholm syndrome. As a researcher, Farfel understood that all men have a breaking point. Begging was part of a predictable chain of behavior. But the boy's perverse gratitude for being hurt and humiliated was unaccountable, a dramatic device used to evoke sympathy.

The Cuban had experienced it too many times.

"Shut up!" Farfel had yelled in English. "You're a disgrace. Show some self-respect."

When the boy continued bawling and blabbering for forgiveness, the Cuban had reached to slap him—something Farfel now had to admit was a rare mistake on his part.

Instantly, the insane young Indian had ceased crying, swung his jaws like a snake, and bit a chunk out of Farfel's hand the size of a quarter.

Maricon! Basura!

In reply, the child's Spanish improved when he used profanity to call Farfel sick names and threatened to kill him in sick ways until Hump finally silenced the boy with a fresh roll of duct tape.

Before Farfel took two steps, he turned and used the hand that wasn't bleeding to toss another clod of sand at the boy and the boy thrust his face forward as if to catch it. Never in the man's life had he seen such wild hatred, such black, crazed eyes.

Insane, yes, but at least interesting.

To Hump, Farfel said, "While I transmit the photo, nail the lid shut and bury the brat. After all the trouble he's caused us? Don't kill him. I want him to have some time with the worms before he dies."

Touching the side of his head gingerly, Hump agreed, saying, "I'm worried I'm gonna lose my ear. You should make a poultice for your hand. The Devil Child's teeth contain a poison, I believe."

Farfel said, "Quit complaining and listen! Fill the hole, then use your weight to stomp around on the sand. Pack it smooth. That's important. We don't want anyone to spot it from the air."

"Pack the sand smooth," Hump repeated, making a mental list.

"After that, connect the battery to the fan and aim it so it's blowing toward the pipe. I don't care how close you put it, or even if the damn thing works, but it's part of the agreement. We should be in Havana by sunset, but if something else goes wrong"—Farfel's expression warned *It better not!*—"it would look bad in court if there was no fan as we promised."

"Connect the fan," Hump repeated, "but after I fill in the hole first?"

"*Yes.* Is that *so* complicated?"

Hump had something on his mind, Farfel could tell by the giant's twitching. He was working up the nerve to say, "My ears are still making a terrible *boom-boom* sound because of the rock the boy attacked me with. Is it possible I have a concussion? Something serious damaged inside my brain?"

Now Farfel's expression read *No . . . even if I said it, he wouldn't get it.*

"Dr. Navárro," Hump continued, "just burying the brat doesn't seem enough. While the coffin lid is off, couldn't I first punish him in some small way by—"

"No! Hurry up and do what I told you. I want to be in the boat, on our way to Cuba, before the FBI starts analyzing the photo."

Farfel walked away, concentrating on his new cell phone, a BlackBerry that could send photos over the Internet. He'd bought it on the black market in Havana using some of the money Nelson Myles, the rich child killer, had provided.

Farfel had first learned of Myles from an American soldier at Hoa Lo Prison, downtown Hanoi. The POW's name was Billy Sofvia, who said he had worked for Myles and helped him bury a girl the rich man had murdered.

The soldier Billy Sofvia had a higher pain tolerance than most Americans—that was the objective of the Cuban Program: chart the pain thresholds of different racial and social groups. But Farfel had finally broken Sofvia using a technique of his own invention. Hump's late father, Angel Valencia Yanquez, an intelligent man, had also contributed, but it was René Navárro's concept.

The method employed a low-voltage wire that was inserted up the urethra into the bladder, harmless in terms of the urinary tract and reproductive function but devastating psychologically. Inserting a low-voltage wire through the corner of a man's eye into his frontal lobe did far more actual damage but wasn't nearly as effective, as data had proven.

Fear, Farfel had learned early in his career, was a far more effective weapon than guns or bombs.

Sofvia had confessed to every sin he had committed and then moved on to the sins of people he knew in the U.S.

Farfel had kept careful notes during his years in Vietnam. He had continued keeping notes as an interrogator-for-hire in Panama and the Middle East. He had cataloged the sins of many prisoners but was particularly interested in the sins of wealthy employers the prisoners knew back home. Farfel had filed that information away, hoping it would be valuable when the politics of Cuba changed.

It had been a wise thing to do.

Nelson Myles was so incredibly wealthy that Farfel had decided to allow him to live. The man might be useful later if Farfel ever made it back to Cuba. But so much had gone wrong that he was beginning to have doubts.

It had seemed so easy in the beginning. As a scientist, he was now surprised by his own naïveté. But he was even more surprised by their run of bad luck.

While living as a peasant in Havana, working as a common barber, Farfel had read about the famous Hamptons. He had often dreamed of visiting the place.

Farfel had imagined himself at expensive restaurants, chatting with famous artists or in bed with the daughter or wife of his eager host. Yet even though Myles had cooperated—with the exception of offering his wife—

Farfel now felt a welling dread when he thought of the Hamptons, all because of the insane boy.

America, with its wealth, was no longer a dream. It had become a nightmare.

That will change soon. Be patient, be precise. Listen to the intellect, not the emotions.

Not easy to do when in the company of a moron. Hump, even though born from the seed of his late friend Angel Yanquez, was just another experiment. And that experiment had gone terribly wrong, as even Angel had conceded on his deathbed.

Farfel had now fulfilled his promise to Yanquez, so never again after this. All Farfel wanted to do was return safely to Cuba, which, unfortunately, required that he trust Hump to drive the boat while he navigated.

It's only two hundred miles. Two hundred miles is nothing! The Gulf of Mexico is only a few kilometers from here.

Here was an island, a place identified as Tamarindo on the GPS in the boat that Myles had made available to them. Farfel had wrestled with the idea of simply killing the boy, using a razor on him, or an open flame perhaps, which might have provided interesting notes. But their run of bad luck worried the Cuban.

Instead of imagining expensive restaurants and sleeping with the daughters of his hosts, he was now envisioning an American courtroom with former POWs who would never fully appreciate the kindness Farfel had demonstrated by not killing them.

Fulfilling the obligations of the ransom note, the Cuban had decided, was the wisest course, although now, looking at his bloody hand, he was having doubts about that, too.

Farfel crossed the beach, hearing the sound of sand being shoveled. The sand made a water-saturated *thump* as it landed on the boy's coffin. Finally, Hump was following orders and filling the hole.

Near the wooden dock, bayside, was a cabin hidden by palms and casuarina pines. Wind in the casuarinas imitated the wash of waves on a distant beach, as Farfel approached a path outlined with whelk shells. The shells were bone white on this breezy, blue tropical day.

It hadn't been easy to break into the cabin. It was made of concrete block, and Myles's construction people had installed a difficult lock system using steel rebar on every door and window. Hump, though, was so freakishly strong that he'd had no trouble ripping off one of the window shutters.

That by-product of Angel Valencia Yanquez's experiment, his spawn's extraordinary strength, had been the only part of the experiment that had gone right.

Farfel entered the cabin, taking comfort in the coolness of the open room. He washed his damaged hand in a bucket and soaked it in Betadine, which he found on a shelf. Then he lay down to rest on one of the bunks.

Farfel was exhausted. His ankle hurt, his hand throbbed and he had been suffering back spasms ever since he'd flinched, dodging the syringe the boy had thrown, and then had to scramble to avoid being crushed by the horse.

Shooting that elephant of a horse was the highlight of this miserable trip.

As Farfel lay resting, his eyes moved around the room. He'd taken a careful look earlier, but the decorations were still beyond his understanding. He was a scientist yet hadn't settled on an explanation for the weird symbols on the walls, on the mantelpiece—everywhere he looked.

There were several prints of an all-seeing eye encased in a pyramid, as on the back of an American dollar bill. There was a pirate flag in one corner, a flag with a large yellow Υ in another.

Pirate banners, showing death's-heads of various designs, marked the entrance to the little kitchen area, where there was a propane stove and oil lanterns. There were skull-and-crossbones symbols on the mantelpiece and a row of Indian artifacts: flint arrowheads, a withered quiver of arrows, a flint knife, an unstrung bow and more than a dozen figurines—cast in plaster, carved from stone—of a dour, flat-faced Indian.

Nelson Myles may be wealthy, but he has bourgeois taste. Or . . . perhaps this is a clubhouse used by children.

Because there was a canoe, two kayaks and a basketball hoop outside, that seemed plausible until Farfel considered several paddles, not for boats but the sort college boys used to spank with. The paddles were covered with more cryptic symbols. There was also a row of beer mugs engraved with such things as MAGOG, SUPERMAN, GOG.

American children don't use paddles or drink beer.

In a glass-sided box, near the fireplace, were bones, which most people couldn't identify but Farfel could. He'd seen them earlier so didn't bother to look. There were human femurs, a partial set of human ribs, carpal remnants and finger segments from a human hand. There were also two ancient-looking skulls.

A section of the parietal bone was missing from one of the skulls. Teeth were missing from the lower mandibles of both.

Myles is a serial killer—that explains it. The murdered girl was his first, and he enjoyed it. Only a ghoul would use bones as decorations.

Or a research scientist, Farfel reminded himself.

The Cuban lay back on the cot and closed his eyes. They would be in the boat soon headed for Havana. He hoped to cross the two hundred miles in less than twelve hours but feared it might take longer.

No matter. The deadline was less than twenty-four hours away. By tomorrow morning, they would surely be close enough to watch the American plane drop the crates of personal possessions that had been stolen from the Bearded One.

Farfel wanted to personally confirm that all records of the Cuban Program had been destroyed—his future depended on it. It also depended on the millions Castro was rumored to have in Spanish treasure.

Once the ransom had been delivered, he would then turn his attention to finding the American who had lied to them, used them, who had demanded half of the money Nelson Myles had sent and who now had abandoned them to rot in an American prison by not sending a boat as he had promised.

Tenth Man, his code name, although in English it was Tinman.

More than anything else, Farfel wanted to confront Tinman. He would use his intellect to find the poorly coiffured American, Hump's strength to subdue him and then . . .

"The job is done, Dr. Navárro." Hump was standing at the open door. His face was grimy, but he was smiling. "Everything you said, I have done. Would you like to inspect?"

Farfel said, "Get on the boat, we're leaving." But as he crossed the room, he stopped and peered into the glass-sided case next to the fireplace. Something was missing.

"Did you take anything from here? I told you not to steal anything, unless it was valuable."

The huge man shook his head quickly. "Nothing. I swear. Look at the grave, how smooth I made it." He smiled, a simpleton who was lying but genuinely proud of his work.

Fifteen minutes later, Hump was standing at the helm of the cabin cruiser, throttle open, and still smiling when he passed to the right of a green navigational marker instead of passing to the left.

The boat was doing twenty-five knots when it hit an oyster bar, the impact so violent that Farfel was catapulted over the railing into water that was less than a foot deep. He had been standing on the forward deck, holding a navigational chart in one hand and waving wildly with the other, yelling to Hump, "Stop . . . stop . . . stop!"

Farfel recovered his glasses and the chart before wading back to the boat. His back was spasming again, his forearms were bloodied by the oysters, but he was still coherent enough to pause and consider the directional flow of the water. The water was moving southwest, toward the Gulf of Mexico.

Next, Farfel looked at the cabin cruiser. It sat atop the oyster bar like a trophy, even its keel showing.

It would be hours, he realized, before they could leave. They would have to wait until the tide turned and was nearly high again. Eight hours at least.

"Stay away from me," Farfel said softly when Hump vaulted off the boat to help. "Stay away."

27

Someone double-crossed the Cuban interrogator. They didn't send a boat. Who?

I was thinking about it as I sat behind the wheel of Nelson Myles's Range Rover, the smell of leather and wood mixing with the unmistakable odor of the man's soiled slacks. Myles and I were only two blocks from the entrance to Falcon Landing. I could see a guard standing beneath a lamppost on a street column-lined with palms.

I asked Myles, "Do your security people carry weapons?"

"If they do, I doubt if they're loaded," he said. "They won't bother us, don't worry. Park by the harbor, if you want." Once again, he was trying to manipulate me into reentering the grounds.

I was tempted. I wanted to check the marina and see if the Cubans had taken the cabin cruiser. If the boat was accurately described, they probably hadn't made it to Key

West yet, not without nosing into the Ten Thousand Islands to refuel. By deadline time, eight tomorrow morning, it was possible they could be in international waters. But, just as likely, they had run aground while leaving Sarasota Bay: Venice Inlet and Snake Island were tricky.

I imagined the Cubans, frustrated and pissed off, sitting high and dry on some bar. Would that be good for the boy or bad?

Could be good, I decided. If they were trapped in U.S. waters, they might keep Will alive as a bargaining chip.

I slowed, watching the guard watch us, then I turned west toward the beach, where I'd parked the rental car. "Now where are we going?" Myles asked.

I said, "To a quiet place. You wanted me to ask questions? It's time."

"I changed my mind. There's nothing I can add. Stop here, let me out, you can have the car. I won't call police, I promise."

"Call them. They can listen to your confession."

"I didn't confess to anything. What I remember is you sticking a gun in my face and . . . and, well, why review the obvious? I leave that sort of business to my attorneys. Or . . . I'll ask my fraternity brother . . . the federal judge." He put his hand on the door. "Let me out."

I stepped on the gas. "Questions first. Who else knew you murdered the girl?"

"I didn't murder her," he said patiently. "It was an accident."

I gave it a moment before saying, "Who knew, besides Norvin Tomlinson . . . and Billy Sofvia?"

It was the first I'd mentioned their names, and the impact made Myles sit up straighter. He tried to recover, saying, "The details are fuzzy, I keep telling you. I might have told someone—I was still drunk and high most of the next day. You can't expect me to remember every little thing. It was a long time ago."

The details were always fuzzy when Myles got to this part of the story. He was lying again.

"How's your memory when it comes to last night? Who shot your prize horse? Cazzio . . . Alacazam . . . whatever you called him. I heard his stud fee was a couple hundred thousand. No matter how rich you are, that still has to hurt."

The man's surprise was palpable. It filled the car with an expanding, pressurized silence, until he said, "Who *are* you?"

I said, "You haven't told me everything, Nels. But you will. You left someone out of your story. He's been helping the Cubans, and you know it."

"You've been *lying* to me."

"And I feel just terrible about it. Trust is so important in a relationship. Answer the question."

"Bullshit. Why should I?"

I said, "You really want me to give you a reason? Someone had to be at your farm to meet the Cubans. Fred Gardiner was drunk and you stayed at the landing strip. That's what you said. Who helped you?"

"*Fred?* How do you know my manager's name? You tricked me! I'm not saying another word."

I kept talking. "I think the person who helped you last

night helped you bury Annie Sylvester fifteen years ago. Or at least provided you with some kind of alibi."

"Just like Fred. What did I tell you?" Myles said. "Why bother with questions if you think you have all the answers?"

I said, "I have a few. Billy Sofvia worked for your family in those days, so it makes sense he helped dig the grave. But he's dead. Died a POW."

The man tried to hide his surprise but was still sitting up straight, listening.

I continued, "Billy knew you killed the girl. So you either had him fired or somehow steered him into the military. You wanted him as far from the Hamptons as possible. That means at least two people knew you killed Annie."

His expression said *Huh?*

"Your parents fired the guy, so one of them either suspected or was sure of it."

"They're dead. Leave them out of this."

"Then there's at least one person still alive who knows—not counting me."

He raised his voice. "Who have you been talking to?"

"Aside from the boys down at the bowling alley, you mean? Skull and Bones doesn't come up that often."

He turned to face me. "What does my fraternity have to do with . . . How do you know about—" Myles stopped himself because he was flustered, getting mad as he tried to put it together. "Look," he said, "enough of your games. What's going on here? One minute, you pretend to be a professional killer. Now you're talking about things that no one can . . . that no one is—"

"Supposed to know?" I offered. "Maybe it would be easier if you answered in code. *Eight* for *yes, seven* for *no.* Did I get it right . . . Magog?"

"*Magog?* My God!" He took a long, slow breath. "That's enough. There's no possible way for you to know that name unless you spoke to—"

I said, "There's always a way. I know a lot about you, Myles. Almost every question I ask, I already know the answer. Lie to me and I'll take you back to that road."

"You sonuvabitch," he said. "You *have* been setting me up!"

"*Eight* for *yes,*" I replied. "Now it's your turn. Besides Billy Sofvia, who knew you killed the girl? Norvin Tomlinson? Or maybe you snuck off to your island hideaway and confessed to all of your fraternity pals."

His voice dropped a notch. "Who told you about the island? There can't be more than two dozen people who know about Tamarindo. Tell me the man's name and I'll tell you the truth. Deal?"

I'd been referring to Deer Island off Maine, not a tropical island. Tamarinds are an equatorial fruit. But I covered my surprise by saying, "How do you know it was a man? It could have been one of your fraternity sisters. Women Bonesmen: Ever think you'd see the day?"

Myles said, "You're wrong about that. There are no women, not in our fraternity. *Ever,*" his tone so bitter that I realized I had stumbled on something important. I let him talk.

He said, "Who sent you? What are you, an attorney?

A private investigator? You're not really a hit man. This whole thing has been an act." His voice was getting louder. "Goddamn it, pull over!"

On the road ahead, just before the turnoff to the beach, was a maintenance shed and parking area screened from the road by trees. I'd seen it while jogging to the Falcon Landing entrance. I swung into the parking area and switched off the lights, listening to Myles rant, "Did one of those bitches send you?"

I replied, "Your fraternity sisters would object to the generalization."

"Those self-righteous, manipulative bitches, that's who's behind this. Are they trying to get even because of my lawsuit? Or because someone took what they think belonged to them?"

I said, "You robbed your own fraternity house?"

"You can't steal what you already own . . . And I'm not saying another word until you answer me. And don't try your tough-guy lines again. I won't fall for it. You're not a killer. You're a goddamn actor!"

When I put the Range Rover in park, he reached for the keys. I pushed his arm away. When he tried it again, I laced my arm around his elbow, applied enough pressure to slam him back into his seat. I brought out the little Seecamp. When he turned to protest, I jammed the gun barrel under his chin and lifted. I continued lifting until the man was half standing, head against the car's roof. He had to grab the sun visor for balance.

I said, "Somehow, Magog, you got the wrong impression about me."

He said, "You're hurting me," but was thinking about it, reassessing, not yet convinced.

When he made an effort to pull away, I wedged a thumb under his jaw and my two middle fingers into the socket beneath his left eye and shook him. My grip was as solid as if his skull were a bowling ball. Ironic. He couldn't pry my fingers loose but kept trying until I banged the back of his head against the window.

"Know what I found out tonight?" I whispered. "I'm no actor. You need to pay attention, Mr. Myles." Slowly, slowly, I removed my hand from his face, adding, "I've killed better men than you."

Myles made the reflexive, mewing sound again as he inhaled. Maybe it was the way I said it or maybe because it was true, but the man became as submissive as he'd been on the dirt road.

"I got carried away," he said. "I'm . . . sorry. But prying into my personal business, especially fraternity business, I lose my temper."

"A club for college boys. Do fraternities have a rule against growing up?"

"You could never understand. Even new members don't understand. It's not really a fraternity. It's a noble society, hundreds of years old, left to a very few of us in trust. I've had a lot of shitty things happen in my life. But being a Bonesman is the one good thing no one can ever take away from me."

"Must have been tough when the court ruled in favor of admitting women."

"That doesn't mean it happened," Myles replied, the softness going out of him.

"Well . . . I don't give a damn about Skull and Bones. That's not why I'm here," I told him. "I'm after the boy." I was holding the cell phone. "This is how it works. You have five minutes. I ask a question, you answer. Hesitate or lie to me, I slam your head into the window." I touched the record icon and placed the phone on the dash. "*Talk.*"

I wanted to know about Tamarindo. How far was it? How private? Had he told the Cubans about the place?

When he said, "I might have," I felt the same weird transference as when I had cupped the little chunk of granite in my hand.

The island was south of Myakka Inlet, he told me, only two miles from the man's beachfront property at Falcon Landing. That put it about forty miles north-northeast of Sanibel, close enough that I was suspicious. I'd never heard of the place. But then he explained, "That's what we've always called it. On maps, it either doesn't have a name or it's called something else. It's about ten miles north of Hog Island."

I had boated past Hog Island, but it took a few seconds to make a more important connection. Hog Island was where police had trapped and arrested Barbara Mackle's kidnapper, Gary Krist. My intuitive senses, never strong, were suddenly and subtly displacing reason. But I continued asking questions to assemble proof.

Myles told me his family had owned the island since

the 1920s. It was small, about fifteen acres, mangrove bushes on the eastern rim, coconut palms, and a section of beach that faced Charlotte Harbor. His grandfather had built a private fishing camp that had become a retreat for three generations of Myles men. Myles had used the island as an occasional meeting place for his Skull and Bones friends.

I listened closely, trying to see his eyes in the dim dash lights, as he told me the island's main cabin was built of block and stone. It had a complicated lock system, steel rods through all windows and doors, to discourage vandals. "Even though there's nothing really valuable inside," he said. "Some fishing gear and canned food, that's all. But we don't want outsiders wrecking the place."

I thought, *Right*.

Like all islands with high ground, Tamarindo would be an easy place to dig a grave. Soft sand and shell, only a few feet above sea level. It's where I would have left the boy if someone had screwed up my plans to use the horse-sized hole in the Hamptons.

My intuitive senses seemed to be right. Will Chaser was on Tamarindo—I knew it on a gut level buttressed by reason. There was a chance I'd find the Cubans there, too.

I checked my battered old Rolex: almost ten p.m. Ten hours nine minutes before the boy's air ran out . . . if he was still breathing.

Hog Island was a little over an hour from Dinkin's Bay in a fast boat, and I owned a fast boat. Suddenly, I was as eager to be free of Nelson Myles as he was eager to be free of me.

But now the man was talking nonstop, glancing occasionally at the little stainless-steel pistol I had placed on the console but also paying attention to the headlights of passing cars. I should have linked his behavior to the way he'd tried to manipulate me earlier, claiming he would talk more freely if we returned to Falcon Landing.

Even when a Wells Fargo security car appeared out of nowhere, skidding in behind us, yellow lights flashing, I didn't grasp the significance.

"Rental cops," I told him. "Keep your mouth shut or we both go to jail."

Myles wasn't much of an actor either. He exaggerated his confusion as he craned his neck around to look, then overplayed his relief. "Don't worry," he said, speaking as if we were partners. "I know these two guys. I see them all the time."

"Then get rid of them."

He tried to lower his window, then tried to open his door, but I'd locked everything with the master switch. There was no override on the passenger side.

"I can't tell them to go away," he said impatiently, "if I can't talk to them, now, can I?"

I was thinking about it as I watched the guards in the mirror. They rested their hands on their holsters as if unconcerned as they approached what had to be a familiar vehicle.

I said, "We're not on Falcon Landing property?"

Myles said, "No, the county maintenance people use this place."

"Then why are they bothering us?"

"Relax," Myles told me. "They're probably bored. They don't get many calls. And they're dumb as rocks. Let me handle it."

I didn't like the man's airy tone. Was tempted to start the engine and drive away, but that guaranteed attention from the police—real cops, not the four-hours-of-training imitators.

The locks clicked in tandem when I touched the master switch, then lowered both windows. A Gulf wind flooded the cabin. I said, "Don't get out," looking at Myles, seeing his sullen face strobe in yellow rhythmic light.

I glanced in the mirror. Christ, now the security guards were drawing their weapons as they separated, one on each side of the Range Rover, crouching slightly as they came toward us.

I slid the Seecamp under the seat, then grabbed the cell phone from the dash. I punched the recorder's OFF icon as I said, "Tell them who you are. That everything's okay. We're just talking."

The man lay back in his seat as if he didn't hear. I hissed, "Do it now!"

He turned to me, a weak, nervous smile on his face. "Sure. But give me the cell phone first. Then I'll get rid of them."

The phone with his recorded confession.

I reached for the ignition. "I'll take my chances with the rental cops."

"Wait!" Myles tried to pull my hand away.

I said, "You're not getting the phone."

"But you've got to give it to me! They're here because I called them . . . with this." He was holding what looked like a garage opener. It had been clipped to the sun visor, the same visor he had grabbed to balance himself. "It's a panic alert that works if you're near the property. Press it and the security guys come running. But sometimes they call police, too!"

He sounded anxious, the way he said it, "police, too!," as if he already regretted pushing the button. Now I understood why he had tried to maneuver me back to Falcon Landing.

"Give me the phone," Myles said.

"Not a chance."

"I'll tell them it's a false alarm. I swear." Then he said, "Shit," leaning toward the window, listening. I could hear what he was hearing: the warble of sirens a few blocks away.

He began to panic. "Give me the phone! The real police will be here any minute!"

I shook my head no. I was still tempted to start the car and run for it, but that would've been the stupidest possible move. I had to let it play out. I said, "There aren't many murderers who turn themselves in. I want to see how the cops react."

"I had no choice. This is your fault."

"It's always someone else's fault, right, Nels?"

"If you don't give me the phone, I'll them the truth . . . that you kidnapped me and threatened to kill me."

Myles didn't know I had a more compelling reason to avoid the police. But I said, "Maybe they'll put us in the same cell. That would be nice, huh? Just the two of us . . . alone."

I was watching the security guards in the mirror. They had stopped behind the car. One of them hollered, "Mr. Myles! Everything all right?," talking loud because of the sirens.

I called through the open window, "Mr. Myles is just fine. We're talking about going into the recording business." I looked up at palm trees where fronds reflected the blue strobes of a squad car, slowing to turn into the parking lot. I looked at Myles. "I think we might have a big hit on our hands, Nels. Can you picture the headlines?"

Talking fast, he said, "I'll help you find the missing kid, I swear to God. Give me the phone. We can use my boat if you want. I'll tell them it was a false alarm. If I tell them, they'll believe me. We don't have to do this!"

"You're right," I replied. "You're taking a stupid risk. Get rid of them. But it's your call. No matter what, I keep the phone."

He was looking out the side window. "Jesus Christ, they're here! Why are you being so damn stubborn? I offered to help you."

I said, "Tell them you hit the button accidentally. You claim Bonesmen are noble? Prove it by helping me help the kid. I'll decide later if I give the recording to police."

A lie. Annie Sylvester's family deserved to know where

she was buried and who had killed her. Myles probably realized what I was doing: The shrewd anticipate deceit by projecting their behavior onto others. But the man had no choice . . . Until a polite policeman told us to step out of the car, then asked me for identification.

"It's procedure," he said, sounding bored until I hesitated, undecided if I should break one of my own rules and lie to a cop. I own several false passports, but it was pointless to carry one in my own home state. All I had was a driver's license.

"Left your wallet at home, did you?" the officer suggested, suddenly more interested. "What's your name?"

That's when Myles surprised me, saying, "I can vouch for this man. He's a business associate of mine." He was standing near the security guards, who had made their deference obvious.

The cop appeared satisfied, but he was also studying Myles—seeing the stained pants, the swollen ear—as Myles turned to me, thrust out his hand and said, "I bet you left your wallet near the pool. Give me my cell phone, I'll call the wife."

I looked at his hand, aware the officer was staring. "I didn't lose my wallet," I said. "I think I left it in the car. I'll take a look."

I opened the car, pretended to look for the license and handed it to the officer. I watched his face, then winced inwardly at the man's reaction as he read my name.

"Marion Ford," the cop said, sounding cheerful, but his cheeriness was steel. "As in Dr. Ford, the biologist?"

"That's right."

Now the officer was smiling but also backing away as he touched a hand to his sidearm and unsnapped the holster. "I have some friends who've been looking for you, Dr. Ford. So what I'd like you to do right now is empty your pockets, then have a seat in the back of my vehicle."

He glanced at Myles, the rich, respected Falcon Landing resident, who looked from me to the cop, his eyes signaling a reminder. The cop's eyes signaled respect in reply.

As I processed the exchange, the image of an iceberg came into my mind. Odd, until I remembered a conversation I'd had on a faraway winter beach. The father of a dead girl, Virgil Sylvester, had described an iceberg he had seen off Nova Scotia, its peaks like fire at sunrise, the ocean dark beneath.

"It's that kind of power they got," the fishermen had told me. "Even when they use it, you don't see it."

I'd heard the man's words but was deaf to their gravity.

"Oh, one more thing, Dr. Ford," the cop said. "While you're emptying your pockets, give Mr. Myles his telephone back, okay?"

28

The police detective, a woman named Shelly Palmer, told me she lived in Cape Coral, not far from Pine Island and the fishing village of Gumbo Limbo, where the late Bern Heller had owned a marina until he was sent to prison and his business went into foreclosure.

On the drive from Sarasota to Fort Myers, she had tried to bait me, saying things like, "I hear the man was a monster . . . Locals say the man who killed Bern Heller did the world a favor . . . What was he like, Dr. Ford . . . your personal opinion, I mean?"

Whenever she pressed, I removed my glasses and leisurely cleaned them, putting space between my anger and my intellect. She gave up after half an hour, as we traveled south on I-75, forty miles between the Sarasota County line and Lee County, our destination.

Now we were leaving a police substation in North Fort Myers after stopping to pick up her boss and assemble paperwork. I listened to Detective Palmer tell me,

"We're going to do what we call a *roll-by*. Attorneys and judges call it a *show-up*. Do you know what I'm talking about?"

A roll-by/show-up was a prearranged meeting with a witness who had consented to look at a suspect. It required two squad cars, the witness sitting anonymously in the back of one vehicle, while the suspect stepped out of a second vehicle and presented himself for inspection.

My guess: The woman Bern Heller had attempted to rape was waiting to inspect me somewhere nearby.

I said, "I wouldn't have agreed if I didn't understand what we're doing." Which wasn't the whole truth.

Truth was, I was more concerned with Will Chaser's deadline, eight hours away, than I was with protecting my legal rights. Under any other circumstances, whether I was innocent or guilty, I would have spent the last hour in silence after demanding an attorney.

It was a gamble, with two lives on the line, one of them mine. But even in a worst-case scenario, they would only lock me in a prison cell, not bury me in a box. I was willing to risk a few weeks in jail, waiting for a court date, on the chance of arriving at Tamarindo Island a few hours earlier.

Detective Palmer said to her boss, Captain Lester Durell, "He's waived all rights, like I told you. He signed the consent sheet. Satisfied now?"

Durell said, "Well, they say scientists are eggheads," exaggerating his southern vowels. "I guess this one's proof enough." He turned to look through the Plexiglas shield that separated backseat from front in this unmarked car, as Palmer drove us across the Edison Bridge into Fort Myers. "What happened to you, Doc? That big ol' football player scramble your brain when he gave you that beatin'?"

Heller had almost knocked me unconscious a year ago only days before he murdered Javier Castillo.

I said, "That has nothing to do with it. I'm in a hurry. You know why."

"Wish I could help."

"I already told you how. Have your marine division get a boat to that island, with a chopper as backup."

"Thirty years, I've fished these bays," Durell replied, "and Tamarindo's a name I've never heard."

Was the man intentionally trying to make me mad? Twice, I'd explained why it wasn't on charts.

I said, "Why not assume I'm right? Your people would get some extra night-ops experience, and just might make headlines if they find the boy."

Durell didn't want to hear it. "Who we supposed to believe? Our local guy at the FBI says you wore out your welcome. Sarasota County Sheriff's Department thinks the same as this here lady detective: You're lookin' for a way to shift attention from a dead-solid murder charge. And even if you're not"—he paused to take a cigar from the pocket of his sports coat—"doin' this without talking to a lawyer is no excuse for bein' so damn dumb."

I wasn't sure if he was putting on a show for Palmer or for me. Durell was a wide-bodied man who'd boxed Golden Gloves and played pulling guard for Florida State before taking his degree in criminology out into the much tougher world of law enforcement.

I had known him for many years. Once upon a time, we'd been peripheral friends. But cops on every level soon develop a social armor that separates them from the civilian world as effectively as it shields them and the inevitable scars that come with the job.

It was unlikely that he considered us friends now. Maybe he wanted to make that clear to Detective Palmer. Or me. If anything, a pro like Les Durell would be tougher on someone he knew. But he'd never struck me as the flaky, scalp-collecting sort of cop who viewed hanging an acquaintance as a badge of honor.

I said, "I signed the release. Isn't that what Detective Palmer wanted me to do?"

Durell turned his back to me, grumbling, "Also a good way to risk screwin' up this case if it gets to court," which the woman ignored until the big man turned to look at me again.

"Shelly?" he said to her. "You got a problem with me sittin' in the backseat with Dr. Ford? There's a coupla things I'd like to discuss with the man. Personally, I think mosta the evidence your team scraped together ain't worth a crap."

When the woman snapped, "Yes! I do have a problem with it," I knew what they were setting up. Good cop, bad cop—an old routine. No, Lester Durell obviously wasn't my friend.

I listened to the woman speak her lines, asking, "Who is this guy, another one of your locker-room buddies?

Captain Durell, the days of the good-ol'-boy system are gone forever. At least I hope to hell they're gone. But if you want to risk me filing an internal complaint—"

"Now, now, Shelly dear. This here's a respected man. Lives out there on Sanibel with the rich folk, pays his taxes and obeys the law—mostly he does anyway. It can't hurt letting the two of us just talk sorta privatelike—"

I interrupted. "Les, save us some time. You have questions? Fire away. I don't mind if Detective Palmer listens."

The woman said, "Should I be flattered?," still in her bad-cop role—or possibly a woman who was naturally foul-tempered.

Durell said to her, "How long before we're supposed to meet our witness?" It was 11:15 p.m.

Palmer replied, "She's covering third shift but can take a break from the floor after she signs in, around midnight."

In the dim light, I saw the man wince. He was pained by Palmer's use of the gender identifier *she*. But the woman had told me far more than either realized with her one-sentence response.

Palmer had just told me that the witness worked at a hospital—nearby Fort Myers Memorial, most likely. Third shift wasn't the woman's normal schedule. It was probably changed to mitigate stress after the trauma of an attempted rape: She didn't want to be alone at night. It also suggested that the witness was single, had no children and was receiving psychological counseling. And she wasn't a nurse. She was either a physician or a physician's assistant. Nurses don't cover floors, they work in units: peds or ER or critical care.

Extrapolating from what I knew about Bern Heller's many victims, the woman was probably Caucasian, between twenty-four and thirty-two years old, drove an eye-catching car and was sufficiently confident to park in unlighted areas of public parking lots. Odds were that she had shoulder-length brown hair, was fit, with small breasts and, although confident, had a friendly, eager-to-please demeanor.

Implicit was a scenario that included a successful young woman who had fallen for one of Heller's many gambits after she'd finished her shift at the hospital and probably after working out at a nearby fitness center. But the witness was also a person with character. She had a strong sense of civic duty. Why else would she risk coming out at night to identify a man suspected of murder?

I said, "Who's the witness? What can you tell me?"

Durell took the unlighted cigar from his mouth, his expression saying *Nothing*.

"Doc, what you'd better concentrate on is getting over your sudden case of the stupids. Personally, I don't think our people got the evidence we need. But if you keep screwin' up the way you are, I'm afraid you'll make the Sanibel papers . . . after they burn you at Raiford."

*N*ever *lie to a cop* . . .

An old rule. This time, I was sticking to it, even though

Captain Les Durell was trying to make it easy to lie, offering ready-made excuses for his pointed questions.

Nudging a suspect into a perjury maze—another police gambit.

Now he was sitting with me in the backseat but with the Plexiglas safety screen open so Detective Palmer could listen. If she missed anything, the digital tape recorder clipped to the Plexiglas was available for her review.

It proved Durell was right. I had acquired a serious case of the stupids. I was answering questions that could lead to a murder charge, the electric chair, without a lawyer present or even a second tape recorder for my own files.

A worthy cause, I kept reminding myself.

My status had been upgraded from *person of interest* to *person of reasonable suspicion,* a legal term. It meant police believed they had enough evidence to warrant temporary detention. But because I wasn't officially a suspect, I wasn't handcuffed. I would have almost preferred it, because I found myself checking my watch obsessively, recalculating the deadline: *eight hours thirty-one minutes . . . eight hours twenty-five-minutes . . .*

So I tried to slow the minutes by focusing on Durell's questions, learning what I could from the few facts he let slip. He didn't slip often.

The man started by stating procedural formalities for the recorder—time, place, subject, names—then began with an easygoing southern congeniality that would have put me on alert if I wasn't already.

"Right off the bat," he said, "let's deal with the sillier

stuff our folks are calling evidence. I'm gonna be right up front with you, Doc. The medical examiner hasn't issued his final report, but he thinks the football player died sometime between midnight and dawn on Friday, January sixteenth. We know you flew to New York Friday morning. Took the six forty-five Delta flight to New York. "

"*Newark*," I corrected, then listened to the man chuckle at his intentional error.

"Newark," he echoed, making a note on his clipboard. "But you're with me so far on the date and time of death? Heller washed up two days ago on Naples Beach, lungs full of water. But he died six days earlier while you were still on Sanibel."

Lungs full of water. Heller had drowned. It was Durell's first slip. I doubted if the medical examiner had issued such a narrow time window for the same reasons I'd explained to Tomlinson: Saltwater creatures eat land-dwelling creatures. Something else an examiner would have considered was the watch I'd planted. Its crystal was crushed, the date frozen on Saturday, January seventeenth, the day after I'd arrived in New York. Captain Durell was setting a trap.

I shrugged and said nothing.

"Our guys took statements from folks who said you and the football player got into a brawl 'bout a year ago. That he licked you pretty good. That true?"

I said, "I still have headaches."

"Kinda surprising to me—you bein' an All-American wrestler back in the day."

"I wasn't. I never made it to the quarterfinals at nationals."

Durell said, "Even so, Heller musta jumped you from behind, huh?," establishing a pattern by offering me an out.

"No," I said.

It threw off his rhythm. "Well . . . that's not the way I figured it. But then Heller was found guilty of murder, second degree. Shot a friend of yours, a Sanibel fishing guide."

"Javier Castillo," I said. "He'd moved his boat to Pine Island a few months earlier. Javier was a decent man."

"He was a friend."

"Close friend. Left a nice family, a wife and two girls . . . and no life insurance." Then I added, "Javier crossed the Florida Straits in an inner tube, that's how bad he wanted to get into the U.S.," thinking Durell might be impressed.

Instead, he ignored me, saying, "I read about your fund-raisers at the marina. Only natural for you to have hard feelings toward a man who shot your Cuban pal. Anyone would."

I didn't respond. After a few seconds, Durell answered for me, saying, "But not enough to try some stupid vigilante stunt by killing him. I've told our people that, personally, I think they're pissing up a rope. That you're an educated man. Bookish and quiet. I told 'em, 'Hell, look at his picture! Looks like a history teacher I had, Mr. Harrison.'"

He was studying the clipboard, the dome light on,

chewing his cigar, as we passed mobile home parks, a Pizza Hut, lighted billboards. He said, "According to these notes, the folks at Dinkin's Bay Marina wouldn't hardly talk to our boys. That surprise you?"

"Next time, come at sunset," I said. "That's cocktail hour."

"We heard that, too! Heard it from someone who went to the marina's Friday-night party. Got a weird name to it, sounds like . . . Epcot?"

"Perbcott," I said. "Sort of a local joke."

"The person at that party said Heller showed up, and you two almost got into it again—this was just two weeks ago. But this person could've been exaggerating. They usually do when a cop shows up asking questions."

I said, "It was the week before I left for New York. We didn't know Heller had been released. And it's not like the marina invited him."

"Heller showed up on his own?"

"That's right."

Durell said, "Hell, then he came to Dinkin's Bay looking for trouble!" He leaned toward the Plexiglas and said to the woman, "That's a detail your team shoulda noted, Detective Palmer. Sorta thing that changes the whole story around." He settled back. "That's why it's good we can talk like this, Doc. Get some of this puny-assed stuff straightened out. You were saying?"

I said, "Heller made a move on a woman who lives near the marina. Her name's Marlissa Engle."

"That the actress?"

He knew who Marlissa was. The islands attract a lot of famous people, possibly because they can leave more than the mainland behind when they cross the bridge. I could see Palmer watching me in the mirror as I said, "We dated for a while, now she's a workout partner, when she's in town. Marlissa told Heller to get lost, but he wouldn't leave her alone."

"Then I don't blame you for getting pissed off," Durell said. "The man's a convicted rapist."

"*Serial* rapist," I corrected.

"Thirty-some women, the feds are thinking now, coast to coast. But like you said, taking the law into your own hands isn't something you would do."

"You said that," I replied. "Not me. If there was a legal way to get rid of Bern Heller, I would have given it serious consideration."

Surprised, the man hunched over his clipboard to regroup. "But you didn't really think about killing him, did you? Not seriously, I mean."

I said, "There is no legal way, so why would I waste my time? But I'm glad he's dead, if that's what you're asking."

Durell was nodding, his expression saying *Nothing wrong with that*, before getting serious, his face showing concern. "But here's the thing, Doc. The football player died between midnight and dawn on a Friday. Our guys spoke to some beach walkers who say they were out before sunrise that Friday morning. Near Lighthouse Point, looking for shells. You know how shellers are, doesn't matter what hour as long as the tide's right. Around four a.m., they said, a small boat came flying around the point. Only one person aboard.

"Then our guys talked to someone who lives bayside near your marina. This person was up at about the same time—I won't say why—but this person says a flats boat came through the cut into Dinkin's Bay between four a.m. and four-thirty. Your flight was at six forty-five?"

"Delta. Right on time."

"Then even if this person was right about seeing a boat, you were already on your way to the airport. Most folks want to be at security two hours before."

"Not me," I said. "I left Sanibel around five-fifteen, got to the gate fifteen minutes before we boarded."

"That unusual for you?"

"Not unless the flight's international."

"And you own a flats skiff?" Before I could answer, he said to Palmer, "A flats skiff's a small boat built for shallow water. No cabin or windows, just a low hull and a big engine. Sorry, Doc. Go ahead."

I said, "Yes, I've owned flats boats for years."

The man nodded, as if pleased I was telling the truth, then demonstrated why. "Gotta admit, I've seen that fancy Maverick of yours. I hear them Mavericks ride like a BMW. They can plane on dew and run in a rain puddle."

"Unusual boat," I answered. "Magic hull. I use it more than my truck."

"Just what I figured," Durell said. "Which brings up something else. This person I mentioned—the one lives near your marina?—this person claims to have recognized your boat. People see that Maverick on the bay so often, you know? But, hell, there weren't no moon at that hour. It was a black night, and sort of windy, too. No fisherman in his right mind would be out on that tide." He paused. "It was a low tide, that right?"

A subtle trap. I watched the man's careful disinterest as I hesitated, then stepped into it. "Dead low tide," I agreed. "New moon wasn't up yet."

Durell took a deep, satisfied breath and leaned toward the front again, speaking to the woman. "You wouldn't understand, not being a water person, Shelly, but no one would take a small boat into the Gulf on that tide. Not at four in the morning, when it's black as the inside of a cow. Too many exposed bars. Even in a shallow boat, you'd have to be a magician to find enough water, running blind, to get around the lighthouse."

Implicit flattery—a nice touch.

He continued, "And even if someone saw a boat coming into Dinkin's Bay, there's no way a lawyer could prove it. It was too blame dark to make a positive ID." Durell returned his attention to me, smiling now. "See what I mean about some of this evidence being weak? A judge would laugh it out of court."

The man wouldn't have asked about it if he didn't think it could be proven. I said, "You're being hard on your witness, Les. The person's right. It was me."

I watched Detective Palmer's eyes staring at me in the rearview mirror as Durell sat back in his seat. "Doc," he said slowly, "you want to run that past me one more time?"

I said, "That was my boat. I was in it. Three hours before dawn, Friday, January sixteenth. It was me."

Durell said, "You're telling me you was out in the Gulf in your flats boat, four in the morning, the same time the medical examiner figures Bern Heller was murdered?"

I said, "I don't know who the beach walkers saw coming in from the Gulf. You're right about that. Too many exposed bars, it would be stupid to go offshore. And why would I want to be in the Gulf anyway? But at four a.m., I was running into Dinkin's Bay, four or five miles to the northwest. I didn't notice anyone watching from shore, but I was out there."

Durell stumbled, unprepared, but managed to ask, *"Why?"*

"I'd been running shark lines, a half dozen hooks on buoys. Sharks die if you don't get to them quick, so I wanted to make a final check, then clear the hooks, before leaving for New York. I don't keep the sharks. I do tag-and-release. There was one small bull shark. I tagged it and let it go."

Durell said, "Tagged it?," and I knew he was wondering if there was a way to prove I was lying.

I nodded. "And while I was out there, I stopped and checked one of the transmitters Mote Marine set near the channel. They've sunk about two dozen between Boca Grande and the causeway. It was buoyed, but it looked like it had drifted off-station. So I stopped."

From the corner of my eyes, I was gauging Palmer's reaction—guilty people get overtalkative—but decided it was okay to add, "Mote sets out underwater monitors to track fish they've tagged—sharks, snook, some others. The transmitter I pulled had some benthic growth but looked okay. So I towed it closer to shore, but not as close as I would've normally, because the tide was so low. I didn't want to risk running aground and missing my plane."

Time for Durell to study his clipboard again. I had just used the man's trap to give credence to my story.

He cleared his throat and said loud enough for Palmer to hear, "Mote's about as respectable as it gets in the fish-research business," but he wasn't ready to abandon his plan because he offered another easy out. "If you work with Mote, there's no judge or jury would question what you was doing on the water at that hour—even if the scientists at Mote *can't* confirm you checked their transmitter thing. What is it, sorta like an underwater antenna?"

I said, "Looks more like a shock absorber on a car. They're called VM-2s. The tags we use, PIT tags, they're miniature transponders. Check with Mote. They might be able to confirm it, even give you the exact time because I was carrying a tag coded with a personal ID. The VM-2 should have transmitted the number automatically. You know, keeping track of who services the equipment."

The man said, "You sure about this?"

"Unless there was a malfunction, my ID should be in their computers."

"Maybe you already talked to them, said you was out there."

I said, "Nope."

All true.

The big man sat back and placed the clipboard on his knees. He mulled it over as if deciding to stop playing games. "Doc, let me ask you straight out. Did you kill Bern Heller?"

Heller had drowned. The Gulf of Mexico had killed him, not me. "Absolutely not."

"Did you have anything to do with it?"

I said, "They found his body on Naples Beach, you said. That's forty miles south of Sanibel. Couch the question any way you want but my answer's not going to change. I didn't kill Bern Heller. I wasn't anywhere near the man, wherever he was, when he died."

Durell said, "Then why didn't you return the calls our people left at your lab? We been trying to get in touch for two days. You don't check messages?"

I said, "At first, I thought it was because you wanted my opinion about how long Heller had been dead. Your department's hired me five times as a consultant. But when I realized it was because you were actually thinking of me as a suspect, I decided, screw you, I'm not in Florida, I have more important things to do."

Suddenly not so friendly, Durell said, "Did you, now?"

"That's right. Finding a kidnapped boy takes precedence over answering questions about a dead man I didn't like to begin with. But if you're interested in my opinion, I'll tell you—no charge."

Unconvinced but wavering, Durell said, "Keep talking," giving me more rope.

"A more reasonable scenario is that Heller, a convicted serial rapist and murderer who had a limited amount of time . . ." I let Durell see me thinking about it before I asked, "How long before they sent him back to prison, a few months?"

Looking into my eyes, Durell said, "A few weeks, no more."

I said, "A convicted murderer who had a narrow window, he might have headed for Mexico. It's only four hundred miles across the Gulf. So he either hired some lowlife to crew aboard his boat or he hired someone else's boat and they pushed him overboard. Took his money and kept going. Can you tell me how he died. A blow to the head? Drowned?"

Durell's expression said no, so before he answered I asked, "How about the exact time the body was found? Six days drifting in the Gulf, his body should have been closer to the Dry Tortugas, not Naples, if he started off Sanibel . . . unless he got swept in by a vortex current. But if he went in the water off Tampa Bay, that would be about right."

"Tampa, huh?"

"I'd check with the port, ask about tramp cargo vessels and shrimpers that left Thursday or Friday. Or . . . Heller could have been killed *on* Naples Beach, above the tide line. This phase of the moon, the tides get progressively higher every day, so it could have taken a while before—"

Palmer interrupted from the front, saying, "Heller was living on a forty-two-foot yacht parked at the marina he used to manage. We know for sure he was aboard the boat early Friday morning. If his body was drifting, how much difference would twenty-four hours make?"

I said, "You mean, if he went into the water on Saturday, not Friday?"

"Yes, off Sanibel."

She was thinking about the watch with the broken crystal.

I said, "That works. Five days, the body would be off Naples or the Ten Thousand Islands. Again, depending on the vortexes."

Durell slid his pen under the clipboard spring and sighed. "What do you think, Shelly?"

The woman said to Durell, "Can we verify what he just told us?"

Durell said, "Well, I dunno . . . ," as I asked, "What did the Coast Guard say?"

There was a silence, the two officers wondering if the other was going to answer. Finally, Palmer said, "They gave us similar information. And . . . they also suggested we contact a local firm named Sanibel Biological Supply. Which is you."

"Me and one part-time employee."

"They said you've got charts and graphs, every missing boat and person, for the last ten years."

I said, "It's a hobby. Currents in the Gulf are tricky, and there's never been a long-term study. I just told you what I think. If you provided more information, maybe I'd have a different opinion."

Palmer said, "Even if we hired you, I couldn't share—"

"Doesn't matter," I said. "I wouldn't work as a consultant in this case. Aside from the ethical conflict, there's a personal conflict: I'm glad the guy's dead. If he was murdered, I agree with the locals: Someone did the world a favor."

The woman's smart, dark eyes filled the rearview mirror, looking into mine. "You realize you're being recorded?"

I replied, "Yes."

"Then I suggest you keep your mouth shut until we do the roll-by. I want to add, just for the record, that you don't have to do the roll-by. Say the word, Dr. Ford, and I'll cancel it. Or we can wait while you consult your attorney."

Once again, I checked my watch. Eight hours ten minutes until deadline. I said, "I signed the papers. As long as we get this done as fast as possible, I'm willing. But, just for the record, Detective Palmer, whatever your witness says won't change the fact I've been telling the truth."

29

At midnight, I stood in the ten-acre parking lot of a retail minicity, Edison Mall, hoping either mercy or bad
memory would prevent the woman, whose killer I had
killed, from sentencing me to a murder charge or, worse,
a night in jail. If Will Chaser was still alive, his death was
only eight hours away.

The lot was empty except for security carts and three
squad cars sitting at angles beneath yellow sodium lights.
I also noticed a fourth car. It was parked on a curb, in
shadows, behind monoxide-poisoned shrubs. Its rear
window was cracked a few inches, the glass tinted.

Durell had told me to walk to the nearest lamppost,
turn left, turn right, then stand until he waved me back
to our black sedan. Because he said it was okay to look at
the squad cars, I did. But I focused on the less obvious
car, using peripheral vision.

When I got to the lamppost and pivoted, I saw a facial
oval—female eyes, a portion of nose and forehead—

studying me from the unmarked car. As instructed, I turned, turned again, then stopped. I wasn't looking directly at the car but could see the rear window. Durell had also told me to remove my glasses, so I did. Cleaned them on my shirt before straightening them on my nose.

The window dropped another two inches. In the sterile light, filaments of hair appeared, framing the woman's face. Something odd about the left eye. It was swollen the size of my fist, I realized, the eye a solitary creature within, as if peeking out from a cave. Six days since Heller had beaten her. No wonder the woman was afraid to be alone at night.

The face disappeared for a moment—the witness was saying something to the driver—then reappeared. Because of the tinted window glass, the face took the shape of an antique cameo. The woman's eyes were intense, unwavering. They invited contact. I refused.

The woman said something else to the driver. A moment later, I heard the radio squawk, then Durell talking before he called to me, "Walk toward the highway."

I started for U.S. 41, with its lighted stream of Saturday-night traffic, pickup trucks, tourist rentals and tricked-out pubescent coupes. When I was within ten yards of the woman's window, Durell hollered, "Far enough! Come on back."

As I turned, the woman and I locked eyes for the first time. The human iris does not communicate, but facial components do. I watched her one good eye focus, then widen . . . and I felt a sickening dread. She recognized me. No doubt about it.

The window dropped another inch. I saw a healthy conformation of cheeks, full lips, hair that was sun-streaked, glossy, one side of her face articulate, thoughtful, but the other side a bloated mask. The woman wanted me to *know* she recognized me, I realized, just as she wanted me to get a glimpse of her face. Her focus was tunneled, my personal conduit into whatever it was she was thinking or had suffered.

Still staring at me, the woman nodded—a slow-motion assent or signal of some unavoidable honesty, I couldn't be sure. She spoke to the driver once more, then disappeared behind the glass.

When I returned to our vehicle, Durell was in the front seat. "Think the witness recognized you?" he asked.

The man already knew if the woman had recognized me or not. He was baiting me once again, and I was tired of it. "Something wrong with your radio, Les? Wait here while I go tap on the window and ask."

"No need to get smart-assed about it."

I'd closed the door but now opened it to get out. "I don't know what your problem is. Too many years, not enough promotions? Whatever it is, I'm done with your chess game. Either arrest me or I'm calling a cab."

Detective Palmer said, "Hold on." She reached to make certain the recorder was off before saying to Durell, "Why not have one of the uniforms take you back to the station? We're done here."

I liked the sound of that but listened closely, hoping for a more definite acquittal.

"What's the problem, Shelly? You got a hot date waiting?"

"What I have is a professional obligation to take Dr. Ford wherever he wants to go. That's why you need to catch a ride . . . *Les*."

"You're not taking anyone anywhere, Detective," the man snapped, "until I say the word."

Palmer's eyes filled the mirror once again, and I was startled when she lifted her eyebrows, sending a message— a private and personal message just for me.

"Captain, what's going on here?" she said. "I don't want to have to note in my report that in my opinion we risked a harassment charge. The witness just told us Dr. Ford's not the man. Absolutely sure of it, no room for error. And Sarasota says there's no reason to hold him. Their resident confirmed he accidentally hit a security alarm, a big misunderstanding. So what I'm going to do now is thank Dr. Ford for his cooperation and take him home—with your permission of course, Captain."

I was trying very hard not to show my relief as she glanced into the mirror again, buckling her seat belt. I was also busy processing what she'd said about Myles not pressing charges. From the way it sounded, the man had covered for me. Why?

Durell was getting out of the car, moving slower than he once had. He'd put on twenty or thirty pounds. "You're gettin' kind of smart-assed yourself, Shelly," he said. "What I think is, you got an itch that's not been scratched in way too long. It's making you snotty. Boys at the station don't say much when I tell 'em. Just sorta look uncomfortable, like I made a bad joke or I might order one of 'em to help you out." He made a hacking sound of laughter before he slammed the door.

In the game of good cop–bad cop, the pros sometimes take the role that least reflects their convictions about the suspect. Not because it's fair—even though it is—but because it can broaden the range of inquiry. Palmer had been the good cop all along.

Before we pulled away, the woman told me to get in the front seat, then handed me her cell phone, saying, "The guy in Sarasota County, Nelson Myles. He passed along word he wants you to call. It wasn't appropriate for me to tell you earlier. While you're talking, you want me to drive you to Sanibel or back where you started?"

I said, "Give me a minute?" then punched the buttons as she read off the number.

Myles sounded relieved when he recognized my voice, which was unexpected. "I've been thinking about the Cubans," he said. "I don't know of any reason they'd want to stop at Tamarindo—the island's only two miles from my property—but I remembered that Fred's GPS was programmed with the route because the channel's narrow and it's not easy even when the tide's high. The island was probably right there on the screen when they started the boat because it's the only place Fred goes when he's in Florida. So I'm heading to Tamarindo—it's only five minutes."

Myles told me he had brought the Tiara around to his private dock, next to his house, and was getting it ready.

I said, "I'm surprised."

"Don't be. No matter what you think, I'm not a monster. I don't want anyone to get hurt, particularly a child."

That isn't what had surprised me. I'd expected his first words to be about Annie Sylvester. Had I told police?

It made Myles more convincing when he added, "After only an hour with you, Dr. Ford, I think I can say with confidence my standards of moral conduct are at least as high as yours."

There was no arguing the point.

I said, "I apologize for being surprised. But it's a bad idea, you going alone, even if it is only a couple of miles from your dock." I noticed Detective Palmer paying attention as I continued, "You have enough political clout with the local police, probably the FBI, too. Have them send a helicopter. Or a boat, if they—"

"It's been taken care of," he interrupted. "The sheriff told me, personally, a helicopter was on its way. They'll use searchlights, and, if it looks like there's a problem, they'll land."

"They need to put down on the beach no matter—"

He interrupted again. "I'm aware of what should be done, Ford. That's why I'm meeting them. Please stop instructing and start listening. I looked you up on the Internet. There wasn't much, but I see you run a little marine-research station. I assume that means you're good with boats. I'm offering you a chance to go with me if you want. But no more rough stuff."

I checked the time: 12:15 a.m. By car, it was forty

minutes to Dinkin's Bay, then another hour-ten, hour-twenty, give or take, to Tamarindo. If Detective Palmer was willing to push it, we could be at Falcon Landing in less than an hour.

It was the quickest way to the island, but I disliked the prospect of being aboard someone else's boat, particularly at night, particularly on an oversized luxury yacht and most particularly when the pilot was an amateur.

I asked, "How many times have you run the Tamarindo channel after dark?"

"A few times," he said, "several," but I suspected by the way he hesitated, he wasn't confident. When he added, "It's certainly no harder then landing a plane at night," I was sure of it. The real reason he was calling was because he'd found out I made my living on a boat.

Two factors tipped the scales. At the North Fort Myers substation, Palmer had let me call and check messages at the lab. It would have been helpful to have Tomlinson along, but he'd left a message saying he wouldn't arrive on Sanibel until nine, Sunday morning. More important, the equipment I wanted to take wasn't at the lab, it was stowed in the trunk of the rental car, beachside, near Shelter Cottage.

To Myles I said, "I'll meet you at your place in about an hour. I need to get my cell phone anyway . . ."—I let that settle before adding—". . . plus one or two other things." I'd shoved the little Seecamp pistol under the seat and I wanted it back.

Demonstrating that he was in charge, not me, Myles said, "I can't wait that long. You've got half an hour . . ."

He stopped, and I heard what sounded like a tapping in the background. Someone at the man's door? Apparently not, because he then finished the sentence, saying, ". . . that's as long as I'll wait. Call five minutes before you get to security."

I touched the SPEAKERPHONE button and said, "Repeat that. I'm riding with a police detective, so it's up to her."

When Detective Palmer heard, she said, "Buckle up," and flipped a toggle. Ten acres of asphalt echoed with blue strobes.

We were on I-75, cruising in silence, lights pulsing, doing ninety-five when traffic allowed, sometimes one-ten on empty stretches. As we'd left the mall, Palmer had asked how I got involved in the search for the missing boy. She seemed interested but preoccupied and soon went silent, her mind on something else. We hadn't exchanged a word in the last twenty minutes.

Now, though, the road ahead was empty, and she spoke again, her tone puzzled, as she asked me, "Was Les always such a jerk?"

I found the question touching. This tough woman was still smarting from Durell's heavy-handed cut: *You got an itch . . .*

I said, "Nope. A real professional, a forward-thinking guy, master's in law enforcement. Maybe he had a rough week."

"A rough *two years*," she corrected. "That's how long

I've been with the department. I won't go into his personal problems, but if you know of any close friends, they should take him aside, have a talk, maybe get him back on track."

"Alcohol? Or diabetes?" I was thinking of the additional weight he was carrying.

The woman shook her head: *Confidential.*

I said, "I don't know who the man associates with, sorry," wondering if Palmer had any friends left outside the profession. Durell had been intentionally nasty, but he was also savvy enough to have ice-pick instincts when it came to veiling an insult. For maximum damage, he would poison his barbs with truth. I suspected the woman had ended a relationship, or an affair, many months ago, probably with another cop. Outwardly, she hadn't shown much and she'd recovered quickly. But Durell had scored a direct hit.

"He's an asshole," she said, barely audible.

"We all have our valleys."

"What's that supposed to mean?" Her tone warned me to keep a professional distance.

"It meant I'm an asshole more than I care to admit. I do and say things that make me cringe later."

"Homicide, for instance?"

I said, "If you're still playing the good cop–bad cop game, I'll sit here quietly until we get to our destination."

"Our witness recognized you. You know it."

"Maybe we share the same flaw," I told Palmer. "I'm suspicious of anyone who claims to tell the truth in situations where I'd be tempted to lie. Familiar?"

"You were factual, not truthful."

I said, "It's an occupational hazard. First day of scientist school, they warn us."

"I spent hours talking with that witness. I *saw* the way she reacted. You're the man who interrupted the rape. Probably her murder, too."

I said, "I'm not that noble."

"I never thought you were. You use facts to avoid the truth. Whoever went aboard Heller's boat that night didn't go there to save anyone, but I'm glad he showed up. Heller had almost beaten her unconscious by then, and I like that woman. She's incredibly smart, and also incredibly stupid to fall for that bit Heller used to trick her into opening the car door."

I replied, "I don't buy the premise that rape victims are somehow to blame for being raped. That includes all variations of bad timing, misplaced trust, sexy clothing and naïveté."

"Well, aren't you the modern male," Palmer chuckled, unimpressed. "A real—what did you call him?—forward-thinking guy, just like sweet ol' Captain Durell."

The way the dash lights framed Palmer's eyes and dark hair brought back the image of the female victim, one side of her face showing an articulate beauty, the other a grotesque mask.

I said, "It was that bad, huh?"

Her silence communicated confusion, so I repeated myself.

She said, "What are you talking about now? I was telling you how Heller tricked the woman. He followed her out of a 7-Eleven waving a twenty-dollar bill, saying it fell out of her purse. Suddenly, you're on a whole different subject. Whatever it is, I don't care to hear—"

"The cop who dumped you," I said, "that's what I'm talking about. Or did his wife figure it out?"

The woman was a solid driver. Hands comfortably at ten and two, when there was traffic. No abrupt lane changes, nothing to surprise the civilians. Now, though, the car veered slightly, as her hands went white gripping the wheel. Lips barely moving, she snapped, "That bastard Durell, he said you two hadn't spoken in years. How much did he tell you?"

I said, "Nothing." Thought about it a few seconds, decided I'd stepped over the line, so explained why I said what I'd said.

Palmer sat fuming in silence as we took the Venice Beach exit and turned west, toward the Gulf. Minutes later, after maneuvering through a red light, she said, "You hit a raw spot. It's been almost two years. But I'm over it now."

"I can see that."

"I *am*. The detective . . . the *man* I was involved with went back to his wife. He didn't want to. I insisted. Then she got pregnant, trapped him, although he was too damn dumb to see it. This was in Pittsburgh, before I transferred. He still calls, wants me back. So I changed my number. I've gone on with my life."

Before I could stop myself, I said, "Who are you trying to convince, me or you?," but then held up my hands before she could respond. I said, "It's your business, Detective Palmer. That was unfair, and I apologize. I should concentrate on what I'm doing. And you still have a report to write."

I was surprised by her smile. It was one of those self-damning smiles that says *To hell with it.*

"Truce," she said. "Okay? And don't worry about my report. I have Sundays and Mondays off, so I can finish in the morning. Officially, I've been off duty since eleven-thirty, so I can take all night if I want." When she realized how that sounded, she amended quickly, "Don't take that the wrong way. It wasn't an invitation."

"For the record?" I asked.

Palmer said, "Isn't everything?," with a bitterness that told me no, she had few friends outside the profession.

People in the emergency services are good at what they do. They have to be. Lives depend on it. They're far smarter than the caricatures fronted by popular media and seldom credited with the sacrifices they make or the emotional dues exacted. The job is thankless, dangerous and underpaid. They deal with the worst imaginable people under the worst imaginable circumstances. Yet it is the toll—the emotional toll—that in the end is the most dangerous occupational hazard of all.

There was nothing I could say to make Detective Shelly Palmer feel better or to bridge the chasm between us. So I returned to business. Business at least guaranteed the comfortable formality of strangers.

"Mind if I use your phone? Myles told me to call." It

was only 12:45. The lady's driving skills had exceeded expectations.

On the third ring, someone picked up, then hung up without a word. I touched REDIAL and got the recorder.

I was thinking about a noise I'd heard when I was talking to Myles, a sound that resembled someone knocking on a door, as I asked Palmer, "Do you have another number?"

She didn't. "The guy's not answering?"

I said, "He's got my cell phone," meaning I'd try that next.

This time, Nelson Myles answered. I wouldn't have recognized him if I hadn't already heard the way his voice changed when he was afraid. It was a note higher. He spoke with a frantic, tonal precision.

He said, *"What?"*

"Nelson?"

"What do you want?"

I heard a click, and the background silence became cavernous. Someone had switched to speakerphone.

I tapped Palmer's arm as I also switched to speaker, then said, "I called about our appointment. Are we still on?"

"No! You . . . should call back tomorrow."

Spacing my words, I said, "Are you . . . all right?," then added, "What *time* should I call?," emphasizing the word, hoping he would use a number.

"I'm fine! Stop bothering me. I'm . . . I'm trying to sleep!"

In the background was a strange whirring noise, high-pitched, like a beehive . . . or a dentist's drill. I looked at Palmer. She was puzzling over it, too.

Again, I said carefully, "Are you sure you're okay? What *time* should I call, Nelson? The time's important, if you're okay. Seven? Or eight?"

It took a moment but he caught on. "Oh! Call at . . . seven. Definitely, seven. That's when you should call. Seven."

Skull and Bones code. *Seven* meant *no*. No, he wasn't okay.

I said, "Will you be alone?," hoping he understood I wasn't talking about tomorrow.

"What does it matter who I'm with! Seven. Didn't you hear me? Call at seven."

No, he wasn't alone.

Palmer was giving me an odd look now, confused but aware something wasn't right. She mouthed the words *What's that sound?* The whirring noise was getting louder.

I shook my head and said into the phone, "I was hoping to meet the other investors, the men from Spain. Did they stop by earlier?"

"Why are you asking so many questions? No! No one has been here. Call at eight, if you want. Eight's fine, but leave me alone until then."

Yes, the Cuban interrogators—the *Malvados*—were there.

"Look, buddy," I said, sounding indignant, "I've invested a quarter million in this project, you need to show me some respect! Should I meet you at the boat or—"

I heard Myles grunt and start to say something but then heard *click*. Line dead.

Palmer said, "What the hell was that all about?"

I told her, "Let's move! The kidnappers have him. Cubans—Spaniards—that's what I was asking about. But I don't know if he's at home or aboard his boat." I was about to add, "You didn't hear his answers?," but realized all she'd gotten from the conversation was that Myles wanted me to leave him alone.

We were a hundred yards from the palm-lined corridor that led to the Falcon Landing entrance. Rental cops would be there. I didn't want them anywhere near me if the Cubans were waiting. Palmer was already slowing to turn, but I slapped the dash and said, "Straight ahead. Drive straight to the beach, I'll climb over the wall. You can cut me loose."

"Ford, have you gone crazy? The man told you to get lost!"

I said, "You heard his voice, and whatever the hell that was in the background. A drill?"

"Drills aren't illegal. Trespassing is."

"Shelly," I said, "something's wrong, and you know it. Get on the radio, call for backup."

"And tell them what? I'm worried about dangerous hand tools?"

I didn't want to wait while she thought it over. "Goddamn it, trust me. Do it! You want proof I'm serious?" My mouth was moving before I'd thought it out. "Okay, here's proof: I killed Bern Heller, I'm confessing. I dumped him two miles offshore. I told him to swim for shore but knew he wouldn't make it."

I expected some word or gesture of surprise. Instead, she took a long, slow breath, before she flipped off the emergency lights, then accelerated through the intersection. "I know that," she said, her voice calm. "It's why I tipped you off about the witness . . . and offered you the chance to cancel. When you stepped out into that parking lot, I thought you were an idiot."

I said, "I thought you'd slipped up."

Palmer shook her head. "I was giving you a chance to put it together. Did you?"

"You tell me. The woman's a physician at Memorial Hospital, right?"

That did surprise her. "How did you know?"

I said, "You told me. The rest I figured out. Mid-twenties, brown hair, attractive. Emotionally traumatized, which is no surprise—"

"No . . . *early thirties,* just finishing her internship. Her name is . . ." Palmer hesitated. Sharing information went against her cop instincts. "Her name's Leslie DiAngelo. She's got the looks, and all the brains in the world. That's why, I guess, it makes me mad, how stupid she was."

Her flat inflection said she knew the price of throwing something good away.

"Call for backup, Shelly. Trust me."

As we skidded into the beach parking lot, Palmer said, "I'll call in our location and schedule recontact every half hour. That's the best I can do," then surprised me by locking her vehicle as I returned from my rental car carrying a foul-weather jacket and the little ASP Triad flashlight.

"I'm going with you," she told me.

Meaning, over the wall.

30

Water was beginning to seep into Will Chaser's coffin. He had told himself things couldn't possibly get any worse, but here it was.

Because his jeans were already soaked, he hadn't noticed the water until it began sloshing at his earlobes. He had been dozing, or drifting, or hallucinating—Will could no longer differentiate—but the sudden reality that the box was flooding caused him to flinch so hard that he'd banged his face against the lid. The thing was only inches from his nose.

He had banged the lid before but intentionally. This was as Buffalo-head began shoveling dirt, filling the grave. That steady drumming of earth on wood was a Sunday sound, a sound that smelled of greenhouse flowers—or suffocation—and Will had reacted by slamming his head against the coffin over and over and over, ramming it with his forehead.

Will had continued hammering until the coffin vibrated like a drum skin. He timed the blows to counter-synch with Buffalo-head's shoveling as he shrieked for the Cuban to stop, please stop!

Incredibly, the man did. After a minute of silence, Will could hardly believe his good fortune when the lid creaked open, sunlight streaming in, and there was Buffalo-head's massive face.

"You have chewed through the tape already?" For some reason, the man had cast a furtive, guilty look over his shoulder, as if fearful Metal-eyes was watching.

"Don't tape my mouth again," Will had pleaded. "Please. I can't breath. Do you want to kill me?"

Hump said, "Yes, of course. But Farfel won't let me. I'm sorry." Again, the man glanced over his shoulder.

Will had almost asked why but decided not to risk a long list of reasons. Hump was an idiot but he had a temper, and it was a bad move to remind him.

Instead, Will had asked, "Why are you burying me if you're not allowed to kill me?"

"We all have our own reasons," Hump had replied. "The *maricon* from Venezuela wants to protect the church from scandal. Farfel wants to protect us from Nazi hunters. And the American—well, who knows? He is a silent one, that man, and I don't trust him."

Will had no idea what Buffalo-head was talking about, but he spoke so earnestly Will didn't doubt the truth of it. But the information wasn't going to help him escape from the damn coffin.

"I have my own reasons for not wanting to die," Will

said. "Let me out—only for a minute or two—and I'll tell you."

"Can't you think of anyone but yourself?" Buffalo-head said, then took another quick look around before leaning closer to whisper, "May I ask you a question?"

Will wanted to spit in the man's face but sensed an opening. "We're friends. You said so yourself, at the horse ranch."

Before Hump could respond with "Where you chewed my ear off?," Will had added quickly, "I would like to be friends. This is a competitive situation, like a baseball game . . . or a gunfight like in the westerns on TV. Of course, we both fight hard to win, but I've come to admire your great strength, and your"—Will couldn't think of another reason—"and your great strength. Ask me anything."

Hump had caught himself leaning yet closer but pulled away when he remembered Farfel's bloody hand. "In Havana," he said, "I know many Santería priests. It is why I wear these beads."

Will hadn't noticed the string of red, black and blue beads around the man's neck, but now he saw them and heard them rattle.

"Very beautiful," Will offered. "Plastic?"

"Yes, and they've been blessed. They are supposed to protect me from things that would frighten any man. Snakes, for instance. Or giant alligators. I've heard there are many on American golf courses. Mostly, though, the beads protect me from the curse of an evil person."

Will nodded as if that made sense.

"That is what I want to ask. Have you placed a curse on me? It is nothing to be ashamed of if you have done this thing. I believe the devil is in you. In fact, I call you Devil Child." The man said it as if Will should be proud.

Will had realized that his answer was important. He glanced at the blue sky, longing to be beneath it. "Yes," he said, "I've placed a curse on your head. The worst curse I know. I've cast a secret spell but now would like to remove it. But I can't—not now."

"*Why?*"

"Because . . . because . . ."—Will was thinking, *Shit, try to remember some Indian superstitions*—"because I am an Indian shaman," he said, "and we can't remove curses unless we are . . . on a boat . . . on the water. I think of you as my friend now. I want to take back my curse. So if you would only—"

"I can't," Hump whispered, suddenly in a rush. "But I'll come back—I promise. Until then, I thought that if I brought you an offering it would help. Something powerful, such as an object used by the Santería priests, that you would at least reduce this curse."

Metal-eyes must have been returning because Hump finished with, "Here, take this. I'll be back. I swear!"

The man had tossed an object into the coffin, something hard and gray and round. Will thought it was a coconut shell at first. But in the last wedge of light, before the Cuban quietly closed the lid, Will realized it wasn't a coconut.

Will was screaming as Hump began shoveling sand onto the coffin. Will twisted his body to get as close as he could to the PVC air tube so Hump could hear him, but Hump ignored Will's screams and only shoveled faster. He was afraid Farfel would return from the cabin to ask questions.

Now, feeling water moving near his ears, Will thought, *He's the devil. The real devil,* picturing Metal-eyes. Then the boy began to buck, thrusting his abdomen upward, trying to crush the hard gray object against the coffin lid. Instead, the thing bounced off his chest like a pinball, then came to rest between the side of the coffin and Will's neck.

It was a human skull.

Water was still rising, and the density of old bone on young skin was maddening. Because there was nothing left to try, Will began using his own skull to hammer at the coffin's lid, hoping to knock himself unconscious before he drowned.

31

When I peeked through a side window of the horse stable on the ten-acre Shelter Cottage estate, I wasn't prepared for the shock of what the Cubans had done to Nelson Myles. The precision wounds, the surgical technique, told me it could have been no one else.

Beyond the windowpane, the source of the odd whirring sound Detective Palmer and I had heard was revealed. It was a power drill. Horror is commonly amplified by imagination, rarely mitigated, because the limits of our fears are boundaryless, or so I'd believed until that moment.

The scene—Nelson Myles, hanging by his feet from a rafter, hands bound behind him—expanded the reach of my secret fears and proved that I at least had found false refuge in my own limited imagination.

No, I wasn't prepared. No one could have been, although I knew the Cubans were nearby when I saw Fred Gardiner's cabin cruiser banging itself to pieces, grounded on the beach at the western edge of the property.

René Navárro and his partner, Angel Yanquez, had already killed one person, used a knife to stab a limo driver to death. Now, trapped in the U.S., they were becoming desperate. They were calling on their old skills, using *Malvados* techniques to help them escape into international waters or to Cuba before the deadline, in time for the C-130's drop of the Castro Files.

Gardiner's boat was as described: a boxy little tincan of a cruiser, aluminum hull, dented cowling, broken VHF antenna. The outdrive was tilted upward like the stubby tail of a scorpion. The boat was a walleyed weekender out of its league in the Gulf Stream.

Navárro and Yanquez had run the cruiser up onto the beach, probably not long ago. I knew because of the tide. It was two hours before high, but the flood had only recently floated the boat enough to swing it sideways, beam to the sea. There was no ground tackle deployed, no attempt to secure the boat. The interrogators didn't plan on coming back to use it again.

It told me their escape hadn't gone well in the tricky backwaters of the Gulf Coast. Now they'd returned to strong-arm Nelson Myles into flying them out of the country or to commandeer his long-range yacht. I hoped Will Chaser was with them. Reason and instinct told me, however, the boy was either dead . . . or dying.

I was on the seaward side of the Myles property. A few minutes earlier, Detective Palmer and I had rung the front doorbell, then banged the knocker, until it became evident that the house either was empty or whoever was inside wasn't going to answer. Through windows, the place appeared peaceful, no sign of a struggle, no indication of forced entry. It reinforced the detective's suspicion that Myles had meant precisely what he'd told me on the phone: He was fine, stop calling, leave him alone.

When I'd suggested we break in, Palmer gave me an *Are you nuts?* look but told me she'd wait for a few more minutes while I circled the property, then added, "If you're carrying a concealed weapon, I swear to God I'll take you straight to jail."

I didn't ask if she planned on arresting me on a weapons charge, or for murder, because I didn't want to force a decision. But I broke the old rule and lied.

There wasn't an option. No competent cop would accompany an armed civilian onto private property. To Palmer, I was a vigilante first, a marine biologist second— nothing more. It was too much to ask of her. So I didn't, even though, in the pockets of my foul-weather jacket, I was carrying items she wouldn't have tolerated, including an old, fail-safe SIG Sauer 9mm pistol.

I had noticed the cabin cruiser as I circled near the beach onto the back lawn. It was visible beyond a stand of coconut palms, beneath a skull-gray moon, bucking and rolling in the random cadence of abandonment as waves rolled landward. The moon, half full, orbited above the Gulf horizon, casting a milky, funneled pathway to Mexico. It didn't generate much light, but I didn't need light to see. Something else concealed in my jacket was a night vision monocular mounted on headgear.

The monocular was a fifth-generation wonder made by Nivisys Industries. I wore it over my right eye like a surgical optic. Flip the little switch and the darkest night became lime-green day, bright as high noon.

Not only did it give me an edge over the Cubans, it provided a comforting safety factor. Palmer had told me she'd stay at the front while I looped the property. But if she got restless, changed her mind and came searching, there was no risk of mistaking her for one of the bad guys.

The interrogators had lied to Nelson Myles about smuggling illegal weapons. But that didn't mean they weren't carrying illegal weapons.

I got close enough to the cabin cruiser to convince myself no one was aboard—no one who was conscious anyway. The random seesaw banging would have made the cabin unbearable.

Behind the main house, near the pool, I'd seen two guest cottages and remembered there was a horse stable to the south. Before jogging toward the cottages, I drew the familiar weight of my SIG Sauer pistol and confirmed the magazine was full, a round in the chamber.

Lights were off in the cottages but the doors were unlocked. I did a quick search: nothing.

Next, I headed to the stable. And there was Myles . . .

The Yale grad and multimillionaire was hanging by his feet, glasses gone, hair in suspended disarray as if he were adrift underwater.

The man was wearing fresh cotton slacks and a gray tailored shirt. He had probably scrubbed himself clean after I left with the police, then dressed in his cocktail-hour best to counter the humiliation he had suffered on the dirt road.

"I feel filthy," he had told me, a psychological reaction to my bullying. Looking at the man now, I found no comfort in the fact that what I had done to him did not compare to the outrage the interrogators had inflicted.

Nelson's head was four feet off the floor. The floor beneath was stained. On a nearby wall hung a phone that had been ripped from its mounting. Beneath it, on a bench, was the electric drill, plugged into an extension cord. They'd probably found the drill in the tool closet. The closet door was open.

The Cubans had done a poor job of duct-taping Myles's hands. They hadn't secured his thumbs, but clearly the Yale grad hadn't realized the opportunity it could have afforded him.

They hadn't bothered taping his mouth. Ten acres of seclusion and the percussion of waves from the nearby beach guaranteed privacy. To bind his feet, instead of tape the *Malvados* had skewered holes in the fleshy space between ankle bones and Achilles tendons to insert the cable hooks that now strained against the man's suspended weight. It was the same technique used in meat lockers to hang beef.

I'm no carpenter, but I recognized the polished drill bit. It was stainless steel, the diameter finer than pencil lead but forged solid, designed to bore through tile or concrete. It, too, was stained.

Myles appeared to be dead. I couldn't be sure.

The stable consisted of a half dozen stalls, doors open. There were also ancillary rooms, but I didn't pause to weigh the possibility that Navárro and Yanquez were hiding inside. I crashed through bushes to the front entrance and kicked open the office door, pistol at eye level, flipping off lights as I hurried to the barn's main area. Darkness was to my advantage.

The ceiling was pitched, twenty feet high, with a loft. On the main beam, a winch was bolted to a boom, used for hauling up bales of hay or machinery that needed to be stored in the loft. It was an electric winch. Tonight, it had hauled up a six-foot man, suspending him like a trophy fish.

Myles heard me as I banged my way into the room, or the sudden darkness had frightened him, because I heard his scarred vocal chords whisper, "Don't! Don't . . . *Please* don't hurt me anymore."

Surprise! He was alive. When he pleaded, "Lights on . . . can't see," I hesitated before finding the nearest switch. I removed the night vision monocular as banks of neon flooded the room with the cheery luminescence of a retail shop. Anyone outside could see us now. I didn't like it, but the man had been through enough without adding to his fear.

I knelt beside him, saying, "It's me . . . Ford. I'll get you down. You'll be okay."

Myles moaned. "No more hurt me . . . Please, can't . . . Sit it . . . ? Can't *stand* it no more!" as the cable made abbreviated pendulum arcs, caused by his recent convulsing, a musculature response to pain. He was having difficulty selecting words and forming sentences. It was because of what Navárro and Yanquez had done to his brain.

I found the winch toggle and lowered Myles almost to the floor before using one arm to lift his weight while my free hand threaded the cable hooks out of his ankles. I attempted a slow, gentle pull, but his reaction told me it was better to do it fast, in one swift motion, like ripping adhesive tape off a wound.

The man screamed again, twice, then began to sob, as I carried him to a stack of hay bales in the corner and placed him on his back. His body felt as light as that of a withered old man.

As I freed his hands, I asked, "Why'd they do this? What did they want?"

Myles's eyes blinked open. *"Dr. Ford . . . ?"* His relief was audible—and also misplaced, considering what I had done to him earlier.

"You're safe. You'll be okay after I call an ambulance."

It was a lie, but he was too damaged to discern truth.

"Where's my phone?"

"Phone," he whispered. "They took . . . your phone . . . the Spanish man . . . sillll-verr-haired man . . . Woman called . . . the . . . the Cuban answered . . . Woman's name is . . . I saw her picture in the . . . *Nawww York Times* . . ." Myles stuttered, fighting to retrieve words. "The woman . . . she is in . . . the Amerr-ii-can Sin . . . Sin . . . *Senate.*"

Barbara Hayes-Sorrento had tried to call me. René Navárro had answered, and still had my phone.

"Did the man know who she was?" A pointless question. Of course he knew, for the same reason Myles knew. I log names with the same exacting consistency I log specimens: last name, first name, title, address. The data would have flashed on the caller-ID screen.

"The Cuban . . . called her . . . Snn-Snn-Senator. He asked her . . . to come . . ."

"Where? Did she agree?"

Myles replied with a helpless shrug: *Don't know.*

I said, "Rest for a second, maybe you'll remember," as my brain began a rapid review of associated data. Barbara had told me that she was meeting Will Chaser's foster grandparents tonight in Tampa, then going to a vacation home owned by a senator from Oklahoma. Barbara would have arrived by now. It was likely she'd called me from the airport. Just as likely, she was in a hurry, as always, and started talking the instant the man answered, telling him, "We just landed in Tampa," or something like that.

I asked, "Your neighbor, the senator, is he from Minnesota?" I was trying to compute the odds. The Senate is the most exclusive club in the country—only a hundred members—but about half spend part of the winter in Florida. A statistical guess: twenty-some on the Atlantic Coast, twenty-some on the Gulf. Still, the coincidence was unlikely, unless . . .

Myles appeared to shake his head—*No, not from Minnesota*—more concerned with what had happened to his wife. He whispered, "Did they . . . hurt her? I didn't tell them . . . where my wife . . . where Roxanne . . . was hiding! They hurt me . . . threatened to kill me . . . but I didn't . . . tell them!"

The man's eyes widened, proud he had defended his wife, but his wife was Connie, not Roxanne Sofvia. It was impossible to know if he'd confused the names or his loyalty. But he had refused. Nothing else mattered.

"Hiding where?" I asked.

"Drove to a friend's . . . house . . . Saw them coming . . . from the beach . . . the . . . Cubans. Told her it . . . was business . . . didn't want her . . . around."

I was thinking about Detective Palmer, worried she would confront the Cubans if they'd gone to the house, searching for Connie Myles. I was also looking around the room for a water spigot and a working telephone, or even an alarm button like the one in the Range Rover.

There wasn't much I could do for the man but summon an ambulance and try to get some water down him. He'd lost a lot of blood and needed fluids. I told myself water might keep him alive, but it wasn't true. Even if he did live, would he want to?

Myles continued talking as I filled an empty Coke bottle from a water-trough spigot, but he was difficult to understand because the wiring of his brain had been scrambled. Most of what he said was disconnected gibberish. He transposed words or selected nonsensical ones that conveyed no meaning. Inside his head, I guessed, the synapse junctions had to be sparking like meteorites. Even so, I managed to piece together the story.

The Cubans had tried to force him to fly to the Bahamas. They didn't believe him when he told them Lear employees had flown his plane to Miami that afternoon for servicing. That's when the bigger man, Yanquez, grabbed Myles and strung him from a rafter.

The interrogators not only wanted the truth, they wanted to neutralize Myles as a witness by erasing his memory but also keep him alive as long as possible. A hostage is still a hostage, whatever his condition, as long as he is breathing.

As they questioned the multimillionaire, the silver-haired Cuban—the veteran interrogator, René Navárro—used a power drill to systematically destroy the cerebral lobes that had just provided the answers he'd demanded. It was a brutal, ingenious way of covering their tracks.

The human brain possesses the symmetry of a walnut, and its similarly wrinkled skin has the effect of increasing the neuron surface area. A channel divides the brain into left and right hemispheres. Like a walnut, the hemispheres appear to be twins, but they function differently.

The right hemisphere is associated with creativity, the left with logic. We remember the lyrics of even inane songs for years yet struggle to memorize poems or numerical chains because the right brain storehouses music while the more tidy, less fanciful left brain organizes linear data and is also quick to trash what isn't vital.

Navárro had a physician's understanding of how the brain functions, the duties of the various lobes and where they were located within the cranial vault. To create maximum terror but minimize damage, he had begun at the back of Nelson's head, on the creative side. That, too, was ingenious. After the first penetration, there was less chance of Myles tricking them by composing a believable lie.

There were several entry points. I didn't count them, but at least one had pierced the cerebellum, which is the command post of coordination and balance. If Myles lived, he would spend his remaining years in a wheelchair.

Judging from Navárro's knowledge of physiology, and his reputation for cruelty, he had probably waited until the end before targeting the man's forehead, behind which lies the highly evolved neocortex.

The neocortex is the oversized mammalian brain, complex in its layering and abilities. Memory is stored in many regions, but it's the frontal lobe that makes us distinctive as individuals, capable of deep reasoning and original thought.

There was no reason for Navárro to destroy Myles as a person before killing him. But he had, needlessly and viciously, used the power drill in the forehead area. Joined by lines, the three holes would have formed a triangle, a one-dimensional pyramid.

I had felt contempt for Nelson Myles. That wouldn't change, not only because of what he'd done long ago to a thirteen-year-old girl but also because he'd gone on with his life while the child's family was condemned to suffer through their lives, scarred by loss and haunted by the unanswered question *Where is our daughter?*

No amount of good deeds or rationalization could

redeem his self-centered cruelty. But in the small arena of large personal bravery, my respect for the man once again was on the ascent. Myles had told me he was a member of a noble society, an ancient and honorable fraternity, that his membership was the one good thing no one could ever take away from him. For the first time, those words—*ancient, honorable*—had credence.

The silver-haired man, called Farfel by POWs, had put a drill bit to the multimillionaire's head and demanded to know where Connie Myles was hiding. Myles had chosen to endure the horror rather than put his wife—or his lover—in harm's way.

We are a much-flawed species, capable of deeds so inhuman that only humans could devise them. But even the worst of us are capable of acts of heroism and sacrifice far beyond the purview of lesser primates. Here was proof.

I said to Myles, "Drink some of this." I was holding the bottle to his lips. When he tried to push the water away, his malfunctioning neurosystem only managed to flop one chilled hand on my shoulder, the hand which still wore the Skull and Bones ring. He was dying before my eyes.

I had been in the stable for less than three minutes, yet the life of a man was flickering away. Rather than drink and preserve himself, Myles continued talking, trying to anchor his presence by jettisoning information.

"I told them to . . . use my boat. Told the . . . Cubans . . . gave them the keys . . . to my . . . crown? . . . No! . . . Keys to my . . . Tah . . . Tah . . . Uhhh! . . . Wrong word!"

He was getting frustrated, trying to recall the make of his luxury yacht, a Tiara. He had told Navárro and Yanquez where to find the keys, hoping they would go away.

"Cubans," I said, trying to reassure him with an easy question. "There were two of them, right?"

"An . . . eight," Myles said, managing a smile as if he'd done something clever. For a moment, I was confused but then understood. It was Bonesman code—*eight: yes*—there were two men.

The death rattle is not folklore. A final spasm of abdominal musculature creates a distinctive crackle. A moment after Nelson Myles died, I flicked off the lights and checked the windows for the first time in almost four minutes.

Standing outside the stable was a silver-haired man and a giant companion. They were staring at me, their expressions amused, as if they'd been watching a television sitcom.

The SIG Sauer was jammed between belt and butt in the back of my pants. I drew it, already leaning toward the window as I leveled the weapon, hammer back, ready to fire. But I caught myself in time. I didn't shoot.

Slowly, slowly, I lowered the pistol, index finger parallel to the barrel. I used the decocking lever to release the hammer, then squatted and placed the weapon on the floor. When the silver-haired Navárro motioned me to step away from the gun, I did so without hesitation.

Whatever they told me to do, I would do—for now—because they had Shelly Palmer.

The giant, Angel Yanquez, had his arm around the woman's throat. He was holding the detective's pistol to her temple, grinning at me, head down as he made eye contact, showing me his stub of a horn like a rhino.

32

The rhino-sized Cuban pushed Detective Shelly Palmer into the stable as the older man, with his neat gray hair and tidy mustache, locked the door, then pointed the pistol he was carrying at me. It had a laser sight. My eyes squinched shut, temporarily blinded by the red dot that painted my face.

"*Sit!*" the man yelled. "Sit on your hands!"

When Navárro emphasized *Sit!* his dentures clicked, just as I'd been told they would. So it *was* Farfel . . . Farfel and his giant assistant, Hump.

I sat immediately. Palmer did not, which gave Hump reason to grab her hair and trip her legs from beneath her. She collapsed on the floor beside me, her body making a bone-on-cement *thump*, as he yelled something in Spanish about her being stubborn like a mule.

Palmer righted herself, pulling her skirt over her knees, then turned to me, eyes dazed. Her lip was bleeding, and there was a cut above her right eye. She hadn't surrendered without a struggle.

"I'm so damn sorry," the detective said, her voice shaking. "I should have believed you. Who *are* these people?"

I whispered, "Did you get a chance to radio?," as Farfel yelled, *"Quiet!"*

I watched the woman's eyes blink *No*, then move around the stable. She froze when she came to Nelson Myles, then leaned away as if to create distance. A corpse is an overpowering presence. It shrunk the room and weighted the air with a tangible dread, an absence of energy and a silence—an inexorable silence.

The nearby power drill was more unsettling because Farfel knew who I was. I could tell by his reaction as he went through my billfold, checking the driver's license, then looking from the photo to me, before pocketing my cash and credit cards.

Maybe he recognized my name from the newspapers: the civilian who'd gone through the ice with Choirboy. I hoped that was the reason.

"Marion Ford," Farfel said with a heavy accent, tossing my billfold aside. "Finally, some luck that is good! It is what we need, an excellent boat captain to drive us to Cuba. Not an idiot boat captain, one who steers like a farmer pulling a plow." He shot a withering look at Yanquez, who looked like he'd been in a minor car wreck: His right ear was scabbed over by a recent injury and there was a goose-egg-sized bruise on his forehead.

Newspapers hadn't mentioned my prowess with boats, so now I hoped Myles had told him about me. What I feared was that Farfel had gotten info from someone else, a person who knew about my former life—Tinman possibly. If that's how the Cuban knew, I wouldn't survive the night.

The drill: I couldn't keep my eyes off the thing. It was a perverse magnet demanding my attention, so I stared at the floor, choosing not to make eye contact. For someone like Farfel, even a poor reason to torture a man was good enough. It was terrifying to imagine him doing to me what he'd done to Myles.

Fear is an antonym of *bravery.* I am often afraid but only occasionally brave. We all deal with small, nagging fears on a daily basis. But I had never been in a situation where I risked the ultimate indignity, the violation of my own skull. The fear I felt was a cloying, physical manifestation. It sucked the air from my lungs, making it difficult to breath or think clearly.

Farfel startled me when he stepped closer, demanding, "In a boat to Havana, how many trips do you have? You are an expert with boats, yes?" The man used reversed syntax characteristic of Spanish.

When I didn't respond immediately, he pressed, "I know of your identity. You are Dr. Ford but not a real doctor. You are the marine scientist. Or . . ."—the little man was examining my face—". . . or the one who is a trained killer, some say. Which?"

Myles could have told him I was experienced with boats or about my role as a hit man earlier, but something in Farfel's eager contempt suggested he knew I hadn't been acting back on the dirt road. The question produced a quizzical stare from Palmer, her expression asking *What's he talking about?*

I glanced at her and replied with a slight shake of the head: *Don't ask.*

"Stop looking at the woman," the Cuban yelled. "Look at me!"

I said, "I'm sorry," gauging the distance to Farfel's ankles, picturing how I might work it. Trip the man to the floor and wrestle the pistol away before the giant crushed me from behind. No . . . both men would have time to shoot. Even if Navárro missed me, he might hit Palmer.

I was also considering the distance to the winch—two bare, bloodstained hooks hanging near the ground—as Farfel said, "Look how I was forced to treat poor Mr. Nelson Myles." He motioned toward the body, enjoying himself. "I considered it yet another experiment. As a scientist, you may appreciate the precision of my technique. I am a real doctor, unlike you. Does that impress you? It should."

I shrugged, a nonanswer that I expected to irritate him. It did.

Voice louder, he said, "The experiment I conducted earlier I can also apply to you. You see, I knew all about Mr. Myles. That he murdered a poor, young girl, as the rich often do, yet he tried to deceive me. When men talk, they tell me everything or they talk never. If you do not cooperate, I will conduct the same experiment on you."

Once again, the woman was staring at me. She had to be wondering what form of insanity I had led her into.

Eyes on the floor, I replied, "Tell me what you want me to do, I'll do it. But I want something in exchange. Tell me where the boy is. Is Will Chaser still alive?"

The man began to pace, checking the windows, checking his watch. "Shut up! What do I care about some American brat? He is no longer my responsibility."

Farfel wasn't just desperate, I realized, he was as frightened as Palmer and me. Until that moment, I hadn't considered his predicament. He had tortured men—American men—a few of whom were still alive. No matter how many years had passed, they would jump at a chance for revenge, to tell their horror stories in a U.S. court or World Court. With the media in attendance, René Navárro would spend his last years like an animal in a zoo, condemned to die in a cage.

Now the man was working hard to project an overbearing confidence, yet it only made his anxiety more apparent. He was terrified because he was trapped. Maybe he'd wanted to recapture power he had enjoyed as a younger man, but it had all gone bad. He and Yanquez had been abandoned by their partners. The boat scheduled to take them to safety—and wealth—hadn't appeared.

There is nothing more dangerous than a killer who has been cornered. But maybe the man was so desperate that I could manipulate him into the mistake of allowing me to help.

"Tell me about the boy," I said, "and I'll cooperate.

You want to go to Cuba? I'll take you. Do you have the keys to his boat?" I motioned vaguely to Myles without looking because I didn't want to take my eyes off Farfel.

The Cuban nodded. "The dock is only fifty meters from here."

I said, "Then let's make a trade. Tell me what happened to the boy, help me save him if he's still alive. I'll agree to drive the boat. I can have you in international waters in less than an hour. By sunrise, you'll be close enough to Cuba to see Havana. But the woman stays here, understood? That's the agreement. Just the three of us go."

I watched the man thinking about it, probably envisioning a scenario that included throwing me overboard once the boat was in open water. He was disgusting to look at, with his rodentian cheek structure, his manicured hair and his crazed metallic eyes. Farfel: a fitting name, not only because of his dentures but because of his precise and delicate physiology.

He was older than I had pictured: mid-sixties. He looked exhausted, in his outdated tweed slacks, torn at the knees, and a white guyaberra shirt that was spattered with sea grass and blood. People who are compulsively neat sometimes react to dirt as if it were physical pain. Farfel struck me as one of those, with his perfect hair and his mannerisms.

"It is easy to pretend driving a boat to Havana is so easy," the little man said, "but the waters of Florida are shallow, as we've discovered. Channels are narrow and the rich man's boat is the size of a house. This imbecile, who is the idiot son of an associate—a medical school colleague—he ran us onto many obstacles: rocks and bars of shell. I had to wade in the water and push!" Farfel was glaring at Hump, who had positioned himself behind me. "This fool also claimed it would be easy to drive a boat to Havana. But you pretend it is different with you. Why?"

I said, "Because I've done it before."

Farfel wanted to believe me, but he also wanted to keep me in my place. "Are you admitting that you are him? The man who trespassed in my country many times?"

I looked at the steel cable as if staring out the window. "Many times, yes."

Was he asking if I was a spy? If so, he was speaking English for the benefit of Detective Palmer. He would have assumed I spoke Spanish.

Yes, he was doing it for Palmer. I understood when Farfel smiled, as if something had been confirmed, saying, "Then you are the one I have heard stories about! The famous Dr. Ford!" He laughed. "The Bearded One hated you. I heard it was because you made him appear foolish, many years ago, at a baseball game in Havana. Is such a thing true?"

I could sense Palmer looking at me, wondering what the man was talking about, thinking, *Who are you?*

The *Bearded One.* During Fidel Castro's reign, Cubans either spoke of the dictator as the Maximum Leader or *El Barbudo,* the Bearded One. They rarely used his name because it was dangerous to risk even a complimentary remark. It could be interpreted as an insult by eavesdropping Party members.

Farfel knew things about me Myles could not have suspected, even from an Internet search. Farfel knew my real identity and that meant I was dead. I was sure of it now. But how I would die, and when, was still within my control.

I asked, "Mind if I stand?," getting to my feet without waiting for permission, then saying to Farfel, "Who are you talking about, the Bearded One?"

"Sit—sit on the floor. On your hands!" *Click*, the man's dentures snapped, adding emphasis.

I ignored him, watching him take another step back, hoping he'd elevate the pistol to improve his field of vision. It would give me room to dive for his legs. But I was unprepared when Yanquez—Hump—hammered the back of my neck with his elbow. Hit me so hard that I dropped to my knees.

Next, as if rehearsed, in one smooth motion Farfel took a dance step forward and kicked me hard in the ribs. When I almost caught his leg as he backed out of range, the man's face spasmed, nervous as a jackal. From behind, Hump kicked me again, then a third time, before I curled up in a ball on the floor.

A moment later, I heard the snap of precision metal. It was Farfel thumbing back the hammer of his gun. As I lay there, some perverse, frightened instinct in me wanted this nightmare to end and hoped he would shoot. I preferred a bullet to a drill.

Instead, Farfel produced a phone from his pocket—my cell phone—saying, "If you do something so stupid again, I will kill you. But I can see that . . ."—he was reading my face—". . . I believe that the threat does not frighten you. So!"—he swung the pistol toward Palmer—"I will shoot the woman first. I will shoot her above the abdomen. The *solar plexus,* I think. Dr. Ford, have you ever seen a person with a wound in this sensitive area?"

Farfel had years of experience reading fear in the faces of frightened men and he read mine accurately. Yes, I knew what he was threatening and I didn't want to see the woman suffer that sort of agony.

"Good," he said, relaxing a little. "You will do what I tell you to do. Understood? Sit! You will look at me when I speak. You will answer when I ask a question."

Slowly, I got to my knees, then sat with my legs crossed, saying, "Anything you want, name it."

The slang puzzled him, because he replied, "The senator who is your friend—what is the name, Barbara Hayes-Sorrento?—the woman from your government who controls the property stolen from the Bearded One. The senator telephoned you earlier. Now you will telephone her."

He placed the phone on the floor and moved away to give me room.

"The senator will be in Florida tonight," Farfel said, sounding proud he'd manipulated information. "She lands at midnight in Tampa. The senator told me this personally, so I know it to be true."

Midnight? It was after one a.m. now. Maybe there'd

been a layover in Atlanta and Barbara called me just before boarding.

I listened to Farfel say, "You will tell your famous friend to meet you, not us. You will tell the senator that you are alone. If you choose, say you have found the obnoxious little brat. I don't care what you tell her but convince her to come."

"Come where?"

"Here! Where the boat is docked. Are all boat drivers idiots? Tell her it is important. You will have the boat running and will invite her for a voyage—" The man paused midsentence, head tilted, his attention shifting to a faraway sound. It was a familiar sound to me: the rhythmic strokes of helicopter blades.

A helicopter . . .

To me, it was the sound of a cavalry bugler. As I listened, I experienced the buoyant optimism it had produced in me years ago in a faraway jungle.

I risked a glance at Shelly Palmer as the chopper approached. She was staring at the ceiling, her expression eager. The helicopter was coming straight for us. No mistaking the thrashing *whompa-whompa-whompa* of its blades.

I moved my head as if tuning an antenna. Was the aircraft descending?

No . . .

The building shuddered as the chopper roared overhead, flying low and fast toward the southwest.

The helicopter wasn't coming for us. It was the aircraft Myles had been promised. He'd been told the sheriff's department would check Tamarindo for unusual activity. But if the multimillionaire wasn't on the island to meet the crew, would they keep looking?

Farfel was rattled. He began to pace again, muttering. His reaction explained why he wanted to lure Barbara onto the boat. He needed a more important hostage to guarantee his escape. He needed his original target, a U.S. senator.

I wasn't convinced that law enforcement was closing in, but the Cubans believed it. It showed.

Farfel used his eyes to communicate something to Hump as he shouted at me, "Why haven't you done what I told you to do? Are you stubborn as well as stupid?" His eyes moved to the phone. It was midway between us on the floor.

I started to reply, but he talked over me, demanding, "Call the senator *now*. Convince her, say whatever is necessary. But I warn you, don't attempt your silly code words to trick me. Mr. Myles told us the meaning of those numbers, *eight* and *seven*. He told me everything I wanted to—"

I didn't hear him finish because Hump collapsed his weight on me. No finesse, just dropped his body down on me with the weight of a floor safe. The unexpected impact dazed me and might have broken my neck if I hadn't turned first, alerted by the sound of his feet.

By the time my head cleared, I was lying on my belly,

struggling to breathe beneath Hump's bulk. He weighed more than three hundred pounds.

I heard Farfel giving instructions, telling Hump to pull my arms behind my back, to make sure I couldn't move. As I looked up, Farfel was walking toward me. He had the phone in one hand, the electric drill in the other, feeding out the extension cord as he crossed the floor.

Palmer was yelling, "What are you doing? This is crazy! *Why?*," as I experimented with Hump's weight, testing to see if I could find purchase with my shoes and create enough lift to get my knees under me. The giant lay atop me like a blanket, most of his weight centered on my upper body. That was good for me, bad for him. So I didn't struggle as he levered my left wrist up behind my shoulder blades.

I was lying on my right arm. He wanted that, too, but I pretended I couldn't move when he tried to thread his hand under my bicep and pry my hidden wrist free.

In Spanish, Hump told Farfel, "I have him, don't worry. He can't move now." He was breathing heavily, already winded.

Hump was wrong. Only another wrestler would understand, but the man had positioned himself too close to my shoulders to control the strongest part on my body: my legs. He was *riding too high,* in wrestling terms, a mistake all beginners make.

Hump could have weighed four hundred pounds, it would have made no difference. Whenever I wanted, I could loop my right hand over the back of his neck, then buck him forward and over my head as I scrambled free from beneath him. *Out the back door:* more wrestling slang.

Next to my head—that's where Farfel would soon be kneeling. He had done the same thing to Nelson Myles when Myles was talking to me on the phone, used the drill to intimidate. As Farfel drew nearer, he pressed the drill's trigger for effect, its cat-high whine like fingernails on a blackboard.

I arched my back to take a look. The little man was grinning, enjoying himself, letting Palmer see the drill, holding the thing like a trophy, revving it like a motorcycle. Showing off his power, as Farfel had probably done a hundred times before to torment prisoners.

The woman was on her feet now, still yelling, demanding that he stop, saying, "I'll make your goddamn call for you. I'll do anything you want, just stop, *please*!"

I wanted her to shut up, to move away and to let Farfel get closer. I wanted him close enough to kneel and to touch the drill to my skull. If I timed it right, if I synchronized the movement of my legs and free hand, Hump would soon somersault atop Farfel, crushing the little man instead of me.

But Palmer didn't move away. She continued screaming, so angry she was now taking zombie steps toward Farfel, who appeared irritated at first, then vicious. Before I could reassess, he used the drill to club the woman. Hit her fast with the butt, knocking her to the ground. Then Farfel dropped down over her, his knees pinning her shoulders and framing her face like a vise.

"This is a better way," he called to me, speaking Spanish now as he returned his attention to Palmer. He released the drill's trigger as he leaned over her but didn't wait for the bit to stop before he touched its steel to the detective's head.

The woman's scream extended into the gradual silence of the slowing drill. There was blood but just a trickle. Farfel had only pierced her skin.

"A hole in the lady's forehead," he called to me. "Even a fish doctor knows the significance of the frontal lobe. Do what I tell you to do or I will begin my experiment. Later, I will make notes!" Because he was more articulate in Spanish, the man sounded even more desperate and insane.

I did what I was told. I called Barbara Hayes-Sorrento. It was maddening how easy it was to convince her that I needed to see her. Barbara said she was in a van, driving from the airport to Siesta Key, only twenty miles north.

I wanted her to be suspicious of my monotone sincerity, of my indifferent urging. She wasn't, and I couldn't risk making my lies more obvious.

But, as I calmly gave her directions, she was curious about one oddity.

"What's that weird whining noise in the background?" she asked. "The phone I gave you is expensive. Did you get it wet or what?"

33

Maybe I've done it, Will Chaser thought. *Some good luck, finally.*

He was hoping he had hammered his head against the coffin so hard, so relentlessly, that he was now unconscious and only dreaming. It struck him as a possibility because the water was up to his cheekbones now, but he no longer cared.

Must be pouring down raining outside.

No . . . He pictured Buffalo-head cracking the lid and remembered the winter-blue sky, the warm sunlight.

Because he had overheard the Cubans talking, Will knew he was on an island, somewhere in Florida, so now he thought, *Could be the ocean is leaking in.*

But that didn't make sense either. He'd gotten a look at the hole dug by Buffalo-head. The hole was about four feet deep, with only a glaze of water at the bottom. Back home in Oklahoma, it took weeks of rain to raise the level of a lake.

Unless . . . unless the leak has something to do with tides.

All the boy knew about tides was that there were high tides and there were low tides. But it was his understanding that ocean tides changed only once a month, somehow related to the moon phase.

Just my shitty luck, he thought. *They bury me on the only day there's a high tide.*

He lifted his mouth to the coffin lid and screamed, "Goddamn it!"

Then he told himself, *Relax, stay cool. Now it really can't get any worse.*

That calmed him. His abrupt, overwhelming anger faded.

Hours ago, the thought of suffocating had terrified Will. He had curled his body, positioning his mouth as close as he could to the PVC pipe that supposedly was providing him with air.

Will had refused to allow his brain to explore how that would feel, running out of air. Gradually, though, he had given in to his fear, opening up his imagination to peek at the horror.

Never again. Not after what he had experienced. The panic his imagination had created now frightened Will more than the reality of death.

For the first time, Will had lost control. It had happened when Hump closed the lid for the second time and had filled the grave so solidly with dirt that the rhythmic *whoosh* of the man's shovel became but a faint, distant whisper.

The panic Will experienced had started at the base of his skull, then burned like a chemical moving through his veins. It had paralyzed his lungs until it was like those terrible nightmares where he wanted to scream, to shout out a warning, but he couldn't.

That had terrified him even more, so Will finally lost his grip on the careful emotional tethers he'd constructed. He had screamed and shrieked. He had gone so crazy with fear that he had broken his fingernails off, clawing at the lid, trying to get out. He had used his face to bang and hammer at the wood until he could taste the blood streaming down from his forehead.

No . . . he didn't want that feeling to return. Anything but that. It was better to drown calmly than to endure that horror again.

Unconscious . . . he hoped he was.

As the water rose around him, the boy settled comfortably. He imagined he was in a swimming pool, floating on his back. Bull Guttersen came into his mind, but there was no longer any comfort in the old man.

Guttersen wasn't his home, not really—probably never could be—because Otto Guttersen was who he was and Will was who he was, a nobody kid from the Rez who most likely would end up a sad, drunken Skin, just another roadside attraction playing dress-up for tourists, pretending to be an Indian warrior, something, Will was now convinced, that had never truly existed beyond the late-night cowboy fantasies of Hollywood.

What was so bad about dying now? Dying in the dead,

dead silence surrounding his own heartbeat and the privacy of his own Indian despair.

Nothing. Not a damn thing wrong about it!

Will chose to allow his mind to float, just as his body was now floating, which took some effort because the skull had wedged itself between his neck and the coffin's air tube. The skull prodded at him as if demanding attention.

After a while, though, Will's imagination drifted free. Images of the Rez came into his brain, the scent of hay and lathered horses, the faces of girls and women he had lusted after, even though he had not experienced even a momentary sexual thought since the Cubans had kidnapped him. Had Will realized it, he would have been surprised, but he didn't think of it.

Fear was to blame for that, too.

Every drifting image was familiar, rooted in some life experience, until Will's consciousness slipped into what he knew must be a dream.

He had never been in Florida, yet he now envisioned the Everglades, which he had seen in *National Geographic*, but never, never anything like what flooded his brain now.

Plains of gold came into his mind, dotted with mushroom domes of mist-blue, a sea of grass clear to the horizon that didn't slow the wind. Wind spun designs in the grass, drifting streaks and swirls on fields as yellow as a pretty girl's hair, then mussed and dust-deviled and spread its way toward cypress hammocks in the distance:

domes of shade in so much sunlight that it hurt Will's eyes.

In the distance, Will imagined a man on horseback approaching. He hoped, as the rider neared, to discover it was himself aboard Blue Jacket. That would have been nice to feel, to see. But it was a man, a large man, a stranger, yet there was a familiar curvature to his jaw, the cheekbones, the black Seminole hair, tied back with a red wind band, that Will knew without thinking was not Seminole, because the man was not Seminole. He was a Skin, but from a tribe that was older than the Seminoles, or Cherokees, or Apaches. Much, much older.

The name *Chekika* came into the boy's mind.

The horse was brown, at first, but faded to gray as it neared, paler than Cazzio, and it did not possess the expensive confirmation of Blue Jacket. Yet the horse had a sweet, quartering gait, bouncing along as if the earth were a trampoline yet smooth as a rocking chair, the way the large man sat the saddle.

When the rider came to a fence—there had been no fence in the dream until now—the horse wanted to open the throttle, speed up and jump, which caused Will to smile, feeling Cazzio's spirit alive again beneath him.

For the first time, the man spoke, but to the horse, saying, "That ain't no fake fence like the horse shows, Buster. You're in the real world now."

The real world? Buster?

An awful name for a horse, but Will accepted it because he now recognized the man, even though the two had never met, and Will had never seen a photograph.

But Will's mother had often spoken of the man—a huge, handsome Skin who the women loved.

That sounds familiar.

When a white bird descended and landed on the man's shoulder, the man's face zoomed closer, smiling at Will, allowing the bird to communicate a name.

Egret. Joseph Egret.

It was Will Chaser's grandfather.

The feeling that came into Will's chest was so powerful that he chose to ignore the rising water that was now lifting him, floating him water light, pressuring his body upward against the coffin's lid.

Will chose to ignore it even when water began testing his lips and nose, finally leaking into his mouth when the boy could not hold his breath any longer.

He gagged . . . tried to hold his breath again . . . then choked as he breathed water into his lungs. After a brief, panicked flurry, Will gave up, before returning his mind to the buoyant, ascending sensation in his chest.

Will clung to that feeling, held peacefully to its warm power, as his lungs ceased struggling . . . as his heart slowed . . . the drumming heart muscles dimming, then losing their electric spark . . . yet Will felt easy, empty of fear, as a small, true voice within him whispered, *You have endured enough* . . .

Will's grandfather remained in focus behind the boy's eyes, a man astride a good horse, a horse bred for business, the dissimilar images joining as a luminous, knowing energy that offered nothing—not pleasure, not even hope—but was *real*, as real as his grandfather's fire-bright face, a face that became serious when Joseph extended his hand, inviting Will . . . somewhere.

Somewhere, Will decided, was good enough.

But as he reached to take the hand, Joseph was abruptly replaced by the fierce flat mask of a plains Indian, his body wind-sculpted, sundried, with two cavernous, red-sparked skull eyes glowing with a scent that Will knew too well: rage.

A mask-behind-the-mask appeared, an old male Skin who was thinking loud enough for Will to hear, even as the boy's heart slowed, slowed, then ceased beating, in a silence that spoke: *Come with me . . . Come with me now . . .*

In what Will did not believe were his final seconds, a windblown name formed. It vibrated drum notes through wood and earth, resonating long afterward in the living flesh of the boy, and the echo of a coffin that housed two skulls.

Geronimo . . .

34

I was on the flybridge of the luxury yacht talking with Hump. I had just maneuvered him into sharing some surprising information when the lights of Barbara Hayes-Sorrento's van swung through palm trees, then hunted for the turnoff to the dock.

Hump was carrying a gun, which was unusual—Shelly Palmer's gun. He touched the barrel to the back of my head and whispered, "The senator is here. Get down."

For the first time in many minutes, my attention shifted from what the rhino-sized Cuban was saying to what I was seeing.

My hands were duct-taped behind me. Hump had looped a braided rope around my neck and knotted the end to the heavy aluminum sun canopy three feet overhead. Aside from concentrating on stretching the duct tape and working myself free, there wasn't much else I could do but look and listen and follow Hump's orders—for now anyway.

I ducked below the flybridge fairing but could still watch the van as it parked and its doors opened. Barbara wasn't alone as she had told me.

On the passenger side was a man, a large man, shoulders twice as wide as his seat in the van. For a moment, I felt hopeful. But then I heard the hydraulic drone of a sidelift and knew it was a van for the handicapped, one of a special fleet maintained for tourists in wheelchairs.

Because it had to be Otto Guttersen, I could guess what had happened.

Barbara had met the man at Tampa International. Because it was the polite thing to do, she had probably invited him to ride with her. They had compromised by driving Guttersen's rental van.

"No problem," she had answered over the phone when I had asked if she was alone. Only now did I realize it was a politician's device. Again, she'd done the polite thing.

And why not? I had already met Guttersen via telephone, so she'd meant it as a pleasant surprise.

Now here she was, walking into a trap, accompanied by this fraud wrestler with his showtime name, Sheriff Bull-something. Will Chaser's male guardian, newly arrived in Florida to find comfort in sunshine and being close to the U.S. intelligence group based at MacDill Air Force Base, Tampa.

Damn it.

I remembered Barbara telling me, "We're flying the foster grandparents to Tampa. After what we've been through, it'll be good for all of us."

Yes, that's what had happened.

I was thinking, *Where's the foster grandmother? Something about the flu?*

Wherever the woman was, I hoped she remained there. A volatile situation was now out of control. Farfel was desperate to get the senator on the boat, but Guttersen? The Cuban would view a cripple as a liability, as useless as empty baggage, and he would dispose of the man.

Otto Guttersen was about to die.

Up until that moment, I'd been mildly optimistic. Things had begun to go my way. It had required subtle countermoves and some risk to convince Farfel that if he killed Shelly Palmer, I wouldn't help him.

The man had agreed for a simple reason: He was afraid. The infamous interrogator, who specialized in using fear as a weapon, was now the hunted, not the hunter. He knew it and was tired of dealing with his mounting problems alone.

So we had left Shelly Palmer, duct-taped and gagged, in one of the stalls. I hadn't been able to say good-bye, but she and I had exchanged a look before Hump shoved me outside. I had attempted an apology by shaking my head, thin-lipped. Shelly stared back with a familiar quizzical sadness, asking once again *Who are you?*

I hoped the woman was still alive an hour from now so I could answer at least part of that question. I was the man who planned to take Farfel and Hump safely into the Gulf of Mexico, then return without them.

The odds had been shifting in my favor . . . until now.

The Cubans had lost their edge. Another rough day for the kidnappers, I knew, because Hump had been telling me about it. We had been alone on the flybridge for about ten minutes before the van arrived, and I'd goaded and plucked information from him.

Hump had run the ugly little cabin cruiser aground while attempting the channel between Tamarindo and the Gulf of Mexico. After Hump finally wrestled the boat free, Farfel took the wheel, then made the same amateur mistake minutes later, running the boat high and dry onto another oyster bar.

Farfel had injured his back. His arms were a mess from the oysters. He had wrenched a knee trying to push the boat, and, as Hump had explained, the man wasn't a hundred percent to begin with.

"His hand was already bleeding," Hump told me, and I felt a charge of admiration when he described the boy decoying Farfel close enough to bite him.

Will Chaser: That's who we had been discussing *finally* when the van appeared. It had required a different style of manipulation to convince Hump that he could trust me, that I really didn't care if the boy lived or died, but that I was talkative just like him.

There was something else he believed we had in common: I was afraid of Farfel. Which was true. Farfel was injured and in pain, so he was even more foul-tempered and more likely to use violence as an easy solution to minor irritants.

"Don't worry about me saying anything to Dr. Navárro," I had reassured the huge man. "What we say here stays here. Maybe tomorrow when we're in Havana we can go out and have a beer together. A man can't have too many friends."

It was a less subtle lie. Truth was, I had come to despise Angel Yanquez almost as much as I despised René Navárro from the very beginning.

Hump had enjoyed putting the rope leash around my neck, then leading me aboard the boat, pausing once to slap my face, then club me with the back of his hand. He claimed it was because I moved too slowly, but I knew the truth. Hump was enjoying this rare opportunity to act out as the alpha male.

By the time we'd made it to the flybridge, my head was pounding, and my ribs ached because of the kicks he'd landed in the stable. Hump's simpleton way of speaking, and the uneasy alliance I had forged with him to protect Shelly Palmer, made me impatient.

I didn't trust Farfel. He had returned to the stable alone as Hump led me to the boat. He'd been gone for several minutes before returning to hide in a storage shed, anticipating the senator's arrival. I hadn't heard a gunshot, but that meant nothing due to the Cuban's fondness for the drill.

Had he used it on the detective?

It made it tough to bide my time but I knew I had to wait. I had to wait until Farfel and Hump were together on the flybridge.

It hadn't happened yet—Farfel was shrewd that way.

He had a jackal's instincts when it came to self-preservation and a professional's gift for tactical positioning.

The man had always stayed just out of my reach, allowing Hump to do the dangerous work, and never getting close enough to his assistant to allow me a single, united target.

But it would happen. Hopefully, my opportunity would come before we cast off, but even if Farfel didn't join us until later I would continue waiting until we were together, then I would kill them both, at the very least leave them miles from shore.

Farfel, with his jackal wariness, had ordered Hump to duct-tape my hands—a mistake. When I'd taped Nelson Myles's hands, I had made sure his thumbs were exposed and that his fingers were not symmetrically interlaced. Myles hadn't protested, and Hump didn't care, because neither of them was aware of that basic escape-artist's ploy.

Hopefully, it was the last mistake the two Cubans would ever make.

Since then, I had been steadily stretching the tape, working it off my hands so it now covered them like gloves. I had been polite and cooperative and acceptably submissive.

I had remained submissive as I listened to Hump warn me, "You will learn to jump if I tell you. You have never dealt with a man such as me."

I had answered honestly, saying in Spanish, "You are very strong—stronger than me—you've proven that."

"Yes, it is true," he had replied. "Many men have said so."

We had been talking long enough by then for me to risk mentioning Will Chaser. I still didn't know if he was alive or dead so I had nudged the truth closer, saying, "With your size, you should have been an athlete in the Olympics. Cuba always does very well. You could have been a great boxer or weight lifter. Boys all over the world would have admired you. Boys everywhere, even here in the United States."

Hump had nodded, his expression saying *If you say it's true, I won't argue.* "When I was only twelve, I could lift the front end of a Lada from the ground! I could have held an entire Calina over my head, but they are difficult to balance, those ugly Russian cars."

I suggested, "By the time you were fourteen, you probably could put a horse under your arm."

The man made the association. "Don't mention boys or horses to me. I never want to hear about them again. I have always distrusted horses, but now I distrust them both. The boy you call William, can you guess what my name for him was?"

I shrugged.

"Devil Child, that is what I called him. I was afraid of that brat, I admit it! What man wouldn't be afraid of a vicious demon? Have you noticed that he ate part of my ear? It is true!"

Hump turned his head to show me and I felt another surge of admiration.

"Perhaps it was because the boy was an Indian, an Apache, he claimed, like the painted ones I watched on television in René's barbershop in Havana. They are savages, you know. Why, the Devil Child even threatened to scalp me." He lowered his voice to confide, "The child put a curse on me. He admitted it, then bragged of it!"

Hump had already let other information slip. I now knew that he and Farfel had planned the kidnapping with men from two different organizations. Choirboy wanted documents that would embarrass Rome. There was an American who took orders from another American, Tinman, although Hump didn't say it. They wanted *all* the files destroyed but were also in it for the money.

I already knew why Hump and Farfel were involved, so now I was concentrating on the boy. This was the first time Hump had spoken openly of Will, but he was using the past tense.

Hump was borderline mentally retarded, I was convinced. It took him many sentences to communicate even simple facts. But he spoke with the carefully constructed syntax of a slow learner. It was unlikely he would confuse tenses, but I refused to be so easily convinced because I didn't want to believe it.

"I wouldn't have wanted to spend much time around William Chaser," I told Hump. "One time, the boy swore at me. He threatened me, too. It's true."

"Hah!" The man was pleased to hear it. "What a dangerous hostage he made. As I said to Farfel"—the man craned his neck to confirm that Navárro couldn't hear—"no one will pay ransom for a demon teenager. We should kill the boy, I told him, before the U.S. demands money from us."

I affected a casual disinterest. "Good. Sometimes, a bullet's the best way."

"Not in this case. Because of the curse, you see. Also, we have made certain promises. Unlike Farfel, when I give my word I keep it! So we buried the boy in a box. He is less than three kilometers from here." The man motioned toward the bay, then stopped to focus on something that surprised him. "What is that orange light in the distance?"

He was looking toward a line of mangrove islands, dark shapes on moon-blue water. Beyond the islands was an orange corona of light. It pulsed like a slow-motion explosion.

I said, "A fire. Maybe a boat," but was thinking of Tamarindo, more worried than I'd been before.

Because his attention was still on the fire, it took a moment for Hump to reply, "We used a little fan. I connected the fan to a battery for air . . . for the boy, I'm telling you. By now, though"—Hump didn't have a watch so his eyes moved to the night sky—"the battery was not strong, and the fan, it didn't work so very well. So the brat, he is probably dead. Although, personally, I hope he is not."

I said, "What?," before remembering I didn't care.

"Before I filled the grave, the boy promised he would remove the curse if I returned. I told him I would come back. I would like to. It would be a wise thing to do. He's going to die anyway, so I could kill him later. What's the difference?"

The man reached and lifted a necklace from beneath his shirt. "These beads are blessed to protect me from evil. I also made a small offering to the Devil Child. But it didn't help. Not ten minutes later, Farfel crashed our boat."

I pretended to look at the beads, as I said, "Well . . . the boy *is* an Indian."

"An Indian priest, he told me, but used a word I do not know."

"Some people scoff at religion," I said. "Not me. I've heard of voodoo curses and Santería curses. People have died—it's been documented. Some say they can bring the dead back to life. That, I doubt. But from an Indian? Maybe your curse isn't fatal."

"You think I don't know of these things? I have Santería priests who instruct me. Don't make the mistake of thinking me a fool. I am not. Even Farfel now takes my advice. Sometimes, I come right out and tell Farfel what we must do! Of course . . . I do this privately. Why embarrass an old man?"

He was swerving off topic, so I said, "Personally, I don't care if the kid's dead or alive. But, if you're asking me to help, the answer is no."

Confused, Hump said, "Help do what?," then demanded, "Why are you refusing me?"

"Because I can't. I'm not taking you back to where you buried the boy just to have a curse removed."

Hump had been leaning against the safety railing, his attention now on the shell road watching for the senator's car to appear. He straightened. "You told me curses sometimes kill people!"

"It's not part of our agreement. I'm taking you to Cuba, that's all. Sorry. I follow Dr. Navárro's orders, not yours."

"But Farfel is not the one who has been doomed by that bastard savage! If you expect me to go with you to Havana and drink beer, then you should at least—"

That's when the rental van appeared.

Hump crouched low as he touched the gun to my head, saying, "Get down."

35

Men shout and bellow when they're angry. But men who have transcended anger, who function daily with murder in their brains, are transformed when the moment finally does arrive.

The normal voice is displaced by a primitive voice that is linked, unencumbered, to the limbic cortex—the *lizard brain*, an aficionado like René Navárro might call it.

I could hear a lizard voice speaking to Navárro now, saying, "Quit lying. You think I could ever forget your face? Those eyes? Stop backing away . . . *Farfel*. You don't have a gun? You always did. Question is, how many rounds?"

Because I had heard the wise-guy bluster of Otto Guttersen, I would not have believed it was him. It was similar in volume yet had a whispered edge that rasped, as if Guttersen's larynx had been scarred by the memory of a long-ago scream.

"What are you talking about? I'm an associate of Dr.

Ford's. He asked me to show you aboard." Farfel the interrogator had assumed the role of Cuban physician after stepping from the storage shed to introduce himself to Barbara and her unwelcome companion.

He was sticking to the role as Guttersen thrust his wheelchair forward, pursuing the man while making rasping accusations. Farfel had been as shocked to see Guttersen as Guttersen was to see his former tormentor.

Where had they met? No idea. Only Barbara had mentioned the showtime wrestler's military background. But all the information I needed was in Guttersen's venom the first time he spoke the name *Farfel*.

The invalid had been a POW—somewhere. As Roxanne Sofvia had said, "Does it matter which war?"

I had thought the woman naïve, although her bitterness was justified. But she was right, I was wrong. These recent seconds had exposed my comfortable certainty as ignorance.

From the flybridge, peeking over the fairing, I had an elevated view of the area. The parking area was directly beneath me.

I could see that Guttersen was getting frustrated because of the sand, as he tried to press his attack on Farfel. And there was Barbara, dumbstruck, standing near the van, where the doors were still open, dome light on. Like the men, she was in shock.

Trailing southward was the estate's private canal, water star-black, roiled by current where it emptied into an ocean inlet near mangrove bushes thirty yards away.

The yacht sat with its bow pointed toward the inlet,

moored portside to a commercial-grade dock. The dock adjoined a party deck, where there was a chiki hut, a grill and outdoor speakers, all of it—parking area included—lighted by low-voltage lamps. The deck extended out over the water on pilings.

Farfel, I realized, wasn't actually fleeing. Why would he? He had his laser-sighted pistol, although he hadn't produced it. Instead, he was leading Guttersen toward the deck, where there was no railing, only a two-foot drop to the water.

Tide had flooded, current starting to turn.

"You cowardly sonuvabitch, why you running? My legs don't work. You know why. You're the one who did it!"

Barbara had finally recovered enough to attempt an intervention, saying, "What's going on here? Mr. Guttersen, I think you're overreacting. Why don't we all calm down and discuss whatever it is that—"

Guttersen's voice sounded close to normal as he snapped at her, "Shut up! If you want to do something useful, call one of them big shots, Minneapolis National Guard. They'll tell you who this snake is! Or the doctors at the VA!"

"But you must be mistaken—"

Guttersen had reared his wheelchair onto the deck and was now using his fist to hammer at sand clogging the brakes. "Are you blind, lady? Look at his face! If you can't see he's lying, you're dumb as rice, I shit thee not!"

Barbara was looking toward the yacht now, calling, "Ford! Where the hell are you?"

Beside me, Hump pressed the gun harder into my neck, and said, "After Farfel drowns the cripple, he'll be mad if you answer. He told me that he would enjoy killing you more than killing the woman."

At first I thought, *Barbara. Farfel's going to kill a senator?* But then I understood. Hump was talking about Shelly Palmer.

"Navárro killed the woman detective?" I demanded.

Hump realized that he'd slipped up. "Uhhh . . . maybe I imagined him saying that before he returned to the stable. Yes, I'm sure now, because of our agreement."

I felt an emotional jolt: a flurry of denial and self-reproach . . . then a flooding change in blood chemistry that was anger.

My arms were extended behind me. With my hands, I was doing what children do when they interlace their fingers and play *Here's the church, here's the steeple, open up the doors and here's—*

"Stop moving," Hump said. "I have never shot a gun, but I know it's loud. My ear, it is already aching."

He was kneeling to my right, starboard side. When I glanced at him, I noticed something in the water, something moving. It was an elongated shadow gliding across the black water toward the dock where Farfel was standing, now taunting Guttersen with his patient denials.

The shape was pointed like the snout of an alligator—a huge gator, if I was right. It had to be fourteen feet long. It was moving fast, propelled by an effortless wake.

"Are you trying to trick me?" Hump was straining to follow my gaze without turning away.

I wanted to remove my glasses and clean them. Mangrove shadows cloaked details, but the speed was right, as well as the low, surface-flush profile. It's illegal to feed gators in Florida, which makes people even more eager to do so. The big ones come to associate people with food. Gators have killed a dozen strollers and swimmers in recent years.

If Guttersen went into the water, drowning was the least of the man's worries.

I whispered fast, "I'll take you to the boy. He can remove the curse like he promised if you help me disarm Farfel. Just show me where you buried him."

My offer keyed an alpha-male response and Hump used his left hand to slap the back of my head. "He was my father's friend! Do you take me for an idiot?"

Behind my back, I snapped my fingers inward, levered my wrists outward and my hands exited the duct tape as if exiting a cave.

"Can you swim?" I asked the man.

"Of course! Not well, but—"

Before Hump could finish, I slapped the gun away, then looped my arm under his crotch as he attempted to stand, using the man's own upward momentum to vault him over the railing. His three hundred pounds felt light because of my adrenal surge.

The man somersaulted backward, hollering, *"Hey!"* as if offended. His body imploded the water surface with the sound of a refrigerator.

I looked to see the gator's reaction, but it had disappeared—in front of the yacht possibly. Or it was now submerged, swimming toward the vibration of the huge Cuban's thrashing.

I looped the noose off my neck, stripped the ball of tape from my wrists and knelt.

Shelly Palmer's pistol was on the deck. A Glock—not a favorite, but it was loaded. I checked to make sure before scrambling down the ladder. As I sprinted across the gangway, I heard a man's scream.

I hoped it was Hump. It wasn't.

Guttersen!

S omehow, Otto Guttersen had gotten to his feet and was choking Farfel. He was wrestling with the Cuban, driving him toward the edge of the deck, as he screamed profanities, sputtering, "Die, you sonuvabitching snake, die!"

Why wasn't Farfel using his gun?

There was a reason.

By the time I got to the men, Guttersen had the Cuban pinned, his body dwarfing the man, but I could see that Farfel was faceup, eyes glassy, as the big wrestler, clearly not a fraud, used an effective choke hold to position Farfel's head over the water. Guttersen was using the wooden planking as a fulcrum, trying to snap the man's neck . . . or snap the man's head off.

Barbara was pulling at Guttersen's shoulders, yelling, "Stop, stop, stop! He's dead! I think he's dead!"

As I helped the woman calm Guttersen, I could see that she was right. But Guttersen hadn't killed Farfel. It took me a dizzying, confused moment to understand. Protruding from beneath Farfel's Adam's apple was the steel point of a hunting arrow. It had pierced an area near the jugular, had maybe nicked it, judging from the amount of blood.

An arrow?

From the adjoining dock, I heard a momentary splashing. I didn't look, assuming it was Hump. But then we all turned when we heard a boy's voice ask, "Where'd I hit him?"

Will Chaser!

Will was no longer dressed like a cowboy, as when I'd first seen him. He was nearly naked, face smoke-smudged, blood-crusted, carrying a bow and withered quiver as he approached, his hair tied back Apache style with a blue wind band.

His black eyes reflected a momentary red-sparked gleam when he looked at me, a look of recognition.

Beneath lights at the dock's edge, where a kayak was tied, Hump, dog-paddling, was now calling, "Dr. Navárro, be careful! Devil Child is back!"

Barbara had sagged against me. I disentangled myself from her arms, saying, "Call nine-one-one. We need an ambulance *now*." Running toward the horse stable, I added, "Then cancel the ransom flight."

When I entered the stable and knelt beside the body of Shelly Palmer, I saw that we could cancel the ambulance, too.

Farfel had used the drill.

36

The morning of the deadline, Sunday, January twenty-fifth, I got five hours' sleep, put my skiff on a trailer, then rendezvoused with Tomlinson near Southwest Regional Airport.

"Any news?" he asked, swinging his backpack into the bed of my old Chevy pickup.

I told him I was too tired to talk, for him to sit back and I'd share everything telepathically. After a few beats, I added, "But the kid's okay. He's not too fond of me, but he's safe."

Tomlinson had already seen news bulletins on CNN while waiting for his flight. But he must have read the weariness in my face because he told me, "The kid's a solid judge of character. Tell me the rest later," then dozed most of the trip.

At two p.m. we met Jibreel Sudderram and two fellow FBI agents at Falcon Landing and chauffeured them to Tamarindo Island. Because it was my boat, I had asked

Sudderram earlier to play the bad guy and inform a U.S. senator there wasn't enough room for her aboard.

Legally, it was almost true, even though my skiff has carried as many as fifteen. But Barbara had been on a combination power binge and talking jag since she'd seen blood pumping from the Cuban interrogator's neck. I didn't want to listen to her endless cell-phone conversations or babysit her questions.

The agents were trained to be patient with civilians. I was not.

The lady's protests were neutralized by the fact that one of the agents was female. Besides, as I rationalized for our little group, Barbara had already acknowledged that Tomlinson was a credible psychic by attending one of his lectures, so she had no choice but to accept the decision that he might be useful.

The agents didn't consider Tomlinson a psychic, nor did I. It was a concession I would never have made but that the senator had, so it was excuse enough to bring him along.

"Right?" I asked Agent Sudderram.

The man looked as tired as me, but the news about the boy had improved his mood.

He replied, "Why bother her with details?"

Will Chaser had been taken to a Sarasota hospital. Procedure and common sense mandated a physical exam and that he be interviewed by child psychologists before he could be questioned by police.

It had been only fourteen hours so it was possible the boy was still in shock, but he appeared to be handling everything okay, Agent Sudderram told Tomlinson and me as I maneuvered the skiff through mangrove cuts, then down the winding channel toward Tamarindo.

Five minutes later, Sudderram was still briefing us as I dropped off plane and idled toward the island's narrow dock, NO TRESPASSING signs freshly guano-streaked as cormorants, spooked from pilings, then struggled toward laborious flight.

"I've worked with the hospital staff before," Sudderram told us, "so the doctor let me stick around as long as I didn't ask any questions. Will said he didn't mind. He seemed fairly cheerful, considering what he'd been through.

"Will told the staff he couldn't remember much after his coffin started flooding. He said he didn't feel scared, just sort of sleepy and dreamy. Maybe he *blacked out*—his words."

A doctor told Sudderram that a blackout was consistent with the results of an EEG test, which measures brain cell activity, and an MRI scan, which doctors said revealed strokelike indicators visible in the boy's brain tissue.

For a short time, apparently, Will had gone without oxygen. Damage appeared to be minimal, however.

"Next thing the boy says he remembers was crawling through sand toward a cabin. He says he also remembers being pissed off at the Cubans. But not crazy mad—he made that point over and over."

Sudderram smiled at me as I secured the skiff. "It seemed very important to the kid that we believed he was only *sort-*

of mad. You know, that it was no big deal listening to his kidnappers stab the limo driver and then bury him alive."

Tomlinson was standing with his back to us, staring at the remains of the cabin, seeing the charred shutters and broken glass, smoke still tunneling up from the collapsed roof.

"Sort of mad, huh? I'd hate to see what happens when the kid gets seriously pissed off."

I was picturing Farfel's lead-glazed eyes, the razor edge of the hunting arrow creating a pyramid of skin beneath his Adam's apple, blood-circled like a third eye.

I asked, "The boy admitted starting the fire?"

Sudderram said, "Too early to talk about that. But if he did, who could blame him?"

We walked single file along a path lined with whelk shells through a heated space of uplands and cactus to the beach. There was the coffin, lid closed, lying next to the remnants of a hole, and a knotted pile of clothing—Will's filthy jeans and western shirt.

The hole was filled with sand that had collapsed, loosened by the last high tide. The coffin had been made from an industrial crate and modified with a plywood lid. As the female agent took pictures, the other agent used a measuring tape.

A three-inch hole had been augured through the plywood lid, then patched over with a chunk of what looked like pine flooring. The hole was cleanly bored. The patch was a sloppy job but nailed tight.

A second hole had been cut into the side of the coffin. It angled vertically at about twenty degrees. Another sloppy job. As Sudderram made notes, I took notes of my own.

Tomlinson, I noticed, was wandering around the area, a familiar *Om*-dazed look on his face. I watched him walk into the remains of the cabin.

Sudderram stopped writing long enough to ask me, "Does he always behave this way at a crime scene?"

I replied, "No. Sometimes he acts sort of weird. I'm warning you in advance."

We both laughed too loud, a symptom of exhaustion.

The agents and I discussed the coffin. Sudderram guessed that the Cubans had planned to bury the boy on Long Island in the horse pasture, but attention from the police had changed their plans.

"The hole in the lid would fit the sort of galvanized pipe they used at the stable when they buried an animal," he said.

Because they'd had to improvise, the Cubans—Hump, who was now in jail—had sealed the first hole with a chunk of flooring, then used a screwdriver and hammer to create a second breathing hole. A six-foot length of PVC tubing lay nearby.

It explained how Will had stayed alive while buried, but it didn't explain how the boy had escaped. Judging from the way the tide had sucked sand into the hole, it was possible the rising water had also lifted the box free.

"The box looks solid enough," Sudderram offered. "Bury a small boat in sand, the same thing would happen. Water exerts pressure as it rises, the hull displaces water, which increases buoyancy. It was a fairly shallow hole—Will told doctors only about four feet deep. A foot or two of lift could have displaced enough sand for the kid to kick the lid open."

I asked, "He doesn't remember at all?"

"That's what he says and I believe him. Said he had dreams—a spacey and free sort of feeling that could describe a sensation similar to floating, couldn't it?"

There was one problem, I reminded him. "You were on Long Island. You remember the backhoe driver saying he used pipe to vent water pressure. If water flooded the graves, the excess would have exited up the piping instead of lifting what was buried."

When agents opened the coffin's lid, though, we saw that Sudderram and I were both right. Sort of.

Inside the box was a skull. The skull was volcanic gray and had the look of centuries. A section of the parietal bone was missing as well as several teeth.

"Jesus Christ, the kid never mentioned this," Sudderram said, kneeling, then stepping back to get out of the way of the camera.

I noticed that Tomlinson was hurrying toward us as if we had waved him over. We hadn't. On the drive to Falcon Landing, he'd awakened in time for me to tell him a little of what had happened, but I hadn't mentioned Myles implying that he'd stolen fraternity artifacts.

Even so, I expected Tomlinson to take one look inside the coffin and make the association instantly. Which he did. But it wasn't just because the skull was there. Nor was it because we discovered several other bones—ribs and segments of finger bones—when agents removed a sodden blanket.

What convinced Tomlinson was the way the skull was positioned. It was wedged into a corner of the box, between two braces, with the back of the skull angled perfectly so that it covered the airhole.

The skull had served as an effective stopper. If it hadn't been there, the box would have partially flooded but wouldn't have floated.

The agents were wearing rubber gloves. I wasn't, so I kept my hands at my sides as I leaned close to inspect. The skull couldn't possibly have formed a watertight seal, but it might have sealed the vent enough to allow the box to drift upward, freeing the boy.

"Geronimo saved Will," Tomlinson insisted as we trailered my boat back to Sanibel. "I can think of only one other explanation."

"Let's share that information telepathically, too," I suggested. "It worked so well on the way here." Traffic was heavy on I-75, lots of Ohio and Michigan license plates and oversized Winnebagos. I was too tired not to concentrate on my driving.

"Be as sarcastic as you want, I'm going to tell you anyway. William J. Chaser . . . " Tomlinson repeated the name twice before asking, "Do you know what the *J* stands for?"

I could see he was disappointed when I answered, "Yes. Middle name, Joseph. So what? If you're going biblical on me, keep it brief. And please don't rehash the whole Judas thing, okay?"

"Doc, have you ever taken a close look at Will's face?" Tomlinson asked. "A really close look, I mean. Cheek-bones and eyes especially."

"Once," I told him, "and that was enough. The kid still blames me for ordering him back into the limo. He didn't say it, but I can tell. The way he glared at me, I think he wants to put an arrow through me, too."

Tomlinson thought that was hilarious. "Birds of a feather!" he kept repeating until we got back to Dinkin's Bay and he sobered up enough to say he wanted to place the boy's photo next to an old photo Tomlinson had of a man we'd both known and admired. A good man I'd been close to as a boy. His name was Joseph Egret.

Tomlinson said, "I think there's something there. Will and Joseph. They might be related. Seriously."

I groaned, trying to tune the man out.

"Doc," he argued, "a lot of Seminoles were sent to reservations in Oklahoma. And you've heard the rumors about how many children Joe fathered. The women loved him! I know, I know, he wasn't a Seminole, but still . . . "

"Tomlinson," I said, shaking my head, "I don't know what planet you're from, but it's short one lunatic. Save it until we get back to the lab. I need to open a beer first, okay?"

37

On the last day of January, a Saturday, I flew to Pittsburgh and attended Detective Shelly Palmer's funeral, accompanied by Sir James Montbard.

Montbard had spent recent days in the Caribbean, judging from his tan, presumably stationed somewhere near Cuba waiting to nail whoever showed up to collect the ransom.

"By coincidence," he told me, "I have business in the Northeast. Happy to tag along."

It was no coincidence. Montbard was still working on some kind of assignment related to the kidnapping—that was my guess. I wasn't certain who was behind the kidnapping, and Hooker might have useful information. As the Brit had said, socializing is a key part of our craft. That's why I suggested we travel together.

Shelly Palmer was buried east of Pittsburgh in Allegheny Cemetery, a park of rolling hills and trees overlooking the Allegheny River. A hundred friends, uniformed cops and family members were there, along with several dozen film crews.

During the service, I noticed a man who was too broad-shouldered for the suit he wore. Instead of joining the others around the woman's grave, he watched alone from the perimeter.

I nudged Hooker Montbard, then drifted close enough to confirm that the man wore a wedding ring. For an instant, he and I locked eyes. He stared until I looked away, unsettled by the absurd notion that the man might perceive the truth of my guilt, a truth his former lover had carried to her grave.

I decided to speak to him anyway. I believed that Shelly might want the man to know how it was the night she died. That he had been strong in her thoughts. But the man froze me with a warning look, then ambled away.

Cops.

The next day, Sunday, February first, Roxanne Sofvia behaved similarly at Nelson Myles's funeral, or so she told me on the phone. Stood off by herself, faithful to the code of the unfaithful, maintaining a fictional distance from the man she had hoped to marry, still playing her role as mistress even though their affair had irrevocably ended.

I chose not to attend the funeral. I could have.

The night before, Hooker and I had flown from Pittsburgh International to JFK. He went to the Explorers Club, while I took a bus to the Hamptons. I hadn't returned to a New York winter to socialize, but that's not why I didn't attend the funeral.

Loyalty can be demonstrated in a garden variety of ways. I admired Nelson Myles for the courage he'd summoned during his last hour, but I felt a more compelling loyalty to a family which had suffered fifteen years of his silence.

Ironic, as Virgil Sylvester had observed, that his daughter's body was found at Shelter Point Stables on the same day the man who had buried her was being lowered into his grave.

It was ironic beyond the fisherman's knowledge, I now believed.

Had Nelson Myles decided the worth of Annie Sylvester's life was equal to his own, he, too, might have benefited, not only from the kindness he would have provided but because the girl's remains would have finally received forensic attention.

It was one of the reasons I had returned to the Hamptons. While confessing to the girl's murder, Myles had unknowingly caused me to doubt that either of us knew the truth.

The details of the girl's death were gruesome to contemplate, but details solve murder cases. Myles had told me he was certain he had used a seven iron. I had double-checked the golf bag in Norvin Tomlinson's room and was equally certain that it was the nine iron that a worried Mrs. Tomlinson had replaced.

Around seven p.m., after speaking to Virgil Sylvester

and talking with Agent Sudderram several times, I checked into a hotel not far from the Tomlinson estate.

I showered and dressed for dinner, then telephoned NYPD veteran Marvin Esterline. I had his cell number. He was off duty but sounded pleased to hear from me.

I told Esterline that the body of Annie Sylvester had been found and then explained about the golf-club discrepancy. I couldn't tell him how I knew, but I gave names and addresses. He agreed to keep me posted on the results of the autopsy.

"If you played golf, you'd know that those two clubs are angled very differently," Esterline assured me. "Depending on the wounds, it might be as obvious as the difference between a .38 slug and a .45. The medical examiner will know."

Next, I telephoned Harrington. He didn't share my interest in the murder case, but he sounded interested in the possible killer after I'd briefed him.

"A smart guy, Ivy League background, who was recruited by one of our intelligence branches. A guy who's spent most of his life outside the country, but also an insider who has something to hide—that works for me," Harrington responded, but there was something oddly dismissive about his tone.

I said, "Are you agreeing just to be agreeable?"

"You were describing the sort of person capable of planning something this big," he replied. "I'm agreeing because I think you're right. I think our guy recruited fringe-group types, already motivated, because he needed feet on the ground and didn't want those feet to be his own. Smart, in other words. He let René Navárro plan and handle the really dirty parts—who better? I think the buried-alive deal was pure Farfel.

"For Farfel and his other foot soldiers, the payoff was a chance to erase the past and also get rich. As in *very* rich—close to five hundred million in gems and gold and collectibles, *if* our people had made the drop."

I asked Harrington, "What was his payoff? The man we're still looking for—what? Money?"

Harrington hesitated long enough that I knew he was holding something back. He told me, "I'll call you on a different network," and he did seconds later.

"Okay, Doc, here it is," Harrington continued. "We're talking about a former black-ops agent. Worked overseas somewhere, using his real-world job as a cover. Exactly as you described. His payoff was a chance to destroy evidence that he was a traitor."

I said, "You've stopped being hypothetical. What am I missing here?"

"You haven't missed a thing. The man who organized the kidnapping *was* a traitor. Back in the sixties, he was studying leaves or rocks or something in South America and went south in more ways than one. He tipped off Castro before the Bay of Pigs invasion. That was his payoff: a chance to destroy the proof."

I was thinking, *Leaves and rocks?*, as Harrington told me, "A payoff the guy didn't expect was a visit from a mutual friend of ours. I just got confirmation. I couldn't cut you in, Doc—you know how things work."

I was confused and becoming frustrated. "Look, I'm

in the area. Long Island. Tell me where you are and we'll talk."

"No need," Harrington replied. "Besides, you have a dinner date, don't you? With the mutual friend mentioned. Maybe he'll give you the details."

I felt a weird cerebral jolt. I was meeting Hooker Montbard at the American Hotel in Sag Harbor in an hour. I hadn't seen Hooker since he'd left JFK for the Explorers Club the previous night . . . or, at least, *told me* he was going to his club.

"Doc?" Harrington said. "You there?"

"Yes."

"I want you to relax, take a few days off. In terms of the business we discussed, you did another competent job."

Competent: wild praise from Harrington. And it was true that Navárro was dead.

I said slowly, "You're not asking me to drop my interest in finding out who—"

"We already know. You need to let it go, because what you're pushing for is a waste of energy. I need you back, rested up, in good shape."

"Don't patronize me," I said. "I won't drop it. We are talking about *Tinman*?"

I didn't have to explain the code name to Harrington.

"You've got the right person. If he murdered that girl, I suspect it was to cover up for his idiot son—even the worst of us occasionally do noble things. But the police will never charge him because the guy we're talking about has taken a long, long trip. Dr. Hank Tomlinson has . . ."

Harrington allowed his silence to provide the word: *disappeared*.

EPILOGUE

In the middle of February, I had a total of two full weeks to myself and I spent them doing whatever I damned well pleased whenever I damned well pleased.

I hung out at the marina. Traded stories with the fishing guides, bought lunch for Javier Castillo's widow and daughters, and got tipsy one night with my sisterly cousin, Ransom Gatrell. We ended up aboard a water-soaked old Chris Craft named *Tiger Lily.*

Tiger Lily's owners, two respectable businesswomen, decided that at least once a year the only rule should be there are no rules, so one thing led to another, as it always does when the destination is known in advance.

I exercised twice a day, running the beach, then swimming to the NO WAKE buoy off the West Wind Inn or jogging through Ding Darling Sanctuary and doing laps at the public pool.

Pull-ups were done on the bar beneath my lab. Descending sets, beginning at twenty, then nineteen, eigh-

teen and on down to one. If my Sunday voice signaled
there was absolutely no way in hell to do one more, I
reprimanded the traitor by starting with one pull-up and
working my way back up to at least five.

Sunday voice: It's the voice we all hear that tells us to
quit, take it easy, wait until tomorrow, why bother?,
what's the use?

To discredit the voice, all I had to do was imagine
Farfel coming toward me with the power drill . . . or
spend five minutes on the phone with Otto Guttersen.

Otto hadn't had much free time either. For three days
after Will Chaser's escape, the man was the darling of
daytime television, although he refused to discuss what
he had endured as a captive after Mazar-Sharif, and he
also insisted on wearing an absurd white ten-gallon hat.

Because Guttersen was funny and honest, and a relentless advocate of his teenage ward—"Toughest little cuss
you ever met, I *bleep* thee not"—network producers tolerated the man's quirks.

But Guttersen finally breached the limits of free speech
by offending the guardians of political correctness. He
told a national audience that Minnesota's ACLU stood
for Adolescent Commie Lutheran Yuppies, then went off
on a tirade about sportswriters, calling them candy-asses
for not voting his favorite Twins pitcher into the Hall of
Fame.

"What crawled up your knickers?" he fired back when
the host rebuked him. "Only thing your screener said was
don't bitch about Ethiopians or call my boy a half-breed
delinquent."

That was the end of the man's TV career. It was also the beginning of unexpected problems.

The Minnesota Family and Children Services Agency decided that Guttersen's remarks justified an investigation. If Otto and Ruth Guttersen had assumed the legal role of guardians, why weren't they in New York to intervene when William Chaser was kidnapped?

The agency sought an injunction through federal courts—the boy was Native American, after all—demanding that he be housed in a neutral place, at least until the completion of three months of post-traumatic stress counseling. When the Guttersens agreed that counseling was a good idea, bureaucrats turned it around like a weapon, charging that a former POW who himself had refused counseling might be a dangerous influence on a fourteen-year-old.

So the bureaucrats had won—temporarily. Will would soon be transported to an Oklahoma safe house administrated by a psychologist who had treated Will earlier. The psychologist told reporters that she had no personal bias in the case other than an interest in synesthesia, a perceptual handicap the boy sometimes suffered.

Twice a day, Guttersen telephoned me. When he lost his temper and went off on some rant, I swung the conversation toward more positive things. The most positive was the fact that Guttersen, a paraplegic, had stood on his own dead legs and wrestled René Navárro to the ground.

Unless a person believes in divine healing—I do not—

there had to have been a cellular awakening in the man's neurological system since his injury.

Otto wouldn't tell a TV host what Farfel had done to him, but he told me. His motor cortex had been damaged. The strip of brain is only centimeters beneath the skull, dead center at the top of the head.

When Guttersen offered to explain, I stopped him, saying, "No need. I already know how he did it."

Farfel had almost done it to me.

With Tomlinson's help, we assembled research papers and forwarded them to Guttersen's neurologist, who probably thought we were a pain in the ass but accepted the data with thanks.

A study from the University of Washington School of Medicine was among several that offered hope. It dealt with brain plasticity, the ability of the nervous system to sprout new synaptic connections and access latent neuron pathways, unused conduits that an emergency situation might unmask.

"Kind of like a lizard growing a new tail," Guttersen had responded when I told him about it.

Lizard?

"Exactly," I said.

What pleased me most, though, during that empty time was being alone.

Low tides were midmorning, and I had my Maverick loaded with buckets, killing jars, a net and a single iced bottle of beer ready to go each day. I walked the exposed bars, collecting anemones, brittle stars and calico crabs for my tanks, and I dug five dozen sand worms—*Loimia medusa*—to fill an order from New Mexico, and then a dozen live angel wings for the Department of Architecture, University of Nebraska.

Angel wings are fragile shells, moon white, thin as onion skin yet durable. A professor wanted to graph the structural makeup and apply the data to an amphitheater his classes were designing.

Because my company, Sanibel Biological Supply, requires a telephone and a computer, I wasn't totally isolated in the world that is Dinkin's Bay. Along with regular business calls, I also began receiving the occasional hang-up call.

It is something that should concern anyone, but I was doubly concerned because I have lived a life that is doubly complicated.

According to caller ID, the calls came from a pay phone in Fort Myers. After the fourth time the phone rang and I listened to an indecisive silence before hearing *click*, I contacted a friend, and discovered the pay phone's location: a health club only five blocks from Memorial Hospital.

That afternoon, I mailed a typed note to Dr. Leslie DiAngelo but left it unsigned.

I hope you have recovered. On Fridays, sunsets are pleasant here.

I also made it a point to speak with Hooker Montbard when I could. He was still planning his expedition to

Central America and I was still eager to go. I was also eager to find out the parallel reasoning the man had pursued to discover the truth about Tinman.

Yet whenever I hinted at the subject, he would demur, saying, "Next time we're at the Explorers Club, old boy, we'll trade stories over a whiskey."

Hooker weakened, though, when I e-mailed him an article from a Cartagena newspaper about the political changes taking place in Cuba. It had to do with an organization that for decades had operated underground on the island because Fidel Castro feared the group might undermine his power. It was about the Freemasons.

Translated, the article read, in part:

The Cuban population, however, has always embraced the secret knowledge that one of Cuba's greatest heroes, José Martí, was a devout Freemason, as was Simón Bolívar, the "George Washington" of South America. In the secret lodges of the island, José Martí's writings were preserved and shared.

In Havana, Freemasons are now uniting and saying publicly what they could not say even before Castro came to power: Independence demands the overthrow of tyrants, including the tyranny of religion.

I could imagine Hooker smiling and chuckled. "Ford, old man, please don't tell me you've joined the lunatic fringe and begun to believe in silly conspiracies."

During those easy weeks, Tomlinson often dropped in, but that was okay. I hadn't told him about his father. If the time was ever right or if he asked, I would. Not until. It wasn't as if the two men were close.

Hanging out with Tomlinson can be similar to being alone, particularly when he loses himself in a marathon meditation session or a research project . . . or a bag of something recently harvested and dried.

My definition of friendship varies with the friend, but certain traits are mandatory. Friends can occupy the same room without robbing the space of solitude. They appreciate the difference between conversation and pointless noise. They don't snipe and bitch about other friends. They do their share of mundane tasks without prompting. They seldom whine, are secure in their own purpose and don't anchor themselves to an energy-sapping cloud of defeat and ready-made excuses when a challenging project presents itself.

In those two weeks, no new projects came along, but inevitably one would. And it wasn't as if Tomlinson and I didn't already have old projects to pursue—or dispose of.

Tomlinson had become obsessed with finding out the truth about the skull that Hump had tossed into Will Chaser's coffin. Was it really Geronimo's?

It's one of the traits I admire in the man and that separates him from at least a few of our fellow boat bums: He's not content to lie around theorizing and yapping. He gets things done, when he's in the mood.

First, Tomlinson conferred with a few of his friends in the American Indian Movement, who then recommended him to leaders of the Chiricahua Apache Tribe, Fountain Hills, Arizona.

With the tribe's permission, he had enlisted the help of a brilliant archaeologist, Dr. William Marquardt, University of Florida, to help lay the plans and also use his credentials to take temporary possession of the skull. Delicate tests would be required.

On a winter-scented Friday morning, I found the two men still awake in my lab, opening breakfast beers while they debated the best way to extract DNA while also preserving the integrity of the specimen.

Tomlinson had been wise enough not to burden Dr. Marquardt with his Joseph Egret theory, possibly because Will Chaser himself hadn't provided support.

"It's none of your damn business," the boy had told Tomlinson over the phone. He was too busy to talk, he said. Will had been selling interviews to newspapers, saving his money to buy an expensive horse.

What Will didn't tell Tomlinson was that he was also fine-tuning plans to run away if government social workers came to take him to Oklahoma.

But the boy didn't run away. He was packed and ready when social services arrived at the Guttersen home.

"Of course he's ready," Otto Guttersen told reporters. "Pony Chaser never had a dumb day in his life and he knows he's gotta play it straight now."

The Guttersens were playing it straight, too, jumping through all the bureaucratic hoops required to adopt Will Chaser as their son.

For people who choose to attack their potential, to live fully, not simply exist, "life," as Tomlinson says, "is a target-rich environment."

As for me, on that tropic-blue Friday, I was taking it easy, hoping there would be a reason to stay up late, to load the boat with ice, a couple of beers or even a bottle of champagne.

Friday sunsets at Dinkin's Bay are pleasant. You never know who might stop by.

Penguin Group (USA) Inc.
is proud to present

GREAT READS—GUARANTEED

We are so confident you will love
this book that we are offering a
100% money-back guarantee!

If you are not 100% satisfied with
this publication, Penguin Group (USA) Inc.
will refund your money!
Simply return the book before
May 2, 2010 for a full refund.

M609G1109

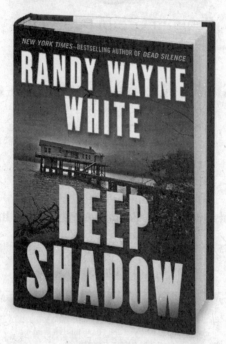

BLACK WIDOW

FROM *NEW YORK TIMES* BESTSELLING AUTHOR

Randy Wayne White

Doc Ford is drawn into a deadly battle when his god-daughter Shay is blackmailed. Someone filmed her at an out-of-control bachelorette party—and they want big money to keep it quiet. When Ford investigates, he finds that the woman responsible is an agent of corruption unlike any Ford has ever encountered before. And she may be the last encounter he ever has.

penguin.com

M611T1109

HUNTER'S MOON
by RANDY WAYNE WHITE

Doc Ford saves a former President of the United States from assassination—and regrets it. Months ago, Kal Wilson's wife was killed in a plane crash. President Wilson is sure it was no accident, and he wants revenge. He needs Doc Ford to spring him loose from the watchful eye of the Secret Service, keep him alive, then get him home. Ford has just been picked for presidential duty—whether he likes it or not.

"Randy Wayne White takes us places that no other Florida mystery writer can hope to find."
—Carl Hiaasen

"Complex and emotionally charged."
—*Sarasota Herald-Tribune*

"Brisk, tense, and tightly wrought."
—*The Miami Herald*

"The plot is twisted."
—*St. Petersburg Times*